PRA[illegible]
NEW YORK TIMES BESTSELLING AUTHOR
JULIET BLACKWELL
AND THE WITCHCRAFT MYSTERIES

"A smashingly fabulous tale."
—*New York Times* bestselling author Victoria Laurie

"It's a fun story, with romance possibilities with a couple of hunky men, terrific vintage clothing, and the enchanting Oscar. But there is so much more to this book. It has serious depth." —*The Herald News* (MA)

"Blackwell has another winner . . . a great entry in a really great series." —*RT Book Reviews*

"I believe this is the best of this series I've read. . . . Juliet Blackwell is a master . . . but truly, reading the entire series is a pleasure." —Fresh Fiction

"[Blackwell] continues to blend magic, mystery, and romance in this sixth novel that shines with good humor and a great plot." —Kings River Life Magazine

"This series gets better and better with each book. . . . A good mystery that quickly became a page-turner."
—Dru's Book Musings

"An enticing, engrossing read, a mystery that's hard to put down, and wickedly fun." —MyShelf.com

continued . . .

"Sparkles with Blackwell's outstanding storytelling skills."

—Lesa's Book Critiques

"Funny and thoughtful . . . an easy read with an enjoyable heroine and a touch of witchy intuition."

—The Mystery Reader

"A wonderful paranormal amateur sleuth tale. . . . Fans will enjoy Lily's magical mystery tour of San Francisco."

—Genre Go Round Reviews

"An excellent blend of mystery, paranormal, and light humor."

—The Romance Readers Connection

Also by Juliet Blackwell

The Paris Key

Letters from Paris

THE WITCHCRAFT MYSTERIES

Secondhand Spirits

A Cast-off Coven

Hexes and Hemlines

In a Witch's Wardrobe

Tarnished and Torn

A Vision in Velvet

Spellcasting in Silk

A Toxic Trousseau

THE HAUNTED HOME RENOVATION MYSTERIES

If Walls Could Talk

Dead Bolt

Murder on the House

Home for the Haunting

Keeper of the Castle

Give Up the Ghost

A Ghostly Light

A MAGICAL MATCH

Juliet Blackwell

BERKLEY PRIME CRIME
New York

BERKLEY PRIME CRIME
Published by Berkley
An imprint of Penguin Random House LLC
375 Hudson Street, New York, New York 10014

ISBN: 9780399584183

First Edition: April 2018

Printed in the United States of America
1 3 5 7 9 10 8 6 4 2

For Hanna Toda
A candle in the darkness
Shine!

Chapter 1

The week had started out with such promise. But now my fiancé was in the slammer, my grandmother's coven had gone missing, my supposed witch's familiar was acting loopy, my powers appeared to have dissipated, and the future of my beloved adopted city of San Francisco was hanging in the balance. Oh, and a man had been murdered.

Maybe I should start at the beginning.

Not long ago I was a simple vintage-clothing-store owner feeling as if she needed to hire an event planner. My own rapidly approaching wedding was on my mind, plus I'd been working with my friend Bronwyn's Welcome coven to plan a mother-daughter matching-outfit brunch, called the Magical Match, as a fund-raiser for the Haight Street women's shelter. It was coming up this very Sunday, and yet it had taken us an hour to agree upon the newly designed flyers.

At long last, we were moving on to item number two on the day's agenda.

We sat in a circle, breakfasting on homemade muffins

and sipping strong cappuccinos and fragrant jasmine tea. Surrounding us was a cascade of crinolines and prom dresses, Jackie O hats and patent leather pumps—all part and parcel of the inventory of Aunt Cora's Closet, my shop in San Francisco's famed Haight-Ashbury neighborhood. Oscar, my miniature Vietnamese potbellied pig—and ersatz witch's familiar—snored faintly on his purple silk pillow on the floor.

"*My* issue is, it feels a bit exclusive to restrict the party to mothers and daughters," Bronwyn mused. "What about fathers and sons?"

"True! After all, gender is fluid," said a coven member formerly known as Amy. Recently Amy had changed her name to Wind Spirit, but I kept forgetting to call her that.

"Or chosen families, for that matter?" interjected Starr, and several women nodded and *mmm-hmm*ed in agreement.

"But I thought everyone was supposed to wear matching outfits," said Wendy, getting back to the point. "How's that going to work?"

A spirited discussion among the members of the Welcome coven followed. This was the Bay Area, after all, and a lot of us who'd landed here were searching for a sense of family and community that reached beyond the lines of blood and tradition. Besides, the women of the Welcome coven were an inclusive bunch and didn't want to leave anyone out.

All of which made it hard to adhere to a talking point.

Bronwyn Theadora Peters was a voluptuous fifty-something Wiccan who favored gauzy purple tunics and chunky natural stone jewelry. Today her frizzy brown hair was crowned with a garland of now-wilting daisies and cornflowers. She ran an herb stand in one corner of Aunt Cora's Closet but was much more than a coworker to me—truly she was one of my best friends.

Bronwyn was one of the first people I'd met when I arrived in San Francisco, and she had welcomed me with a warm bear hug that blasted through my carefully cultivated reserve. Ever since then, Bronwyn had stuck with me through thick and thin, magical and mundane. I adored her, appreciated her, and respected her.

And sometimes she drove me crazy.

This was one of those times. A pair of sweet polka-dot numbers that had come into the store a couple of months ago had reminded me of the early 1960s fad of matching mother-daughter dresses. The garments inspired me to suggest the Welcome coven sponsor a simple brunch fund-raiser for the Haight Street shelter and I offered to hold it at Aunt Cora's Closet. The idea soon took on a life of its own, ballooning into a gala event with such complicated logistics that sometimes I wondered if we were organizing a simple tea or invading a small nation. Planning the event had already taken up far too much of my time and energy, in no small part because—although I loved the Welcome coven—their nonhierarchical structure and commitment to consensus didn't lend itself to quick decisions.

This was *not* our first meeting. The Magical Match Tea was only four days away, but we were still working out details, such as who was allowed to attend.

I sneezed.

"Blessed be!" rang out around the room, accompanied by a few "Gesundheits" and a single "Bless you," which engendered an animated debate over the proper Wiccan response to a sneeze.

"Thank you," I said, accepting Bronwyn's offer of a tissue and sneaking a glance at my antique Tinker Bell wristwatch. I had a lot to do today, not the least of which was to prepare for the arrival of my grandmother and her coven of enchanting, effusive, but elderly witches. Ten days ago the thirteen women had climbed onto an old school bus and taken off on a road trip from Texas to California. Just this morning they had sent selfies to Bronwyn's cell phone—I didn't carry one, because I worried its energy would interfere with my magic—from an In-N-Out Burger drive-through in Salinas, California.

I wasn't entirely sure how they had ended up in Salinas, which was not on the most direct route from Texas to San Francisco, but thought it best not to ask. Miss Agatha, the designated driver of the ancient school bus, didn't especially like driving but had the best eyesight of the bunch. Miss Agatha also had no sense of direction, and so a two-day road trip from Texas stretched into ten days as the busload of elderly witches zigzagged its way through the Western states to San Francisco. Still, Salinas was not far away, and barring any unforeseen problems or yet another spontaneous side trip—at one point they had veered off to see the Cadillac Ranch on Route 66, and they had lingered two whole days in Vegas—they were due to arrive this afternoon, at the latest.

"Sorry?" I said when I realized Bronwyn had asked me a question.

"I saaaaaiiid," Bronwyn teased with a smile, "did you ask Lucille about her progress on the matching outfits for those who couldn't find something in the store that fits?"

The tinkle of the bell over the front door was a welcome interruption.

"I checked in with her yesterday morning," my assistant, Maya, answered for me as she entered the shop, a to-go cup of steaming chai tea in her hand. "She hired a few extra helpers, so they're on track, and still accepting some last-minute orders."

Maya's mother, Lucille, had recently moved her small production team into the space next door to

Aunt Cora's Closet. Lucille's Loft Designs specialized in reproducing vintage fashions, which was great since many women today could not fit into the older, typically more petite clothing.

Chalk one up for good nutrition. Not to mention potato chips.

"Oh, good. I'll be sure to touch base with your mother," I said, jotting down a note to myself. "Thanks for checking."

"Guess who else was there when I stopped in," continued Maya. "Renee Baker, the cupcake lady."

A chill ran down my spine.

"I looooove those cupcakes!" said Amy—er, Wind Spirit. She was short, plump, and sweet-faced, favored ruffled baby-doll dresses, and never let a coven meeting go by without making sure there were ample baked goods available. "Hey, would it be too late to ask Renee about contributing to the Magical Match Tea? I'll bet she wouldn't mind donating a dozen or two."

"Honestly, I don't think we need another thing to eat at this tea," I asserted. It was hard to explain to one and all why I was wary of Renee Baker. But the truth was, the cupcake lady was dealing in more than sugar. "Or no one is going to fit into their dresses."

No two ways about it: the Welcome coven had a sweet tooth. The circle of women was even now feasting on Wind Spirit's chocolate macadamia "health biscuits," which tasted a lot more like dessert than breakfast.

"Sorry to barge in on you," said Maya. "I thought the planning meeting was supposed to be over by nine thirty."

"Actually, it *was*," I said, grateful for the excuse to wrap things up. "We need to bring this meeting to a close for today, I'm afraid. In fact, I think we're just about set. We have a task force ready to move my inventory into Lucille's shop on Saturday, the flyers are approved, and the refreshment committee has put together more food than we'll know what to do with."

"That reminds me," ventured Starr. "Do we think we should find a larger venue for the brunch? No offense, Lily—your store is darling, but it may be too small. We've sold so many tickets already!"

I sneezed again, prompting several suggestions for natural cold remedies.

"Thanks, but it's probably just allergies. I don't get colds. So, back to the agenda . . ."

Wendy—my best ally in keeping the group on task—nodded. "You may be onto something, Starr. But it would be tough to find someplace at this juncture; the event's coming up in a few days."

"What about Aidan's place?" suggested Bronwyn.

"Aidan . . . as in *my* Aidan?" My voice scaled upward.

"Yes! The wax museum would be *perfect*!"

Aidan Rhodes was an important person in the Bay Area's witchy community. He and I had had a few skirmishes in the past, and I still owed him a magical debt. Big-time. Aidan had been nice to me lately, but I didn't trust him as far as I could throw him and had been avoiding him, even though he and I were theoretical allies in the fight against a looming threat to our beloved San Francisco.

Besides, I found wax museums a little . . . creepy. All those human-sized poppets, just begging to be brought to life. I shivered at the thought. Not long ago I darn near burned the whole place down. Not on purpose, of course—but still, I had played a pivotal role in the conflagration. Aidan had only recently moved back into the museum from his temporary quarters in the iconic San Francisco Ferry Building.

Apparently, the coven sisters didn't share my opinion of wax museums. "What a great idea!" was the overwhelming response.

"Bronwyn, would you be willing to ask Aidan?" asked Wendy.

"*I'll* do it," I offered, a little too loudly. "I mean, I have to see him about something else today, anyway. But I doubt he'll be much help; Aidan doesn't own the wax museum, after all. He just keeps an office there. Besides, we're talking about an event happening in four days."

"Roger that," Wendy said. "Okay, Lily will talk to Aidan, but if that doesn't work out, we'll just have to make do right here. Everything's set to move all the merchandise next door to Lucille's, right?"

"She's ready for the onslaught," said Maya.

"One final thing before we go," said Starr. "We need to take a formal vote on whether all are welcome to the brunch, or just mothers and daughters."

I'm no mind reader, but I could have predicted the outcome of this vote: *Yes*, all were welcome as long as the spirit of the mother-daughter bond was in some way honored. The women stood, gathered folding chairs, and swept up muffin crumbs, chattering excitedly and thanking me for hosting them. I assured one and all that I was pleased to offer my hospitality, and gently shooed them out the door, waving good-bye as they departed and nodding my thanks for several more suggestions of home remedies to stave off colds.

"Pay no attention to what they say," Bronwyn said as she started gathering her things. "All you need is eucalyptus oil, hot honey lemonade, and the right attitude."

I laughed. "It's all about attitude, is it? Anyway, I don't have a cold. I don't get colds."

"Yes, just like that! Perfect attitude."

Bronwyn gave me an enveloping vanilla-scented

hug and swept out to meet her boyfriend, Duke, who was driving her to Petaluma for a day of antiquing, with a quick stop at the seed bank for heirloom tomato starts.

Amy—*Wind Spirit,* I reminded myself—lagged behind. "Lily, I hope this isn't too presumptuous, but I came across this wedding dress the other day, and I thought, just maybe . . ."

She handed me a huge paper bag. Poufy clouds of white satin, netting, and lace spilled out from the top.

"Oh, aren't you just the sweetest thing?" I said.

Bronwyn must have mentioned that I had been searching for the perfect wedding dress for my upcoming nuptials. As owner of a vintage clothing store, I was feeling even more pressure to find just the right dress than the average jittery bride.

"It's probably not what you're looking for, but Lucille's so good with alterations, and you should feel free to change it any way you see fit. It was my aunt's, but she got divorced years ago and it's just been sitting in the back of the closet, so no worries at all about cutting it up."

"This is so thoughtful of you. Truly."

"No problem. See you later!"

As the door closed behind her, blessed silence descended over Aunt Cora's Closet. I leaned back against the door and sighed. Maya met my eyes and smiled.

"They're wonderful," I said as I brought the bag with the wedding dress over to the counter.

"They are," Maya replied.

"And it's a great cause."

"It is." She nodded, spraying the glass countertop with my homemade vinegar and lemon verbena all-purpose cleaner. A lovely citrus fragrance filled the air.

"And they wear me out."

"They do."

We shared a laugh.

"Do you think the wedding dress will work for you? It was so sweet of Wind Spirit to bring it."

"It looks a little . . . eighties," I said as I extracted the wrinkled heap from the bag. It was made of inexpensive materials that felt unpleasant to the touch.

"Not exactly your favorite fashion era, the eighties," Maya said with a nod. "Still, it was thoughtful."

"It was. And you never know. . . . Your mother's pure magic with a needle."

"So, where are the grandmas this morning?" Maya asked, stashing the cleaning materials under the counter and turning to the large paper map of the western United States that we had tacked up to a bulletin board behind the register.

What had started out as a joke had developed into a morning ritual: putting a tack in the map to indicate the progress of the busload of witches heading to San Francisco from my hometown of Jarod, Texas. We traced their zigzag route with red string, linking one thumbtack to the next. I told Maya their most recently reported location was Salinas, and she pushed another tack into the soft cork.

"I can't wait to meet them."

"Yes, they're . . . characters, all right," I said, applying the nozzle of the steam machine to a 1950s ecru linen blouse and watching the wrinkles miraculously disappear. Stifling yet another sneeze, I concentrated on my breathing and tried to project an air of calm, because, deep down, I was nervous as a cat on a hot tin roof.

As if the imminent arrival of my grandmother and her coven sisters weren't enough, my *mother* was also on that bus.

My mother and I had . . . issues. First, she had sent me away to live with my grandmother Graciela at the age of eight. Then, when I was seventeen, she tried to "save" me during a nightmarish snake-handling revival meeting designed to drive out the demons she believed to be responsible for my strange powers. Things got out of hand, people got hurt, and I was essentially run out of my small hometown on a rail.

I sent my mother a check every month to help with her expenses, and very occasionally we exchanged an awkward phone call. But I hadn't seen her since that awful day.

"Did you figure out where everyone will be staying?" asked Maya.

"Calypso agreed to have them at her place, thanks be to the heavens. She actually sounds pretty excited about it. Graciela's coven sisters are a font of arcane knowledge about healing herbs and botanicals, so they'll have a lot to talk about."

Calypso Cafaro was an expert in botanicals who lived in a large farmhouse outside Bolinas, about half an hour's drive up the California coast. Calypso had also offered to let me and Sailor have our nuptials in her lush garden surrounded by redwood groves. It would be an enchanted place for a handfasting—a witchy wedding.

Bronwyn had sent away for her license to officiate, and if it got here on time, she would be able to legally marry us. My heart fluttered at the thought: part eager anticipation, part pure nerves.

"Oh, good," Maya said with a quiet chuckle. "I kept imagining them all snoozing on yoga mats here in the store."

"You don't know how close we came to that." I winced at the thought of having thirteen elderly witches—and my mother—literally underfoot.

"How long will they be staying?"

"I'm not sure, but they want to be here for the wedding." On the one hand, it felt as though Sailor and I were rushing into this. On the other hand . . . it meant a lot to me that Graciela, her coven, *and* my mother would be there. At the very least we could have an unofficial handfasting with them all in attendance, and later make it legal at city hall.

I wanted—I *needed*—the strength of my womenfolk around me as I embarked on this new phase of my life.

I sniffed loudly.

"You're sure you're not getting a cold?" Maya asked.

"I don't get colds."

"Lucky you. Is that a witch thing?"

"I'm not sure, actually," I said with a smile. I had a hard time distinguishing my own idiosyncratic weirdness from the traits I had inherited from my witchy foremothers. "But I've never gotten a cold. I'll try some hot honey lemonade later, just to be sure."

"Hey, that reminds me," Maya said. "I stopped by an herb store in Chinatown yesterday to get some ginseng, and ran into Sailor. He hardly even acknowledged me, which was weird. Is everything okay? Did I do something to offend him?"

Sailor is my boyfriend. Correction . . . Sailor is my *fiancé*. Lordy, that was a hard idea to get used to. Still, the thought made me all warm and cozy somewhere deep within me.

On his best days Sailor had a tendency to simmer and to brood. On his worst, he was sullen and irritable and not prone to social niceties. But he liked Maya, and it would be out of character for him to ignore her. Plus, it was hard to imagine what well-mannered Maya could do to offend anyone.

"As far as I know, everything's fine," I said. "When was this, exactly?"

"Yesterday, a little after four."

"That's strange. When I saw him last night, he told

me he had been training with his cousin all afternoon, which is on the other side of town. You're sure about the timing?"

When she nodded, the beads woven into her locks made a soft clacking sound. "I went right after my drawing class."

"Huh," I said.

"He probably just stopped by, and had other things on his mind."

Maya and I had been working together for a while now, and she knew me pretty well. Not to mention she was no fool. She could tell the story bothered me.

I had landed in San Francisco without family or friends, and though I had been working hard to learn to develop emotional bonds, it wasn't easy to shake my loner ways. My childhood hadn't exactly taught me to trust others. If it hadn't been for my grandmother Graciela, I wouldn't have known any stability—much less love—at all. So when Sailor actually proposed *marriage* to the likes of little ol' me, I was stunned. Over-the-moon happy and excited, but stunned. I still couldn't quite believe it was real.

I gazed at the ring he had given me. It glittered in a rainbow of green and blue, pink and orange. The stone, set in antique filigreed silver, wasn't a diamond but a teardrop-shaped druzy, which was the inside of an agate, whose tiny crystals reflected the colorful mineral underneath. I told myself it was just a hunk of metal and rock, not a magical talisman. And yet . . . with every sparkle it reminded me that Sailor loved me.

Me, Lily Ivory. The outsider, the weirdo, the witch nobody even liked, much less loved.

All of which made it harder to understand why Sailor would lie to me about what he had done yesterday. *It wasn't a lie,* I assured myself. Probably just a misunderstanding. Sailor must have taken a break to run a quick errand to the store, just like Maya had. No big deal. No reason to even mention it.

Except . . . Sailor's teacher in the psychic arts was Patience Blix. Patience was Sailor's gorgeous "cousin," but it turned out they weren't actually related by blood. According to Sailor, it was a Rom thing. Patience possessed an hourglass figure, a mass of black curls, and flashing dark eyes, and she took her role of fortune-teller seriously—particularly in the wardrobe department. She was a talented seer, but we weren't exactly buddies. In fact, I felt like her first name must have been meant ironically, because the truth was, Patience trod on my last nerve.

"Lily? Everything all right?" asked Maya.

For the second time this morning, I had lost track of the conversation. *Not a good habit to develop.* Given the way my life had unfolded, I needed to keep on my toes.

"Yes, um . . . sorry. Too much on my mind, I guess." Without meaning to, I had been squeezing the mint green satin jacket in my hands until it was a wrinkled mess. I tried to smooth it out, but no luck. "Darn it. I'll have to steam this again. Let me just—"

Oscar awoke with a loud snort and bolted into the workroom at the back of the store. The nape of my neck tingled.

I turned to see a man lurking on the sidewalk in front of the shop door. He was tall and broad-shouldered, with dark hair and pale, almost colorless eyes. He wasn't trying to open the door—he simply stood there, staring in through the glass. Looming. Threatening.

He looked familiar.

Dangitall.

Chapter 2

I had met Tristan Dupree when I was a teenager. I had traveled alone to Germany in search of my estranged father, who had abandoned my mother and me when I was a toddler. Our eventual reunion had been a disaster on several fronts, though for some reason I could never remember exactly what had transpired—which was odd, since I usually had a great memory. But whatever it was, I knew it had been bad. And Tristan Dupree had been part of it.

If only I could remember the details. Still, I had a vague impression that Tristan was an underling, a minion—not an archfiend himself, but the guy who runs to the corner store to fetch the archfiend's cigarettes.

But even so, I was wary at the sight of him. As a general rule, anything or anyone popping up from my past was a harbinger of trouble.

I stroked the soft leather medicine bag I kept on a braided silk rope around my waist.

"Friend of yours?" Maya asked quietly, sidling up beside me.

"Not exactly," I mumbled.

"Should I call the cops? Or Aidan, or . . . someone?"

Just then Sailor walked up behind Dupree and tapped him on the shoulder. Dupree didn't move a muscle.

Through the glass we heard Sailor's gruff voice: "Can I help you with something?"

As Dupree slowly turned to face Sailor, I rushed across the shop and flung open the door.

The two men were equals in stature and apparent strength. Neither moved or spoke, but instead they stood silently staring at each other, doing that rival-male assessing thing.

"Tristan!" I said. "What a surprise. What brings you to San Francisco?"

He turned to face me and nodded once, very slowly. "Lily Ivory."

"Listen, buddy," Sailor growled. "I don't know what your deal is, but it's time for you to scram."

Dupree stared at Sailor, then back at me, as if a spectator at a slow-motion tennis match.

"You know what?" I said in as chipper a tone as I could muster, though my voice broke slightly. "Sailor, I've got this. Honest. Tristan and I go way back. Why don't you head on back to work, and Tristan and I will catch up over a nice cup of tea?"

"No tea," answered Tristan. His deep monotone was all the more threatening for its lack of animation. "Just the bēag."

"The what?" Sailor and I asked at the same time.

"Is that the way it is going to be?" Tristan asked, his expressionless light eyes never leaving mine.

"Honestly, Tristan, I have no idea what—"

"Forty-eight hours. I'll come back."

"You come back," Sailor said, his voice a study in anger, "and you'll deal with me."

Tristan nodded.

"Listen, Tristan," I began, "why don't we—"

"Forty-eight hours."

"Make no mistake, pal. You come anywhere near her, you lay a hand on her," Sailor threatened, "and I'll kill you."

At that moment I heard a car door slam. Homicide Inspector Carlos Romero, of the San Francisco Police Department, had double-parked his unmarked police car on busy Haight Street, causing an immediate traffic snarl. Relief warred with consternation in my chest. Carlos was a friend. But he was also a cop.

"Everything okay here, folks?" Carlos said as he joined us, his dark brown eyes evaluating the tense scene.

"Just peachy," I piped.

"Lily Ivory stole from me," said Tristan.

"Is that right?" Carlos said. "And who might you be?"

"I am Mr. Tristan Dupree," Tristan replied in his stilted way.

Carlos turned to me, a faint smile on his face. "Lily, did you steal something from this gentleman?"

"This is one of those complicated situations. . . ." I trailed off.

"Meaning what, exactly?" asked Carlos.

"Meaning I'm not sure what he's talking about."

Tristan repeated: "Forty-eight hours."

"What happens then?" Carlos asked, his eyes boring into Tristan.

"Am I free to go, Inspector?" Tristan asked.

Carlos and I exchanged a glance. He was dressed in plain clothes, and no one else had called him by his title. How had Tristan known he was a cop—and an inspector at that?

"Not if you're making threats against Ms. Ivory, you're not," said Carlos.

"I am not the one who is making the threats," Tristan said. He nodded at Sailor. "He is the one with whom you should speak. One moment ago he threatened my life. Lily Ivory, I am staying at the Hotel Marais. On Bush Street, not far from the Chinatown gates." He handed me a business card from a downtown hotel. "Room two seventeen. I shall be waiting to hear from you."

Carlos, Sailor, and I watched as Tristan Dupree turned and walked down the street. He had a slight limp but was nonetheless an imposing figure.

"Lily, you sure do know some interesting people," Carlos said, breaking the silence. "Friend of yours?"

"An acquaintance, at best," I replied. "I met him in Germany many years ago, and haven't seen him since."

"What did you steal from him?"

"Honestly, I have no idea."

"So you *did* steal something?"

"Honestly—"

"You have no idea," Carlos finished my sentence with a nod.

"What brings you here, Carlos?" I asked, changing the subject.

"Just so happens I was down the street at Coffee to the People when Maya called. She thought there might be trouble."

"No trouble here," I chirped.

Sailor glowered.

"That a fact?" Carlos said. "So what's with the forty-eight-hour deadline?"

"I'm sure it's nothing to worry about; Tristan's a bit of a drama king," I said. "I'll look through my old things, see if I might have accidentally squirreled something away."

I was lying through my teeth. I had no idea what a bēag was, much less whether I had stolen one from Tristan. I needed to give this some thought, away from the presence of the police inspector.

Sailor was staring at me, his confusion apparent. Carlos glanced at him, then at me. "All righty, then. Lily, let me know if there's any more trouble. And, Sailor—don't kill anyone. Matter of fact, stop *threatening* to kill anyone. We clear?"

Sailor didn't react. He did this often: The curtain would come down over his handsome features like a wall of ice. On the rare occasions that ice melted . . . well, it made my heart go wonky.

But right now it irritated me. Couldn't he just *once* be cooperative and say, "Sure thing, Inspector"? Then again, I reminded myself, not everyone lies as easily as I've learned to do.

Carlos waited. "Sailor, I'm serious. You got a history with this guy?"

Sailor shook his head.

"Did you threaten him?"

Sailor shrugged.

"Sailor was feeling protective," I volunteered, "because Tristan's a bit of an odd fellow, as I'm sure you noticed."

"And because he gave you a mysterious forty-eight-hour deadline," said Carlos.

"That, too."

"I have no plans to do anything to him," Sailor said. "But if he bothers Lily—"

"You won't back down. Okay, got it. Lily, may I see the card he gave you, please?"

I handed Carlos the business card for the Hotel Marais. He nodded. "I know the place. I'll have a uniform go over and have a chat with this Mr. Tristan Dupree, make sure he understands we don't want any trouble in our fair city. You're certain you don't know what he's after?"

"Very certain. But I'll look into it—that's a promise."

"You do that," Carlos said as he headed for his car.

He paused before getting in and said, "In the meantime, both of you: Keep the peace, will you? I've got homicides to deal with. I can't afford to be riding herd on the two of you."

As Sailor and I stepped into Aunt Cora's Closet, Oscar peeked out from behind the brocade curtain that separates the workroom from the display floor. Apparently relieved to see it was only us, he ran around in circles, his hooves tapping on the wooden floor, then excitedly butted my shins.

"A lot of help you are," I grumbled, but gave him a smile and a scratch behind the ears. "So much for being a fearsome guard pig."

"What was all that about?" asked Maya. "Who was that guy?"

"An old acquaintance. He thinks I have something of his."

"Like what?"

"A . . . blegh, I think?" I tried to recall what Tristan had said.

"A blog?" Maya asked. "That can't be right. You're scared of the Internet."

"No, not a blog. A . . . bag, maybe?"

"Sounded more like a *beeg* to me," said Sailor.

"And what's a beeg?" asked Maya. Without waiting for an answer, she opened the shop laptop—the one I avoided like the plague—and started to search the Internet.

"We don't know," I said, moving to look at the computer screen over her shoulder. "Does anything come up?"

"Let's see. . . . There's a movie review site, and Bleeg is a last name . . . and the Urban Dictionary says 'bleeg' is slang for something sex-related, but no surprise there.

'Beeg,' without the *l*, brings up nothing but porn. Lily, I know your past is a bit mysterious, but were you at one time into pornography? Because that really doesn't sound like you."

"Pretty sure I wasn't," I said, elbowing Sailor, who looked amused—and perhaps a little intrigued—at the idea of my being a secret porn princess.

"None of this makes sense—you say he's looking for an item of some sort?" Maya asked.

Sailor nodded. "He claimed Lily stole it from him."

"Given my previous encounter with Tristan Dupree, it's probably something arcane and magical, or at least he thinks it is," I said. "I have a few boxes of mementos tucked away upstairs; I'll look through them and see if I can figure out what he's talking about."

Oscar rubbed against my legs again, and absent-mindedly I reached down to tug his soft piggy ear. Oscar is a very special witch's familiar. Technically he isn't a familiar at all, but a shape-shifting creature that Aidan Rhodes had "gifted" me upon my arrival in San Francisco.

Speaking of Aidan . . . the self-proclaimed godfather of Bay Area witches might know something about what Tristan was after. Tristan Dupree had an oddly inflected style of speaking—was it possible he was asking about "the bag"? The most significant "bag" in my life was a special satchel Aidan had asked me to guard when he was out of town not too long ago. Could that be what Tristan was referring to? Aidan might know, and even if he didn't, he had an occult research library in his office. Some of his books dealt with obscure aspects of witchcraft.

And Aidan was a night owl.

That decided it: If I had time, I would drop by the wax museum after closing Aunt Cora's Closet this evening, once I'd gotten the busload of witches settled in with Calypso. It was high time Aidan and I had a pow-wow, anyway, to discuss the supernatural threat looming over San Francisco. I would also warn him not to agree to hold the Magical Match fund-raiser at the wax museum, just in case a member of the Welcome coven got to him. And I felt like I should invite him to my wedding, a wedding he was dead set against. That should be fun.

Great Goddess, my life was complicated.

"Hey, Sailor," said Maya. She'd stopped searching for mysterious bleegs and was making sure the store's Web site was up-to-date. "What was the deal with you yesterday?"

"Yesterday?"

"At that Chinese herb place the Lucky Moon, on Sacramento near Grant? A little after four?"

Sailor frowned. "The Lucky Moon is my regular herb shop. But I wasn't in Chinatown yesterday. I worked with Patience all afternoon, then came here for dinner."

Maya tilted her head, the way she did when she was puzzled. "But . . . this is so weird. Honestly, Sailor, you're not easily mistaken for someone else. We were standing right next to each other at the cash register. Motorcycle jacket, black boots . . . ?"

Sailor shook his head again. "I don't know what to say, Maya. I wasn't there."

"Do you have a twin brother, by any chance?"

He let out a quick bark of laughter. "Not that I'm aware of."

"Can you imagine?" I breathed, nearly fanning myself at the thought of *two* Sailors walking around.

"It must have been someone who looks like me," said Sailor.

I stared at him, and my stomach fell. He wasn't being entirely truthful.

Don't overreact, I told myself. Sailor and I were both new to this romantic-relationship deal; it was only natural to experience a few hiccups along the way. I would ask him about it tonight, when we were alone.

"Nice dress," Sailor said, checking out the wedding dress Wind Spirit had brought in. One eyebrow rose. "Or am I not supposed to see that before the big event?"

"You don't find it a little . . . meringue-y?"

He inclined his head. "It does make me think of pie."

"Sailor, did you feel anything when you met Tristan?" I asked, changing the subject.

"No, he was strongly guarded," Sailor said. "All I felt was a simmering threat."

"I would imagine that had more to do with your regular old human radar than anything psychic," Maya said. "That Tristan is one creepy dude. I could feel it through the glass, and I'm about as psychic as my dog, Loretta."

"Actually," said Sailor, "most animals are highly intuitive."

Maya smiled. "Bad example. You know what I mean."

"I do." He returned her smile. "Anyway, I have to rush off; I'm due in Oakland in half an hour. Sorry about yesterday, Maya; I can't tell you who that was."

"No worries," she said.

"What's up in Oakland?" I asked.

"I'm working with my aunt Renna today." Once upon a time Sailor had been a powerful psychic, under the wing—and the thumb—of Aidan Rhodes. He had recently gained his freedom but at the cost of some of his psychic abilities. Ever since, Sailor had been training intensively to relearn how to interpret and control his natural talents.

"Oh, um . . . say hi to her for me. If it feels appropriate," I said. Sailor's aunt Renna was a talented Rom fortune-teller. She was another person who was angry with me. Since I'd arrived in San Francisco, I had, for the first time in my life, made several good friends, but had also made some powerful enemies. I might want to watch that.

Sailor smiled and brushed a lock of dark hair off my forehead. "She'll come to the wedding, and peace shall be made."

"Is that some sort of ancient Rom saying?"

"As a matter of fact, it is. Though I may have mangled the translation. But Renna wouldn't miss out on what I promised her would be some amazing hors d'oeuvres, and in our family, at least, once someone attends a wedding and eats something, they're obligated to support the marriage."

"Well, then," I said, a little fluttery sensation in my stomach. "We'll have to make sure those are some darned yummy appetizers."

"Fried okra, maybe? For the moment, though, Lily, please do me a favor and put some extra protection on the store?"

I nodded. The protection spell I cast each morning was probably the reason Tristan had hesitated to enter Aunt Cora's Closet. A determined foe would be able to find a way through, including by force, but the spell would slow a person down and, at the very least, give a witch like me a few extra seconds to act.

"And stay away from that hotel and this Dupree character," Sailor said, his tone sterner.

"Right back at you, big guy," I responded.

Sailor raised an eyebrow. "So that's how it's going to be, eh?"

"'What's sauce for the goose is sauce for the gander.'"

He smiled. "I'm good with gander sauce. Besides, I'm heading over the bridge, in the opposite direction."

"Good. See you tonight?"

"Actually, probably not. I'll be working late."

"Oh . . . okay."

He looked into my eyes, cupped the back of my head in his hand, and kissed me. His voice dropped to a whisper. "I'll call you."

I nodded and saw him out the front door.

When I turned back, Maya was fanning herself. "I tell you what," she said in a blatant imitation of my Texas twang. "If that man *does* have a twin brother, I call dibs."

Chapter 3

The problem with Tristan Dupree showing up and issuing vague threats was that I was a very busy witch these days, and didn't have a lot of time to look for whatever it was he wanted. In addition to my planning fund-raising teas and my own wedding, not to mention finding the perfect vintage wedding gown, San Francisco was facing a frustratingly nonspecific existential menace that involved the cupcake lady named Renee Baker.

Hard to believe someone who peddled ornately frosted little "fairy cakes," as Renee called them, could pose a danger of any kind, much less supernatural. But that was how my life had unfolded ever since that day years ago in Hong Kong, when I met a parrot named Barnabas in a bar. I had been at a crossroads in my life, and Barnabas advised me to head to the City by the Bay—but warned me to "mark the fog."

And he was right—the moment I arrived in San Francisco, it felt like home, though the fog did seem to inspire a good deal of supernatural mayhem. And now, despite my determination to avoid getting involved in such things, I was smack-dab in the center of local witchy politics.

Which meant it was high time for a visit to the wax museum.

First, though, I wanted to see if I could find whatever it was Tristan was certain I possessed. That entire episode involving my reunion with my father in Germany remained just barely beyond my mind's reach, like the cloudy aftermath of a bad dream. I had occasional flashes of memory, disconnected images in my mind, but that was all. I had never been able to make any sense of them, and a big part of me didn't want to. I was afraid.

Still, maybe I had accidentally purloined the man's heirloom jewelry or some such. If so, I would find it and give it back; then Tristan would go away, and everyone would be happy. As simple as that.

Yeah, right. As they said in my hometown of Jarod, Texas, just because a chicken has wings don't mean it can fly.

"Still, it's worth a shot," I muttered while sorting through a bag of clothing acquired from a woman whose elderly grandmother had passed. It was a gold mine: designer women's dresses from the early 1960s that she had sold to me for pennies on the dollar, just to get them out of her closets.

"Did you say something?" Maya asked as she finished ringing up a customer's purchases. It had been a busy day; the Union Street Spring Celebration and Easter Parade was coming up, and we'd been swamped all afternoon with customers searching for just the *right* outfit. San Franciscans did like their celebrations.

"Um . . . no, sorry. I was just talking to myself." *Lordy, Lily.* Losing track of the conversation was bad enough, but a witch who talked to herself ran the risk of accidentally casting a spell and causing havoc.

"No worries. Hey, Bronwyn just forwarded me another text from your grandmother's coven. They decided to head to the Monterey Bay Aquarium to see the sea otters, so they won't be here tonight after all."

"Oh, that's too bad." The truth was, I felt of two minds. While I was anxious to see Graciela after so many years, I would be happier if I could get Tristan out of my hair before the coven arrived.

"Speaking of the grandmas . . ." I dialed Calypso Cafaro's number.

After exchanging pleasantries, she asked, "What do you hear from Graciela?"

"Not a lot, actually. They keep driving through dead zones. They're in Monterey now, visiting the aquarium. I'm sure they'll arrive soon. Sorry it's been so delayed. I hope it's not driving you crazy, not knowing when to expect them."

She laughed. "It's no problem at all. I'm here, tending my gardens. I've got cots lined up from back when I had foster kids, and several mattresses and air beds on the floor. They'll have to share, but we'll make do. They're welcome anytime."

"This really is so generous of you."

"Are you kidding me? The chance to confer with a coven of botanical geniuses? I'm excited beyond words. Plus, I'm putting them to work: They're going to do some guest speaking at my classes."

"Passing on their knowledge to a new generation?"

"Exactly so. And one of these days you promised to teach a few classes with me, too, remember?"

I smiled. "I remember very well. I keep waiting for my life to settle down a bit, but it looks like that's going to be too long a wait. Maybe I should just jump in—we could do a group event with Graciela's coven."

"I can just see it now," she said with a low chuckle. "They won't know what hit them!"

Hanging up the phone, I looked around the shop to see what needed my attention.

"Laundry," I said. "It's the go-to answer for 'What's next?'"

Maya cast a sidelong glance at the clothes I had separated into three piles: repair, machine-wash, hand-wash. "Why is the 'hand-wash' pile always, by far, the largest?"

"The wonder of vintage clothing."

"Want me to start a load of the washables?"

"Good idea. Let's put a load in, and then close up shop."

"Don't you want to try on the wedding dress? It looks a little out of proportion for you, but you're right—my mom's a whiz with things like that. She could alter it, no problem."

I wasn't sure why I was hesitating. The dress's vibrations weren't negative, but they just didn't feel . . . right. I couldn't quite put my finger on it. "Selena's coming by in the morning to try on bridesmaid dresses. Maybe I'll try it on then. It's almost six o'clock."

"Already? I didn't realize it had gotten so late. That explains why Oscar's so hungry," Maya said, feeding Oscar a handful of the Annie's organic cheese bunny crackers I kept behind the counter for cranky children.

"Oscar's *always* hungry," I said. As I glanced at my pig, I realized he might be able to shed some light on the Tristan Dupree situation.

Maya and I chatted companionably as we tidied up and closed the shop. Then she left to meet some friends at Cha Cha Cha, a Caribbean bar featuring pitchers of sangria, farther down Haight Street. I locked the door behind her, used a candle dressed with olive oil and camphor to cast an extra-strong protection spell as I had promised Sailor I would, then passed through the rear workroom and went up a set of stairs, Oscar's hooves tapping on the wooden planks as he trailed me. At the top of the stairs I unlocked the door to my second-floor apartment.

As I walked in, the day's tension and worries lifted from my shoulders. I was *home*.

This was the first home I had made for myself, and in many ways it was my first *real* home, a refuge from the world where I felt entirely at ease. A wreath of nettles on the door was pretty, and provided some basic protection. As I walked into the small foyer, I was greeted by the subtle scents of lavender and rosemary, herbs I had grown in my garden, dried, and sewn into soft squares of colored silk. I had hung the fragrant sachets throughout the apartment. A mirror on the wall opposite the front door served double duty: It repelled negative spirits and allowed me to primp briefly before leaving to start my day.

The apartment was not big, but it was more than sufficient for my needs. A small sitting room was furnished with a plump sofa and a comfortable chair, and opened onto the spacious terrace, where I had my garden—essential for a witch who worked with botanicals. My cozy bedroom was painted in soothing shades of white and cream that complemented the handmade quilt, in a wedding ring pattern, on my brass bed.

My favorite room, though, was the kitchen. It was a large, airy space. Sunshine poured in through the large windows, the floor was tiled in an old-fashioned black-and-white checkerboard pattern, and bundles of drying herbs dangled from wooden ceiling beams. A moon chart hung by the counter, on which sat a pot of fresh basil. On a high shelf was my battered red leather-bound Book of Shadows, containing spells and incantations, as well as quotes and newspaper clippings—many of which reminded me of events I would like to forget but knew I must not.

"*Oof.* That was a loooong day," said Oscar, sighing wearily, as though he'd spent the day digging ditches in the hot sun instead of snoozing on his silk pillow fifty minutes out of every hour. He perched on the kitchen counter, his snout still covered in orange cracker crumbs. "This ten-to-six business is wearing me out. . . ."

"Is that right?" I said, filling my old copper kettle with water and setting it on the burner. "Napping all day tuckers you out, does it?"

"That's a ruse," Oscar said solemnly. "I'm actually fully alert, ready to spring into action. You think it's that easy?"

I smiled. "Probably not. So tell me: What does a hardworking gobgoyle such as yourself need to revive?"

"A little mac 'n' cheese couldn't hurt."

Oscar remained in pig form only when we were in public. In the privacy of our home, he shifted into his natural self: a cross between a goblin and a gargoyle. It's hard to imagine quite how such a pairing came together, but as with many things in the supernatural world, it was best not to ask too many questions. Oscar's hide was gray-green and scaly; he had large hands and taloned feet, big batlike ears, and a longish snout. At full height he didn't quite reach my waist.

Oscar called himself my familiar and addressed me as "mistress," but at this point in our relationship he was more like my sidekick. A garrulous, ravenous sidekick who was wise in the ways of the magic folk.

"Mac 'n' cheese? What a surprise," I said with a smile, and began to gather the ingredients for Oscar's favorite meal. Luckily, I had replenished my cheese supply last weekend at the farmers' market. Oscar adored cheese. And carbs. Mostly in combination. "Oscar, will you start the pasta cooking?"

"Yes, mistress." He took the large soup pot from the shelf near the stove and went over to the sink to fill it.

"Oscar, do you know what Tristan Dupree was talking about?"

"Don't like that guy," Oscar said, placing the pot on the old Wedgewood stove and lighting the burner.

"So you know him?"

Silence. He stared at me with his wide bottle green eyes, doing his best to look innocent. This was another way in which Oscar wasn't a typical familiar: He only occasionally told me what I wanted to know, or did what I asked him to do. And he was stubborn as all get-out. By now I knew better than to waste my breath trying to get him to tell me something he wasn't ready to reveal.

"All righty, then," I said. "Let's come at this from a different angle: Do you know what Tristan might be looking for? What's a 'beeeuuugh,' or whatever it was he called it?"

He shrugged one bony shoulder. "Beats me. I forgot my Old English. It's been years since anybody talked that way." Oscar was something of a linguistic chameleon. He spoke numerous spirit languages, when speaking English favored a lot of teen slang, and now had a tendency to mimic my Texas twang. Or maybe he was making fun of me; it was hard to tell.

"Just how old are you?"

He looked at me askance. "You're not supposed to ask things like that! *Sheesh*."

It was humbling to be taught social niceties by a gobgoyle.

I sneezed.

"*Gesundheit.* You know what you oughta do for that cold? Find a topaz the color of the sea. Take a boat out to the middle of the bay and—"

"It's not a cold."

"Whatever you say." Oscar shrugged. "How much longer until the mac 'n' cheese is ready?"

"Soon as the pasta's done, little guy," I said, finishing the cheese sauce. "I don't have time to bake it in the oven like I usually do, so cheese sauce and macaroni mixed together in the pot will have to do. I need to take care of a few things."

"I'm sure it will be fine," Oscar said magnanimously. "Whatcha gotta do that's so important?"

"I want to take a quick look through my old suitcase, and then I have to go see Aidan."

"Master Aidan? Why?" Oscar's huge eyes got impossibly wide.

"He's not your master anymore, remember?"

"Listen." He tried to smile, which came across as a grimace, then chuckled, which sounded like a rusty saw. "No need to talk with Maaaiiiister Aidan, no need at all. I know a *little* Middle English—how about this?"

He launched himself off the counter, landed lightly on the kitchen floor, and began reciting a poem, complete with sweeping gestures of his surprisingly graceful oversized hands:

WHAN that Aprille with his shoures soote
The droghte of Marche hath perced to the roote,
And bathed every veyne in swich licour,
Of which vertu engendred is the flour;
Whan Zephirus eek with his swete breeth—

"Stop that Oscar! Stop it at once!" I said, alarmed. "Is that . . . are you casting a *spell*?"

He blinked, one arm still held aloft, frozen in a dramatic pose. "What are you talkin' about? You know my kind don't cast spells."

"Then . . . what are you doing?"

"Duh." He rolled his eyes.

"Duh *what*?" I said, impatient now.

"I'm reciting the prelude from *The Canterbury Tales*." Oscar's tone suggested this was the most obvious thing in the world. When I didn't react, he added, "Hello, Geoffrey Chaucer? Ring a bell?"

"Um . . . sort of," I mumbled.

"I know you didn't finish high school, mistress, but you did go for a couple of years, right? I thought they made kids memorize and recite that in English class."

"Maybe. I don't know. I was sort of . . . absent. A lot. So, okay, I'm not up to speed on Chaucer. The point is, why are you reciting one of his poems?"

"'S not poetry, exactly. More like a prose poem, I guess. It's written in rhyming couplets—"

"Okay, sorry. My fault for asking the wrong question." Oscar was a stickler for precise language. "Let's focus. What is Tristan Dupree looking for? You're saying he used an Old English word?"

He rolled his eyes.

"By that very rude gesture I'm going to assume you mean, 'Yes, mistress.'"

I decided to pursue this line of questioning later, when he might be more forthcoming. Hunger made Oscar a mite testy. No two ways about it, Oscar and I had a nontraditional witch-and-familiar relationship.

I drained the cooked pasta and poured it into a bowl, mixed in the cheese sauce, and grated some Parmesan over the top. Not a gourmet version of mac 'n' cheese, but better than the premade stuff from a box. I set the steaming bowl on the kitchen table. "Serve yourself. There's also a pizza in the freezer if you get hungry later. Unless you want to come with me to visit Aidan?"

"I . . . uh . . ." He picked at his talons.

As nervous as Aidan made me, he had a much stronger effect on my familiar. Oscar had been bound to Aidan for a very long time, until I freed him by stealing back his wings. The wings themselves had been destroyed in the process, but at least Oscar now had his freedom. Ever since, though, whenever Oscar was around "Master Aidan," he was alternately obsequious, giddy, and nervous as all get-out.

"Tell you what: You eat your dinner while I look for something. Let me know what you decide in a few minutes, okay?"

I went into the bedroom, closed the door behind me, and headed to the closet. At the very back, behind the clothes hanging on the rod, sat an old suitcase I had lugged around the world with me but hadn't opened since arriving in San Francisco. It was nothing like today's luggage; heavy and hard-backed, it was a mottled jade green, a 1960s-era suitcase as vintage as any of the clothes in my shop. My mother had called it her "special valise" when she helped me pack it to move in with Graciela, all those years ago. I stared at it for a moment, reminding myself to breathe, before dragging it out of the closet and hoisting it onto the bed.

I had never really blamed my mother for sending me away when I was eight. Children with supernatural powers can be a challenge to raise. I had recently become an unofficial "big sister" to a powerful young witch named Selena, who, despite my own powers, kept me on my toes. My mother, in comparison, was a simple small-town woman overwhelmed with life in general, never mind her magical misfit of a daughter.

But lately I had started wondering. Every once in a while Bronwyn's grandchildren would come hang out at the shop, or customers would wander in with their kids. Seeing children who were about the age I'd been when I left my home made me realize just how young

I had been. How vulnerable. How in need of guidance and love and nurturing.

Of course, it wasn't as if my mother had put me out on the *street*, I reminded myself. She had sent me to live with Graciela, a woman who loved me unconditionally and had the strength and knowledge to handle my talents while helping me to understand them.

Still . . . now that I had made my home in San Francisco and had made friends—*good* friends, who felt more like family—I was beginning to realize that I wasn't so bad, after all. Yes, I was different, but I wasn't wicked and I wasn't a freak. I was a person as deserving of love as any other.

All of a sudden I flashed on a memory of the drive-the-demons-out-of-her ritual I had been subjected to when I was seventeen, and felt a surge of anger toward Margarita Ann Velasquez Ivory. My mother.

Well, I thought. This reunion was going to be interesting. Clearly, I had a lot to say to the mother of the bride.

I pushed those thoughts aside for the moment and concentrated on the suitcase in front of me. I placed my hands on it and took a moment to ground myself before opening it.

The suitcase's old metal fasteners popped open with a loud *snick*. I splayed the luggage open to reveal several tightly packed pouches and small boxes, many of which were bound with magically knotted string, as well as a manila envelope containing loose papers and newspaper clippings. I had traveled the world for many years before coming to San Francisco, and this suitcase was filled with items I needed to keep from each locale. Not the fun souvenirs that I picked up in my wanderings, such as my Bavarian cuckoo clock or stash of antique Chantilly lace. And don't get me started on the vintage clothing I had started to collect and which was one of the main reasons for opening Aunt Cora's Closet. No, this suitcase was filled with mementos too important to discard, even if I wanted to.

"Whatcha doin'?"

I jumped at the sound of Oscar's gravelly voice, right behind me.

"*My Lord in heaven*, Oscar, you scare me when you do that!" Oscar had an uncanny ability to sneak up on me.

He cackled and waved one oversized hand. Goblin humor.

"Whatcha doin'?" he repeated.

"I don't know if you noticed," I said, slamming the suitcase shut, "but the bedroom door was closed."

He stared at me.

"That usually means something," I continued.

He shrugged.

"A desire for privacy?" I suggested.

"Wasn't locked."

"That's true, but you could have knocked. What if I had been dressing?"

"You weren't."

"No, but—"

"So what's the problem?"

I gave up. One day I would have to write a book: *Etiquette Lessons for Gobgoyles*.

"What's in the suitcase?" Oscar persisted, and once again I was reminded of how intelligent he was. He didn't fall for my attempt at diversion.

Keeping things to myself was a lifelong habit, and a hard one to break. It wasn't my default to be open and trusting with others, like Bronwyn was. But I was trying to change.

Besides, the little guy and I had been through numerous adventures together, and he had saved my life more than once. And the truth was, Oscar was probably more likely than I to figure out whether something in the suitcase might be what Tristan Dupree was looking for.

So despite my misgivings, I opened the suitcase. Oscar perched on the bed and leaned in.

"Ooooh! What's this? What's that?" he asked excitedly, poking at one object after another. "What's *this*?"

"Tea from Sri Lanka . . . seashells from a beach in Peru . . . lava rocks from a volcano in the Philippines . . . a handful of wool from Iceland."

"How 'bout this?" His knobby index finger landed on a bundle of postcards.

"Those are postcards I wrote to my mom."

"But you didn't send them?"

I shook my head. Oscar's face was covered in scales and didn't express much emotion, but his big green eyes were another story. At the moment they were filled with sympathy.

He nodded and let out a long sigh. "Mother issues. Those are the worst."

Oscar had been searching for his own mother for years. She suffered under a spell that turned her into a stone gargoyle most of the time. I didn't know many details—I didn't know much at all about my familiar's life before he met me—but I did know Oscar would never stop searching for her. Gargoyles lived a *long* time, he'd informed me.

"What's with all the newspaper?" he asked.

"Those are articles about a fire in Germany a while back," I said.

"What is it with you and fire?" Oscar asked, shaking his head. "'Member what happened at the wax museum?"

Did I ever. I still had vivid memories—and the occasional nightmare—of the wax figures melting, turning into hot molten puddles on the floor, swirling and pooling and streaming as if reaching out to capture us as we tried to escape the inferno. I shivered. I was *not* looking forward to going back there to visit Aidan in his newly renovated digs.

"And what's this?" Oscar asked again, poking a little leather pouch that looked a lot like the medicine bag I kept tied at my waist.

I picked it up, weighed it in my hand for a moment, felt for vibrations.

"This is my land bag. I put a little earth from each place I spent more than a few nights."

He held his hand out and I set it on his palm. He closed his eyes for a moment. "Cool, you went all over. What was Madagascar like?"

"You can sense that?"

He snickered as though I were making a joke. I had known my familiar for quite a while now, but still wasn't clear on the extent of his abilities.

"There's no San Francisco in there," he said.

"That's because I haven't left—" My stomach did a strange little flip. I really needed to speak to Aidan to address the threat posed to my adopted city by Renee-the-cupcake-lady. If we weren't able to defeat her . . . would I have to leave? Would I become a wanderer again? If so, would Sailor come with me? Would Oscar? What about my friends?

Oscar pointed to a battered cardboard shoe box, sealed with duct tape and twine. It was wrapped in long-dried loops of rowan—a plant common to protection spells—and covered with hand-drawn symbols. My teenage attempt to keep evil at bay.

"What's in *there*?" he whispered.

I lifted the box from the suitcase. This was what had come to mind when Tristan accused me of stealing something from him.

The shoe box held the remnants of my meeting with my father in Germany, many years ago. When I was just seventeen and unsure of myself as a person, much less of my abilities as a witch. I had only vague memories of the reunion, lingering, disconnected flashes of images, like the snippets of a vivid dream—or, more aptly, a nightmare.

I hesitated. If I opened this box, would I learn something about my father, or our encounter, or *myself*, that I had suppressed so long ago? Some memory that would be best left in the past, unremembered?

There was a reason I hadn't opened it all these years. But I sensed it was time to deal with it, whether or not it was connected to Tristan.

I took a deep, calming breath and steeled myself. I wasn't a teenager anymore but a grown woman and a powerful witch. The past months in San Francisco had taught me that I was stronger, and more in control of my magic, than I'd ever thought I could be.

"Hand me the pair of scissors on the chifforobe, will you?" I asked, sniffing loudly.

"You're catching a cold."

"I don't get colds."

"I didn't think you were immortal."

"I'm not immortal—I just don't get colds. If my throat gets scratchy, I take garlic and lemon, or a spoonful of honey with turmeric, and then I'm all good."

"'Kay. Maybe you should do that, because you've got a cold."

Oscar leaned over and grabbed the scissors, then slowly, solemnly handed them to me.

His eyes remained on me, steady and wide. I started chanting as I cut through the rowan and the knotted threads, feeling the faint resistance from my teenage spell. I had been only partially trained when I was forced to leave my grandmother at the age of seventeen, but clearly I had done my darnedest to cast a binding spell over this otherwise innocuous-looking shoe box.

I sliced through the heavy packing twine, and finally snipped at the duct tape. The process took several minutes, and my chanting never faltered. Oscar watched intently, his mere presence adding strength and calm to the flow of energy through me . . . though to tell the truth, I felt something resisting my magic. Could the contents of the box be fighting against me, or could it be the remnants of my teenage spell?

Nonetheless, I completed the charm.

Taking one final deep breath, I lifted the lid off the box.

Chapter 4

Something inside slithered.

Oscar let out a screech and leapt onto the top of the armoire.

I managed to slide the cover, still looped in rowan, back into place and jumped back. I grabbed a few crystals and a tiger's-eye talisman from my nightstand and slapped them down on top of the shoe box. From inside the box came a distinctive *thump*.

"What the heck is *that*?" Oscar growled.

"I'm not sure," I choked out, my heart pounding. I met my familiar's eyes. "I think I might need to take a few more precautions before opening it."

"Ya *think*?"

"No need to be sarcastic."

"What you should do is take the whole kit 'n' caboodle to Maaaa*iiis*ter Aidan. See if he can find the whatchamahoozit that Tristan guy's lookin' for."

"I thought you were afraid of Aidan?"

He puffed out his scaly chest. "Oscar's not *afraid* of

anything. It's just that . . . I have other things to do tonight. I was going to use the cloak you gave me."

"The cloak? What will you use it for?"

A while back I had come across an enchanted cloak that had the ability to transport the wearer through time and space, to places one had been before. To compensate Oscar for the loss of his wings, I had given it to him. From time to time, Oscar would disappear for a day or two, but I had not realized he was using the travel cloak.

Oscar shrugged. "You're not the only one with important things to do, ya know."

"Well, now, that's fair," I said.

Now that Oscar and I were no longer truly witch and familiar, he had his own path to follow. And like me, he tended to keep his cards close to his chest. It was entirely possible he was simply meeting some magical friends for a round of margaritas, guacamole, and gossip, though he might also be on some kind of magical mission. Oscar liked to play it cool, but I knew he loved San Francisco as much as I did. This was our adopted home.

Once again, I thought of the impending threat to our beautiful City by the Bay. I wasn't even sure precisely what the threat *was*, but I'd sensed long ago that my arrival in San Francisco wasn't entirely accidental. Aidan and I had banded together to try to strengthen our magical alliances for the big supernatural showdown, whenever that might occur. I knew Renee-the-cupcake-lady was involved, but didn't know exactly how.

Could Tristan's sudden appearance somehow be connected?

"Okey-dokey," I said, trying to sound casual, hoping to reassure Oscar—or myself?—that creepy strangers and sealed shoe boxes with mysterious slithery contents were all in a day's work. "I'm going to just wrap that puppy up and go see Aidan. If you travel tonight, promise me you'll be careful?"

He waved his oversized hand and grimaced, his version of a smile.

I took a carved pendant from the top drawer of my dresser. It was a crescent moon, symbol of good luck for travelers, carved with the Algiz protection rune. I had made it from a branch of an old tree from Calypso's ancient peach orchard, polished it with olive oil beside the flame of a white candle, bathed it in goat's milk, and consecrated it under the silvery light of the waning moon.

I slipped it around Oscar's neck, then patted the pendant against his chest while incanting a quick charm.

Oscar's huge eyes grew even wider, and he looked as though he was about to cry. "Mistress is very good to me."

"Well, I'd surely hate to lose you again." With a pang, I remembered the time he had disappeared: how desperate I had been to find him, and just how far I was willing to go to get him back. "Just promise me you'll be careful, and come back to me safe and sound, yes?"

"I promise," he said with a quick nod. Eyeing the shoe box suspiciously, he added: "You, too, mistress. You, too."

Thank goodness Graciela's coven had been waylaid by the lure of sea otters, I thought as I wrapped the shoe box in red felt, then black silk, before adding beads of lapis lazuli and Apache tears and finishing with a braided cord of black, red, purple, and orange silk threads, which I knotted while chanting a binding spell.

I sat back on my haunches on the bed, letting out a quick breath. I hoped that would be enough to hold whatever it was until I could ask for Aidan's help.

I sneezed again and remembered that, while chanting the spell earlier, I had sensed a resistance, a certain lack of my regular energy. Normally Oscar's mere presence was more than enough to open the portals, to allow the energy to slip back and forth beyond the veil. Was it simply the remnants of the spell I had cast on the box as a teenager, or could I really be catching a cold? And if so, was it having an effect on my magic?

No time to worry about that now. I loaded my woven Filipino backpack with mason jars full of a general protective brew, my special salts, and a variety of small stones and talismans. There was really no such thing as "all-purpose" magical supplies, since the individuality of each situation had to be respected or a spell wouldn't work properly. But I prepared the best I could. After I'd carefully tucked the resealed shoe box under one arm and slipped down the stairs, I walked through the shop and out the front door. The bell tinkled merrily as I slipped out.

I hurried around the corner to the driveway where I parked my vintage cherry red Mustang. As I drove toward the tourist mecca of Fisherman's Wharf, and the newly rebuilt wax museum, I realized: Sailor had promised to call . . . but he hadn't.

The young woman in the wax museum ticket booth didn't like me. I had once saved Clarinda's life, but even that didn't appear to have altered her opinion as to my general character. She wore a lot of white face powder, heavy eyeliner, and black lipstick, and always appeared bored to the point of falling asleep.

A very jaded Queen of the Dead.

"Howdy!" I greeted her cheerfully, because I knew it annoyed her. "Is Aidan in?"

She looked up from the battered paperback she was

reading and sneered. Her eyes flickered down to the shoe box under my arm.

"Gotta buy a ticket," she said.

"Actually, I don't," I replied. We'd had this conversation before. Repeatedly. "I'll just go on up and see him, then, all right?"

She shrugged.

Outside, the newly rebuilt tourist attraction had remounted its old-movie-poster-like placards featuring famous figures from the worlds of sports and popular music, as well as the ever-popular vampires and various torture devices in the Chamber of Horrors. But inside, the wax museum didn't look much like the old one.

I climbed a floating acrylic-and-steel staircase that swept gracefully up to the second floor, averted my eyes from the Chamber of Horrors, which always gave me the willies, and smiled at the figure of local legend Mary Ellen Pleasant, as I passed through the new display featuring Great Entertainers, such as Louis Armstrong and Barbra Streisand. Just beyond Carol Channing was the door to Aidan's office.

Few tourists would ever notice the door. Aidan had cast a glamour over it, so unless you were looking for it, the door appeared invisible.

As I held my fist up to knock, a pure white long-haired cat appeared at my side and wound around my legs. I wasn't fooled by the friendly display—Noctemus, Aidan's familiar, didn't like me and no doubt knew I was allergic to cats. Her greeting was designed to leave me with a special souvenir: a few white cat hairs on the hem of my dress. My nose twitched.

Aidan opened the door and smiled.

"Bless you," he said, in response to my sneeze. "To what do I owe the honor of this visit from my favorite witch?"

Even in a city full of attractive people, Aidan stood out. His eyes were an impossible periwinkle blue, and his golden hair gleamed under the museum's subtle lights. I was one of the few who knew that Aidan's good looks were due in no small part to another glamour; his true self showed dramatic burn scars. This was one reason he was such a homebody and a night owl; it was harder to maintain the glamour out in the open, in full daylight. Every once in a while—more frequently, recently—I noted a shimmer, a sign that the glamour was slipping.

Still, the Aidan who greeted me was lovely—and his aura sparkled still more intensely than his physical shell. Even people who weren't sensitive to auras could sense Aidan's.

"Nice to see you again, Aidan. I'm here for some advice."

He grinned, displaying dazzling white teeth. "It just so happens that advice is my middle name."

"I rather doubt that," I said. "Speaking of which, what *is* your middle name?"

"Whatever you'd like it to be, Lily," Aidan said silkily. "You know my fondest wish is to please you."

Aidan's blatantly flirtatious manner, combined with his incredible good looks, used to fluster me. Not anymore. At least . . . not as much.

"Okay if we step into your office for a consultation?"

"Please, come in," he said, standing back and waving me through the doorway. "I'll just add this to your growing list of indebtedness to me, shall I?"

This was the deal when reaching out to Aidan: Everything had a price.

Aidan's rebuilt office was an exact replica of the one that had burned down, and was decorated in a lavish style I thought of privately as "Barbary Coast Bordello."

Red velvet drapes with gold fringe hid any trace of windows, while a plush Oriental rug in deep red, emerald, and ocher hues covered the floor. A heavy carved mahogany desk and leather office chair dominated the room. Floor-to-ceiling bookcases ran along two walls, their shelves crammed with musty leather-bound tomes. Aidan had lost his last library in the fire, but told me he had managed to replace many of the rare manuscripts by scouring the Internet. I had an inkling there was more to it than that—many of the books in Aidan's collection were arcane depositories of highly specialized magic, with only one or two copies in existence—but since he allowed me to avail myself of his library whenever I wanted, I hadn't pushed the point.

I took a seat in one of the comfortable leather armchairs facing his desk, and he settled into the thronelike desk chair. Placing his hands flat on the blotter, Aidan leaned toward me.

"What can I do for you today, Lily? Is this about Selena, or Renee?"

"What? No." Then I wondered. "Why? Have you seen something?"

"Nothing new, not in particular. But we need to come up with a defensive plan soon. Have you been hunting down some of those names from the Satchel?"

I nodded. Not long ago Aidan had asked me to babysit his special satchel while he was out of town. In it were names of people who owed him favors, and who had pledged their loyalty. As the threat I believed Renee posed heated up, Aidan and I had been shoring up support, preparing to circle the magical wagons.

"We'll need the Gypsies in on this," Aidan continued. "Their support will be essential to our success."

"Sailor told me his aunt Renna is on board, and Patience Blix also agreed, though with reluctance because she's not much of a team player. Where those two go, apparently, so goes the rest of the extended family. Sailor can't speak for any other clans, of course—"

Aidan waved off my concern. "If we have Sailor's people, we're good. What matters is not just that they're Rom, but that they have special abilities."

I nodded. "Also, Hervé Le Mansec is making contact with the voodoo practitioners."

"Excellent. And how is Selena's training coming along?"

"It's . . . coming," I hedged. Selena wasn't the most patient student. Yet another way in which she reminded me of me. "Anyway, none of that is the reason I'm here tonight. I get that we need to deal with whatever Renee's up to, but I have to address something a little more immediate. I'm under a forty-eight-hour deadline."

"What is it?"

I placed the shoe box atop the desk blotter in front of him. Aidan stared at it for a long moment; then his blue eyes met mine. "Intriguing."

I nodded. "In a creepy sort of way, sure."

"Would you like me to sequester it? I know of a rather effective little Etruscan binding spell I picked up in my travels."

"No, I'd like you to open it and tell me what you see."

"Probably best not to open it."

"How so?"

His elegant eyebrows rose. "Is this a joke?"

"Not hardly."

"Why in the world would you want to open"—he inclined his head toward the box—"that?"

"Do you know a fellow named Tristan Dupree?"

"Of course."

"You do?" I had assumed Aidan knew of Tristan Dupree. I just hadn't expected him to admit it.

"How is Dupree doing these days?"

"Seems like his old self." In fact, Tristan looked exactly as he had when our paths crossed more than a decade ago. Exactly. "Anyway, he says I stole something from him."

"Did he?"

"Do you know what it is? He said it was a bleeg, or something like that? I didn't quite catch it. I wondered if he was trying to say 'bag,' and maybe referring to the Satchel you had me watch over?"

Aidan sighed. "It's not the Satchel."

"Then what is it?"

"Lily, Lily, Lily. When will you listen to me? Have I not been nagging you to study your craft more intensively?"

"Just tell me what it is, Aidan."

Aidan rose, pulled a fat volume off the bookshelf, flipped it open, and handed it to me, pointing to a passage on one page.

"I would guess Tristan was referring to a bēag."

I read: *Old English* bēag, *referring most often to circular jewelry such as rings, bracelets, necklaces; also garlands, collars, crowns; might include shackles and coils, or precious objects in general. From the Proto-Germanic* baugaz *(bow or ring); from the Proto-Indo-European* bewg *(to bend). Cognate* baug *in some German dialects (ring, collar), or Icelandic* baugur *(circle). Relative of* bagel.

"Tristan thinks I stole his bagel?"

Aidan smiled. "More likely a ring."

"Or it says here it could be a collar, a garland, or a crown. Any precious object, really." I blew out a frustrated breath. "Could I ask you something?"

"That's why you're here."

"Why do magical folks have to be so gol-durned nonspecific? Why do they always have to talk in riddles?

Why can't they just say what it is they want, in *modern* English? I'd take Spanish, or Nahuatl, for that matter."

"That would take all the fun out of it."

"Not for me. I get plenty of fun with my vintage clothes. Going out to dinner, hanging out with my friends . . ."

"If you're asking seriously, I would say it's because the flow of power we tap into is primordial, beyond language. We are interpreting symbols and sensations, which don't lend themselves to specific meanings."

"Huh. I never thought of that. Good point. Anyway, so what does 'bēag' tell us?"

"Why don't you tell me?"

"I can't—I don't remember stealing anything from anybody, much less Tristan Dupree. Do you think he might be working for somebody?"

Aidan looked thoughtful. "I suppose it's possible, but I haven't heard Dupree associated with anyone in that way. He's generally a loner, and while he might ally himself with folks from time to time, he's more of a contract worker than a salaried employee, if you get my drift. Coming after you in San Francisco indicates something more serious is afoot. Did he frighten you?"

A little, though I was loath to admit that to Aidan. I shrugged.

"Anyway, if I stole anything from anybody when I was with my father in Germany, it's probably in there," I said, pointing to the shoe box.

His gaze fell to his desktop. "The box you're afraid to open."

"Looks like I'm not the only one."

"I wouldn't say I'm afraid, exactly. More like prudent."

I held Aidan's gaze, and after a moment he let out a sigh.

"You don't remember what happened in Germany . . . none of it?"

"Not really. I get little details from time to time, flashes of memory, but nothing concrete, nothing more than a quick picture."

"And yet you remembered Tristan."

"I remember meeting him. But I don't remember what went on."

He gave me a strange look.

"What is it?" I demanded.

He shook his head. "I think the first thing we should do, long before opening this box, is to meld our magic to help you remember."

I hesitated. The first time Aidan and I melded our magic, we ended up melting metal. The second time went slightly better; he was more prepared for my energy, and I was more in control. Still, it wasn't exactly a good experience. It was . . . passionate and sensual, but also overwhelming. Threatening. I lost all sense of time, and it made me feel like I was drowning.

Avoiding Aidan's gaze, I glanced over at the bookshelf, then at Noctemus, and then at a huge brass urn etched with elaborate linear designs. The etchings reminded me of the map of the busload of witches crisscrossing the country, and that thought brought me strength. After all, I was descended from a long line of strong, wild, magical women. Even though I was mostly a solo act, I was but one in a community of witches.

It was time to face what had happened when I went to find my father, so very long ago.

"Are you sure this will work?" I asked.

"Of course not. If you've repressed the memories this long, they won't be easy to retrieve. But it's worth a try. Ready?"

I nodded.

We stood, facing each other. When I interacted with other witches—in coven meetings, for example—we had always come together heart to heart, and hand to hand. Not so with Aidan. He placed his hands on either side of my head, then bent his head to touch mine, forehead to forehead.

A shock of energy reached out, like a sustained spark between us. I could feel the sensation of electricity running from his head to mine.

We breathed together, until it was hard to tell where his breath stopped and mine began.

I reached up and placed my hands over his. A humming began, so low that at first I wasn't sure if it was external or if it was manifesting within myself. The hum grew in intensity, filling the room. Dots swam in front of my eyes, and my vision went black. It was so dark I couldn't see my hand in front of my face. I felt like I was falling, headfirst, down an endless tunnel. It seemed to go on forever.

And I started to remember. A rainy night, the taxi dropping me off at the address I had at long last tracked my father to. Standing at the door, afraid to knock. Without my making a sound, it swung open.

I saw Aidan. *"Am I seeing you?"* I asked in my mind. Was this a memory, or was this now?

He held his hand out. *"Come in,"* he said. *"Remember."*

Everything was shadowy, confusing, like a bad dream. I stepped through the door and into the burned-out shell of a once-grand house. The stench of smoke and soot was overwhelming. A wrought iron circular staircase led up through a gaping hole in the ceiling. I began to climb it, and saw a bird's nest lodged on a timber under the broken glass of an intricate skylight. The light blue speckled eggs were broken. Nestled among them was an old watch, the ticking sound growing louder and louder.

"What is this place?" I asked, but Aidan was no longer there. Instead, I saw my father standing at the bottom of the stairs. Hatred burned in his eyes. He whispered: *"Prophecy."*

My cheeks felt wet with tears. But that was impossible. I didn't cry. I *couldn't* cry.

I turned to go back down the spiral stairs, but they began to disintegrate beneath my feet. Rung by rung, the pinging of metal snapping fought with the ticking of the watch. I lost my foothold and began tumbling, falling headfirst, down and down, into the burned remains of the house, into the thick pile of ashes. . . .

I had been underwater only once, and had nearly drowned. But I vividly remembered the sensation of fighting my way up and out of the watery depths, my eyes searching for the light of the moon dancing on the surface of the bay, streaming toward it, lungs screaming for air, gut spasming. That was what this felt like.

With a violent jolt, I yanked myself out of the trance.

Chapter 5

"Hold on one gol-durned second. *Prophecy?* What prophecy?" My voice ended on a squeaky note.

Aidan and I were standing just as we had been, in the center of the room, but according to the antique grandfather clock, several hours had passed. I felt cranky and mildly nauseated, and my muscles burned with fatigue. Combining energies with Aidan was disorienting, exhausting, and, of course, revelatory.

Aidan nodded. "I believe you were named in a prophecy, yes."

"Me?"

"It wasn't clear until recently, but yes, I believe that's so."

"That's why everyone's always acted so weird around me? You couldn't have *told* a person?"

"The signs weren't clear."

"But now they are?"

He inclined his head, as casual as if he were ordering eggs for breakfast.

"This is ridiculous."

"I believe the timeline sped up a bit when you went up against the demon named Deliverance Corydon. I told you it was a mistake for you to battle her alone. A part of her now resides within you."

Deliverance Corydon was a demonlike creature who had been burned at the stake after being accused of witchcraft, way back in the day. My own guiding spirit, the Ashen Witch, had known—and fought—her back then. So it did seem foreshadowed, somehow, that I would battle her when she tried to rise again. But I rejected Aidan's theory—which he'd espoused before—that Deliverance Corydon was now a part of me.

"That's even more ridiculous. I mean, seriously, Aidan. I know Corydon was bad news, but she's gone. She came back and was destroyed by lightning, no less. Also, she despises witches."

He shrugged. "I can feel it when we meld energies."

"And I have the Ashen Witch as my guiding spirit."

"More evidence for the prophecy."

"And what does the prophecy prophesize, exactly?"

He hesitated, as though choosing his words carefully. "That a practitioner connected to your father would come to town, and spark a kind of supernatural showdown in San Francisco, the results of which would be crucial, and not just for the city. The effects have the potential to ripple out, endlessly."

"That's it?"

"There's a bit more to it, but that's the gist of it."

"And couldn't there be someone else who fits that description? You, for instance?"

He laughed and shook his head.

"And your role in this has been, what?" I demanded. "To help me? To stop me? Both? Was Oscar your spy?"

Aidan sat down in his desk chair, as though tired. "For the moment, I'm here to help you, and to help San Francisco. Lily, you're missing the point: If *I* know about this, it's a good bet other practitioners, like Renee, do as well. And if she does, she'll stop at nothing to siphon off your powers for her own use. Yet another reason this relationship between you and Sailor is a problem. It couldn't come at a worse time."

"Could you please drop it, already? You've made your opinion known, as have I. Can't we please move on? Why do you insist on trying to direct my life?"

"You don't take your magical talent seriously enough."

"That's not true. I mean . . . that might have been true when I first arrived. But things are different now."

"You've gained power, to be sure. And that's no small thing. But you're still not ready. Take this shoe box, for instance. Why haven't you opened it?"

I had no answer to that.

"Because you're protecting yourself—that's why," Aidan continued. "You haven't wanted to deal with your past, Lily, and it's coming back to bite you, the way unsettled pasts tend to do. And now, instead of focusing on developing and controlling your powers, you're rushing into marriage with a man you barely know."

"That's not true! I *have* been working on my powers, and I know Sailor very well."

"Is that right? You asked me my middle name when you arrived tonight. Do you know *Sailor's* middle name?"

"I'll get it off the marriage license. Anyway, I know him in the ways that count."

"You don't know him at all," Aidan said, an uncharacteristic note of anger in his voice. "Let me ask you this: What about children?"

"What about them?"

"Do you want them? Does he? The only thing that will bring a powerful witch down faster than falling in love is becoming a mother. Children will make you vulnerable, Lily, dangerously so. It's one thing to go up against demonic forces when your own life is at risk. Imagine risking the life of your child."

"I don't think—"

I cut myself off when Noctemus leapt down from her perch on the bookshelf, meowing loudly and heading for the door. A moment later there was a soft rapping. Aidan went to answer the door, opening it just a crack. I heard him talking softly to Clarinda.

"Call Maya," Aidan said, closing the door. He took a cell phone from his breast pocket and held it out to me.

"Why? Is something wrong?"

"Maya left a message that you need to call her. That's all I know."

"I didn't know you have a cell phone," I commented, taking the phone.

"Everyone has a cell phone."

"Not me."

He shook his head and gave me a rueful smile.

"And if you have a cell phone, why don't I have your number?"

"Make the call, Lily."

My fingers shook slightly as I dialed. If Maya had tracked me down at the wax museum, it must be important.

"Maya? What's wrong?"

"*Lily.* I've been calling everyone I could think of, trying to find you. Sailor's been arrested."

An entire shelf's worth of books flew across the room and smashed against the opposite wall, falling to the floor with a crash. Across the desk, Aidan's too-blue eyes held mine.

"*My* Sailor? Arrested for what?"

"Murder."

Chapter 6

The knowing look in Aidan's eyes was insufferable. I avoided it while I rummaged in my bag for Carlos Romero's card and called his number. The inspector wouldn't talk about the case over the phone, but to my surprise, he suggested we meet at the Buena Vista Café in ten minutes.

"What did I tell you?" Aidan asked after I had hung up and handed him his phone. "A witch like you cannot maintain a serious romantic relationship. If it doesn't destroy you, it will destroy him. Frankly I'd rather it be Sailor than you, but ultimately it's not good for—"

"Listen, Aidan. If you can't—or won't—help me," I said, enraged, as I grabbed my still-unopened shoe box and stormed out of the office, "then *stay out of it*."

I slammed the door behind me.

The Buena Vista Café sits at the corner of Hyde Street and Beach Street, not far from Fisherman's Wharf and the wax museum. Since it was past midnight on a weeknight, I found a parking spot almost directly across the street, just above Aquatic Park.

Carlos was waiting for me on the corner. I parked and jogged over to him.

"What happened?" I demanded as soon as I was within earshot. "Where is he? How do I get him out? I need to talk to him."

"And a good evening to you, too, Lily."

"Seriously, Carlos. What in the world happened? Sailor didn't kill anybody."

"If you don't know what happened, how do you know he didn't kill anybody?" Carlos asked.

"He wouldn't do that."

Are you sure? a tiny voice in my head asked. Could Aidan be right? How well did I know my fiancé, after all? Sailor had a temper—a sometimes volatile temper. Was it possible he had lost control while facing an adversary?

Once again I sneezed. I was worn-out, tired. It was late, and I was still feeling the aftereffects of melding magic with Aidan, but truthfully I had been feeling off all day. What was going on with me?

"Please, Carlos, tell me what happened."

"It's still under investi—"

"Is it your case?"

"Come, buy me a cup of coffee and we'll chat."

"At this hour?"

"We'll make it Irish coffee. A little whiskey will be good for what ails you."

"I want to see Sailor."

"All in good time. Let's talk first." He gestured to the battered box under my arm. I hadn't wanted to leave it in the car. Just in case. "What's that?"

"A shoe box," I said.

"I can see that. Is it time for show-and-tell?"

I shook my head. “Just worried about car break-ins. It’s a . . . project I’m working on.”

His eyebrows rose a smidgen, but he didn’t pursue it. Carlos held the door open for me and I led the way into the Buena Vista.

Even at this late hour on a weeknight, the place was jumping, with most seats occupied. To the left was a long bar reminiscent of an old-timey saloon, and in front of the windows were tables. We grabbed a small one not far from the door, and I stashed the shoe box on the seat next to me. Until I figured out what was in it, I wanted to keep it close.

“They say the fishermen used to drink here because they could see when the boats came in,” said Carlos after ordering two Irish coffees from the bartender.

“I’ve never been here,” I murmured, not in the mood for small talk. “But what—”

“You’ve never been to the Buena Vista?” Carlos asked. “It’s a genuine San Francisco watering hole, made famous by columnist Herb Caen. He used to ride the cable car down Hyde Street and stop in for Irish coffee. Which was invented right here at the Buena Vista, by the way.”

“To tell you the truth, Carlos, I don’t even know what Irish coffee *is*, and at the moment I don’t particularly care. Please tell me, who is the inspector assigned to this case?”

“As luck would have it, *I* am.”

“You are? But Sailor’s a friend of yours.”

“I wouldn’t go that far.”

“Are you allowed to investigate someone you know?”

“According to General Rules of Conduct Order Number Fifty-seven, ‘Conflict of Interest in Investigations’: ‘If a member is assigned to an investigation in which the member knows or suspects, or should reasonably know or suspect, that the member has a personal or family interest, the member shall immediately report the interest to the member's immediate supervisor.'"

I blinked. "You've got that memorized?"

"I've got several of the General Orders memorized. Comes in handy. Besides, I'm sorry to say this isn't the first time a potential conflict of interest has arisen. San Francisco is in many ways a small town, and I've got a large and colorful family. Ah, the drinks."

Carlos retrieved the Irish coffees from the bar and set before me a stemmed glass of steaming, fragrant coffee topped with a thick layer of cream.

"You're going to thank me for introducing you to this," he said, taking a seat and raising his glass in a toast. "Here's to exonerating your jailbird boyfriend."

"Tell me what happened. Please, Carlos."

He grew more serious, gazing out at the darkness in the direction of Aquatic Park. Finally, he blew out a breath and took another sip of his drink. "Just so we're clear, I wouldn't be discussing any of this with you if the situation didn't strike me as hinky."

"'Hinky' being the official police term for something that doesn't add up."

He nodded.

"Who is the victim?"

"You really don't know?"

I shook my head.

"Tristan Dupree."

My heart sank. *Of course.* "Carlos, honestly, Sailor was headed to Oakland—"

"There are witnesses."

"That's not possible."

"I don't know what to tell you. Except that there are indeed witnesses."

"Well . . . eyewitnesses can be mistaken."

"You think I don't know that? But three different people picked him out of a lineup. *Three*, Lily. Upstanding citizens, with no apparent ax to grind. And if that weren't enough, I've seen the hotel's security camera footage. It was Sailor."

I sat back, stunned. "There has to be some explanation."

"I'd love to hear it."

"Then tell me, what seems hinky to you?"

He shrugged, took another sip of his Irish coffee, and inclined his dark head. His eyes searched mine: intelligent, caring. Worried.

"Sailor denied it. Completely. Claimed he wasn't in that part of town, not there at all."

"And?"

"According to the witnesses and the security tapes, he *was* there. Walked out through the hotel lobby with blood on him, stopping to check his watch, cool as a cucumber. Big as day and bold as brass."

"But that makes no sense."

"No, it doesn't. Frankly, that's what troubles me the most. I can easily believe Sailor could go after someone he thought might harm you—but I can't believe he would be so ham-fisted about it. Sailor's not stupid. If he'd planned to do Dupree harm, why wouldn't he have caught him out on the street, away from witnesses and cameras?"

"Good question."

"And if Sailor *did* murder Dupree, why would he go straight home and wait for the cops to bang on his door? Or if it was a deal where he just went to talk to him, and things got out of hand, why wouldn't he have told us Dupree attacked first, claim self-defense?"

I nodded, and sneezed.

"Bless you," Carlos said. "And finally, according to the witnesses, Dupree must have fought back, because Sailor left the hotel battered—cuts, bruises, blood dripping down his face, the whole nine yards."

My heart flipped. Was Sailor okay? "Was he taken to the hospital? Is it bad?"

"That's another hinky part: When Sailor was arrested, he didn't have a scratch on him."

"He didn't?" I was relieved for Sailor, but Carlos was right—that was hinky.

He shook his head. "Of course, I hear tell there are folks out there with special talents, maybe the ability to cure a person faster than would be normal. So, the crime happened late this afternoon. Where were you this afternoon and evening?"

"I was in the shop, with Maya. We closed at six."

"That the usual time?"

"Yes."

"Okay. What did you do after the shop closed?"

"I went upstairs, made dinner for—" I halted. *I made mac 'n' cheese for my pig* would sound weird. ". . . myself, and did a little housekeeping."

"And afterward . . . ?"

"I was with Ai—" I stopped, remembering how Carlos felt about this particular witchy godfather. But the cat was already out of the bag, so I finished what I was saying. "Excuse me. I met with Aidan Rhodes at the wax museum."

Carlos gave me a look. A cop look.

"He's a business associate, Carlos."

"And what kind of business would that be, exactly?"

"Witchy business."

"Uh-huh. When was this?"

"I probably arrived at the wax museum about seven thirty or eight."

He raised an eyebrow. "And you spent the next several hours with him?"

"Time flies when you're doing witchy business."

"I'll just bet it does." He rubbed his neck. "Okay, it's not the greatest alibi, but they've got security cameras at the wax museum, which can verify your presence. Unless . . . Is this the sort of thing you can do from afar?"

"What sort of thing?"

"Curing Sailor, healing his wounds."

I sneezed again.

"Bless you."

"Thanks." I shook my head. "Lately I can't seem to even heal myself, much less someone else."

He gave me a skeptical look.

"Seriously, Carlos, that kind of healing isn't in my repertoire. My grandmother can cure all sorts of things, usually with the laying on of hands or a brew. But even she can't cast over serious injuries from a distance, as far as I know."

He nodded and lapsed into silence. This was Carlos's way, and although I sometimes had to literally bite my tongue to keep from blathering on in his presence, I had learned to try to respect his silence lest I blurt out something incriminating. I was pretty sure this was what made him such an effective homicide inspector.

We both took a moment, sipping our drinks. I'm not a big drinker, but the Buena Vista's Irish coffee was sweet, creamy, and delicious. It made me feel warm and cozy inside. It occurred to me that I hadn't eaten since lunch, and I hoped the alcohol wouldn't go straight to my head. Clearly, I had work to do.

"Did you find anything interesting in Dupree's hotel room?" I asked.

"Why would you ask that?"

"Just wondering."

"As a matter of fact, we found a root and some unidentified powders; sent 'em to the lab. You know, I had asked a friend of mine, a beat cop, to stop by earlier in the day, after Dupree seemed to threaten you at your store. At that time Dupree said he felt sick to his stomach, and my friend said he looked pretty green around the gills."

"And what does that tell us?"

Carlos shrugged.

"I didn't hex Dupree, Carlos, if that's what you're insinuating."

"I wasn't suggesting that, exactly, but I'm glad to hear you deny it. Is Sailor right- or left-handed?"

"Right-handed. Why?"

He nodded. "That's what I thought. The forensics guys said the blood spatter patterns indicate that whoever attacked Dupree was left-handed. Also, on the hotel's security footage Sailor seemed to favor his left hand: He carried a pocket watch in his left pocket and opened the door with his left hand."

"I hate to say it, but that seems . . . a little flimsy, evidence-wise. A lot of right-handed people use their left for some things."

"I know. It's just another in a long line of hinky aspects. But despite the fact that we found no trace of blood on Sailor, and no discarded clothes anywhere, the eyewitnesses and the security footage place him at the scene and are probably enough to get a jury to swing guilty. Not to mention, Dupree told me himself that Sailor threatened to kill him this morning. I gotta tell you, Lily, it doesn't look good."

"*No*, Carlos, I can't believe this. What can I do to prove Sailor's innocent?"

"Find the killer."

"I . . . um, okay."

"Keep in mind that if Sailor didn't do it, then the person who did looks a whole lot like him."

Suddenly I recalled Maya's story about seeing someone who looked just like Sailor in the herbal store; could that have been the person who killed Tristan Dupree? And if so, why? And . . . who was he?

"Need a refill?" Carlos asked. "It might just cure your cold."

"No, thanks."

"Okay, tell me everything you know about Tristan Dupree."

"I don't know much. I met him fifteen years ago or so, in Germany."

Carlos nodded. "He's a Swiss citizen, here on a standard tourist visa. We've made inquiries about him in Europe. How did you meet him?"

I thought back to the visions I'd had with Aidan. He was right. It was time to remember. Sailor's life might depend upon it.

"He worked with my father."

"That sounds like trouble."

"You're telling me." Carlos had once arrested my father for a crime he didn't commit, either . . . but still, he could tell good old Dad was bad news.

"Really, Carlos, I've been racking my brain ever since Dupree came to Aunt Cora's Closet, but I barely knew him."

"And yet he arrived on the Lufthansa flight into SFO yesterday morning, dropped his bags at the hotel, and then headed to your shop to demand you return something you'd stolen from him fifteen years ago?"

"Are you sure he came directly to Aunt Cora's Closet?"

"We're working on the timeline. The hotel says he left about forty minutes before I saw him at your place, so it's possible he stopped somewhere else. I'm not sure how much it matters. Have you figured out what he wanted from you?"

"Not yet." I thought I heard the box thump next to me. The bar was noisy, though, so it was probably my imagination.

I played with the ring on my finger. The crystals sparkled in the dim light of the bar, casting minuscule rainbows about us. Comforting me.

What bēag had Tristan been after—and what was its significance?

"Nice ring," said Carlos. "Unusual."

"It's called a druzy. Sailor gave it to me for . . ." My voice caught. I cleared my throat. "It's our engagement ring."

He nodded slowly, holding my gaze. "I heard about that through the grapevine. Congratulations."

"Thank you." I was embarrassed that I hadn't reached out to tell Carlos that Sailor and I had gotten engaged. But it had felt awkward to pick up the phone and call him to deliver the news out of the blue. After all, usually I called him about murder. Although I liked to think of Carlos as a friend, the truth was that ours was not a typical friendship. Also, although their relationship had progressed a little, he still wasn't wild about Sailor. "I guess it's been a while since I've seen you."

He nodded.

"Speaking of engagements," I continued, "my grandmother and her friends are set to arrive any day now. I'm not sure how long they'll stay, so we've sort of moved up the wedding timetable. We're having a handfasting in two weeks, in Bolinas."

"What's a handfasting?"

"It's a traditional witchy wedding, usually held outside, in a natural setting. We're not certain if Bronwyn will get her certification to officiate in time, so we might have to do the legal ceremony later. But the handfasting will be the *real* ceremony, the one that counts. I would love it if you would join us."

His mouth kicked up on one side. I imagined he was thinking, *What if Sailor is still in jail?* I decided to cross that bridge if and when we came to it.

"I would be honored, Lily," said Carlos. But there was something else in his eyes, something I couldn't put my finger on. Sailor always insisted that reading minds wasn't all it was cracked up to be, but I thought it would make my life a lot easier if I could do it.

"All right." Carlos finished off his Irish coffee and wiped a little cream from his lips with a cocktail napkin. "So, a man you haven't seen or heard from in fifteen years, whom you barely knew in the first place, arrived in town yesterday, stopped by your shop and threatened you, then got dead at the hands of someone who looks like your fiancé, walks like your fiancé, and talks like your fiancé but who is not, in fact, your fiancé. Is that about the size of it?"

I nodded.

"You know, Lily, if anyone else told me this story, I'd say they were full of it."

"But you believe me?"

"I don't *not* believe you. Did Dupree have any enemies in town that you know about?"

"I have no idea. But I'm going to find out, sure as shootin'."

If only I knew how to get started.

Chapter 7

First things first: I wanted to see Sailor. I pleaded with Carlos. Cajoled. Threatened, even—politely, of course.

Carlos was unmoved. "Do you know what time it is? Visiting hours are over, Lily. You can see him in the morning, and that's final. I'm sure you remember the basic rules: no head coverings, bare midriff, miniskirts, gang-related clothing, orange clothing that resembles inmate clothing, or anything that reveals undergarments."

"You don't know the regulations for visitation by heart?"

"I didn't want to show off," he said with a smile. "And by the way, if I hear there's been any funny stuff happening there, I'm going to be most displeased."

"Funny stuff?"

"Some member of the jail staff suddenly deciding to allow an after-hours visit between you and Sailor, for example. If I catch a whiff of you pulling some sort of magical shenanigans, I'm gonna be pissed. I'm your friend, but I'm also a cop. I'll do what I can to help, but don't push me."

"No shenanigans, magical or otherwise, I promise. Could you at least check on Sailor, make sure he's okay?"

"He's fine."

"Maybe give him a message?"

"That much I can do."

I wrote a note and cast a quick comforting spell over it. Folded it, and sealed it with a kiss.

"I said no magic stuff."

"It's just a kiss, Carlos. It doesn't actually do anything."

"All right, then. You can see him at nine in the morning. I'll leave word."

"Thank you."

"Lily." Carlos hesitated. "I assume you're going to try to find out what's going on."

"Yes. Please don't try to talk me out of it, because it won't work."

"I wasn't going to. Something weird is happening here, and you're probably the only person who has the skills to find out what that is. But *be careful*. It's a safe bet that whoever killed Tristan Dupree and framed Sailor for the crime has targeted you as well."

After declining Carlos's offer of an escort home, I waved good-bye to him and lingered outside the Buena Vista, gazing out at the dark bay waters and trying to decide what to do next.

Where in the world should I start?

A group of young people jostled along the sidewalk, stumbling toward the Buena Vista for a final nightcap before it closed. This area of the waterfront wasn't as mobbed with tourists as Pier 39, a few blocks away, but it enjoyed its fair share of visitors, due to the terminus of the Powell-Hyde cable car line. Couples walked arm in arm, peeking into art gallery windows that displayed watercolors and limited-edition silk screens of the Golden Gate Bridge, Lombard Street, and other iconic scenes of San Francisco. Nearby stood the Cannery and the Ghirardelli chocolate factory, relics of a time when there was actual manufacturing in this part of town. The old redbrick buildings had long since been renovated and turned into boutiques, restaurants, and bars that teemed with people having a good time.

I wasn't one of them.

The thought of Sailor sitting in jail—facing murder charges, no less—clawed at my belly with a mixture of dread and fear and anxiety about the future. He hadn't done it, had he? Surely not. If Dupree had been immediately threatening to me, I could imagine Sailor being capable of violence. But beating a man to death with his bare hands, then calmly heading out of the building while casually checking his watch? No. That was not Sailor.

For want of any other bright ideas, I borrowed a cell phone from the bartender who stood on the sidewalk taking a smoke break. I called a friend, then headed over to the Hotel Marais, on Bush Street.

Sailor was the best necromancer I knew. Second best was Hervé Le Mansec, a voodoo priest who owns a nifty little magical-supply shop on Valencia. I didn't know much about voodoo, but Hervé was a powerful practitioner; in a city full of charlatans, Hervé was the real deal. Also, he had become a good friend—the kind I could call and ask to meet me in the middle of the night.

"What's up?" Hervé asked when we met on Bush Street, just down the block from the Chinatown gates. He looked relaxed and wide-awake, despite the hour. Luckily a lot of us magical folk are night owls.

"A man was killed here earlier in the evening," I said. "I'm hoping you might be able to communicate with him."

Hervé looked skeptical. "You know it hardly ever works that way, right? Even if I am able to make contact, trauma victims rarely remember what happened just prior to death."

"I know. But he might be able to tell you if someone had been threatening him, or what he was after. He came to see me, searching for something he thought I'd stolen from him."

"What was it?"

"That's one of the very many things I don't know. Just . . . Really, I'd rather not say too much ahead of time. But if you can make contact and get any information at all from him, I'll be better off than I am right now."

He inclined his head. Hervé wasn't particularly tall, but he was powerfully built, with the thick physique of a rugby player. In his public role as a voodoo priest, he spoke with a lilting Jamaican accent, but in actuality he hailed from Los Angeles and had been raised Catholic.

"I appreciate your meeting me here at this hour. Please apologize to your wife for me. Again."

Hervé's wife, Caterina, was yet another person who didn't like me, though in this case it was probably for good reason. This wasn't the first time I'd asked Hervé for help after hours. *Well* after hours.

"I see you brought supplies," he said, nodding to the shoe box under my arm and the backpack slung over my shoulder.

"A few. Salts and a basic brew, a few crystals. Just the usual; I try to keep the backpack ready to go."

"In case you need to cast in a hurry?"

"I'm sure you can imagine. With the way life is unfolding lately . . ." I trailed off with a shrug.

He grinned. "Let's give it a go. You really think they'll let us in?"

"Trust me."

"Always, my friend. But just to be sure, why don't I wait out of sight while you ring the bell?"

I saw his point. I wasn't all that intimidating in my floral cotton dress—better suited to a summer picnic than a midnight assignation—tangerine cardigan, turquoise Keds, and ponytail. Hervé was another matter altogether.

The Hotel Marais was a tall, thin Victorian-era building, squashed in between a large residential building and a small theater advertising a midnight all-nude male revue. Along the facade, several flags wafted lazily in the night breeze: those of France, the United States, and California with its iconic grizzly bear, and a blue one with stars that I didn't recognize.

I climbed a short set of stone steps and rang the after-hours bell.

As a child who was shunned by the larger community of Jarod, Texas, I had developed a bit of a complex about having doors slammed in my face. But since moving to San Francisco, I had been so embraced by my friends that I had started to relax. Right now, though, the old feelings of rejection came rushing back, and I was grateful to have a friend like Hervé by my side. Hidden and crouching, but by my side nonetheless.

A thin man peered through the glass door. Young, probably a college student working a second job. He was dressed in dark slacks and a plaid shirt, but his brown hair was tousled and his eyes puffy, as though he'd been asleep.

"May I help you?" he said through the locked doors. He wore a name tag: Shawn.

"Could you open the door, Shawn?"

He sized me up, then buzzed the door open. Shawn's eyes widened in alarm when Hervé joined me at the top of the stairs. Shawn was forced to step back as the three of us crowded into the small foyer.

"Are you . . . I'm sorry. Are you guests?" Shawn asked nervously.

"No, we—"

"Sorry, but we don't have any rooms to let."

"We'd like to see room two seventeen, please," I said, stroking my medicine bag and focusing my intent.

"That's a . . . That room's not available."

"I understand. We just want to take a quick look."

"There's crime scene tape up."

I took his hand in mine, gazed into his eyes, and concentrated. I wasn't always able to influence others, but in general I had good luck with people in the hospitality business, probably because their job was to accommodate their patrons.

"It's so nice to meet you, Shawn. I'm sorry to have awakened you so late. We'll only need a few minutes. Why don't you give me the key to room two seventeen, and then you can go back to sleep? I'll leave the key at the desk on my way out. Don't you worry about a thing."

Shawn relaxed. "Um . . . okay, I guess it'd be all right."

The foyer led into a narrow hall; to the right was a cozy parlor, and to the left a small chamber filled with tiny café tables; a coffee machine, a stack of newspapers, and a platter of cookies rested on a counter. Beyond that was an office crammed with two desks topped by computers.

A statue of Joan of Arc in full armor stood at the end of the hallway; another flag and several maps of France added to the Gallic flavor of the boutique hotel. But what really caught my eye were the delicate, colorful paintings of mythological creatures along the tops of the walls, on the door panels, and winding up the columns. There were allegorical and humorous figures and animals, along with a framework of garlands, borders, fans, piers, and cartouches with landscapes or narrative scenes. Unless I missed my guess, these were copies of the ceiling frescoes from the Uffizi museum in Florence.

"Grottesche," I said. Hervé raised an eyebrow, and I nodded at the paintings.

"Yeah," Shawn said. "They're kind of cool, right? The hotel's former owner was enthralled with these things. When his wife died, he started painting, and didn't stop until he'd painted just about every flat surface he could find."

"They're beautiful. Oh, one more thing," I said to Shawn as something occurred to me. "Did you meet the victim?"

"Sure."

"Did he say anything, do anything odd?"

"He didn't say much. He came down to the office at one point and said he wasn't feeling well, asked for the name of a pharmacy."

"Where did you send him?"

"To the drugstore around the corner. But he said he preferred natural remedies, so I told him to talk to Quan."

"And who is Quan?"

"The day manager. I don't know much about Chinese medicine, but Quan swears by it. She says it's the only thing that really works."

"And was she able to help him?"

"She told him about an herb store, the Lucky something, on Sacramento."

"The Lucky Moon?" I suggested. That was Sailor's favorite apothecary, the one Maya had "seen" him in. It was a popular shop, not far from the hotel, so perhaps it was simply a coincidence.

Shawn nodded. "Sounds about right."

"Did he go, do you know? Any idea what he bought there?"

Shawn shrugged. "Said he felt sick to his stomach and stuff. Gotta say, he looked kind of pale."

"And what about the man"—my voice wavered, as though railing against the idea of Sailor standing accused of murder—"the man people saw leave the scene?"

"He's on our security tapes," said Shawn.

"So I hear."

"I told everything to the police. No one saw him come in, but a bunch of people saw him leave. It was hard not to notice."

"Anything strike you as odd?"

"Besides the fact that he had blood all over him?"

My stomach quailed.

"Yes, besides that."

Shawn shrugged. "People were freaking out at the sight of him, but he was totally calm. He stopped and looked at an old-fashioned pocket watch, and then kept on going. Weird, right?"

"Yep, weird. Okay, thanks. The room key?"

"Oh, yeah," Shawn said, foraging behind the desk and handing me the key. "The forensics people left about an hour ago. I'll be here if you need me."

I thanked Shawn again, encouraged him to go back to sleep; then Hervé and I hurried toward the narrow circular stairs that wound around the elevator.

"Does the pocket watch have any significance to you?" I asked Hervé.

"Maybe he was late for a very important date?" Hervé suggested. "Seriously, the only thing it brings up for me is the rabbit from *Alice in Wonderland*."

Well, that seemed apt. I felt a lot like I'd fallen down a rabbit hole lately.

The elevator was the old-fashioned kind; riders had to pull the grate closed manually, and the shaft was open to the center of the building, with the stairs wrapping around it. As we mounted the stairs, I noticed that even the interior walls of the elevator shaft were covered with the paintings.

"You've got to give the artist props for diligence," I said to Hervé.

"I never knew you were a student of art history."

"I'm not. But I spent some time in Florence, and used to hang out at the Uffizi. The art on the wall is great, of course, but it was the ceilings that really captured my interest. In English they're referred to as 'grotesques,' which sounds like something bad or ugly. But I think they're charming. Bizarre, but charming."

One of the painted grotesques seemed to move, swimming before my eyes.

"Did you see that?" I asked Hervé.

"See what?"

"One of the paintings just seemed to move."

"It's the energy of this place. There's a spirit here, no doubt about it," said Hervé.

But it wasn't necessarily Tristan Dupree's spirit. In a hotel of this age, a resident ghost was practically a foregone conclusion.

"Also, violent death stirs things up," Hervé added as we reached the second-floor landing and headed to the right.

These weren't the long, straight hallways of modern hotels, but were narrow and twisty, snaking through the old building. As we approached room 217, more of the painted figures started to stir, their movements sinewy, lugubrious, sensual. The box under my arm thumped.

Spirits are attracted to me and often try to make contact, but I can't understand what they're saying. I could feel their energy, like an army of ants marching up and down my spine or puffs of cold breath on the back of my neck. But I'm a witch, not an empath, and

I can't communicate with them. It's very frustrating and tends to make all parties concerned a little testy.

Once again, I felt a wave of gratitude for my friend's presence. Not just as a necromancer, but as moral support. I'm not new to murder scenes, unfortunately, but confronting the loss of human life never gets easy.

"There it is," Hervé said, nodding at the bright yellow crime scene tape crisscrossing a door just ahead. I wondered if the hotel's management had removed the guests from the rooms along the hall; it wouldn't be great for business to remind them this was an active crime scene. A *homicide* scene.

"Ready?" I asked Hervé.

He nodded.

I ripped the crime scene tape, used the key to turn the knob, and stepped into room 217.

The room was a shambles. Ceramic lamps had been smashed, nightstands overturned, and the sheets and blankets wadded up as though slept in. Blood was spattered on the white walls and drying in dark pools on the cream-colored carpet. Evidence tags and dark fingerprint dust revealed the forensics team had come and gone.

Nausea seized me. The room shimmered with anger and evil.

"Damn," said Hervé, right behind me.

The box thumped again.

"What do you have in there, anyway?" Hervé asked as I carefully set the box on a chest of drawers.

"It's a little hard to explain. But it's possible that whatever is in here once belonged to Tristan Dupree."

"But you don't know what it is? Or even if it's in there?"

"I don't know much of anything, I'm sorry to say. That's why I'm hoping his ghost might be able to clarify a few things."

"And you brought the box to entice him? Clever girl."

"Not really. I brought the box in because I don't want someone to steal it from my car."

"Shall we give it a go? Again—I can't guarantee anything," Hervé said. "This sort of thing would be better suited to your fiancé."

"He's unavailable at the moment."

Hervé gave me an inquisitive look but didn't ask anything further.

"I appreciate your trying, Hervé," I said. "What can I do to help?"

"You could draw a circle."

I started to bring supplies out of my backpack: my mason jar full of brew, my Apache tears and tiger's-eye stones, one clear quartz crystal, one small amethyst. One small purple pouch full of cemetery dirt, and five lavender tea lights.

Hervé sat on the floor in a corner clear of debris, evidence tags, or any signs of struggle. I started to chant as I poured a very slender stream of brew in a circle around him, invoking my guiding spirit to open the portals, to allow the spirits to cross through the veil but only into the protection of the circle.

Just as before, my magic felt . . . rusty. I had cast this spell a thousand times, knew every word, every movement by heart. Why was the energy resisting me? Could I have done something to offend my guiding spirit, the Ashen Witch?

I tried to focus. To call for grace through humility.

"Angels, guardians, spirits, receive my eternal gratitude for the guidance you provide. I bid you allow the spirits to pass through the veil, to speak through this man, this conduit. Speak to him through his third eye, and I will listen with a sharper ear, and I will see with a sharper eye. Speak to us, we beseech you. With this brew, with this fire, with our presence, so mote it be."

I went back over the circle, widdershins, in salt.

Then, continuing to repeat my charm, I placed the stones at the four directions, north, south, east, west. Then I lit the candles and placed them at the five points of the pentacle: spirit, head, heart, earth, fire.

While I chanted, Hervé arranged himself, sitting cross-legged, breathing deeply and relaxing into meditation. His broad hands rested, palms up, on his knees to receive the energies.

His head fell back almost immediately upon my completion of the pentacle within the circle, and his eyes rolled up. Just like that, Hervé was no longer present. He was a conduit.

When I was focused on a magical spell or incantation, I often went into a trancelike state, but watching Sailor or Hervé at work reminded me that I didn't know what a true trance was. They seemed to actually leave their body, somehow, allowing the spirits or words from afar to channel through them. It was equal parts spooky and fascinating.

I sat silently, watching Hervé. His features suddenly shifted, his eyes flew open, and he stared at me.

"Lily Ivory." Hervé's voice sounded strangely hollow, and he spoke with Tristan's odd inflection.

"Tristan?" I tried to quell the queasy feeling of a spirit speaking through a friend's body. "Can you tell me what happened to you?"

"Your boyfriend."

"Are you sure?"

"Yes."

"Did he say anything?"

"No. He entered the room and began to strike."

"Do you have any other enemies, near or far?"

Silence.

"Come on, Tristan. Surely you have other enemies."

If Tristan had enemies, he wasn't going to admit it. The silence continued.

"What did you want from me?"

"Fire. Time. *Teher* . . . tears. The tears of the daughter."

"What does that mean? I think perhaps what you want is in this box." I held it up. "What is it you're looking for, exactly?"

"Bēag."

"Can you be more specific?"

"Bēag, *bēag*!"

He started spouting something that sounded a lot like Oscar's rendition of the prelude to *The Canterbury Tales*—in other words, some form of English I couldn't understand. Or maybe it was another language entirely.

"I can't understand you," I said.

"Bēag! Silber!"

"Silber?" I repeated. "As in silver? Is the bēag made of silver?"

"Silber!"

Happily, although spirits can speak through a medium, they very rarely "take over" the medium's physical body. I was pretty sure that if Tristan could have, he would have gone for my throat. Or, at the very least, for the box.

"What about Renee Baker? Is she involved in this?"

"Kaka."

Were we talking baby talk now?

He mumbled under his breath, as though searching for a word. *"Kuchen?"*

"*Kuchen*—that's German for cookie or cake?" I ventured.

"Cupcakes!" he exclaimed.

Well, at least I understood that last part. So, Tristan was definitely involved with Renee and he associated her with cupcakes, as we all did. After all, she was the cupcake lady.

"The seers saw. The prophecy."

"What is the prophecy? Tell me."

"San Francisco. The child will come."

I blew out a frustrated breath, more confused than ever. Luckily, I'd been mired in confusion before. In fact, I was beginning to think that this was my process when trying to figure out supernatural mysteries.

Hervé twitched and moaned softly. He was coming out of his trance. The question-and-answer period was over.

Chapter 8

Hervé looked vacant and confused, which was typical for someone coming out of a deep fugue state.

While I gave him some space to recover, I studied the paintings on the door panels and in a border framing the ceiling. It wasn't hard to imagine a brokenhearted hotelier painting yet another door, a wall, a column, one after another. The variations of grotesques were endless, the outlandish combinations of beasts and mythology restricted only by one's imagination. Had the artist been desperate to forget, I wondered, or desperate to remember?

"Did I say anything?" Hervé asked after a moment.

"You said plenty. I'm just not sure what any of it means."

"You never know with these things. Often the meaning is revealed over time."

"I just hope that time comes sooner rather than later," I said.

Hervé stood and brushed off his clothes while I gathered my stones and tea lights. I used a small whisk broom to sweep up the salts, hoping that whatever residue remained behind wouldn't interfere with an ongoing police investigation. Shawn said the forensics unit had already come and gone, but still. I probably should have run this one past Carlos.

I repacked the supplies in my backpack and picked up the shoe box; then Hervé and I made our way down the circular stairs. Shawn was fast asleep on the couch in the front parlor, so I left the room key on the desk and we let ourselves out.

The night was chilly, with a thick blanket of fog blowing in off the bay; I shivered, pulling my cardigan tight. When would I learn to take a coat whenever I was out at night in San Francisco, no matter how warm the day?

A group of five people about Shawn's age laughed and feigned screaming as they ran across the street. Traffic was light compared with daytime, but nonetheless there were a good number of cars cruising the street. It always surprised me that San Francisco had so many people out at night, despite the fact that most restaurants closed by nine thirty. San Francisco was not New York City.

Hervé escorted me to my car and lingered while I stashed my supplies in the trunk. I let out a sigh, feeling decidedly defeated.

"You know this is how it works, Lily. The spirits aren't known for their clear signs. You need more pieces of the puzzle before things start to fall into place."

"I know. It's just that . . . Well, Sailor's in jail."

"Sailor? What for?"

"He's the main suspect for this murder."

"*This* murder? The one in room two seventeen?"

I nodded, glumly.

Hervé paused for a moment, as if searching for the right words. "I don't know Sailor well, Lily, but I know this: I felt the sensations in that room. Sailor is not capable of that degree of violence or unbridled ambition. Whatever was in that room with Tristan wasn't some normal guy caught up in the moment."

I almost laughed. Talk about a good news/bad news scenario. The good news: My fiancé wasn't a murderer. The bad news: The murderer was an ambitious psychopath and I had to track him down. *Oh, goody.*

"Anyway," I said, ready to change the subject, "did you get your invitation to the handfasting?"

"It's on my calendar. Selena dropped by my shop today—she's so excited to be in the wedding. She said something about trying on bridesmaid dresses with you tomorrow."

Dangitall. I had totally forgotten. Another lapse in memory. This wasn't like me. "Yes, of course. I'm looking forward to seeing her."

He looked at me out of the corner of his eye. "You're confident you'll be able to spring Sailor in time for the nuptials? I'd hate for her to be disappointed."

"We'd all be just a tad disappointed. And anyway, I don't have any other choice. Sailor didn't do this, Hervé. I just have to find out who did, and figure out how to prove Sailor's innocence."

"Exonerate Sailor and find the real killer. How hard could that be, right?" Hervé chuckled, his voice sonorous.

"That about sums it up."

A siren wailed in the distance, and several people emerged from the theater next door. Show must be over.

"If I can help, you know where to find me. But, Lily, you mentioned your grandmother's coven is on their way into town. Couldn't they be of assistance with this sort of thing?"

"They're taking a rather circuitous route. Besides, they're all in their seventies and eighties, so I'm not sure how helpful they'll be with the actual running-after-a-murderer part. Also . . . my *mother* is on that bus."

He nodded sagely. "Mother issues. They're the worst."

I smiled. "My familiar said that very thing this morning."

His eyebrows rose. "Your pig talks?"

"I . . . might have interpreted that. You know how it is." *Watch it, Lily.* Only Sailor, Aidan, and Selena knew about Oscar's true form, and it was best that way. Since I had started feeling at home, making friends, creating family, I had been letting my guard down.

Or was it more than that? I had been losing track of conversations, talking to myself, letting things slip.

I sneezed.

"Coming down with something?" Hervé asked.

I shook my head.

"My wife swears by zinc and echinacea, but personally, I think industrial-strength DayQuil's the only thing that works."

"Thanks. But I'm not getting a cold. I don't get colds."

He chuckled. "Of course not. But if you do, DayQuil's the ticket."

By the time I got home, I was exhausted, worried, and no closer to figuring out what was going on, much less how to exonerate Sailor. Walking into the kitchen, I was relieved to see Oscar snuggled in a nest of blankets in his cubby above the refrigerator, snoring away. At least I didn't have to worry about his being out and about.

I yearned for bed, but was so worried about Sailor that I knew I wouldn't be able to sleep. So I rose to my tiptoes to reach a high shelf, and grasped a thick old tome covered in faded red leather: my ancient Book of Shadows.

I had inherited the witchcraft manual from Graciela, who had inherited it from her own grandmother. It was chock-full of spells and incantations, wise words, articles clipped from newspapers—including a few from the *Jarod Weekly Clarion* that accused me of creating havoc at that snake-handling fiasco. I flipped through the yellowed pages, running my fingers along paper made soft from frequent handling, not seeking anything in particular. But every once in a while my Book of Shadows would offer me subtle advice; a familiar spell might be changed ever so slightly, or I would notice a new addition that was useful for my particular situation.

This time my eyes fell on a passage I'd read before, dealing with human-demon alliances:

> A daemonic allegiance is oft betrayed by an outward manifestation of youth and vigour. The maturation of the individual is slowed by the hand of vile iniquity belonging to the servant of the Devil. The soul of the wretch, enmeshed by vanity and greed, is in such manner seduced by the blandishments of an abiding beauty. Alas! doth the sufferer fall victim to the foul trickery of the daemon, the better to employ the truckling knave.

Huh.

Other than that, the old red leather tome remained mute, except for a quote I hadn't noticed before: *Just when the caterpillar thought the world was over, it became a butterfly.*

At the moment, anything that mentioned the world being over sounded a tad ominous, what with prophecies being bandied about, and all. Still, it was a good sentiment to keep in mind, I supposed.

I flipped through to some clippings from my time in Germany. None of them mentioned Dupree specifically, but they reminded me of that time in my life. Of my father, and a terrible fire that consumed an old manor house.

In the bedroom the suitcase was still splayed open on my bed, so I rummaged through the manila envelope of clippings. I found only one mention of Tristan, in which he was described as "Tristan Dupree, aged 45. Resident of Füssen, Bavaria."

Tristan had looked much younger than midforties when I knew him in Germany, I thought. I would have guessed he was in his thirties. In fact, when he stood at my door yesterday, he *still* looked as if he were in his thirties. But if the newspaper article was correct, Tristan would have been sixty today. Also, I remembered that Dupree seemed to know who Carlos was this morning, even though he hadn't been introduced. Not aging and knowing things he shouldn't . . .

Had Dupree made a deal with a demon?

Finally, I bathed and dressed in all black, then sat cross-legged on the floor in front of my coffee table. I grounded myself, stroked my medicine bag, and prepared to scry, or see beyond the here and now, to concentrate while allowing my mind to wander.

My crystal ball was beautiful, and easily my most expensive possession. The base was hand-wrought gold, encrusted with jewels. A grateful client had given it to Graciela, and she in turn had gifted me with it when I was forced to leave Texas.

But all the beauty in the world couldn't improve my scrying. Most witches had at least some natural ability with this sort of thing, but not me. I could brew with the best of them, but seeing something useful—whether in the crystal ball or in a black mirror or in standing water—was almost always beyond my ken.

Tonight was no exception. I had hoped to spy a glimpse of Sailor, or Tristan Dupree, or even the cupcake lady, aka Renee Baker. But all I saw, as ever, was a few fleeting shadows, the significance of which remained frustratingly out of reach.

I turned to the shoe box.

At the moment, I was tempted to open it, but I feared I wasn't strong enough to face whatever it contained, all by myself. Especially now, with the sneezing and fatigue and strangely challenged magical energy.

I cringed at how I'd left things with Aidan. When would I learn not to antagonize him? But I pushed that thought away. Best to focus on the problems at hand. For lack of a better idea, I rewrapped the rowan around the shoe box, braided some threads and knotted them with whispered incantations, added a string of holly and stinging nettles, then put the box back into my suitcase and hid the suitcase in the back of my closet. It would be safe there.

I hoped. Normally I had confidence that my apartment was so protected it was virtually immune to intruders. But since I hadn't been exactly feeling myself lately . . . I wondered whether I should have taken up Aidan on his offer to safeguard the box. He would probably still agree to do so, if I asked him nicely.

I yearned to talk with Graciela, and to convene her coven of elderly wisewomen. Surely they could offer some insight into what was going on? If only they were here and could help me to open the shoe box, figure out what was plaguing me, find a murderer, and get Sailor off the hook.

My mind cast back to the red thread spiderweb forming over the map behind the register. What in the world were the women doing?

Had the coven simply been sidetracked by burgers and sea otters, or was there something else—something more sinister—going on?

Chapter 9

Early the next morning, I headed out to the jail.

The street was quiet at this hour of the morning. Haight Street's boutiques, bookstore and record shop, and myriad bars and restaurants catered primarily to a later crowd. But Lucille's Loft, right next door, was already bustling.

I had hoped to rush past—Sailor was paramount on my mind—but Lucille noticed me and came to the door.

"Good morning, Lily," she said. Lucille is a lot like her daughter, Maya: calm, kind, and smart. Lucille carried a few more pounds and many more laugh lines, and her hair was graying, but other than that, mother and daughter could have been sisters.

"Good morning, Lucille."

"Is everything all right?"

"I—" I wondered whether to launch into the whole story. I didn't have much time. Besides, I wasn't sure I wanted to go around telling people my fiancé was in the slammer. A big part of me expected—hoped, anyway—that Carlos would stumble across some huge hole in the case, the SFPD would apologize profusely, and Sailor would be home in time for dinner.

"A friend's in trouble," I said simply.

"I hope it's nothing serious," she said.

"Me, too. Thanks. Oh, Lucille," I said as something else occurred to me. "Maya mentioned that Renee Baker had dropped by the other day?"

"The cupcake lady? Yes, she did."

"Could I ask what she was looking for?"

"She wanted to know if we would be available to do some alterations for her."

"Really? That's . . . odd."

Lucille's brows rose and she smiled. "Lucille's Loft is the best, after all. Why wouldn't she come to us?"

"Oh, no, I'm sorry. I didn't mean it like that!" I blushed.

She chuckled. "I know. Renee's cupcake shop is across town, so why would she come all the way here? She mentioned she was in the neighborhood visiting a friend who'd placed a big order for an upcoming event."

"Did she say who?"

Lucille gave me an searching look. "Are you sure everything's all right, Lily?"

"There's . . . Not really, no. Sailor was arrested last night."

"Sailor? Is he all right?"

It didn't escape my notice that Lucille didn't even ask what Sailor had been accused of. He had fans. It did my heart good.

"I think so. I'm on my way to visit him."

"And you think Renee's somehow involved? The *cupcake* lady?"

"Not really. I'm just . . . Things are off-kilter right now, so I'm keeping an open mind."

Maya didn't share a lot of the details of my life with her mother, and that was probably best. I doubted Lucille would be on board with the whole witchcraft thing. She was open-minded and openhearted, but she was an active member of her local Baptist church—and in any case, my brand of witchy was a little tough for most people to swallow.

"Did you happen to notice anything odd about Renee's visit? Did she ask anything, do anything in particular, that struck you as"—I couldn't think of a more apt word—"odd?"

Lucille shook her head. "I'm sorry, Lily. Nothing comes to mind. She admired our collection of fabrics, asked about prices, and then left us with a lovely basket of assorted baked goods."

"Did you eat them?" I demanded, a strident note in my voice.

"Sorry I can't offer you any—they didn't last long." Lucille laughed and patted her stomach. "I know I shouldn't, but I had a meat pasty for lunch, and *two* cupcakes for dessert, and enjoyed them thoroughly."

"And you're feeling all right?"

"Lily . . . what is going *on*?"

I had debated whether to tell my friends and acquaintances that Renee was bad news. To all external appearances, she was simply a bakery owner whose intricately iced cupcakes had become wildly popular, and whose baked goods were in high demand all over the city. How did I tell people Renee might well be involved in some sort of supernatural battle for the soul of San Francisco? And that her cupcakes might, or might not, be suspect?

"Nothing, Lucille," I said with a shake of my head. "I'm sure it's nothing. I'm just jumpy, and worried about Sailor. But if Renee comes back, would you let me know?"

She nodded, her soft brown eyes gazing at me intently. "Of course. Please give Sailor my love, and let me know if there's anything at all I can do. I have a niece who works for the sheriff's office. I'd be happy to make a call if you need a personal contact."

"Thank you, Lucille," I said. "I appreciate that, and I know Sailor will, too."

The prosaically named County Jail #2 is located on Seventh Street, not far from the freeway. Many's the time I'd been stuck in traffic in the approach to the Bay Bridge, and gazed at the serpentine building with its partially fogged windows, thinking of those inside, awaiting their fate.

I had been here a few times to visit prisoners.

It dawned on me that my father had once been accused of murder. My fiancé currently stood accused of murder. Perhaps I should wonder about the men in my life.

The check-in process for visitors always seemed to take forever, but at long last I sat at the counter, waiting.

Sailor shuffled in; his dark hair stuck up, uncombed, and whiskers shadowed his jaw in blue-black. He looked pissed off. But that was nothing new. Sailor had his great moments—*amazingly* great—but his default way of looking at the world was grumpy, and his general attitude had not been helped by a night in jail.

We took a long moment, just staring at each other. Drinking in the sight of each other. Then he started talking.

According to Sailor, he had been practicing a new psychic technique in his apartment when the cops came a-knocking. He had been alone since about four in the afternoon, and all evening. There was no more to the story.

"I'm surprised you didn't sense the police were on their way."

"I was in a trance state. And I had no reason to be on guard."

"That's it? You didn't go anywhere near Dupree? You weren't at the Hotel Marais at all?"

He shook his head. "No, I was in the East Bay working with Aunt Renna until a little before four, then walked the labyrinth up at Sibley Park. After that, I went straight home. I was nowhere near Dupree's hotel, Lily."

"So Renna can vouch for you?" I asked, feeling hopeful.

"Only until four. The police seem to think I would have had enough time to get back to the hotel. I guess they haven't sat in traffic on the Bay Bridge lately—even on the bike it's a challenge. But in any case, Renna's a known Rom fortune-teller. The DA will make the case that she's unreliable, and that she's lying to protect me. Doubtful anyone will believe her."

"That's awfully cynical," I said, disappointed.

"And this surprises you?" Sailor's words were sarcastic, but his tone was gentle.

"Is there anything else you can tell me? Anything at all that might help? Have you been able to see anything?"

"Not much. The only thing . . ."

"What is it?"

"It doesn't make much sense. As I've told you, I 'see' things in symbols, usually. And I keep seeing my dad's old watch."

"What would a watch symbolize?"

He shrugged. "Running out of time, maybe? It's unusual for me; usually I see things in the language of flowers. I did also see aspen trees. . . ."

"In my tradition, aspen leaves are used in antitheft charms."

He nodded. "It's unclear what it means. But I had an inkling that someone had been in my apartment yesterday. You didn't go by there, did you?"

"No, I was at the shop all day. I haven't been to your place in a while."

"That's what I thought. I didn't find anything disturbed; it was just a sense I had. I also had a vision of a symbol of some sort. Unfortunately, I haven't been able to fully make it out. I was seeing it in the trance just before I was arrested, as a matter of fact, and tried sketching it, but it still made no sense."

"The man—the fellow who seems to have killed Tristan—stopped to look at a watch."

"Interesting. Still not sure what that tells us, though."

"Hervé met me at the hotel last night," I said, "and was able to make contact with Tristan's spirit. But he couldn't tell me much. He did mention cupcakes, so I suppose Renee's involved in whatever's going on."

"You're suggesting the cupcake lady beat up Tristan?" he asked in a sardonic tone.

"No, of course not. But she has people working for her."

"What motive would she have?"

"I don't know," I said, shaking my head. "Tristan shouted about the bēag again, and I still don't know what he was after, much less why. But . . . when I asked him who killed him, he was very clear. He said it was you."

"He and everyone else at the hotel, apparently."

"Why would they think that?"

He shrugged.

"Sailor, remember the other day, when Maya said she saw you, or someone who looked just like you, in an herb shop in Chinatown . . . ?"

He held my gaze but didn't help me to finish the phrase.

"I had the sense you weren't being entirely forthright."

"Forthright?" The corner of his mouth kicked up in a slight smile.

"All right, let's put our cards on the table," I said, annoyed. I'd been up all night worrying about Sailor and trying to figure out how to prove his innocence—and here he was, being Mr. Cranky Pants? "I had the sense you were . . . lying." When he still didn't respond, I asked: "Were you?"

He glanced around, then leaned forward slightly. "I've been working on projection."

"I'm going to assume you don't mean in a psychological sense, accusing others of the things you are guilty of?"

He shook his head. "No. Actual projection. Psychic projection, which is sometimes called astral projection."

"What does that entail, exactly?"

"It's hard to explain." He glanced at a sheriff's deputy standing, attentive, nearby. "Essentially it means I can project my thoughts to wander elsewhere. I can pick up sensory data: I can see, hear, smell someplace even though my body's not present."

"Could your thoughts go rogue and kill someone?"

"Of course not. It's a spirit projection. It has no impact on the world around it. It's sort of like being a fly on the wall, but it makes even less of a physical impact than a fly would. And even if it did, I wouldn't have. I didn't like Dupree bothering you, and I wouldn't have pulled a punch if he showed up at the shop again. I'm no saint, but to kill a man? I'd need a damn good reason. You seriously think I could have done this?"

Our eyes held for a long moment. I shook my head. He seemed to relax, ever so slightly.

I sneezed. I felt bone tired. I hadn't slept much last night, but usually that wasn't a problem for me. Maybe I was just getting older and finding it hard to bounce back from things like casting all night.

"Are you okay?" Sailor asked. "You look tired."

"Thanks."

"Beautiful, of course. Have I mentioned that? But are you feeling all right?"

His deep voice relaxed me, and I could feel his aura wrapping around me like a psychic hug. I missed him, my Sailor. Cranky pants and all. I wanted nothing more than to throw myself into his arms, have him tell me that everything was going to be all right.

But it was up to *me* to find a way to make it right.

"I'm okay."

"You were probably up all night trying to find a way to get me out."

I smiled. "You promised not to try to read my mind."

"I'm not. I just know you."

Our eyes held for a long, warm moment.

"Sailor, why didn't you call me when you were arrested?"

"I tried—you weren't at home or in the shop. I was able to get in touch with Maya because she has a cell phone. My last phone call was to a lawyer: Henry Petulengro, who's married to a Rom cousin. He's good. I told him you might be calling, so he can fill you in. I don't have his number on me; you'll have to look it up."

I jotted the lawyer's name on the little pad I always kept in my bag.

"Oh, by the way, Lucille sends her love and an offer to do anything she can to help, as does Maya. And Hervé. And Oscar, of course. So, what do we do now?"

"I'm afraid my contributions will be limited, given my circumstances. I can try to use projection to snoop around a bit, but I have to be careful."

"Of what?"

He shrugged. "If it's not done right, the soul can get trapped in the spirit world. The body is left torpid, can't be roused."

"That sounds . . . ridiculously dangerous."

"I'll be careful."

"You'd better be. I'm supposed to be getting married in two weeks, and that will be decidedly more difficult if the groom's trapped in some random spirit dimension."

"Not to mention in jail."

"That, too. It won't happen. We'll figure this out."

"Yes, ma'am." Sailor gazed at me with such intensity I swear his look could have started a fire.

My mind was racing, trying to think of something else to ask him, anything that could help. I didn't know what my next steps should be, or how to go about proving that Sailor wasn't where the police said he was, despite all evidence to the contrary. How could I find out who else might have had motive to kill Tristan Dupree, even though he was new to town?

"I'm hoping Carlos and Aidan may be of some help," I said finally.

"I know I don't have to remind you of this, but I'm not Aidan's favorite person these days. Or Carlos's, for that matter."

"Carlos went over your case with me last night, and for your information, he thinks it's hinky."

"And this is a good thing?"

"In this case, it's a very good thing. He doesn't believe you did it."

"Well, I'm glad to hear it. That wasn't the impression he gave me over the course of several hours of interrogation. I was surprised he didn't step away from the case, actually, since we know each other."

"According to Carlos, his involvement isn't prohibited as long as he's transparent about his connection to you, and lets his supervisor know. Anyway, trust me: We want him on your case."

He nodded. "And Aidan?"

I hesitated. "He might take a little more convincing. But I'll figure it out. I have it on good authority that I can be very persuasive."

He gave me a long, slow smile. Our eyes held. There were no words.

Soon enough our time was up. I didn't want to leave.

"Thanks for your note last night, by the way."

"I meant it."

"I feel the same. And yes, I am fully prepared to marry you, even in front of a coven of grandmas. 'Bout time I met my future in-laws."

I rose to leave, feeling the sting of tears at the backs of my eyes. At that moment I was glad I couldn't cry. It would have embarrassed us both.

"Lily."

I turned to face him.

"It's going to be all right. I have faith in you. In us. Unshakable faith. Do you believe me?"

I opened my mouth, but no words came out. Finally I just swallowed, hard, and nodded. And hurried out of the visiting room.

Chapter 10

My mind raced as I drove back to Aunt Cora's Closet. Sailor's faith in me made it all the harder, somehow.

Just a little pressure. Most brides stressed out over flower arrangements, the reception menu, and the guest list. *I* was worrying about how to spring my fiancé from the hoosegow. And as if that weren't enough, I still hadn't found the right wedding dress. Which reminded me . . . I had an appointment this afternoon to preview an estate sale in Pacific Heights, and supposedly there were two wedding dresses in the lot, one from the 1940s, the other from the early 1960s. Two of my favorite fashion eras.

I had been looking forward to going for the past week, but at the moment it was hard to think about anything except how to help Sailor. I didn't even know where to start.

Also, Selena was scheduled to come by the shop to try on dresses. I had considered postponing when Hervé reminded me of our date last night, but I couldn't bring myself to disappoint her, no matter the circumstances.

Not only did I feel obligated to fulfill my promise to a young girl, but also because Selena didn't react well to disappointment. Controlling her emotions—rather than allowing them to spill out into the world around her, causing all manner of mischief—was one of the things we were working on.

For that matter, it was one of the things *I* was still working on.

I parked the Mustang in the driveway I rented and walked around the corner to Haight Street. Sweeping the sidewalk in front of Aunt Cora's Closet was a tall, lanky young man dressed in dirty clothes. Conrad's eyes were rimmed in red, his dishwater blond hair was shaggy, and a straggly goatee studded his chin. He had recently confided in me that he feared he would never be able to grow a decent beard.

He lived on the street, slept in nearby Golden Gate Park, but fretted over facial hair. I would never understand it.

"Good morning, Conrad," I said as I approached.

He paused in his sweeping, leaned on the broom, lifted his chin, and replied, "Duuude."

Conrad is one of the army of "gutter punks" who pepper the streets of the Haight. He was addicted to something—possibly several somethings—but wasn't ready to accept my offers of help. I was sometimes tempted to force temporary sobriety upon him, but I knew it wouldn't last. My magic is strong, but human nature is stronger. Real change had to come from within. As hard as it was to see Conrad like this, and as much as I wanted to take matters into my own hands, I had to wait for him to make the decision.

Despite all that, Conrad—or "the Con," as he referred to himself—was a good friend, and had become an unofficial part-time guardian of Aunt Cora's Closet. When he wasn't doing odd jobs for me, his usual post was on the curb outside the shop. He might not be particularly effectual, but he was brave and loyal. And that counted for a lot.

I sneezed.

"Dude. Getting a cold?"

I shook my head. "No. Probably just allergies."

"I tell you what: the way I hear it is that a cold means you're resisting dealing with something important. See, it's all in your mind, dude. You can overcome anything with positive thinking. Choose happiness—that's my motto."

I smiled. "Maybe I'll try that. Thanks. Have you had breakfast?"

"Maya already brought me a muffin and a Flower Power. Thank you. Oh, and Selena just got here."

Darn. I had been hoping to have a little time before Selena arrived. Among other things, I wanted to make a few phone calls without her interested ears overhearing. My semi-adopted little sister was a handful.

Selena wasn't a typical teenager. Selena wasn't a typical . . . *anything.* At fifteen years old, she was a powerful but troubled young witch who hadn't been trained to control her abilities. She reminded me a lot of myself at the same age, but in my case, Graciela had taken me firmly in hand. Selena lived with her own grandmother, a *botanica* owner who understood and respected magic but was not a sufficiently strong practitioner to be able to train Selena appropriately. So I had been doing my best to help, as had Aidan. Privately, I thought the biggest influence upon Selena's changing attitude toward the world was her volunteer work at the San Francisco animal shelter. She connected with the animals on a deep level, no words needed. The young witch and the homeless pets had a calming effect on one another.

There was one animal, though, that Selena didn't

much care for: Oscar. The young witch and the gob-goyle had a sibling-type relationship, primarily teasing and arguing, and only occasionally on the same page.

I paused, my hand on the door latch. Before leaving to visit Sailor this morning, I had cast my usual spell of protection over the store, cleansing and smudging and lighting a candle. Now, as I stood looking through the window at the vulnerable necks of Selena and Maya, and Oscar's chubby little form snoring on his pillow, Carlos's words of caution came back to me. I decided to add a little more protective magic to the store. Just in case. I couldn't do a total protection spell, or it would keep everyone at bay, including customers. But a wreath of stinging nettles and a second sage-bundle smudging couldn't hurt.

"Good morning, Selena," I said as I walked in. Selena was sitting cross-legged on the floor behind the register, polishing silver jewelry and cutlery with ketchup. She loved handling silver and liked it to sparkle.

"Hi, Maya," I continued.

"Good morning, Lily," said Maya. Her eyes were full of questions—I'm sure she was dying to ask about Sailor—but for Selena's sake said nothing.

Oscar snorted. "And hello to you, too, little guy."

He closed his eyes, let out a long sigh, and was snoring again before his head hit the pillow.

Selena didn't even look up, but that was par for the course. She was what people in the Bay Area called "socially awkward." Back home we called it "touched."

"Selena?"

After a pause, she glanced up at me. "What?"

"I said good morning. What do you say in return?"

"Buenos días," she said in a slightly mocking tone, wagging her head.

"Y buenos días a tí," I answered.

I was glad to see Selena still wore the *Gutta Cavat Lapidem* talisman I had given her months ago. The teardrop-shaped pendant helped focus her scattered adolescent energies.

"Has the bus checked in this morning?" I asked Maya, noting a new pin on the map.

"Yep," said Maya. "They're headed to Sacramento."

"What's in Sacramento?"

"State capital," said Selena.

"Yes, thanks, Selena. I actually do know it's the California state capital. I'm just wondering why the grandmas are headed there."

"They mentioned something about joining a protest march," Maya responded. "They said they'd be another day or two."

"A protest march. Seriously?"

"That's what the text said," said Maya with a smile. "Can you imagine the busload of grandmas with signs in hand? Those state legislators don't stand a chance. And they aren't even constituents!"

I returned her smile at the image of the coven descending upon hapless lawmakers. Still . . . "What are they up to, do you suppose?"

Maya shrugged and handed me her phone to show me the text. "It says they're joining the march, and afterward they plan to visit the California State Railroad Museum in Old Sacramento. That's all."

"Huh. Who knew they were such train enthusiasts?"

On the one hand, given what I was dealing with at the moment, it was nice not to have to worry about what would no doubt be the boisterous arrival of thirteen elderly witches. Not to mention my mother. On the other hand, the waiting and the anticipation were starting to get on my nerves. Also, I could use some advice. And I couldn't help but wonder if they were just being dotty, or if there was something else behind their erratic route.

"Done," said Selena, the now-sparkling jewelry and silverware fanned out around her. Hers was a rare metal magic. As Selena polished the metal, she imbued it with subtle whispers of energy. Customers could feel it, though they didn't understand the source of their reactions. The items Selena polished flew off the store's shelves—occasionally, quite literally.

I had quickly run out of silver objects for her to work on—Aunt Cora's Closet was a clothes store primarily, not a jewelry store—so I had taken to buying old cutlery and other small silver items at garage sales, just to give her something to do.

"Isn't that pretty? Thank you, Selena," I said. "Now, please put the jewelry back in the display case, and the cutlery can go on the shelves with the kitchen items. If we have enough, maybe we'll use it for the Magical Match Tea."

Instead, Selena craned her neck to look up at the wall behind the counter. She gazed at the map.

"It's a picture," she said.

"A what?"

"Their path is making a picture, see?"

I stood back and looked at the map. She was right; the red thread strung around the pins was starting to look like a figure of some sort.

"What is it?" asked Maya.

The three of us stood in front of the map, tilting our heads this way, then that way, but the shape didn't make sense. There was no obvious figure emerging.

"Huh," I said. "It doesn't look like anything yet, does it?"

"Prob'ly they're still working on it," said Selena.

"I think it's more likely just chance," said Maya.

"The thread was bound to start looking like something to an active imagination. You know, like when you look up at the clouds and suddenly see the spitting image of your great-uncle Ollie?"

Maya was a natural skeptic. And normally I would have ceded her point. But these were the *grandmas*. And Graciela. She rarely did anything by chance. It was a witchy characteristic.

"Okay, well . . . ," I said as I hung my sweater on the antique brass coat-tree behind the counter. "I suppose we'll just have to trust they know what they're doing. And frankly, at the moment, I'm just as glad not to have to deal with them. I've got a few other things on my plate."

Maya raised her eyebrows, but we held our tongues in front of Selena.

"Maya, could you look up Tristan Dupree on the Internet?"

"Sure. With a name like that, I don't imagine he'll be hard to . . . Bingo. He's got a Facebook page."

"Tristan Dupree has a *Facebook* page?"

"I told you, Lily. Everyone and their brother has a Facebook page."

"*I* don't."

"That's my point." Maya had been building a Facebook page for Aunt Cora's Closet, insisting it would benefit the business. I believed her, but computers scared me. Too much scattered energy zinging around in cyberspace. Just like cell phones.

Not for the first time, I wondered whether I was a witch meant for an earlier time. Then again, I thanked the stars not to be living back during the burning days.

"Unless this is a different Tristan Dupree," Maya said. "Hard to imagine there's more than one person walking around with that moniker."

"You never know," I said. "It's a big world."

I peered over her shoulder as she scrolled through Tristan Dupree's Facebook page. His privacy settings wouldn't allow us to view much, but the profile picture was Tristan, all right. I would recognize those pale emotionless eyes anywhere. His location was listed as Füssen, Bavaria.

"Isn't Bavaria in Germany?" she asked. "Why not just say Germany?"

"I think it's a regionalist thing," I said. "You know, like people saying they're Northern Californians to distinguish themselves from LA. Does it tell us anything else?" I asked.

Maya shook her head. "Unless he 'friends' us, the rest of the information is private."

"He's not likely to 'friend' anybody at this point."

"I'll search the Web further, see if I can find anything else."

"Thanks. While you're online," I said, "could you look up Renee's cupcake shop?"

"Sure. Didn't Wind Spirit mention ordering some cupcakes for the Magical Match Tea? That's a great idea."

"I don't agree. In fact, Renee's sort of . . . bad news."

"The cupcake lady?" Maya asked, still typing. "She stopped by my mom's shop just the other day."

"Did you see her?"

Maya nodded. "Yeah, I was there."

"Did Renee do anything odd?"

She shook her head. "Dropped off a dozen cupcakes, as a matter of fact. The chocolate one was pretty astonishing. You should have seen it. I think I may have dreamed about it last night. Also, there were a few savory treats, too, little meat pasties. She said she was developing a new product line. Why?"

"I can't give you many details. . . ."

Maya gave me a look. "It's like that, is it?"

"I think we all need to be cautious around her, that's all."

"She doesn't look like much of a threat, I have to say," said Maya as Renee's smiling countenance popped up on the computer screen, her round face friendly and welcoming. Renee posed in front of shelves of colorful intricately decorated cakes and pastries. She was chubby, like someone who enjoyed her own food a little too much, and about Bronwyn's age. I knew only too well what Renee was really up to, but even so, it was hard to look at her and convince myself she was trouble.

Excellent disguise, cupcakes. They hid a multitude of sins.

Selena had wandered off and was now teasing Oscar with a muffin, holding it over his head. Oscar snorted and looked about ready to head-butt her. I decided to let them sort it out themselves.

I turned back to the computer screen. What was I hoping to get from looking at Renee? Some glimmer of what was going on?

"What did Renee *do* while she was at Lucille's Loft?" I asked Maya. "Did she say anything, ask questions about me, maybe?"

"Um, let me think," Maya said. If my questions struck her as odd, she didn't mention it. Maya had grown used to my bizarrely inquisitive ways. "She admired the fabrics, the dresses, the rainbow of thread choices. She asked for a few samples, and had some questions about prices. Nothing out of the ordinary that I can think of."

"You ate one of the cupcakes? You didn't feel strange in any way?"

She shook her head. "Other than dreaming about it? No. I ate a meat pasty, too. So did you, as a matter of fact."

"I did? When was this?"

"Day before yesterday, I think? I brought you one, remember? Flaky pastry, ground meat, onion, carrots, mushrooms, cheese . . . I'm getting hungry just thinking about it," Maya said.

I did remember, and it was delicious. Maya often brought me things from home, or from the café down the street. It hadn't occurred to me to question its origins.

"Are you worried about it?" continued Maya. "I don't think any of us are suffering any ill effects."

"I suppose you're right. But in the future, we should all be a little wary of Renee and her baked goods. One more thing." I dropped my voice. "Would you look up a man named Henry Petulengro? He has a law office in San Francisco. I need his phone number. He's Sailor's lawyer."

"Have you seen him?" Maya whispered as she located the lawyer's Web site. "Is he okay?"

I nodded, jotted down the lawyer's number, then ducked into the back workroom to call his office. As the phone rang, I noticed several of Selena's drawings scattered on the table. Each featured a cupcake with black icing. Selena drew a lot; this probably didn't mean anything special.

Petulengro's voice mail picked up, and I left a message saying I was Sailor's fiancée, and asking him to get back to me.

I turned around to see Selena standing just this side of the curtains, staring at me.

"What's going on?" she demanded.

"Nothing, I . . ." I was about to brush her off but noticed the matching polka-dot dresses Selena and I had picked out for the Magical Match Tea. She was so much like I was at her age: old enough to pick up on things, but not experienced enough to know how to interpret them. Fifteen was a confusing, disorienting age in general, but even more so for someone like Selena, who didn't have friends her own age to bounce worries off, much less to share carefree activities with.

She deserved the truth.

"Sailor has been arrested," I said.

"For what?"

"For . . ." Okay, the truth was one thing, but the *whole* truth was something else. I didn't want to scare her. "For a crime he didn't commit. He's in jail, but I'm fixin' to figure this out and get him released."

She stared at me for a long moment. Emotions filled her near-black eyes, but the rest of her affect remained flat. Not long ago her grandmother had been held in jail, and Selena had been homeless for a brief time. Just the memory of this vulnerable young woman—barely more than a girl—wandering the streets of San Francisco on her own made my heart skip a beat.

"I like Sailor," she said.

"I do, too."

"You got my *abuelita* out of jail."

"I was able to help her, yes." And now, I thought, I had to help Sailor. I *had* to. There was no other choice. If only I had a clue how to go about it.

"You said I could be a bridesmaid. Me and Maya."

"And you will be," I said, hoping I wasn't lying. "You'll be a great bridesmaid. Selena, what made you draw these cupcakes like this?"

She shrugged. "I like cupcakes."

"Are they . . . burned? Why are they all black?"

"I dunno—that's how they were in my head. So . . . can I help? I mean, with Sailor?"

My heart surged. For Selena to worry about someone else—and to offer to help—showed a lot of growth.

"Thank you, sugar," I said as I crossed over and gave her a little squeeze. "At the moment I can't think of a way for you to help, but I surely do appreciate the offer.

As will Sailor, I know. What you can do right now is to pick out your bridesmaid dress so Lucille will have time to alter it, if need be. Have you found one you like?"

She shook her head. "Nothing fits."

Selena used to be painfully thin and pinched, but had been filling out recently; like Oscar, Selena loved to eat. Today she wore a sweater studded with sparkly brooches that had once belonged to an elderly woman named Betty, who had been kind to Selena. The style was much too old for her, and despite her worn Levi's, Selena could not have looked less like her teenage contemporaries if she'd been wearing one of the shop's spangled, shoulder-padded tops from the eighties.

"Well, we'll just have to find you something, then, won't we?" I looped my arm around her shoulders and urged her out onto the shop floor. It was quiet this morning, with only a single customer flipping through some old leather jackets.

"Let's look through this section, here." Leading Selena to the rack marked DRESSY DRESSES, I said, "I think you may need a larger size than before, that's all."

Her eyes went huge. "I'm getting fat?"

"No, Selena, not at all. You're healthy and you're growing up, that's all. Women have a different shape than girls. We're meant to have curves."

I patted myself on my "curvy" hip.

She didn't look convinced. Given everything Selena had to deal with already—possessing out-of-control magical talent, being abandoned by her parents, growing up without a lot of economic advantages—I had hoped Selena would be immune to the more common concerns of girls her age. I supposed this could be an indication that she was becoming more conscious of the world and social expectations, which in some ways—given how clueless she had been about the impression she made not so long ago—could be a good thing. As long as she didn't start doubting herself and her own worth.

Raising children was not for sissies.

We flipped through the many formal dresses on the rack, and I pulled out several that would fit or could be altered. Selena was attracted to the more garish, poufy-skirted prom dresses, though a more streamlined style would have suited her better. Still, I let her grab whatever she wanted and helped her cart the dresses over to one of the private changing alcoves. She shied away from the communal dressing room.

I tried to keep my mind engaged in the dress search with Selena, but it was hard to focus on the here and now. What was my next step in the search for Tristan's murderer? Should I go speak to Renee? If so, I needed Aidan's help. I thought with a pang about how I'd left his office last night. When would I learn not to lose my temper around Aidan?

The bell tinkled wildly as a gorgeous woman with flowing black hair and flashing eyes flung open the door and stormed into Aunt Cora's Closet.

Patience Blix.

This was all I needed.

Chapter 11

"What in the holy *hell* is going on?" Patience demanded loudly before commencing to swear a blue streak.

The bell over the door rang again as the customer who had been perusing the leather jackets scurried outside. Selena emerged from the dressing room clad in an atrocious lime green prom dress that hung awkwardly from her still-bony shoulders.

"Little pitchers," I said to Patience, giving her a look while clapping my hands over Selena's ears.

"I'm not *little*," Selena said, ducking out from my grasp and glaring at me. "And I'm not a pitcher. That's a stupid saying."

"Sorry," I mumbled. "It was a reflex. But my grandmother used to say that to me, so it's not stupid."

Selena rolled her eyes.

"Hello?" Patience said, her voice dripping with sarcasm. "Focus on *me*, shall we?"

Patience had a lucrative fortune-telling business and was a bit of a local celebrity. Not only was she a powerful psychic, but she had a flair for the dramatic, and played the role of an exotic fortune-teller with gusto, embracing every Hollywood stereotype: long, flowing skirts, colorful scarves, tinkling ankle bracelets adorning her sandal-shod feet. Her big, dark eyes were lined in kohl, and gold coins glinted from the necklace that graced her low-cut peasant blouse. With their dark good looks and striking features, Patience and Sailor could easily have modeled together for the cover of a romance novel.

Patience was, in short, everything I was not. I blew out a breath and stroked my medicine bag for strength. This was all I needed, today of all days.

"What can I do for you, Patience?" I asked.

"What can you do for me? What can *you* do for *me*?"

"That's what the lady said," Maya said with a wry laugh, earning a glare from Patience. Maya shrugged it off with a smile, in typical Maya fashion.

"May I assume this has to do with Sailor?" I asked. "I spoke with him this morning."

"I *know* you spoke with him this morning. Do you know *how* I know you spoke with him this morning?"

"Because . . . you're psychic?" I suggested.

"Because *I* tried to speak with him this morning and they told me he'd already had his one permitted visitor." She glared at me.

"I didn't realize he was only allowed one visitor," I said. "But I am his fiancée, after all."

Patience rolled her eyes. "Is that still happening?"

"Is what still happening?"

"This so-called 'wedding'?"

"Of course it's still happening," Maya said, an uncharacteristic touch of annoyance in her voice. "In fact, Selena and I are going to be bridesmaids. Aren't we, Selena?"

Selena nodded but remained mute, apparently a little intimidated by the force of nature that was Patience Blix. I could relate.

"Great heavens above, someone *please* tell me that child is not going to be wearing *that* bilious little number?"

"Hey," I yelled, planting myself between Patience and Selena. "*Enough*, Patience. Don't you *dare* pick on Selena. Your argument isn't with her—it's with me. She's having fun trying on dresses, and she looks adorable in anything she wears. Now, please apologize to her."

Patience gave me another sour look, then flashed Selena a fake smile. "Sorry. You look super, peaches. You look like you're ready for a Gypsy wedding. I'll give you that much."

I wasn't quite sure what she meant by that, but figured it was the best we were going to get.

"Anyway, Lily." Patience turned back to me. "I only came here to tell you that you'd better figure something out and right quick, or you'll be spellcasting over the warden for conjugal visits."

"I will *not* be . . ." I trailed off, realizing I was allowing myself to be baited. I stroked my medicine bag again and concentrated on keeping my temper. Patience could be of use to me—to *us*. "Of course Sailor won't be convicted. He's not even formally charged yet. All we have to do is figure out who the guilty person is, and he'll be off the hook."

"Oh, that's all, is it? Easy-peasy. Best get right on it, then."

I nodded. "I'll grant you, it's a lot. We have our work cut out for us."

"We?" Patience said. "Who are you calling 'we'?"

"All of us who care about Sailor," Maya said.

"That's right," I echoed, warmed by Maya's defense of Sailor. "Think of it this way: You're not helping me—you're helping Sailor."

She rolled her eyes.

"Have you been able to see anything?" I asked.

Patience's drop-dead good looks tended to distract me from the fact that she was tremendously gifted at reading cards and seeing in her crystal ball. Both would be helpful, and neither was my area of expertise.

A trio of college-age girls came into the shop, chatting and giggling. Maya went to help them, while Selena disappeared into the dressing room.

Patience let out a long-suffering sigh, and gestured with her head toward the back room. We passed through the brocade curtains that divided the workroom from the shop floor, and took seats on either side of the jade green linoleum table.

"Here's the problem," Patience said, looking around the workroom. For a moment I saw it through her eyes: the piles of clothes needing to be laundered or repaired, Bronwyn's collection of kettles, the small fridge that kept our lunches and snacks cool. A few old thrift-shop oil paintings and some framed drawings of Selena's studded the walls. They were amateur efforts, but hanging them on the wall added to my feeling of permanence, the sense that this was my forever home.

She hesitated so long I said, "You realize you haven't finished your thought, right? *What's* the problem? Besides the obvious, I mean."

"It looked like him," Patience finally said.

"What looked like who?"

"I was able to see something from that night, and the truth is, it looked like Sailor."

"What did you see, exactly?"

Patience sighed and looked at me as if I were slow-witted. "I went to the hotel where it happened. Hotel Marais, is it? I was able to 'see' the bloodied man stalking through the lobby. It was Sailor."

Our gazes met over the colorful bowl of fruit I kept

well stocked atop the kitchen table, in the vain hope that Oscar would eat something besides cheese and carbs.

"You're sure?" I asked.

"Very. I assume Sailor had good reason to kill the guy. I just can't figure out why he wasn't smarter about it. He walked right through the hotel lobby, in full view of several guests?"

I nodded. "That's what Carlos says."

"Carlos is your friend, the cop?" Her arched brows rose suspiciously.

"Yes. And good thing, too, since he filled me in on what's going on. He doesn't think Sailor did it. Said it sounded hinky to him."

"Hinky? What's that mean?"

"It means something is odd; the facts don't add up. Like you, Carlos couldn't figure out why Sailor had been so stupid as to murder someone in such a blatant manner. But . . . you're saying you think Sailor is capable of murder?"

The mask slipped. She grew serious, gazing at the pile of laundry, a faraway look in her eye. She seemed to be weighing her words.

"Yes and no. Is he capable of killing someone who is a threat? Yes. So am I. And so are you, notwithstanding your Miss Priss ways."

"My Miss what—?"

She waved one hand. "Not important. The point is, Sailor would not kill someone unprovoked, not like that. He wouldn't lie in wait and ambush someone, much less waltz into a hotel in front of witnesses. Unless"—Patience paused, took an orange from the fruit bowl, nicked the rind with her thumbnail, and sniffed its delicate fragrance—"he was trying to protect someone. *You*, for instance. Heavens to Murgatroyd, I can't figure out why he's such a fool for you."

I opened my mouth, but didn't know what to say.

"Did the victim—this Dupree guy—did he threaten you?" Patience asked.

Now it was my turn to weigh my words. "Sort of. He thought I had taken something of his. A bēag."

One eyebrow lifted. "You *stole* something from him? Not too swift, my dear. That guy was bad news."

"You knew Tristan?"

Her mass of shiny near-black curls bounced when she shook her head. "Not when he was alive. But . . . I could feel him there, at the hotel."

"I didn't realize you're such a talented necromancer."

"I have my abilities; you have yours." After a moment she added, with a grudging shrug, "Actually, I'm not usually able to see dead folks, or things from the past, that clearly. Maybe it's because of my connection to Sailor."

We sat for a few minutes, lost in our own thoughts. On the other side of the curtain were the normal, everyday sounds of Aunt Cora's Closet: the bell tinkling as the front door opened and closed, the murmur of voices, a delighted coo when someone found something she liked, the ringing of the antique cash register, and Maya's calm voice chatting with customers. They were comforting sounds, and I relished them, drew strength from their quotidian normality.

"What can you tell me about psychic projection?" I asked Patience.

"Why?" she demanded, her usual prickly demeanor having returned. So much for being on the same page.

I hesitated, not wanting to speak out of turn. Sailor, like the rest of us, kept the details of his life close to his chest. But then I reminded myself that Patience probably knew more about Sailor's training with Renna than I did.

"Sailor told me he's been working on projection.

Would it be possible for a psychic's astral self to have gone after someone like that? Could Sailor's unconscious or id, or whatever you want to call it, have taken over and killed Tristan Dupree?"

I was hoping the answer would be a definitive *no.* After all, if Sailor had experienced an out-of-control astral projection, however unconsciously, it would mean he was not responsible for his actions. But good luck explaining that in a court of law.

"Are you joking?" Patience studied me. "You're not. You're serious."

"I don't know a lot about this sort of thing."

"Obviously," she snorted. "*Somebody* needs to do her homework. Astral projection, my dear little witch, is a form of telepathy. The spirit leaves the body, but the body stays put. Spirits have no substance—they're immaterial. They can't affect the physical world. So, no, Sailor's astral projection could not have killed Dupree."

"But Maya thought she saw Sailor the other day, in an herb shop in Chinatown. He claims he wasn't there, and when I asked him about it, he hesitated and wondered if it was a result of projection."

"He projected himself to an *herbal* store in *Chinatown*? Why?"

I hadn't thought of that. "Now that you mention it, it does seem odd."

"No shit, Sherlock. Listen, a powerful psychic—and I mean a *very* powerful psychic; this stuff isn't easy—might be able to project an image along with some thoughts . . . but what would be the point? The appeal of projection is it allows you to see without being seen."

"A sort of psychic invisibility cloak," I pondered aloud. I wondered if there was a witchy version. I could dearly use something like that. "Cool."

"But seriously, in answer to your question, no, it could not have been Sailor's psychic projection that killed this guy. For one thing, unless you're lying to me, Sailor doesn't have sufficient motive. We both know he's not a stone-cold killer. For another, unless Sailor were suffering from some sort of schizophrenia or multiple personality disorder, he would have remembered killing a man, no matter what form he took."

"He didn't remember being in the herbal shop, when Maya saw him."

Patience shrugged. "That could be something else entirely. If Sailor's been working on astral projection with Renna, he would start with wandering through areas he knows well, like his apartment or neighborhood, or even this shop. Maybe Maya picked up on his projection, somehow. Does she have abilities?"

"Maya? No."

"You sure about that?"

"As sure as I can be. She's never said or done anything to suggest otherwise, and I'm pretty sure she would have told me if she had. But what if it's not projection at all? Could the man Maya saw in the store have been the same guy? The murderer?"

"I suppose it's possible there's a Sailor look-alike wandering the streets of San Francisco," Patience said. "So that's your plan to get Sailor out of jail? Find Sailor's look-alike, the one who's the real killer? How do you intend to do that?"

"By asking for help. Starting with you. Will you use your scrying skills to find this look-alike?"

"If it will help free Sailor."

"What can I do to help you get started?"

"This is a tricky one," Patience said, looking thoughtful. "Usually I have a clearer idea of who I'm looking for. If I search for a fake Sailor, I'm likely to keep finding the real Sailor, if you see what I mean."

I nodded.

"So what I need to do is a more generalized search

and then eliminate all the signs that point to Sailor. But how do I distinguish Sailor from Not Sailor?"

I remained silent, fascinated by watching an experienced and powerful psychic at work. The magic arts are enormously variable, even within specialties. Some witches are experts at chanting to alter reality, for example, while I shine in the art of brewing. I had been tutored as a witch, and had only a general idea of how psychics functioned.

"Let's try this: I need something of Sailor's. No, wait—I need something that carries energy from both you and Sailor. Your combined energy should work better, help to distinguish between Sailor and the Other Guy. . . . Something you associate with him, a sweatshirt, a boyfriend shirt. You have something like that?"

I glanced at my engagement ring. I hated to take it off my finger for even a moment, but if it would help Sailor, it would be worth it. I slipped the ring off and handed it to Patience.

Her eyebrows rose. She tried to put it on her ring finger, and I took mean pleasure in the fact that it was too small. Instead, she put it on her pinkie.

"Please—," I began, then cut myself off.

"No worries, princess. I'll take good care of it. I shouldn't need it for long."

I gazed at my ring for another moment, not liking how pretty it looked on her graceful hand. The ring made me think of the bēag Dupree had been looking for, and I wondered if Patience could help me with that as well.

Interrupting my thoughts, Patience demanded, "What?"

"What, what?"

"I don't have to be a psychic to know there's something else on your mind. Spill."

"As a matter of fact . . . there's this shoe box that dates from the time I knew Tristan Dupree."

"Where did you know him from?" Patience asked.

"In Germany, half a lifetime ago. He knew my father."

"I hear your father is bad news."

I nodded. "Anyway, I think this bēag Tristan was looking for might be in the shoe box."

"And . . . ?"

"I need help to open it."

"Not a typical shoe box, then."

"Not exactly, no."

She let out a long sigh. "Where is it?"

"I can't do this right now. I have to go try on dresses with Selena."

Patience's jaw dropped. "Excuse me? Sailor's rotting in jail and you're busy trying on *dresses*?"

"First of all, he's not 'rotting in jail.'" I talked a big game, but in truth my stomach was quailing at the very thought. Was Sailor safe? He was healthy and strong, experienced with supernatural evil. But could he hold his own among whatever nefarious characters were behind bars with him? "He's only been there overnight. I'm on it as much as I can be, but I will not disappoint a young girl. Especially since I don't exactly know what to do next."

She stared at me.

"I'm open to ideas at this juncture," I added.

"You're a piece of work, Lily Ivory. Okay, how's this for an idea? We need more help. I assume you have not failed to notice that all signs indicate we are dealing with some kind of supernatural evil. If that is the case, then my visions and your shoe box of whatever will only take us so far. We need more weapons. We need Aidan."

I had been afraid of that. But she was right.

"Aidan's a little . . . He might be a little upset with me at the moment."

"Why am I not surprised?" she said dryly. "Well, then, I suggest you get on Aidan's good side *tout de suite*, because we're going to need him. *Sailor* is going to need him."

"I know, and I will," I said, though I worried about what Aidan would demand from me in return. I pushed that thought aside—one problem at a time. "For the moment, will you stick around while I finish up here, and then we'll take a look at the box?"

Patience sighed. "Fine. But don't dawdle. Time is money."

Chapter 12

"Well, aren't you the businesswoman?" I said to Patience as we returned to the shop floor.

"You'd better believe it. I've got a mortgage and bills to pay, just like everyone else."

Bronwyn arrived and greeted Patience with an enthusiastic hug and lavish praise. Bronwyn had been coaching me to get over my jealousy of Sailor's beautiful cousin and the time she spent with him. Bronwyn was an openhearted, generous person who truly believed that most people were good and loyal, and that jealousy was a reflection of a person's insecurity, not an external reality. Bronwyn was also fascinated by Patience's psychic abilities, and swore Patience had "read her future to a tee." When I pointed out that there was no way to tell how accurate Patience's predictions were since the future hadn't happened yet, Bronwyn laughed and called me a spoilsport.

I had to admit, Patience accepted Bronwyn's effusive greeting with good grace. *A beautiful Gypsy queen accepting tribute from one of her subjects,* I thought, then chided myself for being so mean-spirited.

Then, as Bronwyn stashed her things in the workroom, Patience looked around the store and raised one eyebrow.

"I see nothing's changed. How . . . reliable."

Patience's expression suggested she meant "How boring." So much for the self-chiding.

"Not at all," I replied. "The inventory changes constantly. Only the layout is the same."

"As long as I'm here, I suppose I should look for something to wear," Patience said in a tone that suggested she was doing us a grand favor. "Assuming you're really going to go through with this ridiculous farce."

"For the Magical Match Tea, or the wedding?" asked Bronwyn, who was either ignoring or missing my gestures to keep quiet about the tea.

"The 'Magical Match Tea'?" Patience repeated, looking up from a collection of beaded flapper dresses. "What on earth is a Magical Match Tea?"

"I doubt you'd be interested—," I began, belatedly realizing that anything I didn't want Patience to do, she would be bound and determined to do. Had I been smarter, I would have invited her already and made sure she knew that I would personally benefit from the attention the tea would bring to Aunt Cora's Closet. She likely would have refused to attend just to spite me.

"It's a fund-raiser for a very good cause," interrupted Bronwyn, handing her the little flyer designed by Amy, aka Wind Spirit. It included an illustration: a tiered plate of cupcakes that put me in mind of Renee. "The Haight Street women's shelter."

Patience fixed me with an accusatory look. "Why would you think I wouldn't want to support something like that?"

"It's not that. . . ." I trailed off.

"It says here, 'Wear matching outfits,'" Patience said. "Who am I supposed to match?"

"Perhaps you have a young friend," explained Bronwyn, "and the two of you could find matching dresses here in the shop."

"Lily and I are wearing these," Selena said excitedly, showing off the polka-dot dresses that had sparked this whole idea. She held hers up against herself and rocked back and forth, making the full skirts swish gracefully.

It made my heart swell to see Selena smiling—something she very rarely did—and excited about the dresses. Not to mention she seemed pleased, maybe even proud, to be going as my match.

"How adorable. Tell me, does it have to be a *younger* friend?" Patience asked. "Or could *I* be the younger one?"

"All are welcome, no matter the age!" Bronwyn said gaily.

Patience smiled. "I'll invite Renna."

I blanched. Patience Blix and Sailor's aunt Renna? At the Magical Match Tea? The tea that Graciela's coven might be attending? *What could possibly go wrong?*

"You two will make a cute couple," I said with an inward sigh. San Francisco was my home now, and that meant navigating the byzantine machinations of the magical community, as much as everything else.

"Lily, you should try on the wedding gown Wind Spirit brought you," Selena urged. "Wind Spirit's cool. She gave me a charm, see?" She held up her wrist to show me a small silver bell on her charm bracelet.

"Nice charm. But I don't know about the dress. . . ." I hesitated. "It's not quite right for me."

"I think it's adorable," said Bronwyn. "But Wind Spirit said it would never fit her. In fact, when she came in to find a dress for the tea a couple of weeks ago, I helped her try on a few. I always thought she was chubby, but it turns out she's extremely muscular!"

"Selena and I were just talking about different body types," I said, hoping they'd drop the subject of the wedding dress. It was making me jumpy.

"Lily said I'm fat," said Selena.

Bronwyn gaped at me.

"I said no such thing!" I started to defend myself, then saw a ghost of a smile on Selena's face.

"Does Wind Spirit lift weights?" asked Maya. "My cousin got buff quickly when she started training."

"No, she told me her father was a martial arts instructor; apparently she practically grew up in the studio and achieved expert status when she was just a teenager," Bronwyn said. "Anyway, whether it's plumpness or sheer muscles, I fear it's hard to find true vintage to fit her. I sent her next door to Lucille's."

"Mom will fix her up," said Maya with a nod. Maya didn't always see eye to eye with her mother, but she was proud of Lucille's success—and with good reason. Not only was Lucille making a go of a small business in competitive San Francisco; she was also employing several women from the shelter, training them and giving them an opportunity to get on their feet.

"Are you going to try it on, or not?" Selena demanded, thrusting the wedding dress in my direction. Yards of white silk billowed toward me. "You're not chicken, are you?"

"Yeah, you're not chicken, are you?" repeated Patience. "Go for it, princess."

"It's . . . It needs alteration," I hedged. It was a nice enough gown on its own merits: yards of silk and satin topped by lace. The skirts were too poufy for my taste, and it would need to be altered to my dimensions, but Lucille could easily make those changes. Still, the vibrations didn't quite suit me. I couldn't put my finger on it, but one of my talents was knowing when something fit someone, both physically and psychically, and this dress did not fit me.

Or maybe there was nothing supernatural about my jitters—after all, brides were famous for searching for the perfect dress, and for being eternally dissatisfied, right? Maya informed me there was a whole TV show about it.

I had been scouring my usual sources of inventory, and had gone so far as to see what other vintage clothing stores carried, and still hadn't found a wedding gown I liked better. If I didn't find something soon, I would be in trouble. Hopefully this afternoon's estate sale might have something for me.

On top of everything else, Susan Rogers from the *Examiner* wanted to do a photo layout of the wedding party, as a sort of follow-up to the piece she had written about her niece's wedding—which I'd wound up attending stag, when I alienated my former boyfriend, Max. I had outfitted the niece's wedding party not long after Aunt Cora's Closet had opened, and the article had, in good part, made our reputation when it came out.

"Pleeeeaasse?" said Selena. Like any self-respecting teenager, Selena knew just what buttons to push. It was hard for me to refuse her when she found something that would make her happy. I let her lead me into the large communal dressing room, the poufy dress over her arm. Awkwardly, Selena helped me pull frothy yards of pure white satin over my head. I stood back and looked at myself in the full-length mirror. The shoulders were too wide and the shawl collar—clearly made for a better-endowed woman than I—flopped.

Selena flung the curtain open. "See? She *does* look like a princess!"

"More like a Baked Alaska," Patience muttered.

Selena laughed, and light glinted off the metal dream

catchers in the window and landed on her face. For a brief moment, despite my other worries, I reveled in the pure sound of her teenage joy. Selena had once been so severe that every smile—much less full-blown laugh—now felt like a gift.

The back of my neck tingled. I turned to look out the front window. Conrad was talking with someone on the sidewalk, and eating what looked like a brightly frosted cupcake.

A moment later, a man named Jamie strode into the store, carrying a huge pink box.

Jamie was one of Renee-the-cupcake-lady's minions. He was small and slender, with dark hair and eyes and sharp features. "Weaselly" was the adjective that came to mind anytime I saw him.

"Well, lookee here," Jamie said. "Don't you look just like a princess, pretty lady?"

"See?" said Selena. "Told you so."

Oscar had run up to greet Jamie the instant he spotted the pink bakery box.

Instinctively, I reached out to stop him. Renee wouldn't use cupcakes to cast a spell over us, would she? What was I thinking? Of course she would. But surely she would know I would anticipate such an obvious ploy.

Surely.

I glanced outside; Conrad was chatting with a passerby, apparently unaffected by the cupcake. Still, I didn't want to take any chances.

"Jamie," I said, "what brings you here?"

"Renee heard about the troubles facing your fiancé, and sends these as a peace offering. She says she guesses her invitation to the wedding must've got lost in the mail. Mine, too, for that matter."

"We're good here," I said, physically holding Oscar back from the cupcakes. "Thanks, anyway."

Patience, who had been taking in the scene, stepped

in. "You have something to do with what's going on, you little pissant?"

Jamie cringed. "Jeez, lady. A guy brings a dozen cupcakes . . . I mean, I don't expect a parade, but a simple thank-you seems in order." He shook his head. "I really don't get what's up with folks these days. There used to be a time when people valued simple politeness. . . ."

Jamie didn't look like he was much older than I was, but there was no denying he had a timeless sort of way about him.

He reached out and picked up a flyer for the Magical Match event.

"Hey, is this like speed dating? I might just give that a try. I tried the online-dating thing, but it's a bit of a slog. Also, you never know who's gonna show up—the photos don't always reflect current reality, if you catch my drift. Something like this here might be right up my alley."

"It's not a 'match' in that sense," I said. "It's a tea, a fund-raiser for the Haight Street women's shelter. The 'match' refers to matching dresses."

"Or outfits, for that matter," said Bronwyn. "You're very welcome; it's a gender-inclusive event."

Jamie looked disappointed and shoved the flyer back in its stand. "Sorry. Doesn't seem like my type of deal after all. Good cause, though—am I right?" He dug into a pants pocket and extracted a wrinkled five-dollar bill. Handing it to Bronwyn, he winked and said, "A contribution to the cause."

"Well, now," said Bronwyn, "aren't you kind? Thank you. I'm Bronwyn, by the way."

"Nice ta meetcha," he said. "I'm Jamie. I—"

"Why are you here, Jamie?" I interrupted him.

"What? Like I said, I'm on a mission of mercy. Renee heard your fiancé was in the slammer, and that you were feeling under the weather, so she sent you a little something. That's all. Cupcakes are like her version of chicken soup."

"What makes her think I'm under the weather?"

"The little guy want one?" Jamie asked, holding out to Oscar a yellow cupcake piled high with purple frosting.

"No," I intervened. "He's on a diet."

"Whoever heard of a pig bein' on a diet?"

"It's a Bay Area thing," I said. "He's vegan."

"Well, ain't that a kick in the pants? Just so's happens these cupcakes are vegan."

"Gluten-free, rather." I ignored the indignant squeals emanating from the area near my feet.

"Anyway, you should take these," Jamie said, shoving the pink box in my direction again.

"I want one!" said Selena.

"Maybe after lunch," I insisted, taking the box from Jamie. Selena glared at me, as did Oscar.

"Seriously, Lily," said Jamie. "Renee wouldn't pull anything funny with these here cupcakes, if you catch my drift. These came straight off the shelves at the bakery. You've eaten there before."

I had. But that was before I realized what Renee was all about.

"Please let Renee know I'll pay her a visit soon."

Jamie looked at me sideways. "Why's that?"

"Just to thank her, and to check in." I sneezed. "It's been a while."

"Uh-huh. 'Kay. Look, Lily." He dropped his voice and leaned in, as though sharing a confidence. "You mind if I give you a little advice?"

"Yes, she does," Patience answered for me. "And here's some advice for you: I suggest you leave while you still have all your man parts, if you catch *my* drift."

And with that, Patience ducked into a changing room carrying a 1930s green-and-purple dragonfly-bead cocktail dress, and flung the curtain closed with a flourish.

"Well, here's my advice, anyway," he said in a conspiratorial whisper. "It's not the cupcakes you should be worried about."

"By which you mean . . . ?"

"Not for nothin', but Tristan Dupree was an associate of Renee's."

"Is that right? In what way?"

"'Friend' is what I meant to say. He came to town to work with her."

"I didn't realize Tristan was a baker."

"Heh." Jamie snorted. "Good one."

I sneezed again.

"My mom always swore by hot toddies for colds. A little ginger, dash of cayenne pepper, and a healthy jigger of whiskey. That'll cure what ails ya, and you know what? If it don't, ya don't care!" Jamie let out a phlegmy laugh.

"Thanks, but it's probably just allergies. I don't catch colds."

"Yeah, right. You keep telling yourself that."

"So, why are you saying all this to me?" I asked. "I thought you worked for Renee."

"Are you still here?" Patience interrupted as she emerged from the changing room. The slinky cocktail dress hugged her voluptuous form like a kid glove, and she looked spectacular. Like some sort of exotic plumed bird. Of course.

Jamie let out a low whistle, his eyes raking over her, up and down.

"You had *better* not be making that noise at *me*, creep," threatened Patience. "You don't know uncomfortable until you're suffering under a Gypsy curse."

"Youse two both got a little attitude problem—you know that?" said Jamie. "I'm not gonna hang around where I'm not wanted. Anyway, I'll be the bigger man and wish you ladies a good rest of the day. Enjoy the cupcakes, courtesy of the Renee Baker bakery."

Jamie waved his hand over his head as he walked out the door.

"Who the hell was that?" asked Patience.

"Patience, seriously, would you please watch your mouth around—" I started to say "little pitchers," but caught myself in time. "I mean, in the shop."

She rolled her eyes. "Who's the creep? And what's with the cupcakes?"

"It's probably nothing. Just feeling a little cautious lately."

I changed out of the wedding dress and went outside to check on Conrad, hoping the cupcake he'd eaten hadn't made him feel sick or strange in any way. He responded with his typical "Duuuude!" and didn't demonstrate any obvious symptoms, though with Conrad it might be hard to tell.

Back inside Aunt Cora's Closet, I held the pink bakery box and tried to feel any untoward vibrations from the cupcakes. Nothing. I opened the lid and breathed deeply, but I was stuffed up and had a hard time smelling. I touched one after another, but still didn't sense anything untoward. Still, I wasn't about to run the risk. Shaking my head, I carried the big pink box into the back alley and tossed it in the dented Dumpster I shared with my Haight Street neighbors.

I turned to go back into the shop, only to find Oscar and Selena standing at the back door, gaping at me in outrage.

"Listen, you two, they're just cupcakes. I promise to bring you both something special later. But we do *not* eat gifts from strangers—do I make myself understood?"

"But you knew that man," Selena pointed out. "You called him Jamie."

"I know his name, but he's still a stranger. By which I mean he isn't one of our friends. Our people. Our circle."

Oscar and Selena trailed me back into the workroom, but neither looked convinced. Patience had changed back into her usual Gypsy getup and was leaning against the kitchenette counter, arms crossed over her chest, a smarmy smile on her wide mouth.

I tried again.

"Just . . . for a while, until I figure things out, promise me only to eat things from family, or people like Bronwyn and Maya, our adopted family. Promise?"

Oscar snorted and Selena uttered a sullen "I guess so."

I glanced around the room in the vain hope that I would remember a piece of pie or a few cookies I'd forgotten. I liked to keep the cookie jar stocked for an energy boost during work breaks, but I'd been so busy lately that I hadn't had time to bake. Then I remembered a tin of homemade "energy bars" left over from the coven meeting yesterday. I took the little tin from the cupboard where I'd hidden it from Oscar, and offered one to Selena and one to Oscar.

They accepted the peace offering without enthusiasm—the honey-sweetened oatmeal-and-walnut energy bars looked good but were no match for extravagantly iced cupcakes—and joined Maya and Bronwyn on the shop floor.

Patience was waiting for me.

"I don't have all day, you know," she said, and as much as I didn't want to hang out with her, I couldn't put it off any longer. I left Bronwyn and Maya in charge of Aunt Cora's Closet, encouraged Selena to continue trying on dresses with their moral support, and led the way up the back stairs.

I hesitated when I reached the little landing outside my door. I don't bring many people into my private apartment, so it felt strange to invite someone who wasn't exactly my best buddy. But that was silly; Patience had been here once before, with Sailor.

Sailor.

The thought of him sitting in a jail cell, facing boredom and worry at best, threats and intimidation at worst, made my stomach flip and urged me to step outside my comfort zone.

If Patience could help us, I would do whatever it took.

Chapter 13

Once we entered, Patience looked around the foyer, noting the herbal sachets and protective charms. She sauntered into the bedroom, her tongue worrying the inside of her cheek as she picked up a small photo of Sailor I kept on my bedside table. She set it back down and continued her tour, pausing in front of the bookshelf in the living room.

"Nice crystal ball," she said.

"Thanks. It was a present from my grandmother."

"Can you see anything in it?"

I shook my head. "Not often. I try, but . . ."

"But what? You still can't scry?"

"Not really," I admitted.

She lifted one eyebrow, and I lost what was left of my self-restraint. "I think it's important to remember all the things I *can* do. I really am quite gifted at a great number of things."

She shrugged. Listlessly, she walked around my living room, looking at Oscar's stack of detective novels—he was partial to 1950s noir—running her fingers along the backs of chairs, picking up an old music box and then setting it down in the wrong place. I fought the compulsion to follow her around and set things aright. I realized that the last time she had been here, it had been after a very trying evening, and she hadn't seemed to take it in like she did now.

Finally she finished her tour and faced me. "The shoe box?"

"Yes, the shoe box."

"Why are you hesitating?"

"It's just that Aidan was wary about opening it—"

"Hold on one second. You're saying *Aidan* was afraid to open it? Aidan *Rhodes*?"

"I wouldn't say 'afraid.' More like cautious."

"Uh-huh," Patience said, sounding unconvinced. "So cautious that he refused to open it with you?"

"We were about to. He was going to help me—of course he was. But then—"

"You screwed up."

"Why do you always assume the worst about me?"

"I could ask the same of you, princess."

"Okay, all right, fine. Yes, I screwed up. We got into an argument."

"About what?"

"That's personal."

"Since you're asking for my help to open a potentially dangerous box, I'd say it's my business."

"We had an argument," I said, "about Sailor."

"What about him?"

"Aidan says our relationship weakens me."

"Weakens you how?"

"He says it makes me vulnerable. That I need to concentrate on myself and my powers, and work with him to keep San Francisco safe. He thinks . . . I know it sounds a little strange, but Aidan thinks we're the *coincidentia oppositorum*, the male and female. He says a witch like me can't maintain my power while in a romantic relationship."

"Aidan said that about you and Sailor? That's kind of harsh."

Her response surprised me. "I thought you'd agree with him."

"I don't understand Sailor's fascination with you, but so what? Who am I to question the ways of the heart? I mean, he's pretty over the moon for you—anyone can see that." She shrugged. "I'd love to split you two up by agreeing with Aidan, but I don't. We're women, not nuns. Why can't a woman fall in love and still be powerful? I don't hear anyone saying that about men. Do you?"

"To be fair, Aidan says that's why he's not with anyone."

"I don't know, Lily—maybe he has a point. Maybe relationships do make us vulnerable—but so what? Maybe the ability to connect with others, in this world and in the next, is what makes us powerful. Have you thought about that?"

I couldn't help but smile. Seems Patience and I shared some common ground, after all.

"How about you?" I ventured. "Is there someone special in your life?"

She snorted. "Just because I don't buy what Aidan's selling doesn't mean we're BFFs. I'm not here to share secrets of the heart over flavored coffee and biscotti. We have more important things to do."

"Fair enough," I said. Once upon a time, not so very long ago, Patience's words would have stung. Not anymore. *Not everyone will want to be a friend,* Bronwyn had told me. *If you try and fail, oh, well. Move on.*

"So where's this mysterious box of yours?" asked Patience.

I brought the shoe box out of my bedroom and set it

on the coffee table. I wouldn't make the mistake I had with Oscar, of underestimating the weight of my memories, and the power of my grief. Though I couldn't remember much of what had happened with my father in Germany, I knew it had been traumatic.

The thought of my father in that burned-out manor house . . . it made me shiver.

Then Jamie's words came back to me. He claimed Tristan Dupree had come to San Francisco to work with Renee. But before going to see Renee, Tristan had come here, to Aunt Cora's Closet, to recover something from me. If Jamie was telling the truth, did Tristan's death make me even more of an enemy to Renee? Was I her target now? Did this mean she was after the bēag? What would keep her from sending Jamie—or another one of her lackeys—to ransack my place one day when I wasn't home, in search of the bēag Tristan had been looking for? Could her magic overcome my beefed-up protection spell?

"What's all that?" Patience asked while I gathered my supplies in a basket, then brought them to the coffee table.

I held up a jar with a narrow spout. "These are my special salts—ordinary table salt would do for most threats, but I'm going to pull out the big guns for this box."

"I think that's best," she said with a nod. "What do you need me to do?"

"Watch, don't interfere, and follow my lead."

I poured a thin line of salt in a circle around the box, chanting:

At this place and in this time,
lock tight the doors of our minds.
Spirits who wander, spirits who keep,
do not bring our souls to weep,

guardians of the night and arts,
shield the keys to our hearts.

Glancing up at Patience, who sat silently watching me, I felt a wave of self-consciousness.

"That's how it goes," I said, my tone defensive. "It's a protection spell."

"Rock on, witchy woman."

I almost never cast in front of others. But since this was for Sailor, I repeated the chant over and over, forcing myself to focus my intent.

I wished I had thought to bring Oscar with us. Even though he's not a typical witch's familiar, he shares with familiars one very important characteristic: He eases my spellcasting, helping me to open the portals to the next world and beyond more easily. Still, Oscar wouldn't be able to transform in front of Patience, and I wasn't sure whether he would be as helpful in his piggy form. We'd never had reason to try.

I took out a black tourmaline stone from the basket, repeated my chant, then set it on the table right outside the salt circle, just barely touching the white crystals. One by one I placed the rest of the stones: a slick agate, a bloodstone, a labradorite, a black onyx, a peridot, and, from an old Altoids tin, a tiny chip of precious emerald.

The stones studded the salt circle like ornaments on a wreath.

I sat on the floor on one side of the coffee table and nodded to Patience to sit opposite me.

I laid my hands, palms up, on the table. Slowly, she rested hers atop mine.

A shock of recognition, a tiny spark like an electric current, passed between the two of us. This happened at times with other magical folk, such as Aidan, though with him the recognition was greatly amplified, as if on steroids.

"We surround ourselves with a veil of protection," I intoned. "We are safe within our space."

I felt Patience focusing, lending her powers of concentration to mine. A light began to emanate from the two of us, rising above the salt circle, atop the box, growing brighter with each breath. It was strong and controlled, vibrating at a high frequency.

"No evil can penetrate our combined forces."

The light spread from its origin above the box to fill the room, casting a pulsating glow.

"Guiding Spirit, hear my call." A faint visage of the Ashen Witch appeared in my mind.

And then I opened the box.

Chapter 14

The slithering again.

"Ugh, you didn't say there would be silverfish!" Patience said, rearing back. "I hate silverfish."

"Silverfish?" I peered into the box. There were silvery blue insects slithering all over the cardboard and the items within the box.

"You don't need a psychic. You need an exterminator."

"There aren't silverfish anywhere else in my apartment. Look at them; they seem to be confined to the box."

Besides the admittedly creepy silverfish, there were a few items wrapped in brown paper along with an old newspaper and a photograph.

It was a formal wedding portrait of my father and mother. As I picked it up, I remembered carrying it with me from Texas, hoping it would aid me in my search. But of course my father had changed a lot since then. In the photo, his face was open, hopeful, his smile wide and genuine. The last time I had seen him, when he had come to San Francisco, he looked like an entirely different man. Not just older, but hard, jaded. Bitter.

My mother looked slightly dazed, and very innocent. She gazed up at my father adoringly, a beatific expression on her young face.

What does she look like now? I wondered. What would she be like? Why had she decided to board that bus, with all those elderly witches? When I knew her, she had taken pains to distance herself from anything and everything having to do with magic and witchcraft. Including her only daughter.

When will they get here, already? The anticipation was killing me.

In an attempt to focus my wandering thoughts, I unwrapped a small bundle that turned out to contain an old windup wristwatch. I started to turn the knob to see if it still worked, before I found myself hesitating.

"Maybe not," I said. "Wouldn't want to start the doomsday countdown, or whatever."

"No, indeed," replied Patience. "Wouldn't want that. Maybe you should ask Aidan."

There were several other crystals and stones wrapped in paper, a few herbs so dry they were mostly powder, and one more photograph: of me, as a toddler. Probably taken around the time my father left Texas. Left me, and my mother.

I chose another item, this one wrapped in muslin. Inside was a tiny, ornate glass bottle, encased in silver filigree. I held it up to the light of the candle. Inside, a few delicate crystals tinkled.

"What the hell are those?" Patience demanded. "More salts?"

"In a manner of speaking," I replied. "This is a lachrymatory. In the Victorian days, when someone died, mourners collected their tears in a bottle like this. When the tears evaporated, the mourning period was over."

"I've heard of that. I thought it was a myth."

"Lots of things thought to be mythical are true."

"Okay. I can roll with that. But why is this one important?"

"Renee-the-cupcake-lady has been collecting lachrymatories in her bid to take over San Francisco's magical community. The salts that remain after the tears evaporate are essential to a number of spells. They're quite powerful because they contain the essence of the bereaved. Concentrated grief, in a way."

"Renee-the-cupcake-lady? Wasn't that her weasel down in the shop?"

"Yep. Hard to believe the cupcake lady poses an existential threat to San Francisco, but apparently she does."

Patience looked thoughtful. "She wants to depose Aidan?"

I nodded.

"And would that be such a bad thing?" Patience asked.

"Renee is dangerous. Besides, I thought you *liked* Aidan."

She shrugged. "I like him well enough. I mean, I don't *dis*like him. But I don't get into supernatural politics. They're all a bunch of crooks. As far as I can see, power corrupts."

"What's Aidan's story? Do you know?" I asked.

"All I know is he's not a man to cross. The glamour he carries around with him sort of weirds me out. Makes me wonder what he's hiding."

"You know about the glamour?" I hadn't realized anyone but me knew about Aidan's glamour. "Have you seen Aidan's real self?"

"Naw, I'm just hypersensitive to glamours," Patience said. "I get within ten feet of one of them, it's like nails on a chalkboard. But anyway, I like him for this: He can help us with Sailor."

"Um . . . like I mentioned, Aidan might not be in the mood to help at the moment."

"Then apologize, because we need his help. Either that or eat the cupcakes and get Renee-the-cupcake-lady on board, because—as much as it pains me to say this—I don't think you and I alone have what it takes to get Sailor out of the slammer."

It had never occurred to me to throw in with Renee. But Patience was right: We needed some help. We weren't enough, not even as a united front.

No matter that Aidan and I weren't always pals, and that he and I fought a lot—deep down I felt he was an ally. I didn't trust him completely, but that was not unusual for alliances between magic folk. We were cagey that way. Also . . . I had once had a vision while in Aidan's octagonal room. It included lachrymatories, a rain of blood, and other not-good things associated with Renee. According to Aidan, Renee was seeking a male counterpart for the *coincidentia oppositorum*—a sort of ancient covenant that had to do with the balancing of magical forces between two powerful practitioners. At that point she would be strong enough to go up against me and Aidan.

My thoughts turned to Selena, especially how easily she could be influenced—and her talents corrupted—at this point in her life. Then I considered my father, selling out for power. And I thought of the times I, myself, had been tempted. This was the problem with possessing extraordinary supernatural powers; it was far too easy to get carried away, to believe oneself above others, to manipulate and control. To slide on over to . . . whatever one wanted to call it: the dark side, the left-handed way, the wayward path. The God complex.

No, allying with Renee was not an option. She simply didn't feel right to me. I just wished I knew more about Aidan's background, what he was after as an end goal. I didn't know what could happen in San Francisco, but not for the first time, it felt like I had been urged to come here for a reason. To fight the good fight. To fulfill the prophecy, perhaps.

I glanced at Patience, who was inspecting her perfectly manicured nails, and wondered if I could—or should—ask her about the prophecy. It embarrassed me, to tell the truth.

"What do you think the silverfish mean?" I asked.

"I told you: You need to fumigate."

"But they're restricted to the box. Also, there's a distinct thumping sound coming from the box, from time to time."

I broke the salt circle and went to the bookshelf, then brought my Book of Shadows back to the coffee table and flipped through the pages.

"Doesn't say anything about silverfish in particular. Silver is a traditionally powerful metal for witches, as it reflects the light of the moon. And fish can be a sign of abundance and faith, or of fertility. Insects in general can be considered signs of resilience and steadfastness—or destruction and disease." I shook my head, disappointed. "That's all it says."

I rewrapped the box in the rowan and knotted the twine, then stashed it back in the suitcase. Before leaving, I would ask Oscar to make double sure no one came upstairs and started poking around. No one ever had, but just in case, I wanted to be cautious.

"So you still don't know what Tristan was after, exactly?" Patience asked.

"There's no obvious bēag, no. I know Renee has been collecting lachrymatories, so perhaps it's as simple as that. Or there's the watch—Sailor had a vision with a watch. But that doesn't tell us much or help me figure out what Tristan wanted from me."

"So what's next, then? I'm willing to do what I can to break Sailor out of the slammer, but I don't have time to sit around."

"We could go back to the hotel," I suggested. "Maybe Hervé and I missed something last night. And then . . . it's not too far from Fisherman's Wharf. Probably if you're with me, Aidan will be civil."

"That's your plan?"

"It's not like there's a handbook, you know. I'm open to suggestions."

She let out a long-suffering sigh, whipped her scarf around her shoulders, and said: "I'll say one thing for you, princess—you've got a cool car. I'll drive."

"When pigs fly."

Chapter 15

There were three cop cars parked outside the Hotel Marais, so we rolled right on by, continuing down Bush Street. I pulled over in front of Café de la Presse, across from the Chinatown gates.

"You have a sudden need for an espresso?" Patience asked. "A copy of *Le Monde* to catch up on all the latest French news, perhaps?"

"Just taking a moment to rejigger the plan."

"Is 'rejigger' a word?"

"It is where I come from."

I was half hoping Patience would come up with some bright idea, but she just gazed out the window, arms crossed over her chest.

"You know, last night the hotel's clerk, Shawn, told me Tristan hadn't been feeling well and directed him to an apothecary in Chinatown. The same one Maya saw 'Sailor' in once."

She arched an eyebrow at me. "And you haven't checked it out yet?"

"It's been an eventful day."

"So what are we waiting for?"

I navigated the clogged Chinatown streets to the Lucky Moon herbal shop, and then started the search for parking, never an easy feat in this part of town. The sidewalks were crowded: Fishmongers touted today's catch; produce stands were heaped with a vast assortment of vegetables; golden roast ducks hung in display windows; bakeries featured sesame balls, *char siu bau*, and cabbage rolls; tourist shops hawked silk robes, postcards, refrigerator magnets, and windup cable cars. Gaggles of women and men pawed through the merchandise, bright pink plastic bags hanging from their arms. Double-parked delivery trucks snarled traffic, and small clutches of tourists lingered on corners, consulting their phones and maps, further slowing down the flow of cars.

We wound up circling the block a few times, rolling past the Lucky Moon apothecary repeatedly. I kept pondering Sailor and Sailor's double. Self-doubt clutched my heart. What in the world was going on? How could I prove Sailor's innocence?

I was on the verge of using my parking charm to free up a space when a small hatchback pulled out near the corner of Grant and Sacramento. I parallel parked, smoothly backing my Mustang into the tight space.

"Not bad," said Patience.

I smiled. I was proud of my parallel-parking prowess—I'd had plenty of practice since moving to San Francisco. And in comparison with parking the bulky shop van, the nimble Mustang was a breeze.

The Lucky Moon was a typical Chinatown herb shop in many ways: An innocuous sign outside displayed the name in Chinese characters, repeated below in smaller English letters. I had been inside a couple of times with

Sailor; there were a long counter, and an entire wall full of hundreds of wooden drawers, and shelves lined with dozens of huge jars. Behind the counter stood an old man who served as clerk, diagnostician, and pharmacist. He wasn't an acupuncturist and was careful to explain that he wasn't a medical doctor, either. But he filled scripts, mixing ingredients with a mortar and pestle, filling tiny Baggies with herbs and powders, and vials with pressed pellets.

"I love that smell," said Patience, breathing deeply.

I nodded in agreement. Even with my stuffed-up nose I could sense a bit of the spicy aroma of exotic spices and herbs.

Before we could say anything, the old man called to someone in the back of the store. A boy about thirteen or fourteen, thin and gangly, all elbows and knees, wearing basketball gear, came in to translate for us.

I tried to describe Tristan Dupree, but realized I didn't have a photo or anything to show.

"Sorry," said the boy, shaking his head. "We get a lot of tourists in here. Lot of people from out of town, all the time."

"He was complaining of stomach problems," I said, putting my hand on my belly to demonstrate.

The old man spoke and placed a small plastic bag full of herbs on the counter.

The boy translated: "He says this tea is good for digestion. Brew five minutes, take after meals."

"Thank you," I said, and then sneezed. "But my stomach is fine."

The boy reached up for a packaged product and pushed the small box toward me.

"Good for colds."

"Thank you." I sniffed. "But I'm actually not here for a remedy for myself. I'm interested in the man who came here yesterday."

The phone rang and the old man picked it up, speaking in Cantonese to the person on the other end of the line.

While we waited, I noticed one of the jars. On a square white label, beneath the Chinese characters, was written *Mandrake root*. I was no slouch when it came to botanicals, myself, and I was familiar with the mandrake root. In fact, I had used it to make a mandragora—a sort of household imp—for Aidan. I made a mental note to ask Aidan whatever happened to the little guy.

"What is the mandrake root used for?" I asked when the old man hung up the phone.

The boy translated: "He says it is poison."

I nodded. "I know. That's why I asked what it can be used for."

The boy conferred with the old man, who spoke for a long time. Finally the boy turned back to me and said simply: "It's complicated."

"Seriously?" Patience rolled her eyes.

I smiled. Whether the boy hadn't understood what the old man had said, or simply didn't want to bother to translate, or whether the old man wasn't willing to give away his secrets, I understood. Like practitioners of magic, those involved in health care had to be careful about sharing their rarefied knowledge.

We were about to leave when I had another thought. I didn't have a photo of Tristan Dupree, but I carried one of Sailor—a wallet-sized copy of the one that sat on my bedside table. I pulled my billfold out of my bag and flipped it open.

In general, Sailor avoided having his picture taken. This was common for magical folk; after all, if the photo fell into the wrong hands, it could be used for hexing. But with Sailor I thought it had more to do with something else. He didn't enjoy people telling him how handsome he was. Even me.

But I had talked him into letting me take his snapshot with my antique Brownie camera. I hardly ever used it, but when I did, I loved how imperfect the results were. The photo was black-and-white, fuzzy around the edges, with a streak of light that might have been an orb, but was more likely the result of light exposure from my flawed camera. Sailor was sitting on his bike, his arm resting on his helmet on the gas tank. He looked relaxed, but also happy. Or at least as happy as Sailor got, which was limited. There was the slightest smile playing on his lips. The look in his eye was a little bit lustful, a little bit tender, a little bit cynical.

I wondered what he was doing now, and hoped and prayed that he was all right. And that I could figure this thing out soon and hold him, breathe in his scent.

Patience snorted, pulling me out of my reverie. I realized she was looking over my shoulder at the photo. I didn't know how long I had stood there staring at it, but the old man and the boy were gazing at me as well.

"Sorry," I said, clearing my throat and holding the wallet out to them. "Have you seen this man here?"

Both sets of eyes widened. The old man spoke for a moment, seeming agitated. The boy nodded, then turned to me and said, "He used to be a good customer. But now we would like him not to come back, please."

"Why? What happened?"

"He was asking for *Chuan Wu* tea," said the boy. "But raw."

"What kind of tea is that?"

"Sometimes it is used for pain. But if it is not processed properly, it is a deadly poison."

"Do you know what it's called in English?"

The man looked something up in an old catalog, then showed it to the boy. "Here, it says monkshood, or wolfsbane."

"Those are aconite plants," I said.

"Yes." The boy nodded. "It is a poison. Last year a lady died after drinking some tea that was improperly prepared."

"This man asked for that?" I said, holding up Sailor's photo again.

The boy nodded. "But . . . he didn't look nice—he didn't smile like this. He was sort of whack."

"Whack?"

"Scary. A little bit crazy-seeming. He didn't speak, just wrote things down."

"Did he say—or write—anything else?" I asked.

The boy turned to the old man and translated my question. "He asked for mushrooms."

"What kind of mushrooms?"

"Amanita mushrooms. They are poisonous, too. Grandfather says he does not deal in such things. We would like this man not to come back, please."

"That's a lot of poison talk," said Patience as we walked back to the car.

"True. But many medicines—maybe even *most* of them—are poisonous in the wrong dosage but helpful if administered very carefully. Like the aconite tea, which is used in a number of ways, such as to treat pain or bruising. It's only deadly when not prepared properly."

"So you're saying maybe this fake Sailor guy was in the market for medicine?"

"No, you're right. He was probably looking for poison. The question is, why? I've been thinking . . ."

"Good place to start."

I opened the car door and looked at her over the roof. "Maybe there *was* no motive."

"What do you mean?"

"What if someone wanted to set up Sailor, for whatever reason, and Dupree was simply a victim of opportunity?"

"You're saying some Sailor look-alike wanted the real Sailor out of the picture?"

"It's possible. It would explain why he was so obvious about leaving the scene of the crime."

"Putting aside the fact that this mystery assailant just happens to look exactly like your boyfriend—"

"Fiancé."

"Whatever. How would this person know that Sailor knew Dupree, much less that Sailor had threatened him earlier in the day?"

"Good question. The only ones who heard that were Sailor, me, and Carlos."

"You trust Carlos?"

"I'd trust Carlos with my life."

"How about with Sailor's life?"

"That, too."

"All right. What about that dubious character who hangs out on the sidewalk in front of your store?"

"Conrad? I suppose he might have overheard, but he wouldn't be involved in something like this."

"You sure about that? Needs money for drugs, maybe thinks it's no big deal to do a little informing on the side, doesn't think he's hurting anyone . . . ?"

"No way," I said with a firm shake of my head. "Not Conrad."

She shrugged. "So what's next, then? We go to Aidan and grovel? By which I mean *you'll* grovel, of course. I have no beef with the man."

"I have a better idea. First let's check out Sailor's apartment. We can leave the car here; it's just a couple of blocks over."

"I've never been to Sailor's place," she said.

"Never?"

Patience pressed her lips together, looking displeased at the thought that she had been denied the privilege.

I waved off a man in a Mercedes who had been waiting for my spot. Clearly disappointed, the driver made an obscene gesture, which Patience returned with enthusiasm.

I extracted my supplies from my trunk. After being caught without it the other night, today I had remembered to bring along my Hand of Glory. I also had my woven backpack packed with talismans, salts, herbs, and a widemouthed mason jar full of protective brew.

"What's all this?" Patience asked when I handed her the wooden box.

"Just in case."

"More silverfish?"

"Not hardly."

She gave a wry smile. "What exactly do you think we're going to find in Sailor's apartment?"

"Nothing. Probably. It just pays to be prepared."

"What an excellent Girl Scout you must have been. So you cart around all this stuff in your trunk, do you? You must live a pretty fraught life."

"You have no idea. Hey, it occurs to me," I said, slowing my pace. "Sailor would hate the thought of us poking around in his apartment, looking through his things. He's pretty big into privacy."

"Aren't we all? But at the moment I don't particularly care what Sailor wants. He got himself thrown in jail, so his desires aren't paramount to me right now."

"It's not as though he got arrested on purpose."

"So what? The result's the same: He's detained and we have to spend our time and energy finding a way to get him out. So in this case, at least, the ends justify the means. And anyway, he should have known the police were coming for him." She shook her head. "He's been distracted lately."

"Are you suggesting Sailor 'let' himself be arrested because he's distracted by *me*? I'm sorry, but I'm not willing to cop to that."

"All about you much?" she said. "No, I wasn't blaming you. At least, not this time. There's been something going on with him, with his trance state. I can't say exactly what, but something's been off."

"Off, in what way?"

"He's just . . . not fully himself. You're familiar with trance states, right?"

"Sort of. I approximate a trance when I'm brewing sometimes, or casting a complicated spell. But I don't think it's the same."

"No, not by the sound of it. For a psychic like Sailor, it involves allowing his conscious self to leave his body, to become a conduit for spirit helpers or guardians, or to get in touch with others' auras."

"That's why Renna was working with him on astral projection?"

"He was having trouble—new for him, I might add—with being fully there, fully present."

"And yet not."

"Exactly."

"This is why I don't do well with things like scrying. That whole 'concentrate but let your mind wander' thing isn't easy."

"Tell me about it."

We crossed Waverly Place, and walked past the Willie "Woo Woo" Wong Playground. A few kids were running about, screaming and playing, while their parents sat on benches, chatting. Unlike many of the city's other tourist draws, San Francisco's Chinatown is a vibrant neighborhood full of immigrants and native-born citizens, chock-full of people going about the business of everyday life.

As we turned onto Hang Ah Alley, Patience sniffed the air. "You smell that?"

"I can't smell much lately, but there used to be a German perfume manufacturer here, a long time ago."

A young man was leaving Sailor's apartment building as we approached, and he held the front door open for us. The windowless hallway was dim, lit only by a single bare lightbulb. We climbed the creaky stairs to the second floor. At the landing outside Sailor's apartment, I set down my backpack and took the wooden box from Patience.

"Something happened here," said Patience, a frown marring her brow. "Something bad."

"A fight over a gambling debt that didn't have a happy ending." If *I* could feel the spirit that lingered on this landing, I could only imagine how much Patience was feeling. "Sailor said that's why the apartment's so cheap. He says the spirit doesn't bother him."

"It feels . . . mournful."

"I always thought so, too."

This was surreal. I had spent so much time stressing over Patience, had seen her as so very different from me—and here we were, working together, and basically on the same wavelength.

"What's that?" Patience asked as I opened the box.

"My Hand of Glory."

"You do realize what you just said doesn't actually reveal anything, don't you? What is a Hand of Glory, or do I even want to know?"

"Probably not. A Hand of Glory is a kind of candleholder that opens locked doors—so far it hasn't been foiled by a single one—and illuminates dark spaces with a clear bright light, like daylight. It's made from the mummified left hand of a hanged man, which is kind of gruesome, but if you can ignore that part, it's awfully convenient."

"You're serious?"

"It's very handy." I chuckled at my inadvertent pun and held up the Hand of Glory to her. "'Handy,' get it?"

"Yeah. Hysterical," she said, rearing back and pushing my arm away. "Just open the door so we can get out of this apartment building of horrors, will you? Between the mournful spirit breathing down my neck and this gruesome mummified hand, I'm going to have nightmares tonight."

So much for being on the same wavelength.

I held the Hand in front of the lock, and opened the door.

Patience strode right in, but I lingered in the entrance. Sailor's apartment always smelled great: notes of citrus and exotic spice, mingled with the faint scent of perfume from the alley. But today I could barely sense it. It made me sad.

Again, I wondered if we were crossing any important lines in invading Sailor's privacy in this way. True, we were doing it for him . . . but I felt as though I should have asked him before coming in. I had been here before, of course, but not often. We usually met at my place, and almost always stayed the night there instead of here. But Sailor hadn't given up his apartment, and so far we'd avoided talking about where we would live after getting married. Which was a pretty basic conversation not to have had, now that I thought about it. In fact, it dawned on me that we'd avoided talking about a lot of things. Aidan's words rang in my ears. What was Sailor's middle name? What about *children*?

Time to focus. Inside, the usually neat apartment was a mess. I imagined it had been torn apart by the

SFPD's forensics team, looking for bloody clothing or other clues linking Sailor to Tristan's murder.

"This is pretty bleak," Patience said as she wandered around, her fingers trailing over Sailor's sparse furnishings and piles of books.

"It's usually neater than this; the cops must have tossed it. But even so, you're right. Pretty bleak."

Her eyebrows rose, but she didn't say anything else.

The living room included a small galley kitchen. Several cabinet doors and drawers stood open, revealing only a single bowl, a plate, and one set of cutlery. There were a drawer full of disposable chopsticks, the kind that came stuffed into bags of takeaway, and a bunch of single-wrapped fortune cookies and soy sauce packets. On the one hand it did seem sad; on the other, if a person lived alone in Chinatown, it would be easy enough to pick up inexpensive, delicious takeout every day of the week.

Off the living room was a small bedroom furnished with only a bed, a nightstand, and a bookshelf, along with a small bathroom. The books had been toppled, the bed linens tossed in a heap on the floor. A metal file box full of papers and an empty leather-bound jewelry case stood open in the corner. That was all there was.

"Nothing out of place?" Patience asked after sticking her head in the bathroom.

"I can't really tell, since the police have tossed it," I said. But as I spoke, I noticed a notepad covered with doodles on a small table near the bed. The doodles reminded me of something. . . .

"We have to leave," Patience said, her tone urgent.

"What is it?"

"Now!" She grabbed my arm and yanked me toward the door.

"What—"

"Move!"

I ran after her out the door. On the landing the spirit was agitated; moving across the small space felt like pushing through freezing-cold water. Patience took a moment, closed her eyes, and let out a long breath, as though she was praying.

I heard the sound of heavy boots on the wooden stairs.

Climbing toward us was a man.

Jeans, black boots, motorcycle jacket, helmet under one arm. Scowling, but gorgeous.

"Sailor!" I exclaimed. "Did they drop the charges?"

Patience swore a blue streak as she grabbed my arm and pulled me up the stairs, away from Sailor.

"Lily, come *on*!"

"But what—? Sailor?" I said again, but he didn't respond to me.

His eyes were cold, empty. A chill ran through me.

Chapter 16

It wasn't Sailor. Not Sailor.

We ran up the stairs to get away from him.

Not Sailor paused on the landing, as though having trouble getting past the spirit. It gave us a few precious moments as a head start.

Up the next set of stairs, and then the next. At the top of the four-story building, the door to the roof was closed and locked.

"Dammit!" Patience said, slapping her hand against it. It wasn't fancy, merely a simple door with a knob lock. "Where's your Hand thingie?"

"I left it in the apartment."

We heard the boots on the stairs again. Faster this time, coming closer.

Patience whipped a bobby pin out of her hair and jammed it into the doorknob. She opened it quickly.

We rushed through and slammed the door behind us, but had no way to lock it. A pile of dilapidated wooden crates gave me an idea.

"Grab a piece of wood," I said, planting my feet on the roof and leaning against the door.

"What, those old things? They won't hold the door."

"Not a whole crate, just a piece of one to use as a shim."

Patience ran over to one of the crates and stomped on it. The crate splintered, and she grabbed several of the smaller pieces.

"Jam them in the space beneath the door," I said. "Like a doorstop."

Patience shoved the small pieces of wood between the bottom of the door and the sill.

"That should slow him down," I said. "But it won't hold him long. I'm guessing that's not actually Sailor."

He started banging at the door.

"Of course not." She shook her head. "Don't you feel that?"

"What?"

"A pulsating energy . . . It's kind of making me sick to my stomach."

"I don't feel a thing."

"Lucky you. Anyway, how do we get off this damned roof?"

"We go there," I said, pointing to the roof of the building next door. There was a three-foot gap between the buildings, which wouldn't have seemed like much if we were on the ground. Four stories in the air, though, three feet seemed a lot farther.

"There?" she asked, as the pounding on the door increased.

"You got a better idea?"

We ran over to the side of the building. "Jump. You can do it. It's only three feet," I said to Patience.

"My seventh-grade gym teacher told me one day I'd be glad she made me do the broad jump. I really hate that she was right."

"You're stalling," I said. "I'll go first."

I summoned up my courage and jumped as far as I could, clearing the gap by at least a foot.

"No sweat," I said. "You can do this. Now come on, I'll catch you."

Patience hesitated another moment, then took a deep breath and jumped. I grabbed her as she landed, and we ran for the roof door.

Locked.

"Dammit!" Patience said, examining the knob. "This one's beyond bobby pin technology. Now what? Eventually we're going to run out of roofs to jump onto."

"We have to go down," I said, running along the side of the building and looking over the ledge. "There. A fire escape. See it?"

"Are you kidding me? That's at least five feet down!"

"Go over feetfirst. By the time you let go of the ledge, you'll be almost at the fire escape."

"You say that like you know what you're talking about," Patience said. "Do you do this regularly?"

"Just *go*," I urged her.

Patience sat on the ledge of the roof, rolled over on her stomach, and gradually lowered herself until she let go. A second later I heard a loud *thud*.

"Are you all right?" I said, peering over the side.

Patience was sprawled on the fire escape, glaring up at me. "I landed on my butt," she said. "Ow."

"But you looked graceful doing it," I replied.

Patience snorted. "Your turn, Wonder Woman."

I sat on the edge of the roof, rolled over onto my stomach, and slowly eased myself over. *Props to Patience,* I thought. It took a lot more courage to do this than I had realized.

"Let go," Patience called out. I took a breath, released my grip, and landed lightly on my feet on the fire escape, thanks to Patience's steadying hand.

"When this is all over, you're buying me a drink," Patience said. "Probably more than one."

"Deal," I replied.

"Now what?" Patience asked.

"Go inside, I think." A large window faced the fire escape. We tried raising the window, but it was locked.

"Next time bring the damned Hand with you, will you?" Patience said while knocking loudly on the window.

"It's not like you gave me time to gather my things."

"Graft it onto your body or something."

I glanced up at the roof and saw Not Sailor peering over the ledge. "I'll get right on that, assuming we live."

A very confused-looking man approached the window and threw it open. "Can I help you?" he asked.

"We're on a scavenger hunt," Patience said, climbing through the window and into the man's apartment. "It's for charity. You don't mind, do you? Thanks. You, uh, might want to lock up behind us."

I followed Patience through the window, across the apartment to the door, and into the hallway.

As we careened down several flights of stairs, I realized that I had left not only the Hand of Glory in Sailor's apartment but also my backpack. With my keys.

Finally making it back out onto the street, we paused to take a breath.

"Now what?" Patience asked, holding the apartment building's door open for a young woman to enter. I heard the thundering sound of Not Sailor's boots flying down the stairs.

"Run!"

We hurried down the street, our progress slowed by the usual congestion in Chinatown. The busy sidewalks and streets jammed with cars should have worked to our advantage by making it easy for us to get lost in the throng, but not this time. Patience stood out in the crowd. Not Sailor would spot her in a moment.

"We have to get inside somewhere," I said as we hurried along, dodging shoppers picking over the fresh greens on a sidewalk display. "You're too conspicuous."

"Me?" Patience said. "What about you? You don't exactly blend into the neighborhood, either, in your vintage getup."

"Fine, we both need to get our keisters out of sight. Suggestions?"

Patience yanked me into a large souvenir shop. We moved toward the back of the shop, where we pretended to browse a rack of silk robes. The shop was packed floor to ceiling with colorful merchandise, which, combined with the dim lighting, would make it difficult for someone on the sidewalk to spot us.

"Do you have a cell phone?" I asked Patience, keeping my head low to hide my face, though my eyes were fixed on the front windows. "I think it's time to call Carlos to the rescue."

Patience reached into her skirt pocket and handed me a square piece of glass encased in plastic. It was much more complicated than other cell phones I'd seen. I stared at it and handed it back to her. "I have no idea how to work this thing. You dial."

"What's his number?"

Dangitall. I always thought of myself as having a good memory, but I couldn't remember his number. I was clearly out of sorts lately.

"You don't know it, do you?" Patience said. "Why don't I just call 911?"

"What are you going to say?" I asked. "We're being chased by someone currently in lockup?"

"I'll think of something." Patience rolled her eyes and started to dial. "Aw, crap—duck!"

We crouched behind the rack of silk robes just as Not Sailor paused in front of the store. The shop owner, a petite middle-aged woman, stared at us nervously from her seat near the cash register. Patience put her finger to her lips in the universal shushing gesture, which seemed only to make the woman more agitated.

"Please," Patience whispered loudly. "That man outside is chasing us. He's bad news. Very bad man."

The shop owner glanced at the sidewalk, where Not Sailor was staring into the shop, stone-faced. She stood, grabbed an emerald green silk robe, and marched across the store, flinging open the door.

Patience and I exchanged a worried look. "Be ready to bolt," Patience whispered.

"Robes for sale!" the shop owner shouted loudly at Not Sailor in a heavy accent, thrusting the robe at him. "Very nice robes. I make you good price. Come, come! Come in!"

Not Sailor ignored her. He took an old-fashioned watch out of his pocket, checked it, then turned and left.

The woman locked the door, walked back toward us, and winked. "That should take care of him," she said, the accent gone. "Would you like me to call the police for you? That was one mean-looking fellow."

Patience and I started laughing, relieved and grateful. "No, thank you," I said. "Is there a back door?"

"This way, ladies," the shop owner said, and led us to a fire exit at the rear that opened onto an alley. "Be careful. And if you're ever in the market for beautiful silk robes, you know where to find me."

"I need a damned drink," Patience said, ducking into Brandy Ho's on Columbus. "Your treat, remember?"

It was two o'clock in the afternoon and there were only a few customers in the lounge: a young couple in one booth, a single man sitting at the horseshoe-shaped bar and staring at the baseball game playing on the television mounted on the wall.

"I, uh, don't have any money on me," I said.

She gave me a withering look. "Figures. I'll treat. Like I said, you might want to look into having your things grafted onto your body."

"It's not like I make a habit of forgetting my things," I said. "It was a rather . . . unusual situation."

"Really? I get chased all the time by men who are the spitting image of a dear one, and you don't see me forgetting my wallet."

The possibility that Not Sailor would return to Sailor's apartment and take my things gnawed at me. How could I have left them there? My first instinct should have been to grab them on my way out, no matter how big a hurry I was in.

A waitress came over to take our order.

"Vodka martini, dry, and the salt-and-pepper fried calamari," Patience said, snapping the menu shut. "You?"

"I'll have a Co—ke," I said. I had almost asked for a Co-Cola, which was the way my mama always referred to soda pop. But Patience would never let me live that one down.

"Living life right on the edge as usual, eh, Lily?" Patience said with an ironic smile.

"I think it's best I keep on my toes," I said.

"You're worried about your backpack."

I *had* been worried about the backpack. Now I was worried Patience was reading my mind. I made sure my guard was up.

"And now you're worried I'm reading your mind," Patience said.

I didn't say anything. The waitress arrived with my Coke and told Patience her martini was on the way. I took a sip and let the familiar sensation of sweet bubbles play on my tongue and bring me back to reality. After our adrenaline-filled escape, I was feeling the crash.

"I'm not reading your mind, princess," Patience said, her tone almost kind. "Under the circumstances, it doesn't take a psychic to figure out what you're thinking. Want to use my phone to call the store and warn them, just in case? I'll show you how to dial it."

"Good idea," I said. Patience's smartphone wasn't as complicated as I thought it would be, so I took it and went outside, walking past the Flatiron Building to the corner of Columbus and Pacific. It was a busy intersection, with cars whizzing past and pedestrians hurrying along. The traffic noise made it harder to hear, but I wanted the comfort of people around me. Almost compulsively, I searched the crowd for the Sailor look-alike . . . just in case. When I stopped to think about it, we probably should have left this part of town altogether.

"Aunt Cora's Closet, it's not old. It's vintage!" Maya singsonged as she answered the phone.

"Maya, it's Lily. I need to tell you something important, but you have to promise me not to freak out."

"Okaaaaay," Maya said. "What's up?"

"If someone who looks like Sailor comes to the store, it's not Sailor. Sailor's still in jail. This person is just someone who looks like him."

"Would this be the same guy I saw in the herbal store?"

"Yes, it is. And he's up to no good. Maybe you should close the store and go home; I don't like the idea of you being there by yourself."

"I'm not—Selena and Bronwyn are here, too. I'll close the store if you want me to, but I have a better idea: I'll ask Bronwyn to give Duke a call, and I'll get a couple of my cousins to come by and keep us company for the afternoon. Also, Conrad's outside, so I'll ask him to keep an eye peeled."

"Any hint of danger, lock the door and call the police, okay? Don't take any chances, please."

"No worries, Lily. We'll be careful."

"Good—oh, and one more thing. What's Carlos's cell number?"

I jotted it down and hung up, relieved to think they could hold the fort, the whole gang of them together. I was reasonably sure my protection spell over Aunt Cora's Closet would be enough to at least give Not Sailor pause, but still.

Then I called Carlos and gave him the rundown.

"Well, that explains a couple of weird 911 calls we were getting from Chinatown," Carlos said. "So let me get this straight: You're talking doppelgänger now?"

"No, of course not. There's no such thing as doppelgängers. I don't think. But a Sailor look-alike, for sure."

"Isn't that what a doppelgänger is?"

"I'm not certain, actually. I think the situation may be . . . complicated. All I'm saying is there's someone out there who looks like Sailor, and dresses like Sailor, but isn't Sailor. And he may have my keys."

"All right. I'll send a patrol car by the store. You're sure this Sailor-who-isn't-Sailor will be going after the store?"

"I'm not sure of anything at the moment," I said. "In fact, probably not; at least, I can't think of a reason why he would. I just . . . think it pays to be cautious."

"You're right about that. In fact, there are some new developments in the case."

"There are?" My heart pounded. "Are these new developments positive or negative?"

"Can't say yet. Anyway, I'll go over to Sailor's apartment with a couple of uniforms, see if this look-alike clown is still there, or if we can recover anything."

"Thanks. Could you do me a favor as well? I left a couple of things there. A woven backpack full of stuff including my wallet and keys, and an . . . unusual candleholder."

"How unusual?" he asked, and I heard trepidation in his voice.

"Pretty unusual. And valuable. Please, if you find my things, I really need them back."

"I'll see what I can do."

I returned to Brandy Ho's, where Patience had already downed her martini, ordered another, and was tucking into a tall golden mound of salt-and-pepper fried calamari.

"Adrenaline crash," she mumbled. "I need fuel. I ordered noodles, too."

I sipped my Coke. She pushed the plate of calamari toward me. "Have some."

"Thanks, but I'm not hungry."

"I don't care. You need to eat. And drink up—it'll help."

Listlessly I picked up a piece of calamari. I was not a happy camper. I was no closer to getting Sailor out of jail, there were mysterious "new developments" that Carlos couldn't tell me about, and now my other friends were in danger. And the memory of "Sailor" who *wasn't* Sailor coming up those stairs, no recognition in his eyes, blank stare . . . it gave me the willies.

"On the positive side," said Patience, "at least we know we're not dealing with a case of possession."

"Excuse me?"

She shrugged. "It occurred to me as a possibility, since I 'saw' Sailor at the hotel. It really did appear to be him. But presuming he's still in jail, we can cross possession off the list."

"Oh, well . . . that's good, then."

"As I was saying to you, I couldn't read your mind

if I wanted to," said Patience. "Most people think in pictures, some in words, but a witch like you . . ."

"What?"

"Not only do you have your guard up all the time—and it's a very effective guard, too, kudos—but a witch like you thinks in scents and symbols. I wouldn't be able to figure them out even if I could access your thoughts."

"If I'm so guarded, then how do you know what my thoughts look like?"

"Hey, don't get upset with me. I wasn't trying to snoop around in your mind. Most of the time you're guarded, but when you're really upset or emotional, you throw out images and scents."

"I do? That's . . . weird."

"Not really. You wouldn't believe the way most people's thoughts appear. I could tell you stories that would curl your hair."

"Must be why yours is so curly," I said, and she actually gave me a little smile. Sipping her second martini, Patience seemed to have recuperated from our adventure. I wished I could say the same. Although I hoped I projected an outward calm, inside I was going crazy.

"So, when we were running," said Patience, "you threw out a picture. Something that looked something like . . ." She sketched a symbol on a paper napkin. It was similar to the drawings I had seen on the notepad in Sailor's bedroom.

Seeing it now, I realized what it reminded me of: the strange thread web covering the map in the store where we had traced the route of the busload of witches from Texas.

Chapter 17

"Is it a demon's sigil?" asked Patience.

I shook my head. "If someone with magical power sketches the sigil, it could be enough to summon the demon. Sailor wouldn't have been stupid enough to do something like that."

"But Sailor's not magical, Lily. Not technically. Neither am I. We're psychics. There's a difference. We don't conjure. Magical folks have the power to change reality; we only have the power to read it."

"But when you and I combined forces, I could feel your energy."

"I have remarkable powers of concentration due to my training. I'm able to combine it with others. That's what you were feeling."

"What about astral projection? That seems capable of changing reality."

"No, it doesn't—that's what I've been trying to explain to you. Astral projection, like psychic ability, *reads* reality. It doesn't change it. A person might take the information gathered and make decisions that change reality, but the psychic's act of projection doesn't, by itself, affect anything in the real world. . . . See the difference?"

I nodded, a bit stunned. I'd always lumped psychics in with magical folk, but what she said made sense.

"But my point is this: Because psychics aren't magical per se, we can draw a sigil without summoning a demon. My aunt Renna, on the other hand, would have to be as careful as you are. She's great at hexing, that sort of thing, as you well know."

"Okay, important safety tip. But I still doubt that this image is a demon's sigil."

"What makes you so sure?"

"I think my grandmother's coven is taking a circuitous route on purpose, making this symbol. I can't imagine why they would do that."

"I don't know a lot about demons, but aren't there some good ones?"

"Good ones?"

"Helpful ones. I mean, students used to call on demons to help them with their studies, or artists called on them for creativity. Things like that, right?"

"I'm no demonologist, either, but you're right that people sometimes call on demons for help. It's tricky, though. They're only helpful if they're kept in line, and that's no easy task. Almost always, those who summon demons aren't powerful enough to control them, and so the demon ends up turning the tables and controlling the person, instead." I gazed down at the symbol, and shook my head. "No, I think it's more likely something else. Could it be some sort of protective sign?"

"You're the witch. You tell me."

"I hate to say it, but I guess it's time to go to Aidan for help. I need to ask him if he knows what the sign is, and . . ." I sneezed.

She fixed me with a hawkeye. "You might want to try some of those Chinese herbs for colds."

I shook my head. "I don't get colds."

"Uh-huh."

We sat in silence for a few minutes. My thoughts wandered back to Sailor's apartment, wondering what Carlos would find and how I might gain access to whatever he found. Patience was staring at the tabletop, arranging crystals of table salt into little patterns. Good thing she really wasn't magical, I thought, or merely by drawing things in salt, she might wind up spellcasting by accident.

She looked up at me. "I don't suppose the point of all this could be to get *you* out of the picture?"

"Me?"

"Maybe someone's trying to keep you occupied and therefore out of the way."

"Out of the way of what?"

"I don't know." She shrugged. "But didn't that weasel with the cupcakes—"

"Jamie."

"Whatever. Didn't he say Tristan came to San Francisco to work with Renee-the-cupcake-lady?"

I had wondered about that as well. Could Tristan really have been the male practitioner to Renee's female? Had he been after the lachrymatory in the shoe box? A contribution to her collection of grief and tears, an offering to her foundation of power?

"So maybe now she's angry with you, sending cupcakes and a fake Sailor to confuse you and keep you busy. Out of her way."

"But wait," I said. "The Sailor look-alike killed Tristan, right? If Renee is manipulating the look-alike, and she wanted to make Tristan her male counterpart, then why would the look-alike kill Tristan?"

"Good point." She sat back, defeated. "So much for playing junior detective. I need another drink."

"Have one—you've more than earned it," I said. "But I have to get back to the store, plus I've got an appointment at four to look at some wedding dresses."

Patience let out a bark of laughter. "You really are a piece of work. You outrun a Sailor look-alike one moment and try on wedding dresses the next?"

"At this juncture, it would feel good to cross one single item off my to-do list. Anyway, lend me money for a cab?"

"A cab in San Francisco? Dream on. You'll be waiting an hour. I'll get the food to go, and call us a Lyft. I'll go back with you."

Before we left, I asked Patience to pick up the napkin with the sigil on it and place it in the center of my old-fashioned embroidered cotton handkerchief. Then I tied the handkerchief's corners together, wrapping the napkin up so I wouldn't physically touch it.

"Why are we doing this?" she asked.

"I don't want to take any chances in case it really is a demon's sigil. If I carry it on my person, I might accidentally invoke it."

She looked skeptical. "How does a person 'accidentally' invoke a demon? I would think it would be pretty complicated."

"For a normal person, sure. But I think we both know I'm not particularly normal. You know how, in moments of stress, a person might pray or say, 'Oh please oh please oh please'?"

She nodded.

"When I do that, I could focus my intent enough to set off a chain of events I didn't fully intend. It's been known to happen."

"So you're like a ticking time bomb ready to go off."

"I have the sense neither of us walks the easiest path."

Once we got back to Haight Street, Patience left to

speak with Renna and ask if she was able to see anything useful, as well as to make sure as many Rom were lined up to help as she could get. As Patience sashayed down the street, her swishing skirts turning plenty of heads, I realized I was glad to have her on my side. On Sailor's side, to be more precise, as I was fairly certain she wouldn't go out of her way to help just me. But that was good enough. All I wanted right now was to get Sailor out of jail, figure out what the hell was going on, and find a wedding dress.

I glanced at my watch. I had just enough time to check in with the gang at Aunt Cora's Closet, and then head over to the estate sale. Fingers crossed, one of the dresses would be perfect. That way I'd be all set—just in case I could find a way to spring my man from jail in time for the handfasting.

I always love coming into my shop, to be greeted by the hustle and bustle of business and by the scents of fresh laundry and the rosemary and lavender sachets I hung on the rods. But on a day like today that sensation was multiplied many times over. The shop was crowded, but not with customers. Selena was there, along with Bronwyn and her boyfriend, Duke; Conrad and his friend Shalimar; Maya and her cousins Kareem and Richard.

"Lily!" Bronwyn called out, as she hurried over and gave me a big hug. "I'm so glad to see you safe. What in the *world* is going on?"

"I, uh . . . ran into an old acquaintance," I said, though my attention was diverted by Oscar. Instead of greeting me as he usually did, he was lying on his silk pillow and making strange sounds.

"What's wrong with Oscar?" I asked.

"He's been doing that for a while. I'm starting to get worried about our little guy," said Maya. "It sounds sort of like that hollow cough that dogs get."

A loud, indignant snort, emanating from the direction of the purple silk pillow, expressed Oscar's displeasure at being compared to a dog. Then the sounds began again.

It didn't sound like kennel cough to me, though. It sounded like he was giggling—in a porcine sort of way. What was *up* with him?

Unless . . . it wasn't Oscar? What if *Oscar* had a look-alike, too? I could only imagine the havoc it could wreak. Was a look-alike spirit capable of copying any individual it chose, or did every person—and gobgoyle—have his or her own unique counterpart?

"Sailor's lawyer called back," Maya said.

Dang, I'd hoped to speak with him.

"He left a message," Maya continued, handing me a note saying there was an arraignment scheduled for tomorrow morning at ten.

I tried Petulengro's number, but got voice mail again. I made a face, then saw Maya was watching me.

"I know, I know," I said as I hung up. "I really need to get a cell phone."

"I'm just saying . . . you run around town a lot, so it's hard for folks to get in touch." Maya gestured with her head and I followed her into the back room for privacy. We spoke in hushed tones. "Lily, I don't understand. You're saying there really is a Sailor look-alike walking the streets of San Francisco?"

"I'm afraid so," I said. "I just . . . I'm not sure how to explain it to everyone."

Maya nodded slowly. "How about an evil twin?"

I smiled. "Sounds like the plot of a soap opera."

"I grew up watching a lot of 'stories' with my mom while she sewed. I know it sounds far-fetched, but how else are we going to warn folks that someone who looks just like Sailor isn't to be trusted?"

"Good question. So, you're okay with all this?"

"Okay with it? Not at all. But I *saw* him in the Lucky Moon. It was Sailor, but . . . *not* Sailor. It makes no sense, but I assume from the way you're acting and the fact that Sailor's been arrested that there's something supernatural going on."

When first we met, Maya didn't believe in magic. She'd been exposed to a lot in the last year, and had been on a steep learning curve. I thought about Patience's question, whether Maya might have abilities of her own, but I truly didn't think so. She was simply highly intelligent, and had come to understand there was no way to explain the unexplainable . . . other than magic.

"I really don't want—or need—to know the details," Maya continued. "And I don't want to freak everyone out, but I do want them to be safe."

I nodded. "I agree with you there. Okay, let's go with . . . creepy look-alike cousin."

Maya grinned. "Yes, that's so much easier to believe than an identical twin. Whatever you say, boss."

I took another moment to call Selena's grandmother, briefly explained what had happened, and asked her to be particularly wary of anyone who looked like Sailor, or any strangers that might come into her and Selena's lives in the near future.

Then I joined the group in the shop and tried to explain why they should take care around anyone looking a lot like Sailor.

"I don't think it will be a problem, but I want everyone to take precautions."

"A couple of officers stopped by about ten minutes ago," said Bronwyn. "They said they'll cruise by occasionally, keep an eye on the place."

"That's good. But they won't be here twenty-four/seven, so let's stay on guard, all right? No working alone.

I'd rather close the store altogether than have someone here by themselves. Understood?"

Bronwyn and Maya nodded. Conrad shook his head, blew out a long breath, and said, "Duuuuude."

"Oh, hey, Conrad, did you overhear the conversation I had outside the other day with Sailor and a stranger? The time Carlos arrived and joined us?"

"The fight?"

"It wasn't a fight, exactly."

"Sounded like a fight."

"I'm going to take that as a yes. You didn't happen to mention it to anyone, did you?"

"No, nobody."

I hadn't thought so.

"Except . . . Let me think. . . . I think Wind Spirit came by right after. It's possible I mentioned it to her, just, like, in passing."

"Wind Spirit. You're sure?"

"Yeah, dude. She used to be named Amy, and Wind Spirit doesn't seem to fit her, in my view, but whatever she wants—am I right? Also, that doughnut dude was there."

"What doughnut dude?"

"Not doughnuts . . ." He frowned, as though the word escaped him. "*Cupcakes!* That's what it was."

"The cupcake dude? Do you mean Jamie?"

"Right, Jamie. That's the one."

"He came by? Was he with Wind Spirit?"

"Not 'with her' with her. Least, I don't think so. Not that the Con is always up in everybody's business or anything like that."

"Did he say anything? Do anything? Did Wind Spirit?"

"Don't really remember. I think they just happened to be passing by. Everybody loves the Haight—am I right?"

"Right. Okay, thanks. So, please, everyone," I said, getting back to the subject, "err on the side of caution for the next few days, until I can figure this out."

Part of me hoped if I kept saying I would be able to figure it out, I would manifest a resolution. If only it worked that way.

"And does 'erring on the side of caution' apply to you as well, Lily?" Bronwyn asked, forehead wrinkled in concern.

I smiled. "It does. Besides, I have Oscar to protect me."

"Quite the ferocious guard pig," Maya's cousin Kareem said.

We all glanced at said guard pig, who was now lying on his back on the purple pillow, short little legs kicking in the air, a huge porcine grin on his face.

"Maybe not so ferocious," Duke said dryly. "Lily, I hate to be a wet blanket, but you should take additional steps to protect yourself while you're home alone."

"Yes, please, Lily," Bronwyn continued. "We worry about you."

Maya and Selena nodded in agreement, and I felt a wave of warmth wash over me. With friendship, I was learning, came the obligation to take reasonable precautions with one's well-being. "You're right. I'll be extra careful. And to that end: Maya, would you call a locksmith? I want to change the locks. I left my keys somewhere."

"I'm on it," Maya said, and went to the computer to look up the number.

Oscar huffed even louder.

"When did Oscar start acting like this?" I asked.

"A little while ago," Bronwyn replied. "He just keeps snickering. He's also been eating everything in sight."

"Well, at least that part is nothing new. Maya, while

you're on the computer, any chance you could find a symbol that looks like this?"

I took my handkerchief out of my pocket, unwrapped it, and laid it on the counter. Maya looked at me curiously, but reached out to smooth the napkin.

"It looks like the symbol on the map," Selena said immediately. "When they finish it, anyway."

I glanced at the map with its red thread figure. Selena's drawings of cupcakes with black icing were now encircling it, held up by bits of Scotch tape.

"We don't have a scanner," said Maya, her hands moving swiftly over the keyboard, "so I'm not sure how to search for it, exactly. I can pull up some symbol dictionaries, but it will take time to go through them."

"Maybe . . . check out demon sigils?"

I still couldn't understand why the grandmas would be making a sigil, but at this point I was willing to try anything.

Maya was scrolling through a bunch of them, shaking her head and glancing back and forth from the drawing on the napkin to the images popping up on the computer screen.

"You know what it reminds me of?" asked Conrad. "Remember a while back, the Da Pinchi Code?"

"You mean Da Vinci Code?" asked Maya's cousin Richard.

"Nah, dude. Da *Pinchi*. It was, like, this burglar code. Burglars would put these signs on buildings they cased."

"That sounds a little far-fetched, Conrad," said Duke.

"Dude, it was totally, like, on the BBC. You know how those Brits are—they're real serious."

"He's right," said Maya, pulling up an article online. "I remember hearing about it, too. And here it is. It was on the BBC a couple years back. . . ."

Bronwyn, Duke, and I crowded around to look at the screen over Maya's shoulders.

"But . . . no, Snopes doesn't think it makes sense."

"Who's Snopes?" I asked.

"It's a Web site that investigates rumors, tells you whether or not they check out."

"There's a Web site that does that?"

"Welcome to the twenty-first century, my friend."

"And this one doesn't check out?"

"They don't say it's a fabrication, exactly, just that it doesn't make sense, since there wouldn't be much 'added value' in doing it. It says that criminals have other ways of sharing addresses beyond physical marks."

Not to mention . . . why in the world would a bus full of witches be making the sign of theft? It made no sense.

"Still," I said, "this symbol does look a bit like that one, doesn't it? Maya, would you mind poking around a little more, see if you can find any others like it? The image might not be complete, after all."

"Sure, I'll do what I can," said Maya. "And Kareem is great at this sort of thing."

"I was just going to suggest taking a photo of the symbol," Kareem said. "That way we can import it and Google it directly."

"Good idea," said Maya. The cousins bent their heads together and worked up a plan.

Oscar huffed loudly, then snorted, then "coughed"—which sounded a lot like a snicker.

"I'm going to take Oscar upstairs," I said. "See if I can figure out what's going on with him. Come on, Oscar. Let's go."

He didn't respond, just continued to loll on his bed, so I finally leaned over and scooped him up, then carried him to the stairs. "*Lugged* him" is more apt. Oscar might be a miniature pig, but he was still a pig, and he was heavy. I nearly dropped him halfway up. Finally, we reached the top of the steps and he transformed—while still in my arms, which was a decidedly odd sensation—into his natural form.

There was no doubt about it now: Oscar was laughing. Cackling, more like.

"Oscar, what in the world has gotten into you?"

"Woooo," he said. "The stairs are spinning. It's like a carnival ride! Awesome!"

"Are you *drunk*?" I gasped as I set him down on the landing, trying to catch my breath.

"Of course I drink! Everybody drinks!"

"Everybody . . . ?"

"*Water!* Gobgoyles are ninety-eight percent water! Get it?" Oscar roared, as if this were the funniest joke in the world.

"Oscar, be serious. You know what I mean. Did you drink alcohol?"

More cackling. "Duuuude" was his only response.

"Now you sound like Conrad." A terrible thought occurred to me. "Oscar, you didn't take something of Conrad's, did you? Some . . . pills, or anything?"

Oscar sat up and looked at me intently.

"Oscar . . . ?"

"I've got the munchies," he said, and made a beeline into the kitchen.

"So what else is new?" I muttered as I followed him.

Once in the kitchen, he paused and looked at me with a blank, confused expression on his face. "Wait. Hold on."

"What is it?"

"What were we talking about, again?"

"Oscar, what is *wrong* with you?"

"Dude!"

He laughed again, waving his oversized hand in my direction as though I were saying something hysterical.

He flung open the refrigerator and practically climbed in, emerging with a white carton of leftover pad Thai.

"This here's my huckleberry!" he said, and jumped up to perch on the counter, where he started eating pad Thai noodles with his fingers.

"Oscar, I told you I don't like it when you stand on the counter. This is a kitchen, not a pigsty."

He slurped more noodles, and sniggered. "Pigsty, fit for a pig! 'Cept I'm not a pig, so that there's an example of irony! *Get it?*"

"Off!"

"Geesh," he said as he leapt gracefully to the floor, then somersaulted in slow motion, a surprised look on his face.

"Okay, this is ridiculous. You'd better stay here in your cubby until this passes. Whatever this is."

"Can I have something to drink first?"

"Of course. What do you want?"

"A Singapore sling! With an umbrella, please."

"No. There's water or— Did you just stick your tongue out at me?"

"Of course not, mistress," he said, puffing up his chest. "That would be beneath my dignity as a gob-goyle. Say, could you bring me some more cupcakes?"

"What do you mean, more cupcakes?"

"One thing I'll say for that mistress of the dark: she can bake a mean cupcake."

"Oscar . . ."

He yawned, a huge yawn like a lion's, stretching his arms over his head. "I'm sleepy."

"Don't go to sleep!" I said, suddenly afraid of what might happen. What had Renee dosed the batch with? Conrad didn't seem to be showing any ill effects. But no matter what it was . . . I was going to assume that a gobgoyle's metabolism was different from a human's.

And knowing Oscar, he had probably eaten the whole dozen. I fought panic at the idea that Oscar could be ailing.

"Come with me," I said, grabbing my extra set of car keys. "We're going to see Aidan."

Chapter 18

"Master Aidan?" Oscar's eyes grew huge. "I, um, I don't think that's a good idea, mistress. Let's just hang out here and watch a movie. We can make popcorn! With butter!"

"We're going. Aidan will know what to do."

At least I hoped so.

Oscar put up a bit of a struggle, but though he's normally much stronger than his physical size would suggest, whatever was in the cupcakes had made him uncoordinated and weak as a puppy. I was able to hoist him up and slog him down the stairs again, though for the first time since I'd met him, he had to be reminded to transform into his piggy guise.

"What's wrong?" Bronwyn asked as we came through the shop floor. "What's the matter with my little Oscaroo?"

"Something he ate doesn't agree with him," I said. "I think I need to take him to . . . the vet. Did you see how he got into the cupcakes? Did Renee send more over?"

"How do you know he ate cupcakes?" Maya asked.

"He had blue frosting on his muzzle," I improvised.

"Really?" Bronwyn asked. "I can't imagine where he got them from. Unless . . . he did go out into the alley at one point."

"He raided the *Dumpster*?" I said, outraged, as though a pig ransacking a Dumpster were out of the realm of possibility.

"Sorry, Lily," Bronwyn said. "It didn't occur to me that he'd be able to do such a thing. How would such a little tiny piggy get up into the Dumpster in the first place?"

"Pigs are pretty smart," Maya said.

"Maybe it's something else," I said, worried. "Anyway, I'm going to get him checked out. I'm sure he'll be fine. In the meantime, would it be possible for someone to go pick up my car? I had to leave it in Chinatown. Long story. I'll take the shop van."

"We'll take care of it," said Maya, holding her hand out for the spare key.

I told her where the car was parked. "And can the rest of you hang out here together? I don't want anyone to be alone."

"Actually, we were just talking about that. We were thinking we'd order Indian food to be delivered and have an informal picnic on the shop floor," said Bronwyn. "We're hoping you will join us. Bombay biryani, aloo gobhi, and garlic naan, your favorite."

"Thank you. I'll get back as soon as I can. I'm not sure how long I'll be, so don't wait on my account. If there are any leftovers, I'm sure I'll make short work of them," I said, realizing I was starving. I wished I had eaten more of Patience's calamari.

Through the shop windows, I could see the fog had rolled in. I grabbed my cocoa brown wool coat and rushed out the door, a laughing pig in my arms.

* * *

"You can't take a *pig* into the museum!" shouted the ever-suffering Clarinda from her post inside the ticket booth.

Oscar snickered loudly.

"Take it up with Aidan." I barreled past her as fast as I could, given that I was still lugging my hefty familiar. I was panting and my arms ached. "He asked me to bring the pig."

"He *did*?" she asked while picking up the phone.

"Loves pigs," I called over my shoulder, already mounting the stairs. "Can't get enough of 'em."

Aidan stood in the open door of his office, waiting for us.

"Clarinda wants me to remind you that livestock is not permitted in the museum," he said. He did not seem overly pleased to see us.

"Then it's lucky he's not actually a pig," I said, depositing said creature at Aidan's feet. Oscar rolled onto his back, waved his little hooves in the air, and snickered.

Aidan stared at Oscar. "Is something wrong with him?"

"I was hoping you could tell me. He's . . . I think he ate some of Renee's cupcakes and now he's acting like this. I think she might have poisoned him!" I couldn't keep the desperation out of my voice.

"I'm not a vet, Lily," Aidan said.

"Please? See if you can tell what's wrong?"

With obvious reluctance, Aidan stood back and gestured with his hand to enter his office. He shut the door, and we were plunged into the soft lights and hushed atmosphere of his Victorian fantasy world.

Oscar transformed into his natural state, jumped onto a chair, and said:

"Hey! You know what I just found out? 'Pumpernickel' means 'goblin fart'! Or maybe 'fart goblin' . . . not sure." He dissolved into peals of cackles. "Could I have that grilled cheese on pumpernickel, please?"

Aidan opened an elaborately carved box and brought out a clear pale green crystal.

"Be still," he commanded, and to my surprise Oscar obeyed. Aidan placed the crystal on top of Oscar's muzzle, laid his hands on either side of his face, and concentrated for a long moment.

He picked up the crystal, took it to his desk, and studied it with a magnifying glass.

"He wasn't poisoned," he declared after a long moment.

"Are you sure?"

"Positive."

"What a relief," I said, feeling the tension ease from my shoulders. "Then what's wrong with him?"

"He's high."

"High? What do you mean?"

"Stoned. Baked. Wasted. Stewed. Tanked. Shall I go on?"

"Got it. But . . . is this something he does? Oscar gets *high*?"

"You tell me. He's *your* familiar, if I'm not mistaken."

"He's never done it before, at least not since he's been with me. What is he high *on*?"

"Must have gotten into someone's pot stash."

"Pot?"

Aidan gave me a slow, thoughtful smile. "I know you've led an unconventional life, my dear Lily, and you're remarkably innocent in some ways. But are you telling me you don't know what pot is?"

"I know what it is," I said, rolling my eyes. "I just haven't ever tried it."

"Never snuck off behind the gym in high school?"

"My abbreviated time in high school wasn't like that, as you very well know. Besides, I wouldn't have dared—my grandmother would have killed me."

"She was strict?"

"In a manner of speaking. We had enough going on just trying to stay alive in Jarod. We didn't need drugs complicating matters."

Oscar let out a loud snort, jumped off the chair, and declared: "I have something very important to tell you!"

Aidan and I gave him our attention.

There was a long pause. I was about to ask Oscar if he'd forgotten what he was going to say when he drew himself up to his full three and a half feet, puffed out his chest, and declared: "I'm thinking very seriously about getting a pet. A baby bat, maybe. Or a duck. A duckling! I'm gonna name it Pumpernickel!"

And then he fell back onto his butt and sniggered.

Aidan met my eyes, raised his eyebrows, smiled, and inclined his head. "There you have it. Shall I put on some Bob Marley?"

"So he'll be all right, then?"

"He'll be fine. Let him sleep it off."

"What a relief. Thank you."

There was an awkward pause. "Lily, I don't wish to be inhospitable, but I have some work to do, and if I'm not mistaken, you have a boyfriend to exonerate, despite the fact that several eyewitnesses put him at the scene."

"You heard about that?" Of *course* he'd heard about that. As Oscar would say if he hadn't been currently snoozing in the corner, Aidan *knew* things.

"I know he's not your favorite person," I continued, "but I may have to ask you for help. Sailor didn't kill Tristan Dupree."

"Of course he didn't."

"You believe that?" I searched Aidan's face for indications that he was being ironic, but he looked sincere. Then again, with Aidan, one never knew.

Aidan looked impatient. "If you're asking me if I think Sailor is capable of killing someone, then my answer is 'Yes, he is.' If you're asking me if I think Sailor killed this particular someone, then my answer is 'No, he did not.' Satisfied?"

"But the question is, how do I convince the SFPD of that?"

"Looks like you have your work cut out for you."

"Does that mean you won't help me?"

"If I help you, what do I get in return?"

This was the response I'd anticipated. Aidan's assistance always came with strings attached. "That depends. What do you want?"

"Sailor. Or Oscar. Your choice."

"What?"

"Both of them used to work for me, if you recall. Before you managed to wrest them from my . . . influence."

"Aidan—"

"Nothing in this life comes free, Lily. Haven't you learned that by now? There's always a price. And my terms are not unreasonable—I'm just asking Sailor to work for me. I'll pay him handsomely, and help him to increase his natural talents. Surely he would prefer that over rotting in prison."

"Um . . . I can't speak for Sailor. Or Oscar, for that matter."

"Then speak *to* him, Lily. I will gladly help Sailor, but my offer is contingent upon the terms stated."

"I'm going to have to ponder that one." I would be able to see Sailor tomorrow morning. He was going to just love this. "In the meantime, could I ask for some advice? Or does that have a price tag, too?"

Aidan inclined his head graciously. "As you know, Lily, talk is cheap."

"Patience Blix and I were just chased by someone who's a dead ringer for Sailor—during which I lost my Hand of Glory, by the way, but I'm hoping Carlos can get it back for me."

"Carlos?"

"I told him some of what happened, and he was going to go over to Sailor's apartment to check it out. He'll try to retrieve my stuff. I dropped a backpack full of supplies, too. And my keys."

Aidan shook his head. "You know how I feel about your 'friendship' with an SFPD inspector. You're courting trouble."

"Yeah, I know. Sailor said the same thing."

Aidan looked surprised that he and Sailor would agree on anything.

"But Carlos has been a good friend to me, and he has been keeping me informed of what's going on with Sailor. I think the more salient point, at the moment, is that Patience and I were chased by someone who looks exactly like Sailor. I mean *exactly*. Dresses like him, sounds like him, carries himself the same as Sailor. Except his eyes are empty, he was chasing us, and—according to Patience—he wanted to kill us."

I shivered at the memory of those vacant eyes on the face of someone so familiar, so beloved.

"Have a seat, Lily," Aidan said, as he sat behind his desk. "Tell me the whole story."

"I thought you didn't have the time."

"I'll make the time."

After glancing at Oscar, who was now snoozing, I sat down in the chair facing Aidan and told him what had happened earlier with Patience.

"So you escaped with the aid of a shop owner in Chinatown," Aidan mused. "Aren't you the clever thing?"

"Lucky, not clever. If that shop owner hadn't been so gutsy, we might have been in big trouble."

"I think you may be dealing with a doppelgänger."

He stood up and stepped over to his bookshelves, tilting his head to one side as though reading the spines.

"That's . . . that's really a thing?" I asked. "Doppelgängers are real? Actual doppelgängers?"

"How do you mean?"

"As you know, I'm not exactly clear on what's real and what's just folklore. I sort of assumed doppelgängers might be fictional, like vampires."

"This would be one reason—"

"You keep urging me to finish my training. I know that. And I've been trying to play catch-up, but I keep getting derailed."

"Chasing after murderers?"

"And dealing with whatever supernatural havoc comes my way, yes. So, seriously? Why would Sailor have a doppelgänger? And a homicidal one, at that?"

"I'm not saying he does, but it's a possibility to consider."

He started to read from the splayed book in his hands.

"The application of the German word is relatively recent; it might also be called a 'fetch,' or a 'double walker,' but all refer to the 'apparition of a person living.' *Blah blah blah* . . . The concept of alter egos and double spirits has appeared in the folklore of many cultures throughout human history. Most often they are considered harbingers of bad luck."

"Oh, yay," I said. "How come I'm never assaulted by harbingers of *good* luck?"

Aidan ignored me and kept reading. "The Norse *vardøger* precedes a living person and performs that person's actions ahead of time. The Finns call theirs *etiänen*, or 'firstcomer.' In ancient Egyptian mythology a *kaka* was a spirit double with the same memories and feelings as the person to whom the counterpart belongs. But in most traditions, the doppelgänger is a version of the Ankou, or the personification of death."

"You're saying . . . Wait," I said. "Are you saying that this is a sign that Sailor . . . that Sailor is going to *die*?"

"We all die, Lily," Aidan said in a gentle voice.

"Yes, thank you. I realize that. But no time soon is what I was hoping. Is this doppelgänger a harbinger of Sailor's death?"

He shrugged. "I'm not even saying it *is* a doppelgänger. Just that it's a possibility. And if it is true, then it's a sign."

"A *bad* sign."

He inclined his head.

"How do I stop it?"

"As always, that's slightly more complex than simply identifying what you're dealing with. With doppelgängers, in particular, if you attack them, it can be felt or shared with the original person."

"I could hurt Sailor."

"Possibly."

I leaned back and let out a long sigh.

Aidan looked up from the page. "You okay?"

"It's just . . . I have a wedding to plan. Also, I haven't found my dress yet—in fact, I was supposed to preview an estate sale this afternoon, but instead I'm getting chased by doppelgängers and lugging my high-as-a-kite familiar around. Also, my fiancé is in lockup. I guess I'm feeling the pressure."

"Not to mention the prophecy and the threat to San Francisco posed by Renee."

I sneezed. "Yeah, that, too. Also, I think I'm getting a cold. I've never gotten one in my life."

He gave me an odd look. "Are you feeling any other ill effects? Besides the sneezing?"

"Just tired. And I'm sort of stuffed up."

"So your sense of smell has been affected?"

"A little."

"That could be significant. You often sense things through scent, don't you?"

I nodded. "So, back to the doppelgänger. If he's an omen of"—I cleared my throat—"of Sailor's death, then does it make sense that if I find a way to kill him without hurting Sailor, then Sailor will be okay?"

"Possibly. But if he *isn't* a doppelgänger, then *you'll* be the one sitting in jail facing murder charges."

"Something in what you read rings a bell . . . ," I said, reaching out and taking the book from Aidan. I skimmed over what he had read aloud. "Yes! Right here, it says the Egyptians call their version *kaka.* Tristan Dupree said *kaka* to me just last night."

"You sure he wasn't swearing at you?"

"At the time, I thought he was trying to say 'cake.' He ended up talking about cupcakes."

"There's a lot of that going around. Speaking of which, how did Oscar get ahold of Renee's cupcakes?"

"She sent a box over."

"Interesting."

"Interesting how?"

"It sounds to me like an invitation. Which reminds me, I'm going to guess I've fallen off the guest list. I haven't received a formal invitation to your nuptials. Unless . . ." His blue eyes flickered down to my bare hands. "Dare I hope you've come to your senses?"

"No. I mean, yes. I mean, I was never out of my senses. I lent my ring to Patience to help her distinguish between the real and fake Sailors. But to get back to your question, would you come to our handfasting?"

"Of course I would come."

"Despite the fact that you dislike the idea so intensely."

He looked at me for a very long moment. "I've made no bones about the fact that I think your involvement with Sailor is a bad idea. A terrible idea, in fact. I think you will be diminished by the relationship. And I had hoped for something different for you. For us."

"Us?"

He nodded but did not elaborate. "However, you've made your decision and I will abide by it. I don't believe I have any other choice. You are an important person in my life, Lily, and I want to maintain our connection. As your friend, I would like to be there to support you when you marry. Also, I am so looking forward to meeting your grandmother and her coven."

"Well, in that case, consider yourself officially invited. But fair warning—my mother's on that bus, too."

"Is she? Mother issues." He shook his head. "They're tough."

"Somehow it's hard to imagine you with a mother." For that matter, it was hard to imagine Aidan as a child. He'd been a blue-eyed, golden-haired mischief-maker in an angel's guise, no doubt. "What's she like?"

"She passed a long time ago."

"Oh, I'm sorry to hear that. My condolences."

"Thank you. As I said, it was a long time ago."

"Still . . ." I tried to think of something else to say. Our gaze held for a long moment, until Noctemus jumped into Aidan's lap, demanding attention. He stroked her, his large hand looking tan against her pure white fur. "So," I said, changing the subject, "what can you tell me about silverfish?"

"Nothing I can think of. Why?"

"I found some in the shoe box from Germany."

"You opened it, alone?"

"Patience helped me."

"What else did you find within it?"

"Not much, actually. But there was a lachrymatory; do you think that could be the bēag Tristan was after?"

"It's possible. As a small treasure, that would make sense."

"It has the salts of tears, but I have no idea who it belonged to. Also, there was a watch. Speaking of which, I noticed the doppelgänger has a pocket watch. He stopped to check it, just before he stopped chasing us, and when he was leaving the hotel after killing Dupree."

"A watch could be the bēag as well. Where is the box now?"

"In my apartment. It's hidden, and protected."

"I'd feel better if I could keep it here. It might not be safe at your place. You've been broken into before."

"True. And Jamie—Renee's errand boy who brought the cupcakes—he mentioned that Tristan had come to San Francisco to work with Renee. I'm not sure if I can trust what he says, but it was interesting."

"It would make sense that Dupree was searching for the lachrymatory, to add to Renee's collection."

"It's so bizarre. She keeps them right by her collection of silver spoons."

"And that's significant?"

I shook my head. "No. I just think it's funny that she's collecting the remnants of grief to increase her power, but keeps them in a little cupboard right alongside her collectible silver spoons. She's such an unassuming adversary."

"And yet not to be underestimated."

"I know," I said, feeling glum. My stomach growled.

Aidan looked amused. "Hungry?"

"I haven't eaten in a while. It's been an eventful day."

"What you need," Aidan said as he handed me my coat, "is a delicious cupcake."

Chapter 19

We left Oscar snoozing in the corner of Aidan's office under the watchful eye of Noctemus. My familiar was mumbling, "Fart goblin," and chuckling to himself in his sleep.

As we drove across town, Aidan explained that ours was an exploratory mission.

"Most likely she's just trying to mess with your head," Aidan said. "Which, I might point out, she accomplished—admirably. Don't be such an easy mark, Lily."

"I'm working on it."

"Also—and please note that I'm not telling you what to do—but did you honestly not anticipate that Oscar would go after the cupcakes in the Dumpster?"

"I underestimated him. I often do, I find."

I noticed that Aidan's glamour seemed to shimmer slightly, to be off in the glare of the late-afternoon sun. "Aidan, are you sure you're all right going out this afternoon?"

"Of course. Why wouldn't I be?"

"I, um . . . sometimes I see your glamour slip."

He gave me a quick, sharp look. "I don't know what you're talking about."

"Renee once mentioned . . . She told me that you were looking for a fountain of youth. Was that true?"

He muttered something under his breath.

"Sorry?" I said.

"I said," he replied, "that Renee has a big mouth."

"Does that mean she was right? Is there such a thing as the fountain of youth?"

"Of course not," he scoffed.

"Then . . . ?"

"She's fishing, obviously. But the truth is, Renee knows that my powers have been diminishing over the past year or so. I've told you as much myself. That's one reason why you and I need to work together, now more than ever, to secure the future of the city we love."

"Why have your powers been diminishing?"

"That's a conversation for another time," Aidan said as he turned onto Renee's street. "We're here."

We rolled past a now-closed vintage clothing store, Vintage Visions Glad Rags, whose owner had died not long ago. Renee had mentioned she wanted to expand her cupcake business into the site, but so far the clothing store remained closed, its fine inventory still crowding the unlit display windows, surely growing dusty by now. The memory of finding the owner, poisoned and paranoid, holding a gun came back with full force. It was a haunting image.

Again I wondered, if Renee gained the upper hand in the supernatural battle for control of San Francisco, would I have to leave town? Would Aunt Cora's Closet be left like Vintage Visions Glad Rags, sad and dusty and falling to ruin?

Enough with the catastrophic thinking, Lily, I chided myself.

Aidan found a parking space around the corner

from Renee's bakery. As we approached, we saw the tiers of pretty iced cupcakes crowding the display windows, and inside three customers waited in line. Renee was behind the horseshoe counter, as usual, charming her patrons and chatting about what she liked to call her "fairy cakes." I noticed the new product line that Maya had mentioned: One entire shelf was now dedicated to "savories," such as meat pasties and vegetable cheese rolls.

Also on the counter behind Renee was a large tray of burned cupcakes, still steaming. I sniffed, trying to pick up any underlying scents—or even obvious ones like charred batter—beneath the overwhelming aroma of sugar and vanilla. But Aidan had called it: My sense of smell had been compromised. Last time I was here, I had sensed a very subtle putrid scent amid the delicious fragrances of baked goods.

One by one, the three customers were taken care of, each leaving the shop with a pink bakery box tied up with twine. Renee turned to me and Aidan, her eyes glittering.

"What a lovely surprise! Lily, it's always such a pleasure! And you brought the mysterious and oh-so-difficult-to-pin-down Aidan Rhodes. From what I hear, Aidan, you rarely go out anymore. Are you feeling quite yourself these days? You look a mite peaked."

"I feel fine, Renee. Thank you for asking," Aidan responded, his eyes not leaving hers.

The staring contest went on for several moments. I noticed behind the register a pile of vintage-style fabric swatches and a basket holding spools of colored thread.

"That looks like fabric from Lucille's Loft," I said.

"Yes, I'm planning on coming to the Magical Match Tea on Sunday! Lucille's making us dresses. Isn't she just the most exquisite seamstress you've ever *seen*?"

"Who's your match?" I asked.

"Now, just wouldn't you love to know?" she cooed. "That's a secret!"

"Did you decide on a fabric? The event is just around the corner."

"Lucille assures me it is *all* under control." She glanced at Aidan. "So sorry you can't come, Aidan, but it's us girls only."

"Actually, that's not true," I said. "The Welcome coven voted to allow anyone who wants to come with whatever match they want. The event is gender-inclusive."

Renee *tsked* and made an exaggeratedly angry face, reminiscent of a toddler who didn't get her way. I half expected her to stomp her heel. "Well, I don't like that at all. This local insistence on everything being equal takes away the special, don't you think? After all, men and women are not interchangeable. As we know very well, don't we, Aidan?"

I had the sense she wasn't talking about social norms.

"Renee, why did you send the cupcakes to Lily?" asked Aidan. "I assumed they were an invitation."

"To her, not to you," Renee responded.

"And yet we are here to speak to you together, a united force."

"So I see. You know, Aidan, you really should relinquish your control over these young women," Renee said. Her sweet, almost maternal mien was gone, replaced by steely-eyed ambition. "Lily could be so much more than she is, and Selena is ripe to become a powerful young woman. I think you're afraid of the power they could wield without you and you're holding them back."

"With great power comes great responsibility—a lesson I fear you have yet to learn, Renee," Aidan answered. "As for Lily and Selena, they make their own choices."

"Just as in the case of that dear Calypso Cafaro? Would you say she made her own choices, Aidan?"

"We're not here to speak about Calypso," Aidan said.

"Oh, of course," Renee said, looking at me. "We're here to speak of some sort of unnamed 'threat' to your beloved San Francisco. Though why you think I'm any sort of threat is a mystery to me. After all, what's wrong with trying the Renee way?"

"The Renee way?" I asked. "That's a way?"

"It's a lovely way!" She smiled. "Anyway, I'm just a humble cupcake baker. You two are the ones involved in murder and whatnot. It's a shame, Lily, that your fiancé was involved with such an ugly thing."

"He wasn't," I insisted.

She let out a quick laugh. "No? Strange that all the witnesses say otherwise."

"It might have been a doppelgänger," I said, though I still wasn't convinced.

"A doppelgänger?" Now Renee laughed fully. "You don't really expect me to believe that, do you?"

"It's the truth," I said. "Or . . . maybe not a doppelgänger per se, but some sort of look-alike."

Renee laughed again, and I had to quell the urge to vault across the counter and punch her in the nose.

"Then what do *you* think happened?" I asked.

"I think you sent your boyfriend to take out dear Tristan Dupree, for fear that he'd come to work with me. Very clever of you to pick up on it so quickly, I have to say."

"Except it wasn't Sailor. Oh, and thanks for spiking the cupcakes."

"What cupcakes?"

"The ones you sent over with Jamie."

"Why would I do that?" Still smiling, Renee shook her head. "My, my, my, your man kills my man, and I barely even hold a grudge. And now you accuse me of, what? Trying to *poison* you with cupcakes?"

I didn't want her to know that she had succeeded in affecting my familiar. But still, she got my goat.

I could feel Aidan's hand on my arm, though I couldn't tell whom he was trying to restrain—me, or himself.

"Let's get one thing straight, Renee," I said. "Selena is a child, and she's under my protection. And I'll die before I'll let you get to her."

"That's just fine, dear," Renee said, holding out a cupcake frosted with black icing. "Here, I made this one just for you."

I swatted it away, and the cupcake landed with a splat on the tile floor, icing side down.

Renee made another angry-toddler face. But her eyes seemed as ancient as the world itself as her gaze held mine. She gave me a slow smile.

"You'd best take your witch out of here, Aidan, before you both get more than you're asking for."

"Renee, we're a united front, and we aren't alone," Aidan said, his voice steady and calm. "We have many behind us. You don't stand a chance. Unless you want to leave town altogether, you'll drop this challenge. We can all learn to live together."

"That's a lovely speech, Aidan," said Renee. "Just as pretty and false as that glamour you insist upon hiding behind. Are you sure you don't want a dozen cupcakes for the road? My treat."

"No, thank you," I said. "We don't want anything from you."

We left Renee's bakery without another word. Each lost in our own thoughts, Aidan and I rounded the corner without speaking, heading toward the car.

I heard a rustling, and a man jumped out of the bushes.

Chapter 20

Aidan and I both blasted him with a wall of power. He was thrown back and landed on his butt in a large planter full of geraniums.

"Jeez, you two!" Jamie exclaimed, hands held up in surrender. "Lay off, already."

"Oh, Jamie, I'm sorry!" I said.

Aidan held out a hand and helped him to his feet.

"I gotta say," Jamie said, brushing leaves and dirt from his backside. "A guy tries to do the right thing, reach out, and he gets nothin' but rejection. This is how people become recluses, you know—they can't deal with people no more."

"We apologize," I said, elbowing Aidan, who remained silent but nodded ever so slightly. "You caught us off guard."

"All evidence to the contrary."

"We just left Renee, so we're a bit jumpy."

"She tell you anything?"

"Not much," I said. "She made some vague threats, as usual. Hey, did you come by my shop?"

He gave me a side-eyed look. "Is this a trick question? 'Course I did. I brought a dozen cupcakes over this morning—you forget already?"

"Actually, I meant yesterday morning. Did you happen to overhear me speaking to a man in front of Aunt Cora's Closet . . . ?"

Jamie shook his head.

"You weren't on Haight Street yesterday?"

"I like that Amoeba Records they got there on Haight Street. I like vintage LPs. Sound's much better than the modern CDs, in my opinion. I gotta get your permission to go record shopping, now?"

"No, of course not. I was just wondering. Do you know a woman named Amy? Or Wind Spirit?"

"No." He shook his head and looked around as though worried about being watched. "And I gotta tell you: I stopped you for my own reasons, not to get interrogated."

"What is it you want?" I asked.

"I'm thinkin' this 'cold' you got is a little suspicious."

"How so?"

"I work for Renee and all, but it's not like I wanna be there." He crooked his head in Aidan's direction. "He knows what I'm sayin'. Right, pal? Sometimes that's how it works. You don't wanna be workin' for someone, but you get stuck. There I was, runnin' a nice little racket with the Russian psychics out in the Richmond District, and next thing I know, I'm indebted to the Cupcake Queen over here."

"What did you mean about Lily's cold being suspicious?" Aidan asked.

"Well, now, hold on for just a second here," Jamie said. "What's in it for me?"

"You expect to be paid for information?" Aidan asked.

"No, nothin' like that. But I don't wanna work for Renee no more. I want to throw in with you. Maybe I tell you some helpful things, and I come work for you instead? Whaddaya say?"

There was a long pause. A car honked, and a couple of teenagers walked by.

"You were just saying you needed to do some hiring, Aidan," I said, amusing myself at Aidan's expense.

"It's a possibility," said Aidan. "Depending on the information. Renee holds your marker?"

He nodded. "Even talking to you is dangerous for me, I gotta say." He looked over his shoulder again.

"Then don't waste any more time."

"I'm sayin', are you prone to colds? 'Cuz Renee was workin' on a batter the other day, and I saw her put fingernails, hair, chopped-up feathers, and powdered crab shell in it. Lord only knows what else went in there."

"And that means what?" I asked.

"I figured you'd know. Aren't you the botanical whiz?"

"I'm good at brewing, but I don't have encyclopedic knowledge." But I knew who did: Graciela. Or Calypso, maybe.

"And then she did that mumbling thing that weirds me out. Anyway, she didn't exactly come out and say what she was doing. She just said the batch she was makin' was for a 'special' customer. I'm wonderin' if she sent them to you."

"Wait. Were these the cupcakes you delivered this morning?" But that wouldn't make sense—not only had I not eaten any of those cupcakes, but I'd started sneezing and feeling draggy a couple of days earlier.

"Nah, the ones this morning had pot in them. She sells 'em down at the dispensary. She thought it was hysterical to send some over to your shop. Couldn't stop laughing. It's her brand of humor, which I don't entirely get, if you know what I mean."

"So when did she send me cupcakes before then?"

"Wasn't cupcakes, I don't think. More like her new line of meat pasties."

"Ugh," I said, putting my head in my hands as we left Jamie and approached the car. "I can't believe I might have eaten something dosed by Renee! And fingernails and hair . . . I think I'm going to be sick."

Aidan smiled as he opened the car door for me. "You're being just a tiny bit overdramatic. Don't you know we all eat insects and larvae in our food, all the time? It might be unpleasant to think about, but it won't hurt you."

"But I think she gave me this supposed 'cold.' Maybe you should put that green crystal on my nose and see if I've been poisoned?"

"That only works if you've got goblin blood. I assume that's not the case."

"I don't know," I said as Aidan got into the car. "The way things are unfolding, maybe that's what the shoe box was trying to tell me about my past. Maybe *that's* the prophecy. Maybe I'm not a witch at all, but something evil and unnatural."

Aidan looked at me so long without speaking that I looked up to meet his gaze.

"What is it?" I asked.

"You're not evil and unnatural, Lily. You're . . . extraordinary."

"Um, thank you." I really didn't know how to respond to that. "I thought you were angry with me."

"You're the one who stormed out of my office last time. I didn't ask you to leave. Have you ever noticed that when you get angry with me, you assume I'm angry with you?"

"Okay . . . that's a thought that's going to fester."

"It's all right to be angry with someone," Aidan continued. "And with a friend, it's a sign that we need to talk, obviously. Anyway, to get back to the pertinent question: How would you have eaten something from Renee's shop?"

"It was purely by accident."

"What happened?"

"Renee went by Lucille's Loft with some goodies, and Maya brought me one of the meat pasties."

"Was it good?"

"Very."

The truth was, I wasn't that careful about the food I consumed. I sort of assumed I'd feel anything that had been tampered with, and of course I avoided Renee's cupcakes, but hadn't I been thinking recently about all the enemies I'd made in town? Maybe I needed a taster. Like the European royals of old. I always wondered what that must have been like: to eat for a living, with the expectation that one might die at any meal.

"You know, you could simply have a regular cold. You're not immortal, after all."

"True. Could I borrow your phone?"

I called Calypso to ask her about the odd ingredients Jamie had mentioned Renee had used in the pastry batter.

"I don't recognize the ingredients right offhand, Lily. I'm sorry." I could hear her flipping through pages. "Of course, fingernails are never good."

That was for dang sure.

"But, let's see. . . . You say it's associated with cold-like symptoms?"

"Yes. Sneezing, congestion, loss of smell and lack of energy mostly."

"Okay, yes, here it is. It sounds like it might be a Tiberius Caesar befuddling spell. It says here, 'Sneezing was considered losing part of one's soul through the breath, or having to do with evil spirits. That's why we say *bless you.*' A Tiberius Caesar spell is cast by having the mark ingest the brew, but the mark has to do so willingly."

"Is there an antidote?"

"According to this, it should pass within a week or so. It's not deadly, just a nuisance, really. Rather like having an actual cold."

I thanked her and disconnected just as Aidan pulled into a valet parking spot in front of a fancy restaurant near the Ferry Building.

"What's up?" I asked.

"You need dinner," Aidan responded, "and so do I. Please, my treat."

Coqueta was a Spanish restaurant, decorated in the relaxed yet upscale way of many of San Francisco's bayside eateries. The valet and the hostess seemed to know Aidan, the latter fluttering her eyelashes and fawning all over him when he requested a patio table. Outside, overhead heaters kept us warm and snug despite the cool breeze off the water. The bay itself was dark and still at this hour, but the lights along the Bay Bridge twinkled, and the homes and businesses of Oakland and Emeryville and Berkeley on the other side of the bay led the eye up into the hills.

The usually incessant seagulls were quiet, and I imagined I could hear the water lapping gently at the piers.

I felt weary. If I really was suffering under a befuddling spell, I wondered whether I could will it away with the proper attitude, as Conrad had suggested. On top of everything else, I had missed the preview of the estate sale this afternoon. Then again, maybe I wasn't going to need a wedding dress after all. Just the thought of Sailor sitting in jail, waiting for me to figure this thing out . . . Depression settled over me like a shroud.

"So, what did that little chat with Renee tell us?" I asked Aidan after the waiter took our orders and opened a bottle of wine.

"Not as much as I'd hoped." Aidan waved off the waiter and poured the wine himself into two stemmed glasses. "She's still trying to win you over, I'd say."

"Renee said something about you once . . . ," I began.

"Only once?" Aidan said with a crooked smile.

"She said: 'Who died and made Aidan boss?'"

"Ah. And what did you tell her?"

"I said I had no idea. So, Aidan, how *did* you become boss of the San Francisco magical community?"

I didn't expect him to answer me. Politician-like—or similar to Oscar and so many other magical folk—Aidan almost never answered a direct question with a direct answer. Especially when that question was about his past.

But he didn't immediately dissemble, and seemed to be lost in thought, staring into his wineglass. His golden hair sparkled in the light of the overhead lamp, darker lashes framing his blue eyes. I could see his glamour shimmer, ever so slightly, as he shifted in his seat.

"When I first arrived here from Germany, I was in bad shape," he began. "That was fifteen years ago."

"You were in Germany when I was?"

He nodded. "You really don't remember, do you? I was there. Anyway, after I came to San Francisco, I needed to lie low for a while, concentrate on healing. I arrived with nothing but the injuries of which you've seen proof."

I thought of how Aidan walked around with the glamour that recalled his old self, before the burns. Renee had told me he was looking for the fountain of youth. Was that true, or was he simply trying to heal himself? It took a lot of energy for him to maintain the glamour, energy that he needed now if there was a supernatural battle brewing.

"Maybe you should drop the glamour," I suggested. "Let people see the real you. Your friends won't care."

"Do you really believe that?" he asked, flashing me a mocking smile. "But in any event, it matters to me. And speaking of bad old times, we really should try to help you remember everything that happened. I think we could manage it if you were willing to stay in the trance for a longer period of time."

I nodded, but was still nervous. Maybe it was my imagination, but I'd felt like my energy was drained the last time we melded our energies. Something similar had happened with Patience, though not to the same degree. I just didn't feel up to much of anything, now that I thought about it.

"For the moment, maybe you could give me the broad outline?"

Aidan took a sip of wine and sat back in his chair. "As you know, your father was going down the wrong path."

I nodded. I couldn't remember the particulars, but I knew my father was bad news. He had succumbed to the temptation of power, to the desires that I occasionally felt coursing through my own veins.

"He and I had worked together previously. Your father is immensely gifted, Lily; clearly, he passed his abilities on to you. But as his powers grew, his confidence gradually turned into arrogance. He began experimenting with dark forces, almost as if he were playing a game, tempting fate. I tried to warn him, but he wouldn't listen to me, claimed I was jealous of his power. Which, to be fair, I was."

Aidan paused and took another sip of wine. "*In vino veritas*, yes? Shall I continue?"

I nodded.

"Not long before you arrived in Germany, he had been working on something, but he wouldn't tell me what it was. I had my suspicions. I took note of the books he consulted, and in my free time attempted to discover what he had been looking for. It gradually became apparent that he was researching spells to summon and control not one demon, but a small group of them. A fool's quest, as I am sure you already know."

"Why would he do something so reckless?"

"Perhaps sheer ambition, or maybe he was simply bored. Your father was a very powerful practitioner, greatly admired for the natural ability he had spent years honing and perfecting. Maybe he was looking for a new world to conquer? He became fascinated by the grimoire called the Lesser Key of Solomon, and in particular the Ars Goetia, or the hierarchy of demons. But controlling a demon is a feat few have attempted, and even fewer have accomplished, at least over time. Most are seduced by the power, and the roles eventually shift." Aidan paused. "Do you wish me to continue? You may not like what you hear."

"Go on."

"I tried to talk to him about what he was doing, but I was young and foolish and he wouldn't listen to me. I became angry—how we mortals hate it when our idols are toppled. We argued for some time, but after one particularly nasty blood ritual, I told him that I no longer wished to continue my training with him, that I could do better on my own, without him or his magic. He burst out laughing." Aidan shrugged. "It took a while for my ego to recover from that blow, let me tell you."

"And then? What happened next?"

"*You* happened next. I had no idea you existed, much less that you had inherited your father's powers.

You showed up at the door, and the minute your father laid eyes on you, he began to doubt his path. Your presence finally woke your father up to the risk he was running in his pursuit of power. He faltered in his resolve, dangerously so, and the binding spell he had cast over the demon portal began to slip. You don't remember any of this?"

I shook my head. I remembered the trip to Germany, I remembered taking a taxi to my father's house, and I remembered knocking on the huge oak doors. I remembered the door swinging open. . . . But everything from that point on was a blank.

"Your father hid what he was doing from you, and tried everything to get you to leave his house—he threatened; he cajoled; he promised you things—but you refused to go. This went on for days, with the demons growing stronger as your father grew weaker and less focused."

"Because of my presence?"

"I told you, children make you susceptible, vulnerable. I wanted to leave, but your father begged me to stay while you were there, to help protect you. One night, it was unseasonably hot, with thunderstorms moving through, one after another. At three a.m., the witching hour, while you and I were sleeping, your father called on the demons in an attempt to vanquish them once and for all. But the creatures had grown strong, and at least one escaped the circle.

"You woke me, telling me there were terrible sounds coming from the locked study—the demons were laughing and taunting, demanding your father surrender you to them. I locked you in your room. When the screams began in the study, I managed to break down the door and went to your father's aid, hoping our combined powers would be enough to overcome the demons, to save your father, to save you. By then the other demons had escaped your father's spell. We fought the rest of the night. It was horrific."

"Then how did . . . how did it turn out?"

"You joined us in our fight. We were exhausted. We had been fighting for hours by that time, and just as the rays of the sun appeared in the window, the door swung open on its broken hinges, and there you stood. The demons crowed—a hard, triumphant sound. I can still hear it. They were sure they had won. I thought so, too. I felt your father's strength ebbing away, and mine as well. But none of us, it seems, had counted on you."

"What did I do?"

"You honestly don't remember this part? Even after we melded our magic yesterday?"

I shook my head.

"You rushed to your father's side, took his hand and mine, and started chanting, melding our powers. The demons began screaming, shaking the house in their fury and starting fires in the four corners. If they could kill us before we vanquished them, all three of our souls would belong to them. The demons had grown weaker but continued to fight, and as the fire spread, we were running out of time. Your father ordered me to get you out, to save you. I tried to pull you out of the room, but you were still chanting and fighting them. You were crying, refusing to leave."

"I don't cry."

"You *did* cry."

"Then what?"

"Your father told you he despised you, and your weakness. He told you he had already made an agreement with the demons, for strength. For power. As fire engulfed the room, I was finally able to pull you to safety. We were both burned, but I was able to get you to a safe house in Bavaria, and some friends contacted your grandmother. She was able to heal you from afar, along with some help."

"But not you? Why do you have scars, when I don't?"

"I had to run, no time to heal properly. A struggle with a pack of demons like that—it marks you, whether or not you wind up pledging allegiance to their power. I'm not beholden to the demons, but I paid a steep price for my freedom."

"Where was this safe house? Who helped me?"

"As I said, your grandmother and her coven were able to do much of the healing from afar."

"But where was the house?"

"It was hardly luxury accommodations—more like a basement room. With a former student of your father's who didn't have enough natural talent to continue his training. After he left, he and I remained in touch. He wasn't happy about it, but he did help. It was Tristan Dupree."

Chapter 21

"Tristan helped me?"

"Tristan's mother had a number of magical abilities, and she was very good at glamours—in fact, I learned a lot from her. But as much as he tried, Tristan never lived up to her promise. But he did help you, at least at first."

"And my father?"

"As you know, he survived the fire. During the battle, he pledged his allegiance to one of the demons, and the demon wanted him alive. You healed, and forgot the whole thing. I escaped here, to San Francisco."

"Why San Francisco?"

"Why not?"

"No, I just meant . . . was there some special reason you chose the City by the Bay?"

He smiled. "Besides the weather? Of course. Because of the prophecy."

"The prophecy which says a witch like me is going to come to San Francisco?"

"It's slightly more complicated than that. The prophecy had to do with a witch able to provide a conduit for other powerful witches—in other words, not just your guiding spirit, the Ashen Witch, but others. This witch would form one half of the *coincidentia oppositorum*, and I, of course, hoped to provide the other half. And then she would go up against a primal force of evil. Unless . . ."

"Unless?"

"Unless she herself was seduced to the other side. In exchange for power, or self-interest. In your case I imagine your weakness would have more to do with trying to 'save' loved ones, that sort of thing."

"Caring for other people isn't a weakness; it's a strength."

"Sounds like somebody's been reading some Bay Area–style New Age literature. Of course caring for others is a strength in normal humans, Lily. What you don't seem to have grasped yet is that you're not a normal human. You need to be worried about the state of people in general, not one person in particular."

"Uh-huh. And what if I'm not wild about becoming the queen of the witches, or whatever this position is officially called?"

"It's not like running for office, Lily. You don't get to just decline."

"I don't even believe in prophecies."

Aidan let out a long breath, and took another sip of wine. "Tell you what: when your grandmother's coven arrives, why don't you chat about it with them? See what they have to say?"

I nodded. Good idea. Silence reigned for a few moments. The waiter came with the food: a *paella valenciana* served in a huge flat pan. Bright yellow saffron rice was studded with mussels, clams, and crab.

"So, how do you go on, after battling a host of demons?" I asked him.

"In your case, you block the memories entirely. But I wasn't so lucky. I was in bad shape when I arrived, physically, mentally, and spiritually. An amazing woman helped me, brought me back to life. She was trying to hold the Bay Area magical community together, and passed that responsibility on to me. And then things ratcheted up, becoming increasingly dire. As I told you, I believe the surge in energy has to do with you, or at least with your arrival here in San Francisco."

"Hard to believe this all started with a parrot in a bar," I muttered as I dug into my paella.

"Excuse me?"

I shrugged. "I was just thinking about the decisions we make in life, how they bring us to where we are today."

He smiled. "Waxing philosophical, are we?"

"A little, I guess.

"Are you a Dickens fan?"

"Well . . . I'm not *not* a Dickens fan."

"'Pause and think for a moment of the long chain of iron or gold, of thorns or flowers, that would never have bound you but for the formation of the first link on one memorable day.'"

"That's Dickens?"

He nodded and plucked a clam from the paella. "From *Great Expectations*. Wonderful novel. All about expectations, as the title would suggest."

I sighed. "I admire people who can memorize things. I usually think of myself as having a good memory, but the only actual scripts I remember are my spells."

"Seems to me that's more than enough."

"I don't know. . . . I'm feeling so off, lately."

"With your brewing as well?"

I nodded. "Do you really think Jamie's telling the truth, that Renee slipped me something, and that's why I'm feeling like this?"

"Possibly. But as I said, it could be a simple cold—or it could be connected to your upcoming wedding. I told you your relationship to Sailor would make you vulnerable."

"I thought you meant in the sense of having my energies divided, not catching a cold. You know what we could use right now?" I asked. "A mandragora. Mandragoras are great at sniffing out spells and strange ingredients in food. Whatever happened to the one I made you?"

"I gave it away as a gift."

"You told me you wanted it as a household imp, that you were lonely."

"Did I?"

"Who did you give it to?"

"A gentleman never tells. Anyway, back to the important point: I find it interesting that your brewing has been affected, and now your familiar's out of commission."

"For how long, do you know?"

"It's hard to say. Oscar has a different metabolism than we do, obviously. But now that I'm putting this all together, I realize this might not be about Sailor at all. It's more likely about you. Tristan tracked you down for a reason."

"But I don't understand—why would Tristan show up like this, after all this time?"

"According to what I heard, Tristan betrayed you—and his own mother, for that matter. Before you were completely healed, he tried to strike his own deal with one of the demons, and gave up your hiding place. I'm guessing you stole something from him before you ran, perhaps something he had promised to deliver to the demon."

"Why would it take him so long to follow me here to claim it?"

"I believe it took him this long to become strong enough to go up against his old rival."

"You."

He nodded. "It's also possible Renee's been putting out feelers for a male counterpart, so he decided it was time to make a move if he could secure her backing."

"So, you say I cried when I was there, with my father? Tristan's spirit said something about the 'tears of the daughter'. Should I suppose that was *my* lachrymatory?"

"It seems possible. Imagine what Renee could do with the salt of your tears."

"But why wouldn't I be able to cry now? I always thought it was a witchy thing."

"I think it's part of your coping mechanism, an inability to accept those memories, to delve that deeply into your own psyche. The same reason you've suppressed the memories."

"Who's New Agey now?"

He chuckled.

"Okay, let's recap," I said, and took a deep drink of wine. "Tristan comes to San Francisco from Germany to work with Renee, demands his bēag from me, then winds up dead at the hands of a doppelgänger who looks like Sailor. But the doppelgänger must not work for Renee, because she wanted to ally herself with Tristan to go up against you and me, to form her own version of the *coincidentia oppositorum*. So who would want to ruin Renee's plans? Besides you and me, obviously."

"We're not the only ones in the magical community, Lily. I've got feelers out, but no useful information yet. Still, a man like Tristan might have other enemies."

"Let's start there. What more can you tell me about him?"

"As I said, he's worked on the fringes for a long time.

Known for betraying most of the people he's worked with, eventually."

"So maybe it's someone from his past, come to settle a score."

"Maybe." Aidan sipped his wine.

"Or . . . Tristan never seemed like prime material for the *coincidentia oppositorum*, did he? I mean, he seems more like an underling, a guy who gets used. Maybe Renee gave him false hope because she knew he'd get the lachrymatory for her."

"It's possible. But does that tell us anything?"

"I'm not sure. . . ." Something didn't seem quite right, but I couldn't put my finger on it.

I leaned back in my chair. The paella was scrumptious, but despite my earlier hunger I didn't have much of an appetite. Aidan, in contrast, had finished his healthy portion and was now slathering butter on fresh sourdough bread, apparently relishing every bite.

"Who was the woman?" I asked.

"What woman?"

"You said you took over your responsibilities with the San Francisco magical community from a woman. She wasn't . . . That wasn't Renee, was it?"

He gave me a disgusted look. "Of course not."

"Then who?"

"Calypso Cafaro."

"Are you serious?" That shocked me. "I thought you and Calypso were . . . or that you had been . . . together?"

He gave me a slight smile. "'Together'?"

"As in boyfriend, girlfriend . . . I don't know what gave me that impression."

"You're right, of course. We were the *coincidentia oppositorum*, for a little while, anyway."

"Does *coincidentia oppositorum* imply a romantic attachment?"

"Not necessarily, but it doesn't hurt."

"Wait just a gol-durned second. How come you're going on and on about my romance with Sailor weakening me, but you claim it *strengthened* you?"

"Sailor isn't the other half of the *coincidentia*—"

"Oppositorum," I finished with a nod. "Okay, I get it. I guess. Are you sure this isn't some elaborate plot to get me to go out with you?"

Aidan grinned. "You're pretty special, Lily Ivory, but I wouldn't court demons and the like just to get you in my arms. There are other, much more effective ways of accomplishing something like that."

I looked away, trying to ignore his sultry gaze.

"Okay, so first you and Calypso were a thing, but then you took over completely. Was this with Calypso's full endorsement, or was there a struggle?"

"She agreed, of course."

"Freely?"

He had lifted his wineglass to his mouth, and now looked at me over the rim. "Is anything truly free in this life, Lily?"

A while ago, Calypso had made vague references to wanting nothing to do with Aidan, but she had never given me any details. I knew I wouldn't get much more information from Aidan, though, so I decided to let the subject go for the moment. I would raise it again with Calypso when I had the chance.

Aidan drove us back to the wax museum.

"I should come in with you and get my pig," I said when he pulled up to my van.

"Why don't you leave him where he is for the night? Let him sleep it off at my office. He's more than capable of getting himself back home, as you well know."

"That's true. How *does* Oscar get around?"

"You're quite the curious one today."

"I've always wondered. And he tells me as much about himself as you do."

"I find with this sort of thing it's best to leave the details vague."

"By which you mean . . . ?"

He chuckled. "I'm really not sure. He's a miraculous little guy, on several levels."

"I'm so glad he's all right. He gave me a fright. So, what are our next steps?"

"I'll continue to ask questions of the magical community, see if any useful rumors are flying. You should have Patience check in with the Rom community—I'm sure they're aware of what's going on with Sailor and will want to help."

"She's already on it."

"Good. In the meantime, maybe you'll encounter the doppelgänger again, and get some answers."

"Last time I 'encountered' the doppelgänger, he tried to kill me."

"Are you certain? He was chasing you, but perhaps he just wanted to chat."

I gave him a look. He grinned in return.

"Obviously you need to be careful. But if this is a true doppelgänger, it's here for a reason."

"You said it might be here for me. You don't think it just wants to kill me?"

"No. After all, if that was what it wanted, why didn't it kill you already? Why go after Tristan in the guise of your boyfriend?"

"Fiancé," I corrected him automatically. "Or . . . what if it isn't a real doppelgänger? What are the other possibilities?"

"Endless. You could be hallucinating after eating LSD-laden baked goods."

"Very funny. Patience was with me; she saw him, too."

"Not to mention a shop owner in Chinatown."

"And witnesses at the hotel the night Tristan was killed. Speaking of which, would you be willing to go back there with me, see what we can see?"

"So, is it Oscar or Sailor who will come back to work for me?"

I blew out a breath, but didn't respond.

"Anyway, you have a day to figure it out. I have another obligation tonight. When you figure out which one will come back to work for me, we can go to the hotel tomorrow. Ask Patience if she'll go with us."

"Why Patience?"

"We need a necromancer."

"Hervé's a better necromancer. Though she did see something when she was in the lobby . . ."

"Bring them both, then. The more the merrier."

Hervé's voodoo supply shop closed at eight. I just barely made it to Valencia Street in time. Caterina gave me a cool smile when I entered, then ducked into the back and sent Hervé out to speak with me.

"I think we need to go back to the hotel," I said. "But this time with backup."

"Who is our 'backup'?"

"Aidan, Patience, you, and me."

"So two witches, a Gypsy psychic, and a voodoo priest walk into a hotel . . . ," began Hervé with a low chuckle, shaking his head. "Sounds like the beginning of a joke."

"Yes, but I'm not sure if I'll like the punch line."

"Lily, I'll go with you if you need me, but I believe I did all I could last night. If Patience is half the psychic she's cracked up to be, she'll be able to make contact with any latent spirits."

Caterina reappeared through the beaded curtain that separated the shop floor from their private quarters. She was carrying a canvas shopping bag, which held two smaller brown paper bags. She set it on the counter in front of me.

"One of your friends forgot this when they were checking out earlier," she said without preamble.

"Oh, um, thank you," I said.

She shrugged and went back through the curtains.

Hervé leaned toward me and whispered: "Not your biggest fan."

"Yeah, I get that. Sorry. I hope my coming here doesn't make things difficult for you."

"Don't worry about it."

"Who left the bag, do you know?" I asked as I peeked within the first paper bag. There was a little figure in a coffin, and a hexing candle. They weren't from Hervé's shop but from the *botanica*—a sort of Mexican herb and magical-supply store—across the street. The second bag held various dried herbs.

"Wind Spirit, I believe she's calling herself."

"Wind Spirit?"

"She used to go by Amy."

"Yes, I know she did. I didn't realize you knew her."

"I don't know her well. She comes into the shop from time to time."

"I don't know why that surprises me. . . . A lot of people come to you for supplies, right?"

"True."

"What does she buy from you?"

"Last time it was a cookbook, if I recall." He took a copy off a nearby shelf and handed it to me.

"I didn't know you sold cookbooks."

He grinned. "Very special cookbooks. Look up voodoo bread pudding and love sauce."

"What's love sauce?" I asked as I flipped through the pages. "Or . . . do I want to know?"

"Basically it's a slightly sweet bread with sauce. Orris root gives the bread a subtle violet aroma. The sauce is made from brown sugar, butter, and rum."

"Nothing not to love about that."

"Indeed."

"But when you say it's a voodoo recipe . . . ? Does that mean it's harmful, or special in some way?"

"You tell people it's a love potion, and they'll bake anything."

I smiled, but his words made me think of Renee with her cupcakes.

"Besides, you know as well as I do that if one is able to focus one's intent through true belief, one might just infuse that bread pudding with actual feelings of love."

I flipped through the book. "There are a few negative recipes in here as well."

"Sometimes love goes wrong," Hervé said with a grin.

"Are they actually poisonous?"

He shook his head. "No, of course not. Just contain a few nasty ingredients . . . but I have the sense you're used to things like that. Anyone who brews knows that things can get a bit pungent, from time to time. A secret ingredient, secret revenge."

"Remind me not to get on your bad side," I said, glad in that moment that Caterina didn't have her husband's powers.

He smiled. "We all have our ways, Lily."

Chapter 22

That night I felt lonely. No Oscar snoring above the fridge, no sound of boots on the stairs telling me Sailor was on his way up. I was also anxious and frustrated. Again, I sat for a while with my Book of Shadows, but it didn't speak to me. I was finding it hard to concentrate. My mind ping-ponged from thoughts of Sailor to the grandmas on the bus, to what Renee had put in the meat pasties, to what Aidan had told me about his past, to my role in vanquishing the current threat, to Calypso.

Had her love for Aidan made Calypso vulnerable, the way Aidan told me my love for Sailor diminished me? Or had it made their coalition stronger, and if so, why did she back out and leave everything to Aidan?

I could feel my energies scattering, like Selena's typically did. I wasn't sure whether it was due to Renee's spell, or Sailor being in jail, or the urgency of needing to find the killer. . . . What I did know was that it wasn't helpful in any way.

Maybe I needed to make myself a *Gutta Cavat Lapidem* talisman.

Enough. Time to go back to basics. I stepped out to my terrace, pulled on my gardening gloves, grabbed my spade, and spent some time communing with my garden under the light of the waxing moon. Even when I was a young, out-of-control witch, plants had calmed me, while the rich soil soothed me. Graciela had explained it was because I tapped into—and contributed to—the ancient earth energy. That was my skill, my gift, my soul.

I worked the soil for nearly an hour, pulling weeds, pruning and shaping my herbs, bushes, and small potted trees. Before I realized what I was doing, I had started to gather snippets of plants in my basket: mugwort, jasmine, willow, oak leaves, holly berries, mistletoe, yarrow, broom, orris root, ivy, shamrock, rose, and heliotrope. Ingredients I knew well.

I returned to the kitchen.

Quietly, calmly, I began to cast a spell—not for Sailor, or against Renee—just for me. For strength and wisdom. For inner quiet, so I could remain open to the wonder of the night sky, and serve as the conduit between it and the earth beneath my feet. I filled my cauldron with river water and put it on the stove to boil. I chanted while crushing a few of the plants with my stone mortar and pestle, giving my thanks for their sacrifice. I added the rest of the ingredients to the brew, whole. I dropped in a dollop of goat's milk, a pinch of cayenne, a smidgen of black pepper, and a dash of Tabasco sauce.

After I stirred for a while, the brew began to swirl on its own, and then came to a rolling boil. I cut a small X into my palm and added the secret ingredient: three drops of my own blood.

As always, a great puff of steam exploded out of the pot. I looked up toward the ceiling to search the fog for the face of my guiding spirit, the Ashen Witch.

But she didn't appear to me.

The Ashen Witch didn't come.

Long before I even knew what I was, long before I knew who *she* was—ever since I could remember—the Ashen Witch had come to me when I brewed.

When I looked down into the now-calm brew, I saw herbs floating atop the water. They formed a shape like Sailor's doodle, the one I'd asked Maya to look up for me. The one the busload of witches seemed to be making with their path.

The one Patience thought was a demon's sigil.

As I headed over to Jail #2 for visiting hours the next morning, I kept trying to come up with some way to convince Sailor to go back to work for Aidan. I didn't think I could handle this alone, and Aidan had a point: Working for him had to be a better option than rotting in prison. Right?

I was so wound up by the time Sailor shuffled in that I just blurted it out.

"Did it ever occur to you that maybe *Aidan* is the one behind all of this?" was Sailor's response.

"*No.* What are you talking about?"

He shrugged. "Think about it: It gets me back into his employ, brings you closer to him, and spoils Renee's plans, all at the same time. Seems to me he has plenty of motive. Also . . . Aidan's very good at glamours. Maybe *he's* my mystery twin."

"Could a glamour be used that way? To actually change someone's appearance like that, so completely?"

"You tell me. This is witchcraft—it's your strong suit. Remember?"

"Yeah, well, I might be experiencing a few glitches recently," I said. "But . . . wait a minute. I was with Aidan that night. It wouldn't have been possible."

"Think about it: you were with him in the evening, but the murder happened in the afternoon. He could have gotten back to his office by then. Or knowing Aidan, he would more likely have gotten someone else to do his dirty work. Maybe someone who wanted to get in good with him . . . ?"

I didn't want to admit that Sailor might be right . . . but it did make a certain amount of sense. Was Aidan that ruthless? And if it was true, where did that leave us?

"So, what time is your arraignment today, do you know?" I asked.

Sailor gave me a sardonic smile. "Changing the subject, are we?"

"No, I just wanted to know what time to be here for you. I want to post your bail, take you home, and then attend to some of the other items on my to-do list. Not the least of which is how to exonerate the likes of you."

"You sure it's not because you don't like anyone to speak ill of your precious Aidan Rhodes?"

"Sailor, are you kidding me? You're going to choose this moment to be jealous of Aidan?"

"I wouldn't say *jealous*. . . ." He trailed off with a shrug. "I just don't enjoy being a member of this supernatural ménage à trois we seem to have going. Anyway, to answer your earlier question, the arraignment hearing has been postponed."

"Postponed? But . . . this is ridiculous. Until you're arraigned, I can't bail you out. How long can they hold you without charges?"

"Forty-eight hours in California. But if the prosecutor can show good cause, she can ask for an extension."

"What's the good cause, in this case?"

"Apparently there's a question as to whether Dupree died from the injuries sustained in the beating."

"But . . . what do they think killed him, if not that?"

"All I was told was that the medical examiner had some 'concerns.'"

"Well," I said, blowing out a breath, "maybe that's good news, then, right?"

"When you're facing murder one, any news is good news." Sailor cast a quick glance over at the sheriff's deputy, who appeared to be staring at the wall. "Here's the odd thing: There's a rumor going around that the prosecutor's office received a couple of boxes of cupcakes."

"Cupcakes," I repeated. "You're thinking Renee dosed the prosecutor's office? Why would she want to help *you*?"

"I have no idea, but that's the scuttlebutt."

"And you believe it?"

He shrugged. "I kept seeing red dahlias, and fungus, so it would fit. And these guys in here would have no reason to lie to me, as far as I can tell. Especially about something like cupcakes."

"Renee might be angry with you for what happened to Tristan. We think it's possible he came to San Francisco to work with Renee, to be the other half to her *coincidentia oppositorum*."

"We?"

"Aidan and I."

"Uh-huh. And what makes the two of you think that?"

"Jamie mentioned it, and then Renee confirmed it."

"So we might have to consider the sources."

"True. But Aidan thought it was a good possibility. He says there aren't that many options for Renee, so she might have recruited him."

"Imported him all the way from Germany, like a BMW? I can believe she's put out a global search, but was Tristan that well respected?"

I shook my head. "That thought struck me too. So if they're lying, then what does that tell us?"

He gave me a barely there smile. "You mean you haven't figured it all out yet, supersleuth?"

"Not hardly," I said softly.

"I'm kidding," he said, his voice gentle. "It's been less than two days, Lily. You'll get this."

"One other thing: I saw something at your apartment yesterday."

"You went to my apartment?"

I nodded. I wasn't going to fill him in on the details of getting chased by his look-alike; he had enough to worry about.

"I wanted to see if I could pick up any clues. The police had tossed it pretty well."

"Looking for evidence."

"Exactly. There were some doodles on the table near your bed; did they mean anything to you?"

"I kept seeing that image in my trance, right before the police arrived. I was hoping you might be able to interpret it for me."

"Maya's working on it. I also noticed your jewelry box was empty."

"Men don't have jewelry boxes. We have cuff link boxes, or valet boxes."

"Because you have so many cuff links? Or a valet, for that matter?"

He gave me his crooked smile. "As you would say, 'not hardly.'"

"So, what did you keep in it?"

Now he frowned. "Wait. You say it was empty?"

I nodded. "I found it open and empty. What did you keep in it?"

"My father's watch."

"The one you told me you saw in your vision?"

"The very one. I don't have many keepsakes."

"I know you don't. I've seen your apartment before

it was tossed, remember? You hardly had anything in it, other than books."

He looked troubled. "Maybe the police took it into evidence, for some reason. I'll have Petulengro check for me."

"So, once I manage to spring you from the hoosegow . . ." I trailed off, unsure how to approach this.

"Lily? You're not breaking up with me over a little thing like a murder charge, are you?"

I let out a bark of laughter. "Don't be silly."

"I can't help but notice you're not wearing the ring I gave you."

"Patience needed it, just temporarily. To help her try to find your double."

He raised his eyebrows. "Who knew? All I needed to bring you two together was to get busted?"

"I wouldn't say we're best buddies, but we're working together. Nonetheless, I honestly think I need Aidan's help with this. Would you at least consider agreeing to go back to work for him? It might well be the only way."

A curtain came down over his face. His eyes turned cold and flat, reminding me, ever so slightly, of that horrifying look-alike.

"Is that so?" he murmured.

"Yes, it is. And Patience agrees. Aidan said he'd pay you well."

Silence. Sailor just stared at me, his gaze cold.

"I'm . . . I'm not saying you should agree, necessarily. But if the choice is between being convicted of murder or working with Aidan, then—"

"As I said," Sailor interrupted, "it's only been a couple of days. Let's see what you can come up with, first."

"I can't. . . . There are no visiting hours tomorrow. I won't be able to see you unless you're arraigned, and I guess that might not be until Monday."

He gave a curt nod. "Don't worry about me. Focus on trying to figure this out."

"I miss you."

He smiled. "Miss you, too, my little witch. I'll be home soon."

The bad news was that I couldn't spring Sailor on bail. And that he was annoyed with me for suggesting he work for Aidan, but I wasn't going to think about that part now.

The *good* news was that, maybe, the prosecutor was considering lesser charges than murder one.

I spied a small bank of pay phones at the jail. I fetched the roll of quarters I kept in my car for parking meters, and started making phone calls. I tried Sailor's lawyer first, and this time got through.

Henry Petulengro was brief and efficient. His voice didn't betray a lot of emotion.

"This is the dream, in homicide cases," he said. "Turns out the victim died of some preexisting condition, something like that. Suddenly murder one turns into simple assault."

"But Sailor didn't assault anyone," I insisted.

"Sure, right. I'm just saying, it's a whole different ball game."

"So what happens now? When will I be able to bail Sailor out?"

"We have to wait and see what the new complaint against him looks like. Probably not over the weekend. But this is good news, Lily. Try not to worry. And do me a favor—ask Sailor's aunt Renna to stop threatening to hex me if I don't get him off."

"Renna's threatening you?"

"It's not like I'm not getting enough pressure from my wife. I'm doing the best I can."

I thanked him, told him I'd see what I could do

about Renna, and hung up. I was frustrated. Yes, it was good news. But still it wasn't the news I wanted. I wished Petulengro had said that Sailor would be coming home for dinner. That my fiancé would be in my arms tonight. That this was all a terrible misunderstanding and, oh, by the way, there was no overarching threat posed by a cupcake lady and your cold is merely a case of allergies and all will be well.

As Graciela used to always say, *If wishes were horses, beggars would ride.* I had to deal with the way things were. I had to find a way.

Maybe I needed a different angle. I deposited two more quarters and called Patience.

"What do you know about the Russian psychics in the Richmond District?"

"That's like asking what I think of the witches of Texas," Patience responded. "I'm going to guess there's a lot of individual variation."

"Okay, yes, of course you're right. It's just that Jamie—the guy who works for the cupcake lady—mentioned he used to run some sort of scam with some Russian psychics, so I was wondering . . ."

"I see what you're getting at. I happen to know one person, named Juna. Short for Eugenia. Her grandmother used to have a Russian bakery out in the Richmond."

"Do you think she'd talk to us?"

"She'd talk to a goat as long as it paid her hourly rate. I'll set it up."

"Thanks. Also, Sailor's lawyer, Henry Petulengro, wants Renna to stop threatening to hex him."

Patience let out an exasperated breath. "She always does that when family's in jail. I don't know why she thinks it's helpful. I'll talk to her."

"Thank you. You'll call me when you set up the meeting with the psychic? The sooner, the better."

"Of course. Anything else I can do for you? A nice little massage, perhaps?"

"That'll do for now. See you later."

After several more quarters, and several more calls, I finally got Carlos to call me back. It turned out he was in the building, so he asked me to meet him outside on the sidewalk. He handed me a large canvas shopping bag containing the wooden box that held my Hand of Glory, and my woven Filipino backpack.

"I don't even want to know what that alleged 'candleholder' is all about," Carlos said.

"I think that's best. Thank you so much for getting all this back for me." I checked the backpack; my keys and wallet were still there.

"I live to serve. Protect and serve, actually—that's our motto. Let's stash that bag in your trunk and take a walk," he said.

Jail #2 is not in a pretty part of town. There were a number of industrial buildings and a couple of twenty-four-hour bail bonds offices, but not a lot of restaurants or café options. We walked down Seventh Street, passing a hot dog vendor.

"May I buy you something to eat?" I asked.

"No, thanks." Carlos shook his head and kept walking. "So, it looks like Dupree didn't die from the beating, after all."

"What did he die from?"

"He was poisoned."

"Poisoned? How— Wait. You mentioned finding some roots and powders in his hotel room, didn't you?"

Carlos nodded. "We took them in for testing, but they turned out to be standard herbal remedies for digestive problems, that sort of thing. According to the hotel staff, he had been complaining of not feeling well. But the toxicology report says Dupree died due to complications from mycetismus."

"What's that?"

"It's a kind of mushroom poisoning. There are several local mushrooms that are deadly—Destroying Angel and Death Caps, to name just two with evocative names. They're in the amanita family."

Okay, Lily. Remember to breathe. Should I tell Carlos that someone who looked remarkably like Sailor had tried to buy deadly mushrooms in a Chinatown shop the other day? Or . . . should I play along, at least until I got an inkling of what was going on?

"Where would Dupree have come into contact with poisonous mushrooms?" I hedged.

"That's the ten-thousand-dollar question. Apparently they grow in the woods around here. They look a lot like edible mushrooms. Every year people mistake the poisonous ones for the safe ones, and fall ill from mycetismus completely by accident."

"You're not suggesting that Tristan arrived at SFO on a flight from Germany and immediately went mushroom hunting?"

"No," Carlos said with a smile. "I'm suggesting that someone *else* went mushroom hunting, and somehow Tristan ingested some. Problem is, no one else has shown up at the emergency room with symptoms. Usually with this sort of thing, you see whole families or groups of people who've eaten spaghetti with mushroom sauce, something like that."

"You said Tristan bought things at an herb shop in Chinatown," I said. "The Lucky Moon. Could he have bought suspect mushrooms at the same time?"

"It's possible. But the medical examiner says it's more likely he bought the herbs because his stomach was already queasy from the effects of the poison. That was early in the afternoon, which means he probably ingested the mushrooms sometime in the morning, or even earlier."

"How long does it take for the poison to kill?"

"According to the ME, with amatoxins—the poison present in the amanita mushrooms—it's anywhere from five to twenty-four hours for the victim to become symptomatic. So we're working with a pretty broad window."

"If he had gotten to a hospital . . ."

Carlos nodded. "If he'd gone to a hospital, he'd probably be waiting for a liver transplant now, instead of a funeral. But he didn't seek medical attention. Also, it appears he wasn't in great shape to begin with. The medical examiner says Dupree had the heart of a much older man."

"So the question is, how—and when—did he ingest the poisonous mushrooms?"

"That's it in a nutshell. We know that he ate lunch at the hotel restaurant that day, and ordered the special: pasta with mushroom sauce. But we questioned the chef, who cried like a baby and swore up and down he'd bought the mushrooms from his regular supplier, and his story checks out. We also interviewed the waitstaff, who said Dupree ate lunch by himself, and the security tapes confirm he was alone at a table for one. None of the other customers who ordered the dish had problems."

"So he could have eaten them anywhere."

"He got off the plane that morning, and no one else on board felt any ill effects, so we're assuming it happened at some point after that."

"Did you know if he went by Renee's cupcake shop?"

"It's possible. Why?"

"Renee Baker is sort of . . . a suspicious character."

"I remember you telling me that with regards to her neighbor's arsenic poisoning, but that turned out to be something else entirely. Any reason you have a bee in your bonnet about this particular cupcake lady?"

"Let's just say she strikes me as 'hinky.' Anyway, so

you're saying we're no closer to figuring out Dupree's killer."

"Every step is a step closer. At the very least, this new information may be enough to get the murder charge against Sailor dropped. Unless the DA wants to claim he was responsible for the poisoning as well—but that would be quite a stretch, and an obvious source of reasonable doubt."

Speaking of doubt, self-doubt shot through me. I felt like I was betraying Carlos by not telling him what I knew about the ersatz "Sailor" asking for amanita mushrooms at the Lucky Moon. But on the other hand . . . I couldn't bring myself to betray Sailor by spilling the beans. Besides, what purpose would be served by helping to frame an innocent man?

"The ME estimates several hours elapsed between when Dupree consumed the poison and when he died," Carlos continued. "So at the moment, at least, it's looking like the worst-case scenario for Sailor is a charge of assault and battery."

"Which is an improvement, but not exactly what I was hoping for."

"Baby steps, Lily. Baby steps."

Chapter 23

I was late getting back to Aunt Cora's Closet, but luckily Bronwyn and Duke had already arrived and opened the doors for business. Even though weekday mornings were slow, I liked to open on time. One never knew when a customer would be in a mad rush to find just the right dress.

Also, we'd be closed tomorrow to prep the shop for the Magical Match Tea on Sunday. So today was the last day for customers to find true vintage matching outfits in time for the event, and we still had a few outfits up for grabs.

"Maya and her cousin Kareem are due to arrive within the hour," Bronwyn said. "So please don't worry; you do whatever you need to do, and we'll be just fine and look after the place."

The bell over the front door tinkled as Selena walked in.

"Hi, Selena," I said, though in truth my stomach dropped. I had hoped she would stay clear of the shop for a while—at least until things were settled. "What are you doing here?"

"School's off. And I still don't have a bridesmaid's dress. You left yesterday, 'member?"

"Yes, right. Of course. Good idea. Let's get you outfitted."

I turned to the "Dressy Dresses" rack and started rummaging through it with gusto. There was one thing in this life I was still good at: finding the right dress. If I couldn't do it for myself, the very least I could do was to come through for Selena.

As usual, Selena gravitated toward rather garish flounces, but I convinced her to take a few of my choices into the dressing room as well.

The first was a late-1950s claret red sleeveless number with a wide skirt and charcoal gray fabric roses peppered along the neckline, down to the waist, and over the straps. The next dress was a simple ice-blue tea-length A-line chiffon, with a sweetheart neckline and a swishy skirt. The last was a true antique, a genuine flapper-era dress. The top was made of the palest blush silk with satin ribbon and lace details, and a vintage lace sash. The long skirt was made of ashes-of-roses cotton embellished with appliqués and overlaid with a pink cut silk velvet overskirt, with pink tulle and lace trim at the hem. It was finished with a large pink satin rose at the waist. Unfortunately, the last dress, in particular, hung rather limp and uninspiring on the hanger.

"I'm telling you as a professional, Selena: Not many women can wear true vintage from the twenties. You should try it on, see if you like it."

"I guess," she said with a shrug. "Want to try on your wedding dress again? We could use the big dressing room, together."

"Of course," I said. "I'd love to."

We passed the next forty-five minutes trying on dresses, laughing as Bronwyn added more items to our rack, urging us to try on silly items from the sixties, seventies, and eighties. We had the shop to ourselves this morning, so it was like playing dress-up. I reveled in such a relaxed, unguarded, *normal* time with Selena.

As I had predicted, the twenties ensemble was exactly right for Selena. It needed to be taken in a bit here and there, and the cotton skirt was much too long, but otherwise, it was perfect.

She emerged from the dressing room to show Bronwyn and Duke, delighted and blushing as they made a fuss over her.

"I do look pretty good, don't I?" she asked shyly, observing herself in the three-way mirror.

"So good I'm going to have to keep up my search," I declared. "Otherwise you'll outshine me at my own wedding!"

She grinned, and light danced around her.

I had put on the dress Wind Spirit brought again, because Selena asked me to, though I had already decided no amount of alteration would transform it into what I wanted. I considered several of the fancy dresses in the shop—who said I had to wear an actual wedding gown? In the old days, people simply wore a nice dress that they could wear again and again for special occasions.

As we were changing into our everyday clothes—a few customers had arrived, so it was time to get back to work—Selena wrinkled her nose.

"That wedding dress smells kind of funny."

"It does?" I sniffed, but didn't pick up on anything. "My sense of smell is terrible these days. What does it smell like?"

"Like . . . musty, sort of. And kind of like cupcakes? But in a bad way. Burned cupcakes."

"Like the ones in your drawings?" I asked, concerned.

"How did you know they were burned?"

"I saw some burned cupcakes recently, and they reminded me of the ones you drew. I just can't figure out what it means. Do you have any thoughts about it?"

"I see things, sometimes, that's all," Selena's tone was defensive, and a blush stained her cheeks. "I don't know what they mean, but I feel like I want to draw them. Like how you smell things, or at least you used to, and the scents tell you things. It's not like I'm weird, at least no weirder than you are."

Selena turned away and ducked out of the changing room.

"Selena, wait." I followed after her, wrestling with the wedding dress, trying to get it to stay on its hanger. "No one said you were weird."

The shop phone rang, and Bronwyn answered.

I watched as Selena disappeared into the back room, clearly unwilling to talk. For the third time, the wedding dress slipped off the hanger before I could manage to tie it on. I swore under my breath as I picked it up from the floor.

"Patience, Lily," said Bronwyn.

"I'm trying, believe me. But I'm so frustrated by—"

"No, no," Bronwyn said with a laugh. "I meant the phone is for you. It's Patience."

"Oh, right. Thanks."

"I made an appointment with Juna at eleven," said Patience when I answered the phone. "Pick me up in half an hour. And bring your credit card, 'cause Juna's not cheap."

When I first arrived in San Francisco, I assumed the neighborhood known as Russian Hill would be home to a lot of Russians. While that may have been true at one time, these days "Little Russia" referred to an area of the Inner Richmond, along Geary, where Russian restaurants and bakeries flourished. There was an occasional sign in Cyrillic, and a higher-than-average number of hunched, scarf-wearing elderly women making their way along the sidewalks. But the neighborhood's most obvious cultural marker was the spectacular Russian Orthodox Holy Virgin Cathedral, also called Joy of All Who Sorrow. Its onion-shaped domes were covered in gold metallic tiles, and tall mosaics of saints adorned the cathedral's facade.

Geary is a busy commercial boulevard, but the narrower side streets are lined with stucco row houses. We parked on Twenty-seventh Avenue and walked around the corner, where Patience paused in front of the cathedral's open doors.

"Do you mind if I go in, just for a minute?" Patience asked.

"Of course not," I said. We stepped into the hallowed space. The ambience was hushed inside, with a few solitary worshippers in the pews. Patience walked toward the front. I lingered near the entrance, taking in the colorful murals and the elaborately carved, gold-leafed woodwork.

In general, witches had a fraught history with traditional churches; my own personal experiences hadn't been particularly positive, either. On the other hand, some of the best people I knew were believers. People of faith had accomplished some amazing—some might even say miraculous—things for the betterment of humanity. I supposed it was like what Patience had said with regard to the Russian psychics; it was best to take people as individuals, rather than as members of a group.

Patience came back to join me, and we walked out the tall doors together.

"My mother never passed a church without lighting a candle for her mother. It used to drive me nuts. Now I find myself doing the same."

"Has your mother passed?"

"Car crash on my sixteenth birthday."

"I'm so sorry."

"Sailor didn't tell you? My mother was with Sailor's mother; they both died. That's why Renna stepped in, tried her best to be our mom. But Sailor . . . he's complicated. He distanced himself from the Rom for a while and has only recently come back into the fold. And even then . . ." She trailed off with a shrug, and pressed her lips together.

This was the first time I had heard about the death of Sailor's mother. Once again, I realized how many things he and I should probably talk about before we actually tied the knot. Presuming I could figure out how to prove his innocence.

"Did Renna say anything about Sailor's situation?" I asked. "Any ideas how to get him out?"

"She's working it on her end. She keeps 'seeing' Sailor at the crime scene, just like I did, though she thinks he looks short."

"What does she mean, he looks short?"

"She says the 'Sailor' she sees in her visions is too short. And he uses his left hand."

"Carlos mentioned this guy appeared to be left-handed as well."

"I thought maybe it was just symbolic," Patience said. "For you guys, left-handed means evil, right? Although that hardly seems fair."

"Sometimes we refer to the 'left-handed' way when we speak of negative magic, it's true. I think that's based on some outmoded beliefs that it was somehow unnatural to be left-handed."

Patience nodded. "That's what I figured. Anyway, I

told Renna to lay off the lawyer. Also, she's lining up family to stand behind Aidan for whatever showdown is coming, for what that's worth."

"Did she see anything with regard to Renee?"

"Black cupcakes? Something about a rain of blood . . . basically, not good things. Anyway." She gestured to a nail salon, and I noticed she still wore my engagement ring on her finger. "Over there is where Juna's grandmother, and then her mother, used to run their famous Russian bakery. Blintzes and pierogis to die for. Now it's for pedicures—how depressing is that?"

"Could I . . . Do you still need my ring?"

"What?"

"My engagement ring?"

"Oh. Oh, right." She took it off and handed it to me. "I couldn't see any more than I had before. I mean, I saw cupcakes, but that's not helpful. Sorry."

"Worth a shot," I said as I slipped the ring on my finger. I let out a sigh. It felt good to have it back. "Thanks for trying."

She shrugged. "Juna's place is right down here, in the back of the jeweler's shop."

I couldn't help thinking of Selena as I walked through the store. Though most of their jewelry was gold, there was one whole section of silver necklaces, rings, and brooches arranged on a black velvet cloth, twinkling under the bright lights of the display.

Also on display were a number of watches, some antique, others new and shiny. One pocket watch made me think: Why had the doppelgänger stopped to check his watch? Apparently he'd done so when walking out of the hotel, after assaulting Dupree, which seemed like odd behavior for a murderer fleeing the scene of a crime. Had he paused simply to give witnesses a chance to see him, the better to finger Sailor? If not, why would he be so concerned about the time?

I followed Patience down a narrow hallway to the back of the building. She rapped on a plain wooden door, then walked in without awaiting a reply.

I don't know what I'd been expecting from a Russian psychic's office, but it wasn't this. Patience's fortune-telling business was located in an old Victorian, with the mystical accoutrements one might expect of such an establishment. But then, given the way Patience dressed, I supposed that was no surprise.

Juna's place, in contrast, was about as romantic and otherworldly as an accountant's office. There were two file drawers in one corner, a messy desk in front of a small window that looked out onto an alley, a crowded bookshelf, and one plain round oak table with four chairs.

"Thank you for meeting with us," Patience said. "Juna, this is Lily Ivory. Lily, Juna."

Juna was tall and thin. She wore an expensive-looking navy pantsuit and her dark hair framed a rather severe face that would have been at home on a runway model: sunken cheeks and deep-set eyes, more chic than pretty.

"Please, have a seat." She gestured to the table. "So. You want to know about a man named Jamie," she said without further niceties. She spoke with an almost imperceptible Russian accent, the kind of slight lilt one might have if raised in the US by Russian-speaking immigrants. "No last name?"

"No, sorry."

She brought out a stack of cards and started to handle them, mixing and cutting. They weren't a traditional tarot deck, nor were they regular playing cards. They had Cyrillic symbols and Byzantine drawings, reminiscent of the cathedral walls.

"Actually, I didn't come for a reading," I clarified. "I was just hoping you might know him, or perhaps you've heard about him from the talk around the neighborhood."

Her elegant eyebrows rose and she looked down her patrician nose at me. "You're paying for the hour. You're certain you don't want a reading? I'm quite good."

Patience let out a small bark of a laugh. "This one's a special case, Juna. Take my word for it. You don't want to read for her."

"The price is the same."

"I understand," I said. "Really, all I want is information. Have you heard of Jamie?"

"Of course," she said, setting the deck of cards aside. "He used to run a few of the psychics with the carnival, did tourist scams, that sort of thing."

"He wasn't associated with you?"

"Please," she said with a snort. "Jamie didn't deal with *real* psychics. I mean, I knew a couple of his girls, and one or two might get lucky occasionally, but that's about it. Then he screwed up—not sure what happened, but he became indebted to a woman. . . ."

"Renee Baker," I said.

"I don't know her name, but she's bad news."

"They're all politicians," Patience said. "You can't trust politicians."

"Do you know her?" I asked.

"No. But I have heard rumors. . . . She shouldn't be crossed. She's got people paying for protection now. Jamie makes the collections."

"And if you don't pay?"

"People have gone missing."

"We're talking about the cupcake lady?" Patience asked, clearly unconvinced. "Seriously?"

Juna made a face. "Everybody loves cupcakes. Good cover."

"That's what I thought," I said. "So, Renee is extorting people and Jamie does the collections. Is that right?"

"If people don't pay, he threatens that his boss will place a *domovoi* in your store—that's like a poltergeist—or maybe give your name to the Rusalka."

"Rusalka?"

"She's a water demon. Lures people to their watery deaths."

That reminded me of *La Llorona*, a water demon I'd dealt with not long after I had arrived in San Francisco. It seemed a lifetime ago. I blew out a frustrated breath. None of this told me anything helpful.

"Witches, spirits, demons. They're what we call unclean forces," Juna continued. "Generally bad news. We tend to be a very superstitious people, especially the newcomers or the country people. The crossroads, thresholds, that sort of thing, can be zones of danger. It probably has more to do with the insecurity of an immigrant population than anything else, but Jamie knows how to exploit such fears. To tell you the truth, I sort of feel bad for the guy. He used to run a racket, but he was always pretty nice about it. More of a player, a fast talker. Not a leg breaker, like you see in the movies. Jamie's strictly small-time. He seems almost embarrassed to threaten people."

"So he's not responsible for the 'disappearances'?" I asked.

"I wouldn't think so. But then again, I hardly know him. The only time I really interacted with him was when he was looking for *Lepisma saccharina*."

"What's that?"

"I really don't know. Some sort of sweetener? I sent him to the little grocery on the corner; they have a lot of Russian specialties. Anyway, he wanted that, and the recipe for my grandmother's famous meat-and-mushroom pasties."

"Did you give it to him?"

She nodded. "A man who has an in with the Rusalka

gets what he wants." A cat-and-the-canary smile lit her face. "But you know, my grandmother always left something out of her recipes. The secret ingredient was just that, secret. That way no one could ever copy her. Not even I know it."

I felt a quick shiver of premonition and glanced at the little window over the desk just as a bird hit the glass with a loud *thump*.

Juna jumped out of her chair, eyes wide, and crossed herself.

"Death," she said in a fierce whisper, then pointed at me. "That is a harbinger of death! You have brought death to this place. Unclean forces! You must leave, *now*."

"Gotta hand it to you, Lily Ivory," Patience said as we were unceremoniously escorted through the jewelry store and out onto the sidewalk. Juna slammed the door behind us, and threw the lock with a clank. "You do have a way with strangers."

I ignored her. "I think we can access the alley over here."

"Why on earth . . . ?"

"Poor little bird. I want to see if it's okay."

She snorted, crossed her arms, and told me she'd wait for me. I edged along the side of the building to the back. But there was no sign of the bird on the ground, and no blood or other obvious signs of trauma on the window. As I was looking around, Juna spotted me through the glass, made some sort of hand gesture, and then spit three times over her left shoulder.

I didn't have to be up on Russian culture to know what that meant. Juna was spitting on the devil.

"It's not there," I said as I rejoined Patience, who lingered in front of the store. "It must have flown away."

"Oh, what a relief," she said in a voice dripping with

sarcasm as we started down the block. "And here I was, about to call in the animal rescue squad."

"I'm guessing you didn't tell Juna I'm a witch."

"I may have neglected to mention it. She doesn't care for witches."

"Because we're 'unclean'?"

Patience shrugged. "It's a cultural thing. Not like you haven't been called worse, I'm guessing."

"True. Let's stop in at the grocery and ask about the leprous saccharine, or whatever it was."

"*Lepisma saccharina*. Best be quick about it, before Juna makes a phone call."

The cramped grocery offered the usual corner store staples: a lot of cheap American beer, small liquor bottles, potato chips, candy bars, and Slim Jims. But one aisle boasted several items labeled with Cyrillic script. Up by the register homemade pickles floated in a five-gallon container, and a refrigerated display case held an impressive selection of sausages and headcheese.

A very old man stood behind the counter, silent and watching.

"Hello," I said. "Juna sent us. Might you have any *Lepisma saccharina*?"

I tripped over the pronunciation, and the man frowned and shook his head.

I tried again. "I might not be pronouncing it right. *Lepisma saccharina*. I think it's a sweetener of some kind?"

"I have no bugs here!" He spoke with a heavy Russian accent. "My place is clean. I keep my store very clean! What are you saying? Nasty woman! You get out!"

Patience and I scooted outside, and I heard her low chuckle as we hurried toward the car. "O for two, Lily. In less than twenty minutes. Is that a personal best, you nasty woman?"

"I don't understand what just happened. What did I do?"

"Maybe you need a course or two in cultural sensitivity before you think about coming back to Little Russia. Otherwise somebody might put something funny in your pierogis."

"It wasn't my fault a bird hit the window," I said, feeling defensive.

"What about the poor little man in the corner grocery?"

"I have no idea what *that* was about. Either I horribly mispronounced something, or Juna called him and told him I was 'unclean,' maybe?"

"So, you have no idea what that saccharine was? Or why it matters?"

"Not really. I thought it might tell us something pertinent. But it's a bust, like everything else."

"Well, as much as I've enjoyed watching you make an ass of yourself, I have things to do. Drop me off at my place?"

"Sure. The Nasty Woman Express is at your service."

Chapter 24

I found Conrad sitting on the curb outside Aunt Cora's Closet, as was his wont.

"Dudette!" he said when I approached. "You still need my help tomorrow? Want me to bring a coupla friends? Will work for food, as they say."

"Yes, please, we'll need help. I'm more than happy to provide breakfast and lunch for anyone who puts in a couple of hours."

"You're on, dude," Conrad said.

Tomorrow we intended to virtually empty Aunt Cora's Closet to make room for the Magical Match Tea. Hard to believe we were going through with the event with Sailor still behind bars and an unsolved murder on my plate, but canceling it wouldn't achieve anything more than frustrating our friends and disappointing the Haight Street shelter, which needed the funds to help women facing much more difficult lives than mine.

Besides, Renee had promised—or threatened—to show up to the tea. I had no idea what to expect from that, but I certainly wanted to be here when she did.

I couldn't put an impenetrable protection spell over the store, or it would keep out all our visitors. But that didn't mean I couldn't take precautions. I would have to brew. And . . . possibly approach Aidan, one more time. Surely there was something—or someone—else I could appease him with? What about Jamie? He *wanted* to work for Aidan.

Conrad followed me inside Aunt Cora's Closet. Bronwyn was consulting with a customer, her wildflower-crowned head bent low as she concocted a custom tea blend at her herb stand. Duke sat on a velvet bench near the dressing rooms, reading a thick novel. Maya was straightening several brightly colored prom dresses, circa 1980, while half a dozen customers roamed the crowded aisles.

After trading greetings and making sure everyone was still on for our big move tomorrow, I asked Maya: "Did you get any hits on that drawing?"

"Unfortunately, there wasn't anything that matched one hundred percent." She called a file up on the computer. "But you said to keep in mind that it might not be complete, so these are some of the signs that looked similar."

I studied the computer screen, which showed thumbnails of several signs that did seem similar, though none was exact.

"What do they mean?" I asked.

"Depends on which one you're referring to. They're all over the map. This one's an ancient Hebrew sign for water; this one's a petroglyph. This one here"—she clicked on the thumbnail to make the picture larger—"is from the Da Pinchi Code that Conrad mentioned, and it actually looks pretty close. But the interesting thing is that it seems to be based on a much older sign. I'm still trying to track down its origins, though."

"Thanks so much for looking."

"You're welcome. It's sort of fun, like a treasure hunt."

I smiled. "I never think of anything computer-related as 'fun,' but I'm glad *you* do. Hey, could you look up something else for me while you're on the Internet? I think it's Latin, and it's probably an ingredient for baked goods, or a sweetener of some kind. *Lepisma saccharina.*"

"Spell it for me?"

"I'm not completely sure, but *L-e—*"

"*Dude*, what kind of baked goods are you eating?" interrupted Conrad, who had been playing with a heap of colorful Mardi Gras beads.

"What do you mean?"

"That means silverfish."

"Silverfish?" I asked. "As in, the bug?"

He nodded. "*Lepisma saccharina* is the Latin name for silverfish."

"I didn't know you knew Latin," Maya said.

"I don't. I know *bugs*, dude."

"So then it's not an ingredient for baked goods," said Maya, looking it up online. "At least, I sincerely hope not. Yep, the Con's right, as usual: *Lepisma saccharina*, commonly known as 'silverfish.'"

So Jamie had been asking around the Russian psychics for silverfish? That made no sense at all, of course, but there had to be a connection to the bugs in the shoe box.

I felt lost. Whom could I talk to about this? I glanced at the map: The grandmas were in Sacramento. If they were completing this same sign, and it looked like they were, they'd be headed somewhere north next: maybe to Napa for a little wine tasting. Aidan wasn't going to be much help if he kept demanding I turn over Oscar or Sailor; I would save him as a last resort. But there was another wise woman out there, someone I had, perhaps, underestimated.

I knew Calypso Cafaro had a magical way with plants, but according to Aidan, she was more than that. She "used to be" a witch. In my book, once a witch, always a witch.

What's more, she also used to be in charge of the Bay Area's magical community. She had had Aidan's job.

Determined to speak with her, I asked Maya and Bronwyn to stay and close up shop, and made sure Conrad and Duke would keep them company. Then I ran upstairs and managed to corral one of the silverfish from the box into a jar, rewrapped the shoe box in rowan, and returned it to its place on the shelf. Next I jumped in my car, stopped by the wax museum to pick up my pig, then headed north across the Golden Gate Bridge.

"I take it you're feeling better?" I asked my familiar in greeting.

Oscar—or Aidan?—had anticipated my arrival and he'd been waiting with the highly disgruntled Clarinda at the front ticket office. He remained in piggy form until we exited the thick traffic of the Golden Gate Bridge and Highway 101. Now we were winding through the hills, with no witnesses to notice Oscar's true form.

"Hey, mistress, you know when I'm going to do *that* again?"

"Never, I sincerely hope."

"When pigs fly," he said, slapping his knee and cackling. "Get it? 'Cause I was high, like flying?"

"Very funny. Seriously, Oscar, you scared me. What were you thinking, going into the Dumpster for something I told you not to eat?"

"They were *cupcakes*," he said, as though that explained everything.

As we neared Bolinas, it occurred to me that a normal person might have called ahead to warn Calypso that she was coming, or to make sure it was a good time. But in the past, Calypso had always known I was arriving. Whether she was psychic, or someone informed on me, I had no way of knowing.

I turned off the main highway, into a long drive that was virtually invisible unless you knew to look for it. A massive hedge leaned so far in on both sides that it was difficult to pass, the branches scraping the sides of the car as I squeezed through. I cringed, thinking of the Mustang's cherry red paint job, but forced myself to stay focused on the important things. After all, paint jobs could be reapplied.

I had only one fiancé, and there was only one San Francisco.

Beyond the hedge was a clearing, backed by a redwood forest. An old butter yellow farmhouse was fronted by a deep porch filled with white wicker furniture and colorful flowering pots. A calico cat was curled up on a porch swing, while a tabby lingered on a windowsill. A vast vegetable garden sat out back, and a greenhouse was attached to the rear. The little brick walkway leading to the front door was lined with rose trees, and everywhere one looked, plants were in abundant bloom.

"It looks like a picture in a calendar," said Oscar, a note of awe in his gravelly voice.

"That's what I think every time I see it."

"It's pretty early in the season for peaches, isn't it?" asked Oscar.

"Things bloom on a different schedule in Calypso's world."

"That's some powerful plant magic."

"She's a whiz at everything botanical," I said, glancing over at the copse of redwood trees that edged the back garden. My heart fluttered. I had imagined my handfasting with Sailor taking place right there, at the edge of the woods, to invite the blessings of the fairy folk. Soon Graciela's coven would be here, filling the house with laughter and wisewoman energy. Or . . . would those things happen, after all? I knew it was dangerous to anticipate something so fervently.

Be careful what you ask for, my grandmother had always told me. *The spirit world might become jealous; it's best to let the world unfold at your feet, as it will.*

The first time I visited Calypso's home, I had felt conflicting feelings: On the one hand, it was gorgeous. A fantasy setting, a fantasy farmhouse, a fantasy garden. On the other . . . Calypso was a virtual recluse. By choice, of course. But it made me realize that, after years of wandering alone, I wanted something different for myself: I didn't want to be a solo act anymore. I wanted friends nearby. I wanted a family. And most of all, I wanted Sailor by my side.

As she had in the past, Calypso seemed to have sensed our arrival and met us at the door, wearing a bright blue tunic with deep pockets over flowered leggings, a jaunty scarf tied around her neck. Her silver hair was braided, the heavy plait hanging over one shoulder.

"Lily, what a lovely surprise. And Oscar, too!" she said as Oscar and I got out of the car. Even though Calypso knew Oscar was a magical creature, he didn't show her his true form but adopted his porcine guise. "Welcome. Have you heard anything from your grandmother's coven?"

"Not recently. But I don't think they'll be here for another day or two. In fact, that's one of the things I wanted to talk to you about."

"Of course. Please come in and we'll have tea and talk."

Oscar trotted out toward the woods.

"He loves the redwoods," I said.

"Don't we all."

Calypso's huge kitchen was warm and welcoming.

Bundles of drying herbs hung from the rafters, filling the air with the heady aroma of sage, rosemary, and oregano. Rustic shelves held old crockery and wide-mouthed mason jars full of spices and powders. A variety of kitchen utensils hung from pegs on the beadboard wainscoting; there were a number of mortars and pestles, electric grinders, and drying racks on shelves. Some of these might have been used for cooking, but most were for the processing of herbs. Calypso ran a profitable business selling herbs, fruit, and vegetables to Bay Area restaurants that were able to boast they used only "organic, locally sourced" ingredients.

Out of the corner of my eye, I saw something scamper by. It was too big for a mouse, and didn't have the shape of a cat. But it moved too fast for me to get a good look at it.

Calypso put a huge copper kettle on to boil, and I took a seat at the big pine farmhouse table. Leafy green plants hung in baskets in the sunny bay window, and African violets crowded the windowsill.

"Calypso, what are silverfish used for?"

"What do you mean?"

"Are they an ingredient in anything?"

"Silverfish? The insects?" She made a face. "They weren't in that suspected Tiberius Caesar spell you were asking me about, were they?"

"No. At least, I certainly hope not. They're a little creepy."

"A lot creepy. The only insects I really like are the roly-polies. Remember them?"

"I do. We had fireflies back home. I loved those."

"Butterflies are amazing, of course, and moths, too. And bees, and ladybugs. But I don't enjoy a lot of the crawlers."

"I agree. So you don't know of any use for silverfish? Could they be symbolic of something, maybe?"

She shook her head. "I can't think of anything. But . . . Selena has silver magic, doesn't she?"

"She does. That had never occurred to me. Do you think it's connected?"

"I have no idea, Lily," she replied. "You haven't given me any context, or told me what's going on."

"Sorry. You're right, of course. If only I *knew* what was going on."

I gave her the story in brief: about Sailor being in jail and Tristan's death and the contents of the shoe box. About the grandmas making a sign with their wandering travels, and Sailor's doppelgänger.

"Aidan says doppelgängers can be a harbinger of imminent death," I said, a catch in my voice. I hadn't realized how upset I was, how close to breaking down. Calypso wasn't motherly, exactly, but I had been yearning for the opportunity to speak to a wise woman.

"I've always heard that as well," Calypso said in a steady voice. I noticed that a couple of tendrils from the plants behind her seemed to edge closer to her, as though reaching out. This was how plants responded to Calypso. "But you really don't know that this look-alike *is* a doppelgänger, after all. That's not the only possibility."

"True." I knew she was right. But I had been feeling negative lately. I sneezed.

"Are you feeling all right?"

"I think I'm coming down with a cold." For some reason I didn't want her to know I might have fallen victim to Renee's spell. It made me feel foolish. I also held back from asking her if she thought I'd offended my guiding spirit, the Ashen Witch. I trusted her . . . but perhaps not entirely. When it came right down to it, I didn't know Calypso that well.

"I'm sure that's unusual for you."

"It is. How could you tell?"

She simply smiled. Her smile was knowing, reassuring . . . and yet a teensy bit annoying. I wished I knew what she was thinking, how she knew the things she knew. Was she psychic, or simply wise and intuitive?

Calypso got up, turned to a bookshelf stuffed with books, old and new, and files with clippings. She searched for a moment, then brought down a thick tome whose leather binding was so old it was slightly crumbly. She set it on the table and I read the title: *Royal Entomological Society: A Treatise on Taxonomic Specifications*.

"I used this long ago to develop my natural pest-control system in the garden. I'm sure you know I shy away from pesticides. Let's see. . . . 'The silverfish is small and wingless; largely harmless, it does not sting or bite. The common name is derived from the insect's blue-gray color and sinewy ways of moving. The scientific name, *L. saccharina*, indicates the silverfish's exclusive diet of sugars and starches.'"

"Ah, that explains something," I said. "I thought *saccharina* referred to the sugar substitute. But . . . could it be used as an ingredient in something?"

"That kind of information won't be in here. Let's see what else I've got. . . ." She trailed off as she searched the bookshelves. She pulled out one volume, then another, shook her head, and put them back. "I don't see any symbology associated with it or any recipes. I take it you've already checked your Book of Shadows?"

I nodded, joining her at the bookcase and studying the spines. Her collection was almost as fascinating and arcane as Aidan's. "It didn't say anything at all."

"Perhaps we're thinking too specifically. Maybe it's simply indicative of an insect."

"But there are silverfish in the shoe box."

"Only in the box?"

"I've never seen them elsewhere. They appear to be contained."

She met my eyes and our gaze held for so long I became hyperaware of the sound of the ticking clock. I heard a soft cat's meow, a bird's faraway call. I noticed the African violets turning their faces toward her. Finally, she nodded.

"I'm not psychic, Lily. I have my magical moments, but they have to do with plants, nothing more."

"But it was more before, wasn't it? Aidan told me that you used to be in charge around here."

She shrugged it off. "'In charge' makes it sound much more official than it actually was. You've been in San Francisco long enough to know there are a lot of disparate personalities, and yet sometimes the community needs to band together. Especially when going up against outside threats."

"What kind of threat were you facing when Aidan arrived?"

A profound sadness came into her eyes. She crossed the room to stand near the plants, checking their soil for moisture, snipping off a few dead leaves. "It was . . . it was difficult. A challenger came under the influence of the wrong elements. She called on a demon to act as her *coincidentia oppositorum*."

"That sounds like a really bad idea."

"It was. It made her witchcraft incredibly potent, but she was willing to do just about anything to gain power."

"What happened to her?"

"She departed, to the spirit world."

"How?"

"Aidan killed her."

Chapter 25

"Aidan did *what*?"

"He did it to save my life. I begged him not to, to let her live. I never wanted to be saddled with the guilt of anyone's death, to trade my life for another. But Aidan said he did it for everyone's good, that more than just my life was at stake."

I sat silent, stunned by what she had said.

"I never wanted that legacy," she continued, angry now. "Aidan wouldn't listen; as usual he did what he thought best. He's ruthless. Not uncaring, but ruthless."

"But if he loved you, of course he did what was necessary to save your life."

"Who said he loved me?"

I remembered seeing a photo of the two of them on her mantel. It had been taken many years ago; Calypso looked much younger in the photo than she did now, while Aidan looked exactly the same. But what had struck me was the expression on his face: open and guileless, an easy smile. In all the time I'd known him,

I had never seen him smile like that, or seem so relaxed and natural.

"I know you two were once together, so I assumed . . ."

"People can be together without being in love," she said, her tone bitter and dismissive. The tabby seemed to sense her discomfort and leapt into her lap. She caressed him, and calmed. "Anyway, I'd rather not talk about this anymore."

"Could I just ask you—how does the *coincidentia oppositorum* work, exactly? I thought it involved a man and a woman, but you say a demon could be the other half . . . ?"

"It's all about balance. Traditionally it was a man and a woman, but as you know, gender is fluid. As are so many other things. People interpret the world differently these days."

"Interesting. I . . . Well, Aidan says my relationship to Sailor makes me vulnerable."

Calypso didn't answer immediately. Her hands slowly stroked the cat in her lap. He purred so loudly I could hear him from where I sat.

Finally, she let out a sigh. "In a sense, any relationship makes us vulnerable, don't you think? I've always thought that was at the core of our strength as magical women, to allow ourselves vulnerability. It certainly does make things more complicated, however. If Aidan feels he must stand alone, that is his choice. It doesn't have to be yours."

Something skittered past again. Low to the floor, but not a cat.

"What was that?" I asked. "Did you see something run by?"

"That's Finnall," said Calypso.

"What's a Finnall?"

She gave a soft, low laugh. “That’s his name. He’s my mandragora. Aidan made him for me.”

I opened my mouth to inform her that I had made it, but decided against it.

“Do you know mandragoras?” Calypso continued. “They’re a kind of household imp. They can be very useful in sussing out poisons, rotten fruit, that sort of thing. Finnall is priceless in my produce business. And he keeps me company.”

“Where did he go?”

“He’s sitting on the shelf,” she whispered, gesturing with her head. “He’s shy.”

I glanced at the bookshelf and there he sat, legs entwined primly. He looked like a little carved doll. No one would assume he was anything more.

I was happy to think Finnall kept Calypso company, but was suspicious enough of Aidan to wonder if he had an ulterior motive in giving Calypso the mandragora, especially since he had claimed to have made it himself. Could Finnall be acting as a spy of some kind, as I had long suspected Oscar of doing?

“Now that I think about it,” said Calypso, “Finnall might be of help with this. I don’t suppose you brought one of the silverfish from the box?”

“I happen to have one right here,” I said as I extracted the small jam jar from my backpack. “Do you think it’s safe?”

“Safe? That’s a tough one. I’m not overly worried, though. Also, we’ll need an image of Sailor, or some item of his,” Calypso continued as she gathered, then began grinding dried leaves and seeds in a massive marble mortar and pestle.

“Why do we need something of Sailor’s?”

“Isn’t he what all this fuss is about, at the end of the day?”

I took the small photo of Sailor out of my wallet and set it on the counter.

Calypso continued mashing herbs and pods together, then added club moss from the redwood forest.

"I didn't know you brewed," I said as I watched, fascinated. Most practitioners weren't so transparent about their methods.

"I don't brew, per se," said Calypso. "But I do mix."

I didn't see the mandragora move, but suddenly he was sitting near the mortar and pestle, the photo of Sailor in his lap.

In one smooth motion she opened the jar, scooped up the silverfish, and tossed it into the mortar and started to smash it with the stone pestle.

Sparks flew, as though the creature were actually made of silver. Apparently, this particular silverfish wasn't easy to kill. Then Calypso showed a side of herself I hadn't seen before: She attacked the silverfish with a fierce expression on her face, her hair escaping her braid and flying wild around her, all the plants and flowers in the room turning their faces toward the action. She reminded me of the medieval woodcuts that showed wild-eyed women, hair unbound, brewing or dancing or calling to the devil.

"Do you smell that?" Calypso asked, grimacing.

I tried to inhale. "I can't really smell much lately."

"Smells like something burning."

Again, I saw something scamper just out of my field of vision. I turned just in time to see a man run out of the room.

It felt like a bucket of ice water had been poured over me. I stood in shock, paralyzed over what I had just seen.

Sailor's doppelgänger?

Finally I regained the use of my limbs and ran after the man.

By the time I turned the corner into the next room, it was empty. All I saw was the mandragora sitting on the floor.

Oscar came barreling in the room from outside in his fierce, natural guise. "Mistress! Are you okay? I got the strangest feeling."

"Thanks, Oscar. I'm fine."

He looked at the mandragora and grimaced. "Oh, hey, I remember that guy. I don't like him."

"His name's Finnall. He belongs to Calypso now."

Oscar poked at Finnall with his muzzle. "Why's he just sitting there? What, is he playing dead?"

"I think he's shy."

I picked him up and brought him back into the other room, where Calypso waited. Oscar transformed into his pig form, and followed me.

"What's going on here?" I demanded.

"Did you see Sailor?" Calypso asked.

"Yes."

"It's the silverfish. I heard of this charm, long ago. It didn't occur to me before because it doesn't require silverfish per se, but will work with any insect or sea creature with an exoskeleton. Something about their outer shells . . . They can be enchanted, and then used to throw powerful glamours."

"Like the one Aidan maintains?"

She nodded.

"So I have a shoe box full of magical silverfish," I said. "Will wonders never cease?"

"Unassuming creatures—like household pests—are perfect hosts for this sort of glamour charm."

I remembered Aidan mentioning that Tristan Dupree's mother was gifted at glamour charms. And *Silber* was German for silver; maybe when Tristan's spirit spoke through Hervé in the hotel room, he was mentioning his silverfish. So I had "stolen" not only my lachrymatory from him but also a box full of his mother's silverfish glamour charms. I may have suppressed the memories of that time, but I felt a little thrill of pride. Apparently I'd been quite the resourceful teenager.

"I've never thrown glamours," I told Calypso. "I mean, I've done minor masking brews, things like that, to make others less likely to notice something like a pimple. But not full-on glamours like your mandragora just did: making myself look like someone else entirely. How does that work?"

"If one has the skills, the possibilities are endless."

"It would be difficult to maintain a glamour for long, wouldn't it? How does Aidan do it?"

"It takes an enormous amount of strength to maintain a glamour as Aidan does, day in, day out. But in the case of this fake Sailor, one would only need to maintain the guise for a few minutes at a time. Walking through the hotel lobby, or at the bottom of the stairwell. Wouldn't take that much, especially when the onlookers are scared. When people are afraid, they tend not to notice details."

"And it's helpful to have an object belonging to the person you are trying to look like?" I asked. "That makes sense."

"As you know, our possessions sometimes carry traces of our energy. Especially something that means a lot to us."

I thought of how it felt to see my engagement ring on Patience's finger. I hoped I could trust her. As with Calypso, I *thought* I could. But I wasn't entirely sure. The story of my life.

"You know who has a surprising expertise in glamours?" asked Calypso as she cleaned her mortar and pestle, rubbing it with salts and olive oil.

"Who?"

"Your friend Wind Spirit."

"You mean, the witch who used to be called Amy? From the Welcome coven?"

"Yes. She came to talk to me a couple of weeks ago, and she noticed the moss and mentioned using it in glamour spells."

"How did you meet her?"

"Bronwyn gave her my name and suggested she speak to me directly. Wind Spirit's been interested in developing a small agricultural business, but doesn't have any garden space. She said her landlord agreed to let her use the basement, which is mostly dirt."

"What can she grow in a basement?"

"Not much," Calypso said with a laugh. "But the girl's quite determined."

"I've heard white asparagus is grown in the dark."

"That's not a bad idea, but that's not what she cultivated."

"What was she growing?"

"Mushrooms."

My car was alone on Highway 1 as we headed down the twisty route back to San Francisco, so Oscar sat in his natural form in the passenger seat, gazing out at the view. It was bucolic and spectacular: redwood and fern-filled glens, deer and wild turkeys.

Not that I noticed. I was a mite distracted.

"Maybe Renee was telling the truth," I said. "Maybe she's not responsible for any of this. What if Wind Spirit wants to work with Renee? I thought the *coincidentia oppositorum* had to be a male and female, but according to Calypso, that's not true. Gender's fluid, after all—I remember Wind Spirit saying that once herself! So maybe Wind Spirit is making a play for power. Maybe she knew Tristan had come to town to work with Renee, and wanted to stop him."

"So she could take his place and rule with Renee?" Oscar asked.

"Exactly."

"But she's a girl. Tristan was a big guy. How'd she beat him up?"

"According to Carlos, Tristan was already sick by then, so it's likely he was in a weakened state. And Wind Spirit is stronger than she looks. She has a black belt in some form of martial art; Bronwyn mentioned Wind Spirit was all muscle under those baby-doll dresses she always wears," I said, starting to weave the threads together. "The fake Sailor kept checking a watch—maybe the clock was ticking on how long Wind Spirit could sustain the glamour. Also, Patience said Renna thought the fake Sailor looked short. Maybe Wind Spirit couldn't get the glamour quite right. I wonder if she's left-handed. . . ."

"All these people trading places with other people." Oscar shook his head. "It's a downright shame, is what it is."

"Hey!" I said so loudly that Oscar jumped. "Sorry. But it just occurred to me: You're a shape-shifter."

"Yeaaaah . . . ?"

"Is that anything like a glamour?"

"What are you talking about?"

"When you're in your piggy guise, is it a glamour of some sort?"

"Like you just said, I'm a shape-shifter."

"So it's not the same thing?"

He started snickering, then cackled loudly as tears of mirth ran down his scaly cheeks.

"You absolutely *slay* me when you say things like that!"

I blew out a frustrated breath and sat back in my seat. One of these days I was going to lock myself in Aidan's office and read every tome in his library, and then I would go to Calypso's house and read every book in *her* library, and then I would know things. All the things. What was real and what was not, what was merely magical, and what was impossible.

Even so, not everything I wanted to know would be found within books. Probably I needed another decade or two of instruction with Graciela's coven. Imagine what I could learn, how powerful I could become. . . .

I wrenched myself out of that daydream as we reached the Golden Gate Bridge. That sort of thinking was dangerous. Just as the wild, savage ocean met the serene bay under this bridge, the wide-open world of magic could entice a person to explore too far. Where currents became irresistible, and the force of the tides might drag a person out to parts unknown, drowning her in the process.

Then again, I was a witch. Last time someone attempted to drown me, I popped up like a cork.

Witches don't sink.

Aunt Cora's Closet was closed up tight by the time we got back to the city, though Haight Street was hopping as usual on a Friday night. A thick layer of fog had rolled in off the ocean, blanketing the streets and sidewalks and lending a spooky atmosphere to the neighborhood. I kept thinking of that parrot, so long ago, telling me to go to San Francisco, but to "mark the fog."

An inebriated couple sang "Over the Rainbow," loudly and off-key, as they reeled down the sidewalk; I brushed past them and quickly let myself—and Oscar—into the shop. I could hear them crying out, *"Oh my God, a pig!"* as I quickly shut and locked the door, waved without turning around, and scurried into the back room.

I was in no mood for fun this evening.

As we hurried up the stairs, my mind raced. What

should I do with my concerns about Wind Spirit? Should I ask Carlos to check her out? As usual, my suspicions were based on very little substance.

I would call Bronwyn first, I decided. For all I knew, she might have been with Wind Spirit when Tristan was attacked, and could offer her coven sister a hard-and-fast alibi.

"I'm feeling a mite peckish, how 'bout you?" Oscar said as we entered the upstairs apartment. "I thought Calypso was gonna whip up something good in that mortar of hers, but it turned out to be nothing but some crazy-ass glamour magic."

"There's some lasagna in the freezer; why don't you preheat the oven while I make a call?"

Then I went into the bedroom and dialed Bronwyn's number. I explained to her I had reason to suspect Wind Spirit was involved in Tristan's death, and in setting up Sailor.

Bronwyn sounded stunned and stammered, "I—I just can't imagine how that could be true, Lily. I mean, I . . . Wind Spirit is an initiate to the *Welcome* coven. We're all about peace and light."

"I know it's hard to imagine, Bronwyn, but maybe she was just using you, and the coven, to get close to what's going on. Or as cover, so no one discovered her motives."

"I simply can't believe it."

"I know it's hard to wrap your mind around. But sometimes friends aren't all we would want them to be. Of course, I could well be wrong, but if you give me her last name and a phone number, I could ask Carlos to speak with her and see whether or not there's anything to worry about."

"Carlos will speak to her personally?"

"You know he'll be polite, and discreet. It's . . . You're

right—I'm probably wrong. But we have to check this out. Just imagine if I'm right."

"Of course." Bronwyn gave me Amy's last name and phone number. "What will this mean for the Magical Match Tea? She's part of the steering committee!"

I didn't point out that the entire coven was part of the steering committee. "We'll be fine. Oh! See, that's another thing—remember how insistent Wind Spirit was that we should serve Renee Baker's cupcakes at the Magical Match Tea?"

"They really are wonderful cupcakes, Lily. I don't understand why you're so mistrustful."

I realized it was difficult not to fill my friends in on all the goings-on. How best to tell them what I feared about the cupcake lady?

"I have reason not to trust Renee, Bronwyn, and so do you. I can't fill you in on all the details right now, but please believe me when I say she's not what she seems."

"If she concerns you, Lily, that's good enough for me. We can make our own cupcakes, after all!"

"I believe I'm down for three dozen cookies, as a matter of fact."

"Oooh, your special macadamia nut chocolate and butterscotch chip?"

"Of course," I said with a smile. "I've already bought all the ingredients. Oscar and I will whip up a batch right after dinner."

"Wonderful! Oh, by the way, did you pick up your messages? Maya found something she thought might interest you, about that symbol she was researching. She left a note with your mail."

"Thanks, I'll go check it out."

As I hung up, I wondered whether it would be better not to involve Carlos. After all, what could I tell him? That Wind Spirit was stronger than she looked, and that she was fond of cupcakes? I could hear him laughing now. Carlos was far too polite to actually laugh at me, but he'd give me that incredulous look of his, which was even worse. I could mention the mushrooms, I supposed, but that was about the only possible tangible link to Tristan's murder.

Maybe it would be better to talk to Wind Spirit myself at the Magical Match Tea and try to coax her to admit her involvement. I had it on good authority that I could be very persuasive. . . .

While I sat on my bed, pondering, my gaze alighted on the closet door. It was slightly ajar.

I hadn't left it that way.

I *knew* I hadn't left it that way. I might leave dishes in the sink, toss my nightgown in a corner, or let my Keds lie where they fell, but I was a nut about closing drawers and closet doors. It was the result of early training; in Graciela's house, there were things that had to be kept secured behind closed doors.

I surged off the bed, threw the closet door open, and looked for the shoe box.

Gone.

"Did I hear something about whipping up some cookies?" Oscar called out from the other room.

"Oscar." I ran into the living room. "Did you go into my room, or my closet?"

"'Course not. I haven't even been around for the last day, remember? What's wrong?"

"My shoe box is missing."

"The creepy one? No offense, mistress, but no great loss as far as I'm concerned."

"It's important, Oscar. Who could have taken it? Among other things, whoever came in here was able to overcome my protection spells. Think about it that way."

"Good point. See what happens when Oscar isn't on the job? You think I'm just sitting around, but I provide what I like to call 'preventive services.' You sure you didn't leave it somewhere else?"

"I'm absolutely sure." I sneezed once again. Had Renee really cast a befuddling spell over me? And if so, had it dulled my senses enough so that I couldn't call out to the Ashen Witch? Had it diminished my abilities even to cast protection over my store and home?

Unsure where to even start looking for the shoe box, I decided to check out the information Maya had left me.

"Oscar, I'm going down to the shop to get the mail. Want to be my guard pig?"

Oscar's green eyes widened. "You're really that spooked, mistress?"

"Just trying not to act a fool, as my mother used to say. If someone was able to waltz in here and take something from my closet, all bets are off."

"All right, then," Oscar said, puffing out his chest. "Let's go."

We descended the stairs carefully, keeping our eyes and ears peeled. We had rushed through the store earlier, so now I looked for anything that looked out of place. I flicked on the lights in the back room and the store, but everything seemed as serene as ever. Oscar made a big deal about trotting through all the aisles of the shop floor and investigating behind the mannequins.

I was checking behind the register when I noticed Oscar had opened the door to the mini-fridge.

"Pretty sure no one's hiding in there, Oscar," I said.

"You never know," he said with a quick cackle. "In fact—*Wind Spirit*."

"Excuse me?" I went to join him in the back room, and Oscar ran to hide behind my skirts, pointing toward the green linoleum-topped table.

Hiding underneath the table was the witch named Wind Spirit, formerly known as Amy.

Chapter 26

I stroked my medicine bag, assessing the situation. According to Bronwyn, Wind Spirit was a martial arts expert. And if she had been ruthless enough to go after Tristan Dupree, she was more than dangerous—she was homicidal.

Then again, I had Oscar with me. Currently he was cowering behind my skirt, but I'd seen him in action; once Oscar got riled, he was a force to be reckoned with. Still, what if Wind Spirit had a weapon? Her hands were tucked into the pockets of her baby-doll dress, so I couldn't be sure. Even a gobgoyle couldn't fend off a speeding bullet.

"*Wind Spirit.* What are you doing here?" I demanded.

She shook her head, but said nothing.

"Come out from under there, and let's talk," I said, trying to keep my tone steady and as light as possible. "What are you looking for? Did you come for the shoe box?"

She continued to stare. I realized her eyes looked

hollow, as blank as those of the "Sailor" who wasn't actually my fiancé. A shiver ran down my spine.

"Are you . . . are you the doppelgänger?"

She shook her head again and jumped out and up from under the table. Now I was sure. It was Wind Spirit, and yet *not* Wind Spirit. Her face looked like her, but she seemed much smaller than she had before. It was confusing, disorienting to see her like this.

She moved slowly, lurching toward us, her movements jerky, as though her muscles were rusty or out of practice. Oscar and I stumbled back another couple of steps. I could hear my familiar mumbling: "*Gack!* She's like the Mummy!"

Yes, she was creepy, but I thought of what Aidan had said: Maybe the doppelgänger had chased me all over Chinatown because he'd been trying to communicate.

"Amy!" I yelled. I never could get used to her new name. "Stop, and talk to me. Tell us what you want."

And then I remembered the boy in the Chinatown apothecary telling us that the supposed "Sailor" didn't—couldn't?—speak. I grabbed Selena's drawing pad and pencils, and handed them to the "Amy," who was still clumsily moving forward.

As she reached out to take them, I noticed something shiny tinkled on her bracelet. It was the little silver bell charm Amy had given to Selena.

Just then I saw a silverfish scurry past Amy's foot. I followed its path to the old shoe box, sitting open under the table. It crawled inside.

"Selena?" Oscar said.

When I looked up, "Amy" had become Selena. Tears poured down her cheeks, and she was furiously writing on her drawing pad: *I'M SELENA!!!!! DON'T KILL ME!!!!!*

"Selena?" I said, relief warring with anger in my chest. "What in the world . . . ?"

"I'm sorry! I'm sorry! I'm sorry! I just wanted to see what all the fuss was about."

"How did you even know about the box, or where to find it?"

She flipped the pages on her drawing pad to show me a sketch of the box sitting on a shelf in my closet.

"I *told* you, I see things sometimes. I don't know why. It's not like I ask for it. I could tell it was your closet because of the old green suitcase. That's the only place I've ever seen one like that."

"Do you mean to tell me you're running through the streets of San Francisco at this hour, breaking into my shop, and my apartment, and stealing things from my closet?"

She exchanged a guilty glance with Oscar. He shrugged in response, as if to say,"She's got a point."

"When you put it like that, I guess it sounds pretty bad," said Selena, twisting her mouth. "But nobody tells me anything, except for weird things like 'Don't trust Sailor if he comes around,' even though Sailor's supposed to be part of the family. It's confusing."

"That's no excuse, young lady."

"Also, these bugs are silver, and I love silver. But I accidentally stepped on one. He's okay, though. He crawled back into the box."

"And when you stepped on the bug, you changed?"

"I couldn't talk, and I felt funny, and you started calling me Amy, and then I saw my reflection in the chrome of the table leg, and then I sort of freaked out. It wasn't *me*."

I blew out a long breath. Now that my heartbeat was returning to normal, relief was winning out over anger. In fact, the situation was starting to feel pretty funny. But still. I was the grown-up.

"Does your grandmother know where you are?"

"I told her I was sleeping over here so I could help you move things tomorrow."

"Let me see the charm Wind Spirit gave to you."

She held out her slender wrist, and I clasped the charm and tried to feel for vibrations. Nothing felt off, or strange. Probably it was pure chance that Selena had taken Amy's image for a moment, since she was wearing something that had once belonged to Wind Spirit.

"All right, let's go upstairs and get some dinner. But this isn't the end of this. I'm going to give your grandmother a call and we're going to talk about you lying, and stealing, and sneaking out at night—you hear me?"

She nodded, eyes downcast. I noticed a small smile on her face, and looked to see Oscar aping me from behind.

"Oscar," I said, "you are not helping the situation."

They both cracked up.

I couldn't help but smile along with them as I grabbed the shoe box and my mail, turned off the lights, and shepherded my two unrepentant wards up the stairs.

"Hey, Selena, guess what," Oscar said. "Lasagna for dinner! And after, we're gonna make *cookies*!"

"Cool!" said Selena.

It was always dangerous to solicit Oscar and Selena's help making cookies. Odds were good not much of the actual batter would wind up as cooked cookies. Still, there were always more chips where those came from, and I had another night to bake before the tea, if need be. The truth was, if I couldn't have Sailor by my side, I could use a mellow evening with my familiar and Selena, just being normal. Or what passed as normal for the likes of us.

As I followed them into the apartment, I sorted through the pile of mail and phone messages. Bills, advertisements, a postcard from the Grand Canyon sent by Graciela.

And the note from Maya:

Hey boss lady,

I don't know if this is what you're looking for, but the Da Pinchi Code sign was taken from an ancient mark known to have been a witch's sign, in a town not far from Salem, during the witch hunts. It seems to be connected to a woman who was burned at the stake, which was actually very unusual back then—most were hung. Her name was Deliverance Corydon.

So much for my hopes for a normal evening.

The next day I went down to Aunt Cora's Closet, bleary-eyed despite two big cups of strong French roast. I hadn't slept much last night. I hadn't made cookies, either, despite Oscar and Selena's whining.

Instead, I had installed the two of them in front of the TV to watch a movie, and then spent most of the night consulting my Book of Shadows, brewing, and making protective sachets and talismans to pass out to my loved ones. Aidan kept warning me that I had defeated Deliverance Corydon too easily, that part of her had somehow become a part of me. But I hadn't wanted to believe it.

What did it mean that Deliverance's sign kept showing up? Was it a harbinger that I would become evil, like she was? Is that what had happened to Deliverance Corydon? . . . Had she once been a well-meaning witch who was seduced by malevolence, until she became demon-like herself?

And why in the world was a busload of elderly coven members making her mark with their path?

A terrible thought occurred to me: Could the grandmas have been kidnapped, somehow? Were they safe? Anyone could have been sending those text messages, right? How could I be sure?

By midnight I had worked myself into such a tizzy I even called and woke up poor Maya, who assured me that the grandmas had indeed sent the pictures of themselves having a grand old time in various locales, and that it was highly doubtful they had been kidnapped. I apologized and urged her to sleep in the next day. After all, I had extra labor in the form of Selena, and Aunt Cora's Closet wasn't going to be open for regular business on Saturday, anyway.

Instead, we were going to clear the place out to get it ready for the Magical Match Tea on Sunday. The plan was to move most of my inventory into Lucille's Loft for the event, then set up small folding tables and refreshment stands here in the store. On the one hand, I could hardly believe we were going ahead with the Magical Match Tea, given everything else that was going on. But the more I thought about it, the more I was sure it would give me the chance to catch Wind Spirit in an unguarded moment.

Speaking of Wind Spirit, seeing her double last night had knocked me for a loop. But in the end, I didn't think the apparition was anything more than chance. Selena had been fooling around with the silverfish, and happened to be wearing the charm Wind Spirit had given her, so she took on Wind Spirit's appearance for a few minutes. That was all there was to it.

I was pretty sure.

When Bronwyn arrived—cream cheese and two dozen bagels in hand—I asked her to remain discreet about my suspicions.

"Does this mean you've reconsidered? I really don't think dear Wind Spirit could be—"

"Let's just say I'd like to keep a low profile."

"I understand," she said as she laid the bagels out on a platter. "Oh, how is poor Sailor doing? Has there been any progress on his case?"

"Sort of," I hedged. "I'm still working on it."

Duke arrived, and on his heels came Conrad with Shalimar and three other friends happy to work for food.

Every time someone asked how Sailor was doing, my stomach clenched with anxiety. All I could say was that things were still up in the air, but that we might be getting closer to figuring things out. *Fingers crossed.* I handed out the talismans, and hung the sachets around the store, explaining that we still had to be on our toes, especially if someone showed up looking like Sailor. Or Renee-the-cupcake-lady, for that matter.

I wore an apron over the old cotton dress I usually donned for doing laundry. Bronwyn and Duke were clad in jeans and sweatshirts, and Conrad and several of his "gutterpunk" friends wore their everyday attire. Maya, of course, had refused my offer to sleep in and showed up early along with everyone else, also wearing moving clothes. She waved off my apologies for robbing her of sleep.

"Maya, could I ask you about the symbol you found? You said it was connected to Deliverance Corydon?"

"Yes, isn't that wild? I found a reference in a book by a Berkeley professor who had done research on the witch hunts. I even tried calling him, but it turns out he's no longer at Cal."

"Did the sign have any particular meaning that you could find?"

She shook her head. "Just that it was associated with her, and I guess whoever came up with the Da Pinchi sign based on it."

"And what does it mean in the Da Pinchi Code?"

"I wrote it down: 'a rich house, worth burgling, but high risk.'"

"Huh. That doesn't tell us much."

"No, it doesn't. Oh, also, you'll be glad to hear that Graciela's coven checked in this morning," she said as she put a thumbtack in the wall, not far from Napa, as I'd predicted. "They're going wine tasting today. And their path has definitely formed Corydon's sign," said Maya as she looped red thread around the tack. "They said they'd be here tomorrow, for sure. They were in a dead zone for talking, but I texted them about the sign, and whether they were kidnapped."

"You did? How did they respond?"

"'LOL.'"

"'Lots of love'?"

"'Laugh out loud,'" she said, chuckling. "The thing is, Lily, with you I don't know if that's a joke, or you're serious."

I smiled in return, but didn't clarify. Oscar often said, "OMG," but otherwise I wasn't exactly up on my texting acronyms.

"So, let's get to work, shall we?" Maya said.

We trooped next door and, with the help of Lucille and her seamstresses, pushed the sewing machines and worktables to the very back of Lucille's Loft, opening up space for the racks and the shelf contents we would bring over from Aunt Cora's Closet. Lucille had already moved the custom orders to the front of her shop, and every once in a while one of her clients would drop by to pick up her dress, excited about tomorrow's event.

Which reminded me: "Lucille, who is Renee Baker bringing to the tea as her match? You made their outfits, didn't you?"

"I really don't know," Lucille said. "Renee gave me the measurements for her match's outfit, but she didn't come in for a fitting."

"That seems odd," I said.

Lucille shrugged. "It happens that way sometimes. People get busy."

"Has she picked up the dresses yet?"

"No, I have them here." Lucille held out a large dress, along with a smaller one. They were made of matching material, colorful little cupcakes somersaulting across a beige background. Cupcakes. How unexpected.

I tried holding Renee's dress in my arms, hoping to sense any wayward vibrations. No luck. I doubted she had worn it long enough for me to sense anything, anyway—and the befuddling spell I was suffering under didn't help.

The smaller dress could have fit Amy—Wind Spirit—though I couldn't be sure. Would it even make sense that she would come with Renee? Wouldn't that be an obvious tip-off to me? Or would that even matter? Once Renee allied herself with someone magical, I imagined it wouldn't remain a secret. So far, her intentions to mount a challenge to Aidan had been surprisingly straightforward.

Despite everything, I relaxed as I spent a pleasant day with friends, a welcome change from business as usual. We turned up the music—Maya had put together a great mix of upbeat hits from the eighties and nineties—and busied ourselves packing and hauling, fueled by bagels and chips and soda. Luckily Lucille's Loft was right next door to Aunt Cora's Closet, so we were able to roll some of the racks over just as they were, full of hanging clothes. Smaller items such as hats, scarves, and gloves were packed in boxes, which we then stacked on the worktables in the rear of Lucille's shop. We carted over armfuls of dresses, skirts, blouses, and coats that weren't on racks, stashing them atop workbenches or on clean blankets laid out on the floor.

We covered my main display counter with a heavy

brocade cloth; it would serve as a refreshments stand. The shop was nearly emptied of merchandise, but I kept the too-fragile-to-wear dresses hanging on the wall as art pieces, their gossamer skirts fanning out. We outfitted the mannequins in the store's window displays in sets of matching dresses that hadn't been purchased for the tea. When, at Maya's suggestion, we fitted them with hats and gloves, they looked very smart.

By early afternoon, we were done. Duke ordered pizza and the whole crew sprawled on the floor of the shop admiring our handiwork, and taking a well-deserved food break before starting on phase two of the preparations: giving the place a good scrubbing. I wanted to take this rare opportunity to clean thoroughly—using both standard and magical means. Sweeping and mopping under and around racks of clothing is no easy feat, and though I "cleansed" the shop every morning, given the circumstances, I thought it best to add a little extra magic. After the shop had been thoroughly vacuumed, mopped, and wiped down, I smudged widdershins, then sprinkled saltwater deosil, all over the store.

Next we set up several small folding café tables, and ringed the room with long tables for refreshments. There wouldn't be enough room for everyone to sit at a table, but we wanted at least some chairs for those who needed them. Tomorrow morning we would put out the fresh flowers, dishes, and silverware. I was happy to have a reason to put all that vintage cutlery Selena had been polishing to good use.

I had noticed Conrad and his friend Shalimar whispering throughout the day; she seemed to be urging him to do something. Shalimar left after our pizza feast, and I asked Conrad if everything was okay.

"Dude, I'mma turn twenty-five next month," he said. "I wanted to ask you . . ."

"Would you like to hold a party here?" I asked.

"Naw, it's not that. It's more like . . . I'm, like, tired. I was thinking I want to change things. Maybe visit my mom."

"I didn't know you had a mom."

"Dude. Sure. We . . . we haven't been close; but lately I've been thinking. I mean . . . a person never knows what's gonna happen, y'know? I'm not getting any younger, and neither is she. It's easy to act like you've got plenty of time, but when you really think about it, no one really knows how much time they have."

"You are a very wise man, Conrad," I said.

His words made me think of my own mother. Yes, I was anxious to see her, but part of me had been hoping she wouldn't come. It was going to be hard to face her—wonderful, but hard. In some ways it was tempting just to avoid the whole thing. But Conrad was right. How did I know how much time I had, or how much time she had? I had faced disaster, and even death, several times in the past couple of years. I couldn't take life, or time, for granted. None of us could.

"So, when you say you want to make some changes," I continued, "what do you mean?"

His eyes shifted around the newly cavernous shop, as though he was embarrassed. "Dude. Sobriety. You've offered to help me get sober, before."

Inside, I was jumping up and down in excitement. But I didn't want to come on too strong, afraid to scare him off. So I played it cool. I kept my focus on the glass front of the display counter I was cleaning. "Oh, sure."

"Is that, like, difficult?"

"Making any sort of serious change in life is always difficult," I said. "But sometimes that's an indication of how important it is to do."

He nodded. "I guess I'm up to the challenge."

"I *know* you are." I smiled, and hugged him. Conrad

was shaggy, his clothes threadbare. But he was kind-hearted, and intelligent, and a good friend. "And I'll be there beside you, every step of the way."

"Thanks, Lily."

"It will be my honor, and my pleasure. Now, care to help me set up some tables?"

"It will be my honor, and my pleasure."

We had started our day before eight, so by four we had finished all we could do in preparation for the big Magical Match Tea. Tomorrow we would do all the last-minute tasks, like laying out food and flowers. Tonight everyone had baked goods to make, not to mention matching outfits to perfect, so we dispersed early.

I drove Selena back to her grandmother's house, and we had a long talk about enforcing rules. We decided Selena would come to the tea tomorrow, but be grounded for a week after that. And any further shenanigans—especially putting herself in danger—would mean she might not be allowed to attend my wedding.

Afterward, I hurried back home to bake a few dozen macadamia butterscotch chocolate-chip cookies and wash all the silver cutlery Selena had polished, and I also wanted to brew to help Conrad.

And then I would brew for our safety tomorrow at the tea. I was profoundly worried about the Ashen Witch not appearing the last time I'd brewed, but I didn't know what else to do but what I'd always done. I flipped through my Book of Shadows, but found no answers. How should a witch respond to such a thing?

As Oscar and I were finishing up our third batch of cookies, I asked: "Oscar, you know how my guiding spirit shows up when I brew?"

"It's awesome when she does that!"

"What do you . . . I mean, what would it mean if . . . I mean . . ."

"Mistress?"

"What if she didn't show up?"

He blinked.

"What if she started not showing up?" I rephrased as I used the spatula to transfer a dozen cookies, hot out of the oven, onto the rack to cool. Oscar's huge eyes followed the progress of each and every cookie.

"I never heard of that," he said.

"Surely I can't be the first—"

"Oh, I dunno. Seems to me you're the first at a lot of things."

"You're saying it couldn't happen?" I gestured with the spatula. "Once a guiding spirit, always a guiding spirit?"

"Pretty much. Maybe she's just being shy. Or maybe you just didn't notice her, somehow."

"Maybe. Hard to imagine, though," I said as I deposited the empty cookie sheet into the sink. I sensed movement behind my back. "I'm serious, Oscar—you've already eaten at least a dozen cookies' worth of batter. Those are for the fund-raiser tomorrow, and it's a good cause. So *no more cookies*, understand?"

"Yes, mistress." He grumbled something about me having eyes in the back of my head.

"Oscar, I'm not your mistress anymore. You know that, right?"

He nodded. "And I'm not supposed to call Master Aidan 'master' anymore. I remember."

"Right, because he's not your master. But . . . do you ever miss it?"

"Miss what?"

"Working for Aidan."

"How do you mean?"

"I just wondered if you would ever consider going back to work for Aidan."

His bottle glass green eyes grew even bigger than

normal, and started to glitter with the beginning of tears. "I won't eat any more cookies! I promise! Don't send me away, mistress!"

"No, Oscar, that's not what—"

He hopped up onto the sink and started scrubbing the cookie sheets. "Let's get this kitchen spic-and-span, shall we?"

"Oscar, honestly, I appreciate the help, but—"

"Yup, you and me, mistress. We're gonna make cookies, and clean up right after, and—"

"It's not about that. Oscar, would you please calm down and listen to me?"

"It's that mandragora, isn't it? I never liked him. He's the sneaky sort, going behind a guy's back—"

"No, I promise you. Finnall belongs to Calypso. This isn't about replacing you, Oscar. I've told you before: You're family. It's you and me, for better or worse."

"Really?"

"Really."

I couldn't help but notice that, once reassured, Oscar abandoned the dishes in the sink and went back to staring at the cookies cooling on the rack.

"Feeling better now?" I asked.

"Much, mistress. Why were you asking about Aidan?"

"Aidan told me he wouldn't help me get Sailor out of jail unless either you or Sailor went back to work for him."

"Oh."

"It wouldn't be like before, though. You would be a regular employee. He would pay . . ." I trailed off. What was money to someone like Oscar? "Never mind. I don't know what I was thinking. I don't need Aidan. I can pull this off myself."

"Without Aidan, and without your guiding spirit?"

"It looks like it."

"If . . . if it means saving Sailor, I'll do it."

"Oh, Oscar. Now that I think about it, I realize I can't ask you to do that."

"You said I could be the ring bearer at the wedding. How'm I gonna do that if there *is* no wedding?"

"I tell you what, Oscar. I appreciate the offer so much, you have no idea. But let's get through the Magical Match Tea tomorrow. Also, Graciela's coven is set to arrive tomorrow as well. Maybe things will shake out differently, and we won't need Aidan's help at all."

"Maybe. You still think it's Wind Spirit?"

"Maybe. I'll talk to her tomorrow, see if I can get her to admit what's going on. But for right now, I have to brew, guiding spirit or no. Will you help?"

"Of course, mistress. It was real classy how you said to Conrad, 'It will be an honor, and a pleasure.'"

"Thank you, Oscar."

"It will be my honor, and my pleasure."

Chapter 27

After the brewing—which went well enough, though the Ashen Witch once again failed to appear—Oscar curled up in his cubby over the refrigerator, and I took a long shower, then dressed in a fresh white cotton nightgown I had bought from a lovely elderly woman in North Beach. Its vibrations were sweet and calm. I could use all the help I could get at this point.

I wanted to look through the shoe box alone. I sat cross-legged on my bed, centered myself, set out my stones, chanted for a minute, then slipped off the top of the box.

Despite Selena's perusal, everything looked just as it had. Ignoring the squirming silverfish, I gazed again at the photo of my mother and father on their wedding day. Instead of putting it back, I propped it up against the frame holding Sailor's photograph on my bedside table. No matter how fraught our personal history, these were my parents. And, according to the expressions on their faces, they had once loved each other. Perhaps they had once loved me, too.

Next, I unwrapped the lachrymatory and held the small bottle up to the light. I gazed at the tiny crystals within, tumbling as I turned the glass bottle. Were these the vestiges of my tears? Had I cried? I remembered Tristan saying—via Hervé—"The tears of the daughter . . ."

If these truly were mine, they were too precious to keep in a shoe box. I secured the stopper with some soft wax, then cleaned and anointed the bottle with olive oil, and added it to my leather medicine bag.

Next, I took the stones and crystals from the shoe box and added them to my basket of stones. Several hummed with teenage angst and energy, a few with great sadness. But as I knew only too well, negative forces could also be useful in spells. It was all about balance.

Finally, I picked up the watch. The glass face was scratched, the brown leather band worn. Had my father given this to me? Or had I nabbed it? It put me in mind of Sailor's missing watch. I wondered whether the police had taken it into evidence, as Sailor had suggested . . . or if someone had stolen it from him to cast a Sailor-looking glamour. If so, it would suggest this person knew where Sailor lived, as well as Sailor's connection to Tristan Dupree. And this person wouldn't want Dupree horning in on Renee's attention.

I considered winding the wristwatch to see if it worked, but remembered seeing this same watch nestled with the broken eggs in my vision. Probably it was merely symbolic of my father betraying me, but just in case . . . I set the watch, unwound, on my bedside table, alongside my parents' wedding photo, and the one of me as a toddler.

All that was left in the box were the last vestiges of herbs and the silverfish. Very special silverfish, apparently, which could be used to cast glamours. They might come in handy someday, if I took the time to experiment a little and discover how to use them.

As I went to close the box, I noticed with astonishment that the creepy little fellows had arranged themselves in the shape of Deliverance Corydon's mark.

The day dawned bright and cheery, a beautiful spring morning for the Magical Match Tea. Officially the event started at eleven, but the steering committee showed up early to finish setting up.

Tables were covered with colorful cloths, plates were stacked, and silverware was put into jars. Food arrived by the carload: platters of cookies and petits fours, trays of finger sandwiches and cupcakes, and bowls of fruit. There were vats of coffee and tea, and pitchers of juice and punch. Maya had put together a playlist that featured a mix of old and new tunes, and there was a good deal of dancing while we finished our preparations.

We were a raucous, excited, and extremely well-dressed crowd.

Maya and Lucille wore matching turquoise dresses patterned with little sprigs of bright red cherries. Bronwyn's twelve-year-old granddaughter, Imogen, wore an actual vintage dress in a pretty butter yellow with white embroidery, while Bronwyn wore a version that Lucille had skillfully produced to match the original. Selena and I were matching in our polka-dot dresses, and the rest of the coven sisters came with an assortment of daughters, nieces, and granddaughters. Starr brought her two foster daughters, forming a matching trio instead of a pair. Wendy brought her barista buddy, Xander; they were outfitted in matching corsets and black boots with faded jeans. They both looked quite fetching.

"Where's Wind Spirit?" I asked the group, checking my watch. "It's almost ten thirty."

"She texted me that she had to pick up some cupcakes," Starr said. "Said she was running late."

"Looks like we have plenty of cupcakes already," I said.

"She wanted to be sure there were more than enough, Lily," Bronwyn explained. "It's just the way she is."

If Wind Spirit really was working with Renee, I reflected, she wasn't trying to hide it. Then again, why would she? How in the world was I supposed to prove that she had cast a glamour to look like Sailor while attacking and murdering Tristan?

Conrad declined to attend the actual tea, but accepted a muffin and the smoothie I had made for him with the special brew I concocted last night. He announced he would stand outside and act as doorman.

"I'll keep our little porker friend out here with me if you want."

"Good idea. That way he won't be underfoot. I'll bring you both some snacks later." Something occurred to me. "Conrad, do you know what time Amoeba Records opens?"

"Dude, I love that place. It opens at eleven, every day of the week. Want me to run and buy you an LP? I didn't even know you had a record player."

"I don't, actually. I was just wondering. Thanks for staffing the door."

"Happy to do it."

I looked up and down the street. Still no sign of Wind Spirit or Renee. But others were beginning to arrive; from both directions, women—young, old, and in between—wearing matching dresses were walking toward Aunt Cora's Closet. It was a sight to see.

"Dude," said Conrad.

"Dude," I echoed in agreement.

Soon the shop was crowded with chattering partygoers. Most were women; other than Xander, only one brave man had taken us up on the invitation and wore a sort of late-1970s jumpsuit that matched the one his daughter wore. The two of them stood together, beaming with pride. I welcomed several Aunt Cora's Closet regulars, as well as Haight Street neighbors.

"Here comes Renee," said Maya quietly. She had sidled up to me without my noticing, so intent was I on the arrivals.

I stroked my medicine bag for strength, and to help me focus.

"Accompanied by Wind Spirit, in matching cupcake dresses." Just as I'd thought. They carried large pink bakery boxes, which they set down on a nearby refreshment table. Wind Spirit started removing the cupcakes from the boxes and setting them on plates, while Renee worked the crowd, the picture of ease and contentment.

Surely she wouldn't have dosed cupcakes that were for the general public, would she? Was I willing to take that chance?

"How does Wind Spirit know Renee, do you suppose?" asked Maya.

"I'm not sure, but I'll bet it has something to do with cupcakes." I continued to watch Wind Spirit, trying to determine if she was left-handed. She was using both hands to put out the cupcakes, not seeming to favor either one.

"You want me to . . . keep an eye on them, or something?" Maya asked. "I'm not sure what I should be on the lookout for, but I'm happy to try."

"That's okay, Maya. Thanks, though. Mostly I want to get Wind Spirit alone to see if I can get her to tell me anything," I said.

"Wind Spirit? I thought you told me you were worried about Renee?"

"I'm worried about both of them. It's . . . a long story."

Maya nodded. "So what else is new, right? I'll go ask Renee to tell me about her cupcake business. That ought to keep her busy for a little while."

"That's a great idea."

She moved across the room to join Renee, then subtly steered her over to chat with Lucille on the other side of the room. I approached Wind Spirit as she was arranging the last of the cupcakes on a tiered glass stand. At least they hadn't brought meat pasties, so I didn't have to worry about poisonous mushrooms.

"Are those 'special' cupcakes?" I asked Wind Spirit.

"Oh, yes, indeed they are! From Renee's bakery!"

"So I hear. Wind Spirit, I have something in the back for you that you left at the voodoo supply shop the other day. And, oh! Look at this!" I said, picking up the tiered cupcake stand. "This platter needs to be tended to. . . . It's not shiny enough. Let's bring it in the back with us. Would you grab the bakery box with the rest of the cupcakes? There are more platters in the back."

"Oh, um . . . sure."

I led the way to the rear workroom, where it was slightly quieter. We set the cupcakes down on the kitchen counter.

"That is *such* a cute dress," I said. "How in the world did you and Renee decide to come together, as a match?"

"It's the craziest thing! I'm wild about her cupcakes, but then, isn't everyone? So anyway, the second time I went into her bakery, she remembered my name—I have people I've known for *ages* who can't remember my name. She's so thoughtful."

"I'll bet. Here's the stuff you left at Hervé's shop," I said, handing her the canvas bag.

She took it from me and peeked inside the bag. A blush stained her cheeks. "Oh, thank you. Did you, uh, see what's in here?"

"The hexing supplies? Yes, I did."

"Please don't tell the coven sisters," she said, stashing the bag under the table. "They wouldn't approve. It's just . . . I'm trying to get this little side business going, believe it or not, growing mushrooms in the basement of my apartment building. The super gave me permission and everything. But then my cousin stole my idea, and she's trying to edge me out. . . . I know it's silly, and I shouldn't resort to something like this, but . . ." She trailed off.

"What kind of mushrooms are you growing?"

"Champignons de Paris," she said. "Otherwise known as button mushrooms."

"Not amanita?"

Wind Spirit looked shocked. "Those are poisonous! I would never grow something so dangerous. I took classes—I know what I'm talking about. I won't even forage in the woods around here because unless you really know what you're looking for, it's easy to make a mistake. No, I get the spores from a reputable source in North Beach, and sell to a couple of local vendors."

"I went out to visit Calypso Cafaro recently, and she mentioned that you had been out there."

"Isn't she amazing? But, Lily, shouldn't we bring the cupcakes out for everyone and join the party?"

"Soon," I said, deliberately taking my time as I arranged the cupcakes on a painted ceramic platter. As far as I could tell, I thought Wind Spirit was telling me the truth, but I was hesitant to trust my dulled senses. "Calypso mentioned you knew a lot about glamours."

Wind Spirit looked away and blushed again. "I've been reading up on them. But no matter how hard I try, I haven't been able to manage much."

"Why would you want to cast a glamour?"

She shrugged. "I know it's silly. The coven sisters always tell me I'm beautiful, just as I am. But I've always wanted to be . . . lithe—d'you know what I mean?

I'm short and not exactly petite. I've always wanted to be sort of elfin, for want of a better word. I know it's foolish."

"Bronwyn tells me you're an expert in a martial art."

"It's called *eskrima*," she said with a nod. "I practically grew up in my dad's studio. I've known how to fight since before I can remember. I'm strong, but not . . ."

"Elfin," I said. "I get it."

"It makes it hard to fit into your vintage inventory. I'll tell you that much. Anyway, the glamour thing might be silly, but I thought maybe I could make people see me in a different light, somehow."

"Well, I agree with your coven sisters—I think you're beautiful just as you are. And I think being strong and skilled in *eskrima* is more impressive than being thin, or even elfin."

She smiled. Beyond the brocade curtains, the noise was ratcheting up. There was the usual chatter and music of a party, with the occasional raised voice as well. Wind Spirit looked longingly toward the curtains, as though anxious to join the party.

"I suppose we should be getting back," I said. "Let's bring some fruit with us."

I picked up an orange and tossed it to her. She caught it with her right hand. So much for that theory.

"Lily, are you sure everything is all right?" she asked curiously.

"Yes, Wind Spirit. It's fine. Sorry. . . . I just thought we should get to know each other better. Let's go join the party. Do you happen to know what time it is?"

She took her phone out of her pocket and checked the display. "Almost eleven twenty."

"I guess no one wears a watch anymore," I said.

"I know I don't," she said with a laugh. "Want me to bring the cupcakes with us or save them for later?"

I hesitated. I hadn't felt anything from the little cakes,

and I truly couldn't imagine Renee would ruin her reputation by putting anything frightening in this batter for such a public event. Still . . .

"Let's hold on to them for later," I said. "Just so people don't pass up the home-baked items in favor of Renee's cupcakes. We wouldn't want anyone to get their feelings hurt. And besides, who would eat fruit if they could have one of Renee's cupcakes? We'll bring them out when the food runs low."

Wind Spirit looked disappointed, but agreed. She grabbed the bowl of fruit, clearly unconvinced it was an adequate substitute for Renee's elaborately frosted cupcakes.

"Lily!"

I ducked through the curtains as soon as I heard someone scream my name.

Out on the shop floor, I discovered all hell had broken loose.

Chapter 28

"What is going on?" I asked Bronwyn as she approached.

"The-there are bugs!"

Dozens of silverfish scurried around the crowded shop floor, light glinting off their little writhing bodies.

"Ew!" Starr cried out, and she and her foster daughters laughed and tried to step on them, as though it were a game. I heard one of them starting to sing "La Cucaracha" as she stomped.

Bronwyn reached out her foot to step on one, and for a brief second, she looked like her granddaughter, Imogen. I watched as Starr appeared to resemble her older foster daughter for a moment.

These were certainly no ordinary silverfish. *But how did they get out of the shoe box?*

As I looked around the shop, I saw people's appearances changing as soon as they stepped on the slinky little bugs. One mother in a bright pink sundress took on a glamour of her daughter for a few seconds before changing back into her own likeness once again. The father-daughter couple each looked like the other for a quick moment, before regaining their normal appearances.

Some guests were laughing, others shrieking, and one young girl started crying.

I searched the crowd for Patience and Renna, hoping to find a magical ally to lend a hand, but either they were running late or they'd decided against coming altogether.

"It's like *Freaky Friday*!" exclaimed Starr, smiling. "How did you manage this, Lily?"

"I . . ." What could I say? If I admitted I wasn't orchestrating the mayhem, it would only frighten everyone further.

As an enchanted atmosphere took over the store, the antique dresses that had been hanging on the walls ripped free of their pins and started to dance in the air above our heads, like a Halloween haunted house. More people started laughing, *ooh*ing and *aah*ing, believing it was all some sort of elaborate trick designed for their entertainment.

Then an iced cupcake—one of Renee's—sailed across the room and landed with a *plop* on Maya's back, icing side down.

"Hey!" Maya cried as she turned around, but there was no obvious culprit. Another cupcake, then yet another, flew across the shop.

Next the silver cutlery crashed to the floor, skittering across the wooden planks as the tea goers inadvertently kicked the forks and spoons. The lamps glinted off the silverware, casting orbs of light on the walls and the ceiling.

It was bedlam.

Xander came up to me; then the glamour slipped and he transformed into Wendy before my eyes.

"What can I do to help?" she asked.

"Just try to calm folks down," I said. "These bugs

aren't going to hurt them, and the glamours don't last. And if it doesn't weird you out too much, try to corral these silverfish? They aren't normal bugs."

"Yeah, I got that impression," Maya said as she joined us. "Come on, Wendy. I'll help."

"Hey, Maya, have you seen Selena?" I asked, searching the milling crowd.

"Not lately."

"She was headed over to Lucille's Loft for something, last I saw," said Wendy.

Panic crept up on me. "Where's Renee?"

"I was talking to her earlier," said Maya. "But then she put out more cupcakes. . . ."

I pushed my way through the chaos. How could I have been so foolish? I had been so focused on Wind Spirit and her connection to Renee that I utterly failed to make sure Selena was safe.

"Dude," said Conrad as he held the door open for me. "You know how to throw a heck of a party. Did someone spike the punch?"

"Did Selena come out here? Or Renee?"

"Didn't see them, but I have to confess I was off duty for a coupla minutes. Nature called."

"Where's Oscar?"

"I thought he went back in with you. What's wrong? Hey, where are you going? Want me to come with you?"

"No, thanks. It's best if you stay here and watch over things."

"Watch for what, exactly?"

"Just please try to make sure things don't get out of hand, okay? And if someone who looks like Sailor arrives—"

"Don't trust him. I got it, dude."

I ran next door to Lucille's Loft as quickly as I could. The lights were off, and the curtains drawn across the front windows.

I tried the door; it was unlocked. So I pushed it open very slowly.

"Hello?" No response. I tried again. "Anyone? Selena?"

I felt magical vibrations, but they seemed . . . off. It wasn't Renee. Renee was driven and determined, but she was in control.

What I felt was entirely different.

The floor space was crowded with racks of clothing, cardboard boxes, and piles of dresses and blouses from my shop. A narrow passageway led to the worktables at the rear of the store.

I paused briefly and stroked my medicine bag before proceeding any farther. I started chanting, casting a charm for strength and focus. Unfortunately, I was more of a brewing witch than a battling witch. But when I was properly focused, I could send out a blast of energy, as I sometimes did when startled—as Aidan and I had when we last saw Jamie.

"I *hate* it when you guys do that weird mumblin' thing," said Jamie as he emerged from the shadows. He held Selena in front of him, his right hand over her mouth, his left holding a knife to her throat. As usual, Selena's affect was flat. But her eyes were screaming.

I kept on "mumbling."

"Seriously, you don't shut up, and the chickie here is gonna get cut."

I stopped chanting, but continued stroking the medicine bag. I could feel the outline of the lachrymatory within the fabric. The vial with the salts of my teenage tears.

"I'm surprised at you, Jamie," I said. I glanced at Selena, trying to telegraph to her that I would take care of her, that I would make sure she was safe. "I mean, I knew you were working for Renee, but I guess I assumed you were sort of a 'bad guy with a heart of gold.'"

"Yeah, I get that a lot, actually. Don't know why, except I really am a nice guy a lot of the time. But the truth is, people underestimate me. I got ambition, which is somethin' a lot of people don't understand these days."

"So, is that what you're doing over at the party? Creating a distraction? I must say, I'm impressed." We could hear the cacophony next door, the mingled shrieks of delight and surprise.

"That? Naw, that ain't me. Truth is, I don't have that kind of skill. That's all Renee. Shoulda seen her, laughin' her ass off, cookin' it up." He shook his head, and nudged something with his foot. There was a soft moan. Only then did I realize—what I had assumed was yet another heap of clothing was actually Renee, lying on the floor.

"What did you do to her?" I asked.

"She'll be okay, prob'ly, just a knot on her head. Maybe her ego will be a little bruised—you catch my drift. I gotta say, Renee and me, we don't share the same sense of humor. That's one reason, maybe, why this whole *coincidentia* deal isn't gonna work between us like I hoped it would."

"The *coincidentia oppositorum*? You wanted Tristan out of the way so you could step in and be Renee's partner?"

He nodded.

"Why did you set up Sailor?"

He laughed. "That part was sheer luck. Renee just couldn't stop talkin' about him, how unfair it was that you was gonna get married and be happy when no one else in your—how do you call it?—'profession' did. Gotta say, you have a way of getting under her skin. She sent me to your boyfriend's apartment to steal something of his. No offense, but that's a pretty depressin' place."

"He's not big on home decorating," I said lightly,

hoping my tone would help to ease Selena's fears a little. "Why did you steal his father's watch?"

"Renee was gonna use it to hex him, get control over him. Maybe change who he was fond of—you catch my drift. But then she got lucky when Maya brought you one of her pasties—it had a charm in it, made just for you so it wouldn't affect anyone else if they happened to eat it. She didn't want to totally do you in or nothin', just distract you. Guess she managed that, right?"

"Yes, I guess you can say I've been a little distracted lately."

"I happened to have Sailor's watch on me when I tried my first silverfish deal. Looked in the mirror, and voilà! No wonder you people enjoy this magic thing so much. Anyway, I got a few of those special silverfish from a Russian out in the avenues who I was able to persuade to help me with the spell. Took some practice, but I got to where I could keep up a glamour for, like, twenty minutes. Which is pretty darned good, if you ask me. Had to keep checking the time—wouldn't do to transform back to little ol' me in the middle of things."

"Again, I'm impressed. When you chased after us at Sailor's apartment, I had no idea it was you."

"Yeah, that was just dumb luck. It's like I'm charmed lately, excuse the pun. I went by Sailor's building just to practice this glamour deal. Gotta say, it's a little addictive once you start doing it. I thought I'd see if I could fool folks who really knew Sailor, up close and personal, like his neighbors or landlord. Couldn't believe it when I looked up the stairs, and there you stood, with that Gypsy lady."

"Why did you chase us?"

He grinned. "Just to see if I could. A guy like me, in my normal form . . . well, I don't exactly inspire fear and trembling just by looking at me. You get my drift.

It was a hoot to see how scared you guys got. You just about jumped off the roof!"

"That we did. And before that, while you were in Sailor's form, you figured you could kill Tristan with impunity."

"Impuni-what? I figured I could get away with it, if that's what you mean. Went there to get the lachrymatory Tristan promised Renee, and figured he'd be a goner by then. But he came at me, really made me mad. He was sick as a dog, but he still thought he could take me. I guess I showed him what for, but it sure did make a mess."

"Your use of poison surprises me. I thought you'd be a gunman."

"Why's that?"

"You pulled a gun on me once, a while ago, remember?"

"Oh, that wasn't a real gun. It was a starting pistol. Nabbed it from my nephew's track coach. I support gun control, tell you the truth. Bunch of nutcases walking around with concealed weapons, what's that about? No, thank you. Besides, poison's got lots more advantages. Slip some mushrooms into one of Renee's pasties, wait a few hours, and it's vomit city. After all, who could resist one of Renee's creations—am I right?"

I nodded. "That makes a lot of sense. You're pretty smart, Jamie. You thought this through."

"See, you get me. You suppose me and you got a shot at this *coincidentia oppositorum* deal?"

"I thought you were partnering with Renee?"

He glanced down at her crumpled form. "Yeah, that might not work out so good. Seems like we weren't on the same wavelength, after all. Plus, she's prob'ly gonna be pissed when she comes around, so I really could use someone on my side. Not sure my Russian connection can handle someone like Renee. Also, here I thought she was the big threat to you and Aidan, but now I guess there's something else happening."

"Something else?" I kept my eyes on Jamie, but tried to convey calm and strength to Selena, who hadn't made a sound other than a muffled whimper.

"You don't know?" Jamie asked. "Yeah, turns out, Renee's just an underling, too! She likes to talk a big game, but she's takin' orders, just like the rest of us."

"Orders from whom?"

"Hey, lady, if I knew everything you think I know, I'd be running the show already, wouldn't I? All I know is she started burning some batches of cupcakes, and it was a bad sign. That's why she was kind of freaking out, and thought if you were sick, she might be able to pry you away from Aidan, and then you and she could get together. It wasn't that great of a plan, though. And she hadn't really counted on Tristan showing up—she was so excited to get her hands on that lachrymatory, thought it might solve all her problems. Whatever happened to that, by the way?"

I could feel the lachrymatory humming in my medicine bag. "I don't even know what you're talking about."

"*Heh.* Good one. So back to what I was saying: I'm gonna need a strong ally or two. You and me, maybe we could be partners."

"It's not such a bad idea, actually. But . . . somehow I doubt I could trust someone who would hold my sister at knifepoint."

Jamie looked down at Selena, a confused look on his face, as though he had almost forgotten the teenager was still in his arms, at his mercy.

"This is your sister?"

I nodded. Behind Jamie, I spied the glow of Oscar's green eyes peering out of the dark rear of the store. I wasn't certain how this situation would end, but my confidence was growing. It felt as though the befuddling spell was lifting, and I could sense my powers more clearly than I had in days.

"See? Matching polka-dot dresses. Selena's my magical match," I said, holding out my skirt. "Mess with her and you mess with me."

"Now, see here—that's not my fault. I didn't know that. How am I supposed to know something like that? She walked in here with Renee, is all." He licked his lips and seemed to be trying to think of his next move, or how to stall for more time. "So, I gotta know, how'd you finally figure me out?"

"Amoeba Records doesn't open till eleven."

"How'd you know I didn't come to Haight Street early, to get a coffee or something?"

"I didn't. Not really. It just made me wonder."

"That's it? Ah, jeez, gave myself away for no good reason. Story of my life."

"Also, I tried to think of anyone who might want to move up in this world, to partner with Renee. Like you say, you've got ambition. And—no offense—but you're a little bit crazy."

"*Heh*, good one." His hand had slipped down a bit, but that knife was still too close to Selena's vulnerable throat. One quick jab would be enough to end her life.

"Jamie, do you know what it's like to get on the bad side of a witch? I mean, like, the *really* bad side of a witch?"

It was hard to tell in the dim light, but I thought he blanched a bit.

"Take a moment and think about that," I continued. "Really ponder it, roll it around in your mind, meditate on it. And then think about what it might be like to be on the bad side of *several* witches. A whole coven, or maybe two."

I could feel strength surging in me. I didn't dare turn

around to look, but I wondered whether Aidan might have shown up after all, or Patience and Renna, or maybe even my grandmother's coven. There was definitely something going on. Somebody—maybe several somebodies—had my back.

"What . . . what are you smiling about?" Jamie asked.

"Ever have a day when you're just feeling good?" I said, now grinning. "*Really* good. Like the fog has lifted?"

"What are you . . . ? What's goin' on?"

I heard chanting behind me. It started as a low hum, almost undetectable, but gradually grew in intensity.

"I hate that mumblin' thing!" Jamie said. "How are you doing that?"

"Witches come from a long line of powerful women, Jamie—you should know that. We're never truly alone. We come by the dozen, plus one. That's what a coven is."

"Stop it!" He brought the knife closer to Selena's neck. "Stop mumblin'!"

"I'm not saying a word."

I concentrated on his forehead. Kept my gaze there, my eyes piercing and focusing intently. The chanting continued, filling the room and lending me strength. Oscar's presence was helping to open the portals, to let the spirits slip through. But this time, there was more than one spirit guiding me.

Jamie's forehead started to smoke. He cried out. A charred symbol took shape: the sigil of Deliverance Corydon, seared into his flesh. He dropped the knife and fell to his knees, screaming in pain. Oscar moved in on him then, looming over him, snarling.

"Lily!" Selena ran to me, throwing her arms around my waist. "I'm sorry! I'm sorry! I'm sorry! I let the bugs out accidentally. And the cupcake lady said she would help me and we could find a trap for them here, so I came with her—"

"Shhhhh, later, *m'ija*," I said, hugging her to me with one arm. I kept my other hand on my humming medicine bag. "Jamie, the only way to save yourself is to confess everything to the police. Do you hear me? You will get Sailor off the hook, or so help me . . ."

Behind me, the chanting continued until it was loud enough to drown out the raucous sounds emanating from Aunt Cora's Closet.

"I'll do it! I'll do anything! Just stop!" Jamie lay on the floor, crying out and writhing.

"Basta, m'ija," I heard Graciela say from behind me. "Enough. Stick a fork in him, as you young people say. He's done."

Chapter 29

"Looks like we got here just in time," said Graciela.

She looked much older, and even shorter, than when last I'd seen her. But just as beautiful. Her stubborn chin, black eyes, and broad cheekbones . . . she was a sight for sore eyes.

I couldn't stop hugging her. Finally, she pulled away and chided me: "Enough, enough, *m'ija*. You never did know when to stop."

But she was smiling, patting me with her soft hands. The feel of those hands on me made me feel like a cherished child again.

Graciela's coven members seemed unfazed by the scene they'd walked in on. Oscar had shifted back into his pig guise, but three coven members circled Jamie, instructing him to stay where he was on the floor, or else. The others kissed and hugged me with cries of *"Merry part and merry meet!" "It's been so long!" "You've become such a witch!"* And then they peppered Selena with kisses and hugs, even though they'd never met. To my surprise, she gave them each a shy smile, and didn't pull away.

Darlene, one of the coven sisters skilled in healing, knelt over the still prostrate Renee, and declared her alive but in need of medical care for an apparent concussion. Apparently someone had already called for help, because we could hear the noise of a siren growing nearer.

"Where's my mother?" I asked.

"Still on the bus," answered Agatha, another coven sister. "Give her a little time."

"You know how she is," said another. "She's never been one for parties. What's happening next door?"

"Yeah, it's some out-of-control magic. We might need to calm that down," I said. "Especially before the authorities get here."

Outside, the school bus was double-parked and creating a jam on busy Haight Street. I tried to catch a glimpse of my mother, but couldn't see her inside the bus. Conrad was helping to direct traffic around the bus.

Graciela and the rest of the coven waved hello to Conrad—apparently they were old friends by now, since he was the one who told them where I was—and then entered the mayhem of Aunt Cora's Closet, snacking on leftovers as they used their talents to help calm things. Several of the tea patrons had left, but most were still there, apparently enjoying the dancing dresses and the ghostly food fight.

I wasn't sure how Renee had pulled that last one off, but I was impressed. I would have to ask her about it when she was feeling better.

Selena apologized again, and managed to herd the remaining silverfish into a jar. The light glinting off the silver cutlery bounced around her, making her smile.

Graciela's coven formed a circle around the room, and they started to chant, intoning with the ease of a coven of powerful women who had known one another for decades, and who weren't put off by much of anything.

The dancing dresses fell to the floor, and the last of the baked goods stayed on their platters.

By the time the police and the ambulance arrived, Aunt Cora's Closet was quiet. It was one royal mess, but it was quiet. The remaining partygoers started to drift off, but Selena and Maya and Lucille and Conrad, and most of Brownyn's Welcome coven, stayed behind to help clean up. They were excited to meet Graciela and her coven, and the chattering didn't stop.

The police officers admonished me for letting my party get out of hand and asked us to move the bus out of the way, but, most important, took a very eager Jamie into custody. He was confessing before they even read him his rights. His forehead was no longer smoking, but I imagined he would be left with a scar for some time, as a souvenir of Deliverance Corydon. The paramedics took Renee to San Francisco General.

"I think we might want to leave the rest of the cleanup until morning," I said, looking around at the dispiriting mess.

"Nonsense," said Darlene. "If we all work together, we'll put this place to right in an hour!"

Several of the elderly witches—including Graciela—took seats and "supervised" while the rest of us cleaned. But the talking didn't stop. It seemed my friends had been very curious about my background, and they peppered the Texan witches with questions.

"You should go on out and talk to your mother," Graciela told me. "Or likely she's never gettin' off that bus."

"Really?"

"Go, *m'ija*. There's nothing to be afraid of. It's time."

By that point Conrad had parked the bus on a side

street, where it was still double-parked but at least not obstructing bustling Haight Street.

The door was open. I stroked my medicine bag, took a deep breath, and climbed aboard.

Toward the back sat an older woman, a big embroidered handbag sitting primly in her lap.

Margarita Velasquez Ivory. Maggie. My mother.

We had both aged, and changed. Her once-chestnut hair was liberally shot through with white, and she seemed smaller than I remembered. Her face was fuller, but still carried a sweet, somewhat bewildered expression. As with Graciela, she looked beautiful to me, wrinkles and all.

"Hi, Mom," I said as I walked down the aisle.

I sat on the bench across from her.

"*Lily.* You look . . . It's . . . I'm so glad to see you."

"Me, too."

A long moment passed.

"I have to explain myself."

"Mom, you don't have to—"

"No, please. Let me. I've wanted to talk to you for so long; I've done so endlessly in my mind."

I smiled. "I've had a few conversations in my mind with you, too."

"I'll just bet you have," she said, playing with her handbag. She released a long breath. "I was so young, Lily, younger than you are now. That's not an excuse—I know you would never react that way, had you been in my shoes. But you're much more worldly than I am, Lily. Than I'll ever be. In fact, you were *born* more worldly than I've ever been. I don't know if you got that from your father's side, or it was just the way you were, but it's true."

I tried to think of something to say, but just sat there, silent, and listened as she continued.

"And what I went through with your father . . ." She

shook her head. "I'm a small-town girl, Lily. I was a beauty queen, and I thought that was important, for land's sakes!" She laughed. It was a throaty, deep laugh that I remembered from childhood.

"I had never met someone like your father," she continued. "Why, the things he said, the things he knew, the things he did . . ." She trailed off and a blush crept up her cheeks. I wasn't entirely sure I wanted to know about all the things he did. "Anyway, he was a wonder. And I never knew Graciela beyond the rumors, really, until after I married your father. My people never went to her. And then, what he put me through, well, I can only hope you have better luck. That's why I made you a trousseau, so you will have the support and advantages upon your marriage that I never had. I've been learning knot magic from Graciela."

I gaped at her. "You've been learning *what*, now?"

"Knot magic. It's when you imbue the threads with your thoughts and desires as you tie the knots—"

"Yes, I know what knot magic is. But you say you've been learning this from Graciela?"

She nodded. "I went to her, asked her for help. Believe it or not, Lily, my estrangement from you has been the saddest aspect of my life. If only you knew how much I regretted that day in the tent, at that terrible revival meeting. I never knew. . . . First, I was so ashamed. Just so ashamed of myself, and of you, or what I feared you were." Her voice dropped to a hush. "Can you comprehend what it feels like, to be ashamed of one's own child? It's like a sin against nature."

How many times, I wondered, had I dreamed of my mother acknowledging my pain and apologizing for her role in it? I felt myself letting go of the years of festering bitterness, felt myself accepting that my mother had truly loved me and had done the best she knew how.

"I imagine I was pretty scary," I said in a quiet voice, thinking of Selena.

My mother shook her head. Again, the gray hairs startled me. I still remembered her as she had been when last I saw her, in that tent with those hateful people. When I was seventeen. A lifetime ago.

"Yes, you were scary to an uneducated person like me, who didn't know better. I'm . . . I'm sorry, Lily. What you were was a child who needed her mother. Thank goodness Graciela was able to take you in, to understand you and help you to control your talents."

How many times had I dreamed of this moment? I wondered again. I reached out and put my hand over hers. She patted it. Her hands were soft as velvet and warm as love, just as I'd imagined them for years.

"Since then . . . Well, it took a while, but I've educated myself. I've read a lot. And I've come to understand that 'strange' isn't a synonym for 'wrong.'"

I smiled. "And I'm strange, am I?"

She looked at me, startled, as though worried she'd hurt my feelings. She relaxed upon spying my smile, and returned it.

"Oh, aren't we all, darlin'? Aren't we all?"

Half an hour later, the bell tinkled over the door as I led my mother into Aunt Cora's Closet.

She lingered in the doorway, as though unsure about whether to enter.

"Come on in, Mom," I said. "Welcome to my store. It doesn't usually look like this, though, I have to say."

"You named it after my cousin Cora?"

"I used to love playing dress-up in her closet, remember?"

My mother had insisted on bringing a big sewing bag in with her, and it slipped off her shoulder, falling to the floor.

"Oops," I said. "Nothing breakable, I hope."

"Not at all. It's a . . ." She looked around at everyone in the store. "I didn't mean to make a scene in front of everyone, all your friends. . . ."

"Everyone, this is my mother, Maggie. Mom, these are very important people to me. They're my San Francisco family." I was proud to introduce her to Bronwyn, and Maya, and Conrad, then Lucille and Selena and Imogen, and Wendy and Starr and Wind Spirit and the others from the Welcome coven. I only wished Sailor could be here, but I trusted that he would be in my arms soon enough.

"Well, then," said my mother, bringing a gown out of the bag. "I thought I should bring this to you. Maybe it's too soon, but I wanted you to try it on here because Graciela said you had a seamstress who could make alterations. . . ."

"That would be me," said Lucille, stepping forward. "That looks like a lovely gown, Maggie."

"I wore it when I got married," my mother said. "It was also my mother's and her mother's before that. My mother told me my grandmother's mother and sisters sewed it for her."

The dress was from the late 1920s, and was made from a champagne-toned slippery silk satin. The bodice featured a sweetheart neckline, a high back, and dolman-style sleeves. A self-sash was looped through the neckline and finished at the shoulder, where it could be used to tie the sleeve. Tea-stained floral lace appliqués highlighted the front of the bodice. The skirt was asymmetrical and fell from the banded drop waist, which was adorned with sparkling rhinestones in a swirling pattern. There were a few snags in the fabric, and a couple of the rhinestones were lost or loose. A little smudging at the neckline, no doubt evidence of a former bride's lipstick.

But otherwise the dress was pristine. Lucille would be able to alter it to fit me, and I felt confident I could remove the lipstick stains with a tiny bit of ammonia or hair spray—an old vintage clothes dealer's trick.

"It's . . . stunning," I said when I was able to catch my breath. "Truly, absolutely stunning."

Best of all, without even trying it on, I knew it was perfect for me. The vibrations were strong and happy and hopeful, and I detected something I had never before felt in a vintage garment: family. This dress had been made by my great-aunts, worn by my mother, and my mother's mother, and *her* mother.

I had never before worn a family hand-me-down.

"I know there are some issues with it, but Graciela said you'd be able to fix it up, no problem."

"Lucille is amazing," I said with a nod.

"Mom will be able to make it perfect," said Maya, looking over at her mother, who nodded. "And with a good laundering, it will be right as rain."

"Try it on," said Bronwyn.

"Yes, try it on, already," urged Graciela.

"Dude," said Conrad.

I felt shy, and finally realized why some of my customers held back a little. Even though the vibrations felt right and the dress beckoned me, it was a little bit scary to be the center of such attention.

"I'll help you," said Selena, taking my hand and leading me into the big dressing room.

I took off the polka-dot dress that matched Selena's; then Selena helped me to pull my mother's family wedding dress over my head. The fabric slipped easily down my body, encasing me in silky softness. It fit loosely, in the style of the twenties. And though I didn't have a boyish body, it was big enough in the right areas. It needed some alteration, but not much.

"Wow," said Selena.

"Really?"

I stepped out of the dressing room. You could have heard a pin drop.

"Well?" I said, wondering at their silence.

Bronwyn gasped and teared up.

"What?" I looked down at myself, suddenly doubtful.

My mother came up to me, gave me a hug, and then turned me around so I could look into the three-way mirror.

I looked beautiful. I looked like a princess. Best of all, I looked like a very happy witch.

Everyone started talking at once, *ooh*ing and *aah*-ing, pulling a little here, a little there.

"All you need now is the perfect veil," Maya said. "We must have some in boxes next door, right?"

"I have one here," my mother said as she pulled a lace veil out of her sewing bag. It was attached to a tiara. It was antique, but not fancy, made of cheap wire and rhinestones that had been cleaned up and polished.

"I know it's silly," my mother said. "But that's the tiara I won when I was crowned Miss Tecla County. That was the closest I've ever come to feeling magical."

"It's amazing," I said, wishing I had a better word for it. I smelled daisies, and my mind was flooded with images of home, and Texas, and sitting in my mother's lap while she read me a story when I was little. I thought of what Patience had said, that my thoughts were expressed in scents and symbols. Maybe this was what she meant.

"Thank you," I said, tears stinging the backs of my eyes. I knew if I had been able to cry, I would have done so. "It's amazing. It's exactly what I've been hoping for."

While saying, "No time like the present," Lucille trailed me back into the changing room and pinned the dress for alterations, then helped me to take it off without stabbing myself.

After I had changed back into my polka-dot dress, Bronwyn excused herself to take Imogen and Selena to their respective homes, Maya and Lucille begged off as well, and the last of the crowd began to disperse. My mother and the Texas coven climbed back onto the school bus to drive to Calypso's house in Bolinas. Only my grandmother and Oscar stayed behind to accompany me in my Mustang. Graciela insisted on hunting for a sparkly jacket in my inventory piled in Lucille's Loft, and then wanted to ride with the top down, because she'd once seen a movie in which a glamorous actress—was it Audrey Hepburn, or Grace Kelly?—drove across the Golden Gate Bridge in a convertible and she wasn't about to miss a chance to do the same before she died.

"You really taught my mother knot magic?" I asked her while we packed the last of the leftovers into boxes to take to Calypso's.

Graciela laughed. "She's atrocious. Truly. Still and all, it'll be interestin' to see what she came up with in that trousseau. Have you looked yet?"

"She told me not to, yet."

Graciela lifted an eyebrow.

"I'm respecting her wishes," I said, a defensive tone to my voice.

"That's a first."

I remembered snooping around in Graciela's things, which was how I'd found out more than I should have about my father. "I was just a child, after all."

"A nosy child."

"You're right," I said with a laugh. "A nosy child. I guess I still am, in lots of ways. I seem to stick my nose in all sorts of things around these parts—that's certain."

I looked up from the Tupperware container I was

closing to see Graciela—clad in a silver bugle-beaded jacket much too large for her—standing and gazing at the map behind the register, where the red thread now displayed Deliverance Corydon's entire sigil.

"So you and the coven deliberately made Deliverance Corydon's sign?" I asked as I joined her.

She let out a sigh, and nodded. "Yes, we cast at each point to rally her strength for you—you needed it. You now have two guiding spirits, *m'ija*. And they are at war. It will not be easy."

"I don't understand. Two spirits? That sounds bad."

"It is not all bad. There is great strength in the negative, as you know. You are on track to become very powerful now, *m'ija*. More than before, much more. But you must fight to maintain control. Otherwise, one spirit will win out over the other."

"Is that why the Ashen Witch didn't come to me the last time I brewed?"

"She didn't?" Graciela looked surprised, and it scared me to see worry in her eyes. But then she chuckled ruefully and patted me on the shoulder. "I guess we'll have to work on that. She hasn't abandoned you. Don't worry. But she might need to be invited back."

"I'll do whatever it takes."

"I know you will, *m'ija*. You have always been brave. To the point of foolishness."

"So you've told me."

"You must take precautions. But there is no denying what you are, so you must deal with it, embrace it, learn to best use it while maintaining balance and control. That's the way life is. You must work on your training; you cannot keep running away from that. But we are here now, *m'ija*. We will help you figure this out."

"Thank the heavens for that," I said. "So, does this have to do with the prophecy?"

"What prophecy?"

"Aidan told me there was a prophecy about me, that my father knew about it. And . . . a demon knew about it, too."

Now in addition to the worry in her eyes, I saw pain. She turned away.

"Graciela? Is it true?"

"I don't know."

"I don't believe you."

"I know there's a prophecy, but it had to do with your father, not you specifically."

"But through him, me, right?"

"Maybe. Maybe not."

"Graciela, you aren't making any sense. Please don't talk in riddles."

"I was going to wait to tell you this, but I guess there's no point. The truth is, the prophecy referred to your father's child."

"Right. But I'm an only child."

Graciela held my gaze for a long moment.

"You're saying . . . ," I ventured, "I'm *not* his only child? You're saying I have a *sibling*?"

"I thought he was dead. We all did. But lately there have been some signs. . . . Anyway, it's possible he's coming to San Francisco. Lucky we're here, right? Let's get going, *m'ija*. We should consult with the coven about this."

I mulled over this disturbing revelation while I loaded the boxes of leftovers, plus Graciela and Oscar, into the car, and ran back to Aunt Cora's Closet to grab my bag and coat and lock up.

As I grabbed my keys, I felt a shiver of premonition, the bell over the door tinkled, and I turned around to see Sailor stride into the store.

I blasted him with a wall of energy, and he hit the wall with a loud grunt.

"Ow," he said as he straightened, rubbing his shoul-

der. "I *really* dislike it when you do that. I hope you don't plan on resorting to violence after we're married."

"*Sailor?* I'm so sorry!" I threw myself into his arms. "It's you!"

"Of course it's me." He chuckled and hugged me. "What is going on?"

"How did you get out? Are you off the hook?"

"I don't know if it was Carlos, the cupcakes, or what, but apparently they figured they didn't have enough to make the charges stick. Since Dupree died of poisoning, and they couldn't find any blood evidence to link me to the beating, they're dropping the complaint. Also, now they've got some guy in custody who claims he was responsible . . . ?"

I hugged him again. "Oh, I can't believe you're here. I want to introduce you to my grandmother. She's waiting in the car. Can you come to Bolinas with us?"

"Why not? I'm free as the proverbial bird."

We went around the corner to the car.

"*Abuelita*, this is Sailor. Sailor, this is my grandmother Graciela."

Sailor took her hand in his, and they stared at each other for a long while. Finally, Sailor said, "Nice jacket."

"It's new. I like how it sparkles."

"It suits you."

Graciela stuck her chin out, and nodded. "He'll do. It'll be a challenge, but he'll do."

One side of Sailor's mouth kicked up in a crooked smile. "I'll take that. And I guess I'll just climb on in the back with the pig, unless you want me to drive."

I smiled. "I've got this. You just relax. We're going to drive our convertible over the Golden Gate Bridge, like— Was it Grace Kelly or Audrey Hepburn?"

"One of those," said Graciela with a wave of her hand. "I looked just like one of them when I was your age. Especially in a classy getup like this one."

Chapter 30

Calypso's house, as predicted, was full of laughter and lively discussion about everything from the proper way to brew lavender lemonade to the best order in which to plant the "three sisters": maize, beans, and squash.

Sailor, as the only male on the premises besides Oscar, held up well under the ardent grilling of Graciela, my mother, and the other coven sisters. It got so intense that Calypso stepped in to help him out from time to time, but I figured he could hold his own.

Just watching him sitting there, patiently answering questions, cracking the occasional joke, and sending me steamy looks across the room, made me feel flushed all over.

Sailor was out of jail. Exonerated. And he would be in my bed tonight.

Okay, Aidan was right: Sailor and I should probably talk and get a few important things worked out prior to the handfasting. We had some time—not very much, but a little—before we got married. And I didn't want to put off the ceremony, among other reasons, because I could not *wait* for the honeymoon.

The only thing that worried me now was Oscar. He was decidedly mopey. Oscar wasn't one to hide his feelings.

I called him outside, and we walked along a path into the redwoods so he could change into his natural form. I took a seat on a fallen log and patted the space next to me. He sat.

"What's up, little guy?" I asked him, nudging him with my elbow.

He shrugged and looked petulant, refusing to meet my eyes.

"You know, just because I'm getting married doesn't mean anything changes between you and me. We have a special bond. You're the only familiar I've ever had, or ever will have."

"It's not that," he said. "It's just . . . I heard Conrad say he's gonna go see his mom. And *you're* talking to *your* mom after all these years."

"You're missing your mom?"

His eyes were huge, and I saw tears in his eyes.

"I don't know if I'll ever find her at this point," he said.

"Oh, come on, now, what kind of attitude is that? You told me gargoyles live for centuries. I mean . . . have you even checked the top of Notre-Dame?"

"She wouldn't be someplace as obvious as that," he scoffed.

"How can you be sure? Have you been?"

"No, I figured that couldn't be right. It's too touristy."

"It wasn't touristy when the gargoyles first went up. And that's not the only place in France: there's Mont-Saint-Michel, in Normandy. Or how about Spain?

There's San Juan de los Reyes Monastery in Toledo, and the Palau de la Generalitat de Catalunya in Barcelona. I remember seeing a bunch on the cathedral in Quito, Ecuador, too."

"I heard they had gargoyles in the Forbidden City, in Beijing," Oscar said, warming to the theme. "And you don't even have to go that far. Someone told me there are gargoyles at Princeton University, and that's in *Jersey*."

"See? There must be a million places to check out."

He deflated again. "That's sort of my point. A million's a lot."

"True enough. But you only need to be right once."

"But . . ." He shrugged again.

"Now what?" I asked.

"I don't think I can leave you all alone. You get into a lot of trouble."

"Well, now. That's a fact. What if . . . what if we went with you?"

"What do you mean?"

"What if, after the handfasting, Sailor and I go on a honeymoon and you come with us? And we'll check out some of those gargoyles together."

He sat up a little straighter, and a hopeful gleam entered his green eyes.

"Prob'ly a long shot," he said.

"Maybe. But think about this: Most of what you and I get up to is a long shot. Why don't we ask Patience to read for you, see if she can give us any hints about where to start searching?"

"You'd do that for me?"

"Wouldn't you do the same for me?"

"Of course, mistress."

"Well, there you go. Works both ways."

"Mistress!" Oscar leapt up, suddenly full of enthusiasm. "Does this mean we can have *pain au chocolat* for breakfast in Paris?"

"I think that's practically a requirement," I said, laughing.

Now I just had to break the news to Sailor that we would have a porcine chaperone on our honeymoon.

And I still had a lot of wedding plans to follow up on.

Not to mention a vintage dress to make perfect. My professional reputation was on the line.

And then we would go on an international search for a stone gargoyle, one among thousands.

After all, it only took one in a million.

Continue reading for a preview
of the newest book in Juliet Blackwell's
bestselling Haunted Home Renovation
mystery series,

A GHOSTLY LIGHT

The tower reached high into a gray sky. A faint glow—dare I say a ghostly light?—seemed to emanate from the lighthouse's narrow windows. Probably just a trick of the light, the afternoon sun reflecting off curved stone walls.

Just looking up at the tower through the cracked bay window made me dizzy.

"I'm thinking of calling the inn 'Spirit of the Lighthouse.' Or maybe 'the Bay Light,'" said Alicia Withers as she checked an item off the list on her clipboard. Alicia was big on lists. And clipboards. "What do you think, Mel? Too simple?"

"I think you need to figure out your plumbing issues before you worry about the name," I replied. That's me, Mel Turner. General contractor and head of Turner Construction.

Also known as Killjoy.

Alicia and I stood in the central hallway of the former lighthouse keeper's home, a charming but dilapidated four-bedroom Victorian adjacent to the lighthouse tower. The structures had been built in 1871 on the small, rather unimaginatively named Lighthouse Island, located in the strait connecting the San Francisco and San Pablo bays. Not far away, the Richmond–San Rafael Bridge loomed, and barely visible to the southwest was the elegant new span that linked Oakland to Treasure Island and on to San Francisco. The nearest shoreline was Richmond, with San Rafael—and San Quentin prison—situated across the normally placid, though occasionally tempestuous bay waters.

It was a view to die for.

Lighthouse Island's foghorn and lamp had been staffed by full-time keepers and their assistants and families for decades, the flashing light and thunderous horn warning sea captains of the bay's surprisingly treacherous shallows and rocky shoals. But the humans had long since been replaced by less costly electronics, and the island's structures had fallen into disrepair.

The house itself had once been a beauty, and still boasted gingerbread trim and a cupola painted an appealing (but now peeling) creamy white. Also in the compound were a supply shed, the original foghorn building, and a huge cistern that collected rainwater for the keeper and his family on this otherwise dry rock. The only other structures on the island were the docks and lavatory, located in a small natural harbor to the east, which were still used occasionally by pleasure boats seeking refuge from sudden squalls—and by those interested in exploring Lighthouse Island, of course.

"I'm just saying," I continued. "There's a lot of dry rot to contend with before you start inviting guests to your Lighthouse Inn."

"Oh, *you*," Alicia said with a slight smile, which I answered with a big one.

I had known Alicia for quite a while before spying an iota of good cheer in her. She was still a serious, hardworking person but had relaxed a lot since I first met her on a historic restoration in Marin. We had bonded late one night over a shared love of potato chips and home renovation television shows. And then we quite literally kicked the butt of a murderer, which had definitely improved her attitude.

"I'm sure you know I haven't lost sight of the all-important infrastructure," continued Alicia. "But I need to register my domain and business names, so no, it's *not* too early to think about such things."

She whipped out a thick sheaf of lists and flowcharts and handed them over. I flipped through the papers. There were preliminary schedules for demolition and foundation work, electrical and plumbing and Internet installation, Sheetrock and mudding, overhauls of baths and kitchen, and installations of moldings and flooring and painting and light fixtures.

I raised my eyebrows. "Thanks, Alicia, but I usually work up the schedules with Stan, my office manager."

"I know you do, but I was up late one night, thinking about everything that had to be done, and figured I might as well get the paperwork started. I based these on your schedules for the job in Marin, you see? I can e-mail everything to Stan so you can rearrange it as you need, and plug in the actual dates and the like. I hope you don't think it was too presumptuous—I couldn't help myself. Ever since Ellis agreed to back me on this project, I can hardly *sleep* I'm so excited!"

Several months ago Alicia's boss, Ellis Elrich, had asked me to evaluate "a property" he was considering. It wasn't until he told me to meet him at the Point Moro Marina that I realized this would be no ordinary renovation: It was Lighthouse Island, and the Bay Light.

I—along with much of the population of the Bay Area—had watched over the years as the historic

Victorian-era lighthouse descended into greater and greater decrepitude. Every time my family drove over the Richmond–San Rafael Bridge, my father would shake his head and grumble, "It's a damned shame." Mom would shush Dad for swearing in front of the children—"Little pitchers have big ears, Bill"—but, craning her neck to watch the sad little island as it receded from view, she would add, "You're right, though. Someone really ought to save that place."

Never did I imagine that, decades later, *I'd* be that person.

But historic renovation was my business, and Alicia's boss was filthy rich. Which was a very good thing, because this lighthouse was in need of a serious infusion of cash. I already had in hand the architect's detailed blueprints, as well as the necessary permits and variances from the city and county, which had also promised to fast-track the code inspections. The Bay Light's renovation would be a highly unusual public-private partnership that cash-strapped local officials had agreed to in the interest of saving the historical structures. I was impressed at the city's eager participation but didn't ask too many questions. Ellis Elrich had a way of making things happen.

"So, here's what we're thinking," Alicia said, making a sweeping gesture around the former front parlor. "We take down this wall, combine the space with the smaller drawing room next door, and make this whole area the bar and restaurant."

"It's not very large," I pointed out, comparing the blueprints in my hand to the existing floor plan.

"It doesn't have to be. There will be at most ten overnight guests, so only five small tables are required for their meals—or we might just do one big table and serve everything family-style, I haven't decided yet. And visitors won't be that frequent—there aren't that many people who stop in at the yacht harbor, and even with our boat ferrying people over from the mainland, it will still take some planning to come to the island. It's not as though we have to take into account foot traffic! So I'm thinking we'll be at capacity with about twenty guests for drinks and dinner. But for those that make it, we'll be a gorgeous little oasis in the bay."

Alicia sighed with happiness.

I was pleased for my friend, but experienced enough to be a wee bit jaded. At this point in a renovation, most clients couldn't see past the stars in their eyes and the longing in their hearts. Starting a historic renovation was a lot like falling in love: a blissful period of soaring romantic hope and infatuation that lasted until the grueling realities of sawdust and noise and confusion and delays—not to mention mounting cost overruns and unwelcome discoveries in the walls—brought a person back to earth with a resounding thud.

"We'll keep the bare bones of the kitchen, but include updated fixtures and some expansion, of course. But we'll make the study and part of the pantry into a first-floor suite for the live-in manager—"

"That would be you?"

"Oh, I dearly hope so, if I can find a replacement to serve as Ellis's assistant. I can't leave him high and dry."

"But he wants this for you, right? Isn't that why he's bankrolling the project?"

Alicia blushed. "Yes, he does. Ellis is very . . ."

"Sweet," I said when she trailed off.

She nodded but avoided my eyes. Now that she had loosened up a little and was no longer the tight-lipped martinet I had first met, Alicia was charming. The scar on her upper lip and another by one eye—relics of difficult times at the hands of her abusive (now-ex) husband—only served to make her pretty face more interesting.

The wounds on her psyche were another matter altogether, but through therapy and a whole lot of emotional hard work, Alicia had made great strides toward healing.

And now, unless I was mistaken, she had developed a serious crush on Ellis Elrich, her boss and savior. Ellis was a good guy, surprisingly down-to-earth for a billionaire. Still, the situation seemed . . . complicated.

Oh, what tangled webs we weave.

"Anyway, that will leave three guest suites upstairs, each with an attached bath. And one in the attic, awaiting renovation. Oh! Did I tell you? The attic is full of old furniture, and there's a trunk of old books. There are even the original keeper's logs!"

"Still? No one took them after all this time?"

"I suppose that's the advantage of being on an isolated island. Can you imagine? We can put some on display to add to the historic maritime ambience!"

I smiled. "Of course we can. I can't wait to look through everything. You know me and old books." Me and old everything, actually.

"We might be able to create one more bedroom in the foghorn building, unless we decide to turn that into a separate office. The problem, though, is the noise."

"What noise?"

"The foghorn still sounds on foggy days. It's not the original horn; it's an electronic version. But still, it's loud."

"How loud?"

"*Really* loud."

"That could be a problem. So, what do you want to do with the tower itself? The architect hasn't specified anything here."

"That—" She stopped midsentence and her face lost all color.

"Alicia?" I glanced behind me, but didn't notice anything out of place. "What's wrong?"

"I thought I saw . . ."

"What?"

"Nothing," she said with a shake of her auburn hair.

I turned back to scan the scene, paying careful attention to my peripheral vision. Fervently hoping not to see a ghost. Or a body. Or both.

Because I tend to see things. Things that would make many people scream, run, or faint dead away. Not all the time, but often enough for it to make an impression. Due to my profession I spend a lot of time in historic structures, so it probably isn't surprising—for the open-minded, anyway—that I've been exposed to more than a few wandering souls who aren't clear on the veil between our worlds.

The fact that I trip over dead bodies, on the other hand, is . . . disturbing.

For me most of all, I should add.

Happily, in this moment I saw only the debris-filled main parlor of the old Keeper's House. My mind's eye began to imagine the space filled with vivacious guests sharing meals and stories, children holding cold hands up to the fire in the raised stone hearth, perhaps a calico cat lounging on the windowsill. The visitors warm and happy, safe from the chill winds blowing off the bay, the occasional mournful blast of the foghorn or flash of the lamp atop the tower adding to the dreamy atmosphere, to the sense that they were a world away from a major metropolitan area, rather than minutes. Alicia was right; with Ellis's deep pockets and Turner Construction's building skills, the inn could be magical. *Would* be magical.

Who's the romantic now, Mel Turner?

"Let's . . . I think we should go, Mel," Alicia said, her voice tight.

"What's wrong, Alicia? Are you okay?"

"I'm fine. It's just . . ." She walked toward the front

entry, its charming beadboard paneling buckling in the center, and led the way out to the deep wraparound porch. Thick wooden boards had been laid over rotten sections of the porch floor to allow safe passage to the steps. "I think I'm just spooked."

"Did you see something . . . ghostly?" I asked, surprised. Alicia had never mentioned being sensitive to the supernatural.

"No, it's nothing like that. It's— Well, I'm a little jumpy. I received a letter not long ago."

"And?"

"It was from Thorn."

"Thorn?"

"Thorn Walker. He's . . . he was my husband. Thorn's my *ex*-husband."

"How did he find you? I thought you changed your name, covered your tracks."

"I did," Alicia said with a humorless laugh. "Ellis hired a lawyer and a skip tracer, and they helped me to create a new identity. But . . . it's all my fault. I haven't been as careful as I needed to be, and have let my guard down lately. When Ellis bought this island and announced plans to renovate the buildings and open an inn, I was photographed next to him. The photo appeared in several news outlets—it seems everyone loves stories about historic lighthouses! What was I thinking? Thorn's not stupid. I should know better than anyone that when he puts his mind to something, he can be quite determined."

"What did Ellis's security team suggest?"

She didn't answer.

"Alicia? Did you show Ellis the letter?"

She remained silent, heading down the shored-up porch steps, past an old NO TRESPASSING sign, and into a cement courtyard that had been built on a slight incline to funnel rainwater into the underground cistern.

Back when these buildings were constructed, access to freshwater would have been a priority. Living on a virtually barren rock wasn't easy, and similar challenges had ultimately closed down Alcatraz, the famous federal penitentiary that still held pride of place on another island in the bay, much closer to San Francisco. When everything had to be brought in by supply boat, priorities shifted.

There would be no pizza delivery while on *this* job.

In fact, any and all construction supplies—lumber and concrete, nails and screws, equipment and tools—would have to be brought to the dock by boat and hoisted up with a winch.

The prospect was daunting, but exciting. I had been running Turner Construction for a few years now, and while I still enjoyed bringing historic San Francisco homes back from the brink, I had been itching for a new challenge. For something different.

And this was a *lighthouse.*

Still, one aspect of this renovation gave me pause: The lighthouse tower was several stories high, and ever since an altercation on the roof of a mansion high atop Pacific Heights, I had found myself dreading heights. Where once I wouldn't have given a second thought to scrambling up a tall ladder or hopping out an attic window to repair loose shingles, now the very idea made me quail. I told myself I was being silly, and that these feelings would dissipate as the memory of the attack faded. I would *not* let fear stop me.

If only my vertigo were subject to my stern general's voice.

Because this was a *lighthouse.* What was it about lighthouses that evoked such an aura of romance and mystery? Was it simply the idea of the keeper out here all alone, polishing the old lamps by day, keeping the fires burning at night, responsible for the lives of the equally lonely sailors passing by on the dark, vast waters?

"Alicia, I—"

My words were cut short when I realized she had frozen, a stricken look on her face.

A man stood in the greenery just past the edge of the courtyard. Smiling a smile that did not reach his eyes.

At least it isn't a ghost, was my first thought. My second: *Aw, crap. Is this Alicia's ex? And he tracked her here, to a secluded island?*

A ghost would have been a better bet.